The
GUARDIANS
of the
COVENANT

The
GUARDIANS
of the
COVENANT

TOM EGELAND

JOHN MURRAY

First published in Great Britain in 2009 by John Murray (Publishers)
An Hachette UK Company

First published in paperback in 2010

1

© Tom Egeland 2007

© H. Aschehoug & Co (W. Nygaard), Oslo 2007

English translation © Kari Dickson 2009

This translation has been published with the financial support of NORLA

A CIP catalogue record for this title is available from the British Library

ISBN 978-0-7195-2153-9

Typeset in Monotype Sabon by Servis Filmsetting Ltd, Stockport, Cheshire

Printed and bound by Clays Ltd, St Ives plc

John Murray policy is to use papers that are natural, renewable and
recyclable products and made from wood grown in sustainable forests. The
logging and manufacturing processes are expected to conform to the
environmental regulations of the country of origin.

John Murray (Publishers)
338 Euston Road
London NW1 3BH

www.johnmurray.co.uk

Contents

*Egyptian
ankh*

*Rune
tiwaz*

*Christian
Cross*

Pentagram

'So Moses the servant of the LORD died there in the
land of Moab,
according to the word of the LORD.
And he buried him in a valley in the land of Moab,
over against Bethpeor:
but no man knoweth of his sepulchre unto this day.'

DEUTERONOMY 34: 5–6

'My cavern is open; the glorified spirits in the darkness fall.
The Eye of Horus sanctifies; the Opener of Ways has nursed me.'

EGYPTIAN BOOK OF THE DEAD

'Tore Hund went to where King Olaf's body lay, took
care of it, laid it straight out on the ground, and spread
a cloak over it. He told later that when he wiped the
blood from the face it was very beautiful; and there was
red in the cheeks, as if he only slept, and even much
clearer than when he was in life.'

SNORRI

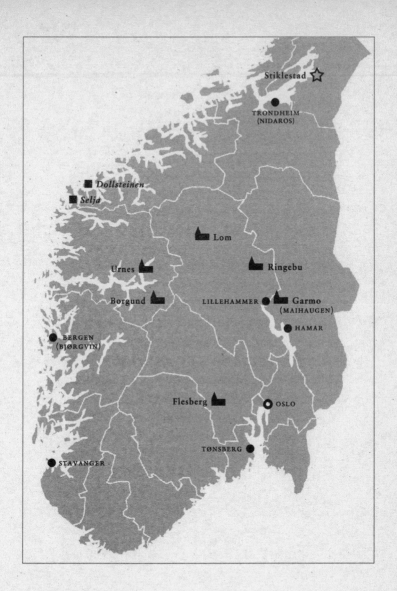

Prologue

☿ ↑ †

'There is but a step between me and death.'
FIRST BOOK OF SAMUEL 20: 3

'Therefore also said the wisdom of God, I send them
prophets and apostles, and some of them they shall
slay and persecute.'
GOSPEL ACCORDING TO LUKE 11: 49

H E SLOWLY lifted the cup of poison to his lips.
Through the haze of heat, he could see Nile glittering, far below the palace. The sun shimmered in the clear sky like molten copper. In the distance, the desert sand blew up an arc of brownish-grey mist.

Beads of sweat trickled down his neck and back. The sand stuck to his skin like a stubborn scab.

Though they had blended the poison with honey and wine, the potion still had a harsh, bitter aroma. They had allowed him to choose how he would die. And now they stood around him, the viziers, high priests, officials and generals, waiting for him to empty the cup. Only the pharaoh and queen were absent. They did not wish to be there.

A white dove flew past the window, a fleeting shadow over the sun. He followed the bird with his eyes, then raised the cup to his mouth and drank.

'Beware, reader of the mystic runes. The torments of Duat, Helheim and Hell await those who decipher the mysteries of the runes without leave.

'Chosen are you who guard the secret with your honour and your life. Your Divine Helpers, Osiris, Odin and the White Christ, will follow you and assist you. Hail, Amon!'

OLD NORSE MANUSCRIPT
AD 1050
(incorporated in the *Codex Snorri* in 1240)

T HE OLD Viking looked out through the small window of his cold cell in the monastery at the foot of the mountain. He coughed. A huge bank of fog was rolling in from the sea, but he could not see it, as he was almost blind. Down by the water's edge, the seagulls were screeching around the rotting carcass of a seal caught between the rolling rocks and seaweed. He coughed again and bent his arthritic fingers round his quill.

Odin, grant me strength.

My hands, they shake. My gnarled fingers resemble more the claws of an eagle. My nails are scabrous and broken. Each breath is a rattling wheeze. My eyes, which once could see a buzzard high beneath the clouds, or a flag atop the mast of a ship over the horizon, are now prisoner to an eternal mist. Only when I bend close to the page can I discern the faint scribblings of ink. I hear the nib of my pen scratch across the parchment and recognise the smell of tannin. So it is, to suffer the slow death of old age.

Bragi, grant me the hand to put down my memories on this whitened hide. More than forty years have passed since my lord and king, the man they called Óláfr hinn helgi, or Holy Olav, was struck by a sword at Stiklestad. I was his squire and friend. Still I see him standing before me, fearless and firm in his belief, as Kalv dealt him that fatal blow. He found his god, my king.

To please my lord, I let myself be baptised in the name of the White Christ. But through all the years, I have, in secret, never ceased to worship the gods of my ancestors. I did not dare confess my betrayal to Olav. In secret I paid homage to Odin and Thor, Balder and Bragi, Freyr and Freyja. My own gods, who have protected me throughout my life. What has the White Christ done for you, my king? Where was Olav's god when he fought so valiantly in the name of the Lord at Stiklestad? My own gods spared my life. They have let me live so long that this miserable frame of mine is failing. My bowels are rotting. My flesh hangs loose from bone and joint. The gates of Valhalla have never been opened for me. And yet a doubt gnaws at me: why did they not let me die in battle? When Olav and I were but young lads and sailed with the Vikings, I looked death in the eye in distant realms. But never did the Valkyries come to take me. I can taste still the thirst for blood and feel the frenzy that seized me when we neared foreign shores. I envisaged the treasures that awaited us, the fear in our enemy's eyes, the pale breasts and thighs of the women we would ravish. We fought bravely, as our fathers and their fathers before had taught. How many did we kill? More than can be counted on a thousand men's fingers. In my mind, I can still see the eyes of the men that I killed in the service of Olav, my king. We captured men and women whom we sold on as slaves and whores. We burned houses, laid villages to waste. That was our way.

But in later years, Olav struggled with his conscience. He prayed to his god for forgiveness. His god did not respect the honour of battle. But when this god's servants folded their hands to him and begged, he smoothed over the sins that had tortured them so. Hypocrisy. I do not understand this fork-tongued god and his holy son. Therefore I still make sacrifices to my Odin and Thor. And to Bragi, the god of poets and skalds. They call me Bård the

Skald. Not one of my songs has been written down; they live on the lips of others.

I have lived here in this monastery some twenty years now, and they treat me well. They hold me as a saint, for my closeness to King Olav and the Egyptian, Asim. Both now rest in Asim's secret tomb, together with the treasure and scrolls that only he could read.

For those twenty-five years, from when we were but lads until the life seeped out of him under the punishing July sun in Stiklestad, up there in Trøndelag, I stood steadfast and loyal by my king. I am old now. I have my mind set on writing down – on the best parchment to be found, with a stripped quill and the finest ink – a secret from the life that I shared with my king. Before I die, I wish to tell the tale of a raid to the kingdom of the sun and the temple of strange gods.

Again, the old man looked out of the window. The monastery was swathed in sea mist. The seagulls were silent. He peered down at the words he had written. Runes filled the white parchment in symmetrical lines. He struggled to his feet and shuffled over to the window, where he leaned his elbows on the ledge, and stared into his memory. The salty sea air took him back to his youth, when he stood at the prow of the Viking ship, Sea Eagle, together with King Olav, their hair blowing in the wind and their sights set on unknown kingdoms.

'The Sacred Cult
Of Amon-Ra
Worthy GUARDIANS
Who know the runes'
Sonorous secret.'

Rune stave
Urnes stave church

T HE FACE of Cardinal Bishop Benedictus Secundus appeared waxen in the light of the smoking oil lamp. He threw a pile of parchments on to the table and fixed the archivist with gimlet eyes: 'Why has this manuscript not been given to me before now?'

'Your Excellency! The Coptic document was one of the countless manuscripts confiscated by the Vatican over a hundred years ago. They have lain untouched in the vault ever since. That is, until Prefect Scannabecchi ordered that the documents be tidied and catalogued. The Coptic manuscript is one of many that were recently translated. We had no idea . . .' The archivist hesitated as he looked from the cardinal bishop to Clemens de'Fieschi, the Pope's trusted knight, who stood like a shadow in the half-dark. '. . . what the nature of the text was.'

'And who was responsible for the Coptic manuscript?'

'An Egyptian, Your Excellency . . .'

'Ah, I should have guessed.'

'. . . a certain high priest . . .'

'Hah!'

'. . . by the name of Asim.'

'And where is the original manuscript now?'

'As far as we know, the papyrus scrolls are in . . . Norway.'

The cardinal's eye flickered, perplexed, as he sought to understand.

'*Noruega*,' the archivist repeated. 'The land of snow. To the far north.'

'*Noruega*.' The cardinal bishop was struggling not to lose his temper. 'How did a collection of holy scripts fall into the hands of those . . . *barbarians*?'

'We do not know,' the archivist whispered.

'I am certain there is no need to explain how important it is that the original is returned to the Vatican?'

'That is why I asked for an audience with Your Excellency.'

The cardinal bishop turned to Clemens de'Fieschi: 'I want you to go there, to this country . . . *Noruega* . . . and to find the original!'

Clemens de'Fieschi stepped into the full light with an elegant bow.

'Your Excellency,' the archivist interrupted, leafing through the parchments until he found what he was looking for, 'the directions given by Asim the Egyptian are only approximations . . .'

'Find it!' the cardinal bishop cut in, with his eyes pinned on de'Fieschi. 'And bring it back.'

'Your Excellency,' de'Fieschi responded with a nod. The swish of his cape made the lamp flames flicker. They heard his footsteps retreat down the corridor and then the slam of the door.

'De'Fieschi *must* find the original!' the cardinal bishop exclaimed, more to himself than the archivist. 'If this manuscript should ever fall into the wrong hands . . .'

'It must never happen.'

'Not a word! Not a word to anyone!'

The cardinal's eyes ran over the archive shelves that went from floor to ceiling, full of parchments, manuscripts, documents, letters and maps. He folded his hands and with the words 'O Lord God, help us to find the papyrus manuscript', he left the archivist alone with his fear and the smoking lamps.

'HIR:HUILER:SIRA:RUTOLFR
Here rests Sira Rudolf'

Tomb inscription
Lyse Monastery
AD 1146

'Honourable GUARDIAN
Who deciphers the mystery of the runes
You alone will find the rune stone
In the final tomb of the rune rose
Where Bishop Rudolf lies.'

From the *Codex Snorri*
AD 1240

O N T H E night they came to kill him, he stood out in the yard for a long time, gazing at the stars. Something ached inside him. A premonition. He shivered in the cold northerly wind. He had sat in the outdoor hot spring for an hour, before drying himself and getting dressed again. The steam from the hot spring glittered in the moonlight over the roof. The glimmering sheen made him think of the Northern Lights. He pulled his fingers through his grey beard and kicked a withered tuft of grass with his boot. How he loathed the icy-cold feeling that had penetrated his very soul. He had so much left to do. His age did not worry him yet; far from it, he was still as spritely and quick as a lamb. Ah, well. A shooting star flared across the sky. Was that an omen? he wondered. He filled his lungs and held in the frost. Somewhere on the farm a dog barked. A horse snorted in the stable.

The world fell silent again.

'Well, well,' he mumbled to himself. 'Well, well, well.'

He went inside and mounted the stairs with the creaking seventh tread. Closing the bedroom door behind him, he sat down heavily on the bed, on the sheepskins that the maid had shaken and folded. And so he fell asleep, with his clothes on, and his head leaning against the coarse timbers of the gable wall.

*

Horses neighing.

Loud shouts.

A wooden gate opening, creaking, slamming shut.

Someone calling out a name. His name.

The sounds wove themselves into his dreams. His eyelids twitched. Then, in an instant, he was wide awake. He leapt up, and had to hold on to the bedpost to keep his balance. He heard shouting and barking outside. He looked out through a peephole. The farm was crawling with armed men. In the midst of them, he saw Gissur in the light of the torches. His face stiffened. Gissur! In a moment of rashness, he had allowed his daughter, Ingibjørg, to be wed with that worthless dog. Was it this knowledge which had been eating him? He and Gissur were bitter enemies. But this? Yet what more could you expect from a coward who ran errands for the Norwegian king?

His heart was thumping, but he did not want to feel his fear. Death would not come on such a night, he thought to himself, such a peaceful, starry autumn night.

He opened the chest that stood by the wall and rummaged around among the heavy clothes until his fingers found the lock of the secret drawer. The lock snapped open. His hands closed around the parchment scrolls. These must never fall into the hands of Gissur and the Norwegian king! He stowed the scrolls carefully under his homespun jerkin before sneaking down the narrow stairs and into the outside gallery. Under cover of dark, he skirted the walls of the buildings until he came to the house of Arnbjørn the Priest.

The priest was sitting up in bed, with his sheepskin pulled up to his chin. He heaved a sigh of relief when he recognised the chieftain. 'Who . . .'

'Gissur and his men!'

'Gissur!' The priest crossed himself and tumbled out of

bed. 'You must hide! I know where! In the cellar. In the storeroom there . . .'

'But first you must swear to help me!'

The words had a strange ring to them. Calming. Imperious. Bold. He pulled out the parchment scrolls. 'Arnbjørn, heed my words closely!'

Arnbjørn's mouth was half open. His breathing echoed his pounding heart. 'I am listening.'

He handed him the parchments. For a while, they both held the vellum scrolls.

'If I am no longer living by daybreak, Arnbjørn, you have a mission. A mission that is more important than your own life.'

The priest nodded in silence.

'You must, in secret, take these parchments to Thordur the Stammerer.' He fixed the priest with his eyes. 'And you must never say so much as a word about it. Never! Not a word! To anyone! Do you understand?'

'What should I say to Thordur?'

'He will understand.'

Thordur was the next Guardian on Iceland. If there was anyone on this earth that he trusted, it was Thordur the Stammerer, his brother's son.

He let go of the scrolls. 'Guard them with your life! Even if someone should gouge out your eyes . . .' The priest gasped and took a step back. 'You must never give the scrolls to anyone or tell that you have them, or even that you so much as know about them! Can you give me your oath, Arnbjørn, in the name of God?'

The priest hesitated for a moment, no doubt while he considered the prospect of having his eyes gouged out. Then he answered: 'Of course!'

'I trust you, my friend. Peace be with you, Priest Arnbjørn!'

With these words, he turned on his heel and went out into the night. The dark was cold on his skin. He heard the shouts of Gissur's men as they scoured the farm, the neighing and pawing of the horses, the baying of the dogs and angry protests from the farm folk, who were aggrieved by the men's behaviour. He opened the trapdoor behind the tool shed that led down to one of the passages in the cellar. He had to crouch as he ran down the narrow passage in the pitch dark, with his hands on the stone walls to feel his way. After ten or twelve metres, he ran straight into a wooden door. *Damnation!* He fumbled for his keys, opened the door and entered the storeroom. The air smelt of corn, mould and yeasted mead. He squeezed in behind some barrels of corn that stood against the wall. He knew they would not give up until they found him.

When they found him, there were jubilant cheers as they kicked the barrels aside and dragged him from his hiding place. In the light of their torches, he could see that there were five of them. He recognised Arni the Bitter and Simon the Knot. But Gissur was not with them. The coward.

He then saw Arnbjørn the Priest in the dark passage behind them. 'My lord,' shouted the terrified priest, 'they swore they would show you mercy.'

'So be it,' he said, so quietly that the priest could not have heard him.

'Be silent, priest,' Simon the Knot demanded.

'Gissur has promised to spare your life!' Arnbjørn continued. 'He said there could be no reconciliation if he did not meet you . . .' He fell quiet as he realised that he had been fooled into betraying his chieftain.

One of the men laughed.

'Where are the parchments?' Simon the Knot demanded.

'Where have you hidden them?' Arni the Bitter shouted.

Who did they think he was?

Simon the Knot thrust his face up close. 'You know that we will find them, old man! Even if we have to pull down the farm, timber by timber!'

And so they carried on. Until they lost all patience.

'Strike him!' Simon the Knot said to Arni the Bitter.

The warriors looked at him.

'Talk!' Arni the Bitter screamed.

All he felt was a deep peace. The knowledge that his life was over. A rich and dramatic life, that he could not deny. A life not dissimilar to those he had portrayed in the sagas.

'No one shall strike!' he said in a steady voice. *Eigi skal höggva.*

'Strike him!' Simon the Knot repeated.

He was not afraid. But he wanted to die with honour. He did not want to leave this life with his face mutilated by axe and sword. A sword through the heart would be more honourable.

'No one shall strike,' he said again with authority, and stared his slayers in the eyes.

Arni the Bitter was the first to strike. His sword struck an artery. The blood pumped out with great force. The sap rises in me still, he thought to himself as he sank to the floor. They all started to hack at him. From the tunnel he heard the whimpers of Arnbjørn the Priest. Please let him keep his promise and deliver the scrolls to Thordur the Stammerer, he prayed.

And so the life of Snorri Sturluson ebbed away, bathed in his own blood, surrounded by enemies.

'Thord carved these runes far from the land of
his ancestors
Over stormy seas and unknown mountain ranges
Through forests and over peaks
We have carried the Holy One
We were born to protect.'

Rune stone
Miércoles Palace
AD 1503

Pope Julius stared dumbfounded at the Vatican's newly appointed Cardinal Bishop Giuliano Castagna. 'Please be so good as to repeat for me,' he said. '*Where* are the papyrus manuscripts?'

'Your Holiness, I know it sounds utterly inconceivable . . . But the letter was delivered this morning by a messenger from Queen Isabella. And as you can see from the seal, it is authentic.'

The Pope took the paper scroll with the broken seal. He shook his head as he read. When he was done, he handed the letter back to the cardinal bishop. 'And this is the papyrus originals of the Holy Scriptures, of which we have the Coptic translation?'

Cardinal Castagna nodded.

'The same papyrus scrolls that your predecessor, Secundus, tried to trace nearly four hundred years ago?' the Pope asked.

'Indeed so.'

'How do these papers come to be *there*?'

'That too is an astonishing story,' the cardinal said.

The Pope looked up at the starry dome of the Sistine Chapel. 'We really must get something done with the ceiling,' he muttered, turning his gaze back to the cardinal. 'It would be a catastrophe if this gets out! For the Church. For the Vatican. For the world.'

'May I propose a bold solution?'

PART I

The Manuscript

♀ ↑ ✝

'. . . and killed three priests and burnt three churches,
and then they returned.'
SNORRI

'A Knight Templar is truly a fearless knight, for his
soul is protected by the armour of faith.'
BERNARD OF CLAIRVAUX

'All will prove true
That thou askest of runes.'
HAVAMÅL

A Priest is Murdered

ICELAND, 2007

1

SIRA MAGNUS is dead. He is floating face down in the hot spring, as if he has just taken a deep breath and is looking for something on the bottom. His shoulder-length hair radiates out like a grey halo in the water. His pale white hands bob on the ripples.

'Magnus?'

My voice sounds thin and feeble.

His clothes billow on the surface of the water, like seaweed. Coins thrown in by tourists shimmer at the bottom of the pool.

I call his name again. Somewhere a raven caws.

I can't move. Perhaps I'm just trying to postpone the inevitable – that I will have to pull him out of the hot spring and look into his lifeless eyes.

He did not fall in by accident. The pool is not deep. He could easily have got out.

Someone has killed him. Someone has drowned Sira Magnus.

I kneel down, grab his ankles and haul him out of the water, which smells faintly of sulphur. He is heavy. His clothes are sodden and dripping. When I turn him over on to his side, water runs out of his mouth. I try to find a pulse that I know ceased to beat some time ago. His face is red and bloated. He has lost his glasses. His eyes are wide open. And empty.

'Oh, Magnus,' I whisper, 'what have they done to you?'
Or maybe I only think it. I take his hand in mine. I'm
shaking. Water drips from his beard. His clothes cling to his
plump frame.

The round pool is surrounded by uneven slabs. Here
and there, defiant plants have pushed their way up through
the cracks. A gust of wind whistles over the barren
landscape.

I let go of his hand and ring the emergency services.

2

While I wait for the police, I run up to the house to see
whether they have stolen the manuscript.

The door has been left wide open. I storm down the hall,
through the drawing room and into the study. This is
where we sat, last night, studying the fragile parchment.
Codex Snorri. A strange collection of codes, texts, maps and
occult symbols. It was nearly two in the morning by the
time we finally stopped for the night. I remember how
carefully he packed the manuscript away and locked it in
the drawer of his desk. He kept the key on the keyring that
hung from his belt.

The key and keyring are now hanging from the open
drawer.

The Snorri Codex has gone.

Someone has stolen the ancient collection of texts.

I can just picture it. They held his head under water. They
threatened him. And finally he gave in. He told them reluctantly where the manuscript was. Of course. I would have
done the same thing. Some of the thugs had run up to the
house. And once they had found the codex in the drawer of
his desk, the bastards pressed his head under water as he
struggled and fought, until eventually he stopped breathing

24

and was floppy and still. Then they just left him floating in the water, like any other corpse.

In Snorri Sturluson's hot spring.

3

The sirens rip through the silence.

A flock of ravens takes wing and disappears over the ridge of the hill in a cackle of complaint. *Lögregla* and *sjúkrabíllin* – the police and ambulance – arrive at such a speed that I wonder whether they have raced each other from Borganes, and in fact do not want to stop at all, now that they have got up speed. They obviously don't know that the call ceased to be urgent hours ago.

I wave the police car and ambulance over, down the track to the pool. Blue lights flashing. The sirens whimper and fall silent, first one, then the other. Through the windscreen, I see their faces: sceptical, expectant, perplexed.

Sira Magnus?

Dead?

In Snorri's hot spring?

Murdered?

They can scarcely believe it. Reykholt is tucked away in a peaceful corner of the world. The last murder in Reykholt took place some 766 years ago. One night in September 1241, Snorri Sturluson was murdered by Gissur Thorvaldsson's men, on the instructions of King Håkon Håkonsson of Norway.

At present, I am the only one who knows that there is a connection between the two.

The Discovery

S IRA MAGNUS was a priest. He saved lost souls. I
myself am an archaeologist and I save the past from
oblivion.

Let me take you back a few days, only two days in fact.
Let me fast-rewind to Saturday morning:

'I have found something fantastic, Bjørn!'

Sira Magnus was standing in the sun, smiling and full
of anticipation, when I turned into the parking place at
Reykholt, Snorri's old kingdom on Iceland. When I close
my eyes, I can still see him in front of me, through the
glare of the front screen – excited and very much alive. I
stopped the car. Sira Magnus opened the door for me. We
gave each other an awkward embrace, in the way men do,
too afraid to show the admiration we really felt for each
other.

'Thank you for coming, Bjørn. Thank you. You won't
regret it!'

'When were you thinking of telling me what you've
found?'

'Soon, Bjørn, soon.'

We met three years ago at an interdisciplinary sympo-
sium on the chieftain and saga writer Snorri Sturluson. Sira
Magnus gave a talk on the similarities between Snorri and

Socrates as carriers of wisdom and mediators of knowledge in medieval Iceland and Ancient Greece. I myself gave a paper on Snorri's difficult relationship with Håkon Håkonsson, who became king of Norway in 1217, following the victory of the *Birkebeiners* in the civil war.

That is how we became friends.

A week ago, he phoned me and invited me to Iceland. I did not have the time. I explained that I was extremely tied up with the excavation of Harald Fair Hair's royal farm on Karmøy. But he would not listen. I *had* to come. He had found something. Something historical. If I had not known him so well, I might have thought that he had lost his marbles. But Sira Magnus was a sensible priest in a rural parish, who seldom lost his composure.

'So, what have you found?' With suitcase in hand, I followed a few steps behind Sira Magnus, as he strode down the path that led to Snorrastofa, the research centre attached to the church and museum. He had a very particular rolling gait, as if his legs were slightly too short. Two cars stood parked in the large car park: Sira Magnus's four-by-four BMW and my hire car.

'A codex! A collection of documents . . .'

'About?'

'Written on the finest, softest calfskin! A handwritten collection of mysterious texts and verse, maps, directions, symbols and codes.'

'What are they about? From which century? Who wrote the texts?'

'Patience, my friend, patience!'

Sira Magnus always spoke slowly. In time with the metronome of the soul, as he used to say.

'But why did you ask me, specifically, to come?'

'That, my dear Bjørn, is obvious.'

I don't know whether he meant because I was his friend,

or whether he was referring to an incident a few years ago. I was the Norwegian inspector for the archaeological dig that discovered the Shrine of Sacred Secrets, a gold chest that contained a manuscript which gave me some degree of fame within academic circles.

Sira Magnus unlocked the door to the flat for visiting research fellows, where I was going to stay. I put my suitcase down in the hall. Then I grabbed him by the arm of his jacket and pulled him into the sitting room and pushed him down into a chair.

'There. Now tell me!'

His face, if you took away the goatee and the spindle web of wrinkles, could have been a child's. With gravity and ceremony, as if he were about to give a sermon, he cleared his throat: 'Allow your friend to tell the story chronologically.'

'Oh, get on with it!'

'It all started about two weeks ago. There was a death in the parish. An elderly, paralysed man. So not unexpected. After the funeral, I was asked to help the family who had looked after the old man, on behalf of the congregation, to go through his considerable collection of documents. The old man was obsessed with genealogy. Family trees. His collection contained everything from reports on recent research to Icelandic family trees and manuscripts. The couple on the farm where he lived are very active in the congregation. Friends of mine. They were his inheritors. They asked me for help when the Icelandic company deCODE, which does gene research for the development of bio-pharmaceutical medicine, asked if they could buy the collection.'

'What was deCODE going to do with it?'

'Iceland has the world's best gene bank. The genealogical history of the greater part of the population can be traced back to the days when Iceland was settled. No doubt, deCODE hoped that the old man's collection might shed new light on unknown family relations. My old friend, the farmer, wanted an expert to look at the stuff first so that the company didn't walk away with something that should go to the manuscript collection in Reykjavik.'

'What did you find?'

'The collection is unique. Truly unique! Ancient books. Letters. Parchments. Manuscripts. Some were barely in one piece. Maps. Property conveyance documents. Among all the papers I found an overview of the Sturlung family, Snorri's family tree, from 1453.'

I tried to sneak in a question, but he held up his hand to stop me.

'Just when I was about to pack away all the parchments, I noticed a bulge in the leather holder . . .' He coughed guiltily. 'So I cut open the darkened seam to see what was inside.'

'You did *what*?'

'Just listen! In the holder I found an even older text.'

'You split open the holder?'

'The parchment collection inside the holder was sewn together like a book. A codex.'

'To split open something antique is vandalism. And you know that.'

'I know that I did something terrible, Bjørn.'

'Absolutely! You should have let a curator open the leather holder.'

'No, there's more to it.'

'More to it? The fact that you cut open the holder is bad enough.'

'More to the text.' His focus became distant and dreamy. 'Something about the words, about the handwriting, about all the geometrical characters . . .'

'What did you do?'

'You know that I am an honest and righteous priest!'

'Magnus, what did you do?'

He looked at me, full of shame. 'I hid the parchments under my jacket and took them home with me.' His eyes crawled over the floor to meet mine. 'I stole them, Bjørn.'

2

Later that evening, with a chilly wind blowing from the mountains, Sira Magnus showed me the codex. We sat at a cracked table in one of the rectory sitting rooms, a stone's throw from Snorrastofa.

I could see that his face was distorted with pain.

'What's bothering you?' I asked.

He shook his head dejectedly.

'Do you feel ashamed that you stole the parchments?'

'It's more than that. I . . . nothing. Not now. Maybe another time.'

He took out a box wrapped in brown paper and newspaper from a locked drawer in his desk. He then folded back several layers of paper, before handing me the manuscript. The collection of parchments was remarkably intact. I ran my fingertips over the golden tan leather. 'What is it?' For some reason it felt right to whisper. With great care, I opened the codex. The first five pages were written in runes. Then I came to a section with paler leather and Latin letters. Three symbols were scratched into the leather: an Egyptian ankh, the rune *tiwaz* and a Christian cross.

The next page showed two maps of southern Norway and western Iceland.

And a pentagram.

'Sacred geometry,' Sira Magnus said.

That was all we needed.

'To be honest,' I said patiently, 'I have never really understood whether sacred geometry is a myth or a science.'

'Or something in between . . .'

'You're the priest.'

We had had a guest speaker at university who had managed to convince even a diehard sceptic like myself that our ancestors were influenced by ancient Greek and Egyptian concepts of maths, astronomy, geography and geodesy, the discipline that underpins cartography. With the help of satellite pictures and maps he had shown how medieval sacred sites and landmarks were positioned in accordance with geographical, geometric and mathematical patterns.

All the same . . .

Sira Magnus leafed back a few pages to the Latin letters and pointed at the handwriting.

'Look! This script is called Carolingian minuscule. It's what our modern letters are based on. A milestone in calligraphy.'

I gave him a look that I knew would be irritating, especially as it would be magnified by my thick glasses. Sira Magnus pointed to two tiny letters at the bottom of the page and handed me a magnifying glass.

'Do you see those two S's?'

'Yes.'

'Then perhaps you can understand what I'm talking about.'

But I, unfortunately, had not understood a thing.

'S.S? Combined with Carolingian minuscule? Bjørn? You still don't get it? S.S: Snorri Sturluson! The Latin letters were written by Snorri!'

Astonished, I looked down at the text. The wind complained and whistled around the corners outside.

'The text was written by Snorri, personally,' Sira Magnus continued.

'Are you sure?'

'Isn't it incredible, Bjørn?'

If Sira Magnus was right, the codex would be a historical

sensation. A piece of world history. Snorri handwrote hardly anything. He dictated. Surrounded by a host of scribes, Snorri composed his opus of sagas and myths about Viking kings and Old Norse gods. Scholars are still arguing whether an addendum in the margin of an Icelandic *máldagi*, a written agreement, was handwritten by Snorri himself or one of his scribes.

'The fact that Snorri himself has handwritten parts of the text, and not left it to his most trusted scribes, must mean that the content is extremely sensitive,' Sira Magnus said.

'But why would Snorri mix his own parchments and texts in with an even older manuscript, written in runes?'

'Well, if I knew . . .'

We leafed back and forth through the parchments with great care.

'What is the text about?'

'Instructions. Rules. Prophecies . . .'

He turned back a page and found an old Icelandic text:

The High Priest Asim declared that a time will come when the GUARDIANS will bring THE HOLY ONE back to his resting place, under the sacred sun, in the sacred air, in the sacred rock; and a thousand years will pass; and half of this period will be shrouded in depravity and corruption; and of the great multitude of GUARDIANS only three shall remain; and they are true, they are pure of heart and their number is three.

'What on earth does all that mean?' I asked.

'No idea. But at least the words are legible.'

'What do you mean?'

'The greater part of the text is completely incomprehensible!'

'A foreign language?'

'Parts of it are in code.'

'. . .'

'Can you believe that, Bjørn?'

'Code?'

'It's completely unbelievable. Some verses and paragraphs are written in code.' He realised that I needed a bit of time to digest this. 'Why are you so surprised? Codes have been used for thousands of years!'

'Yes, but . . . Snorri?'

'If he wanted to write something that was secret, then he had to disguise the meaning.'

He turned to the last page of the parchments and showed me a beautifully written verse surrounded by elegant borders. I tried to read it. But even for a relatively bright associate professor who understood Old Norse, the text was complete gobbledegook.

'Thirty-three words divided over six lines,' Sira Magnus said. 'The text is incomprehensible. So I have tried to find the different meanings of the number thirty-three.'

'And what have you come up with?'

'That's how old Jesus was when he died. It's also a key number in magical numerology. Thirty-three is a sacred number for the Freemasons.'

'The Freemasons didn't exist in Snorri's day.'

'Exactly! That's why I think it's completely arbitrary that the message has thirty-three words.' He burst out laughing and leafed back through the manuscript. He pointed at an eighteen-line text. 'More gibberish!'

'Can you crack codes?'

'Not at all. And you?'

I shook my head. 'But I do know someone who can.'

3

I can't decide whether Terje Lønn Erichsen is more friend or more colleague. Like me, he is a social amoeba. He is a linguist and associate professor at the Institute for Linguistics and Nordic Studies at the University of Oslo. He is working on a research project looking into the division of Old Norse into Norwegian, Swedish, Danish and Icelandic. I would go so far as to say that Terje is a linguistic genius. Cracking codes is one of his hobbies. When he was sixteen, he single-handedly, and without consulting Thomas Phelippes, worked out the codes used in the correspondence between Mary Queen of Scots and her supporters when she was in jail.

When I rang Terje and explained what I needed help with, it was easy to hear how excited he was. Word by word, line by line, I dictated Snorri's code. Sira Magnus watched with a wry smile, as if he could not believe that anyone would ever be able to understand Snorri's medieval codes. Not even my nerdy friends.

4

A dreamless sleep can be a bit like death, apart from the fact that you wake up. There are mornings when I open my eyes with sunshine in my soul and Prokofiev's *Romeo and Juliet* playing on my mobile phone.

'Great news!' Terje shouted down the phone.

'Hmm?' I grunted, trying to shake the sleep from my vocal cords.

'I've cracked the code!'

'Don't tell me you've been at it all night?'

'You have no idea how much fun it was!'

'Fun?' I squeezed the phone between my ear and shoulder as I opened the window a crack. The North Atlantic wind immediately chilled the temperature in the room to around minus two hundred.

'The runic code is a straightforward C3 code. Caesar 3.'

'Caesar 3?'

'Caesar shift cipher. The name of the simple code that

Julius Caesar used to confuse curious eyes whenever he sent important messages to his generals. Caesar substituted every letter with another letter a given number of places down the alphabet. C3 means that every character in the text has been substituted with another character four ahead in the alphabet. So, for example, A becomes D, B becomes E, etc.'

'Does that mean that you have a translation?'

'Isn't that why you asked me to help? Let's start with the first verse.' He cleared his throat before starting to read:

'Seek the answer in the saga of the cross
For the number is magic
And the number is the word of God
And the number you will find
In the tree of life and the lost tribes
And the number of the sacraments will show the way ahead.'

'Oh,' was all I could muster.

'Isn't that great?'

'Well, yes.'

'Don't you get it?'

'Not really.'

'Well, *the saga of the cross . . .*'

'*The Saga of the Holy Cross*. The last saga that Snorri wrote before he died.'

'*For the number is magic and the number is the word of God.* The word of God could be the Ten Commandments, for example. *The tree of life* is a reference to the Kabbalah and Judaic mysticism and boils down to God's appearance in this world in ten stages. *And the lost tribes* – well, what else could they be other than Israel's ten lost tribes?'

'Ten,' I said, 'the number ten keeps coming up.'

'Bingo!'

'And the *number of the sacraments*?'

'Is seven. The seven sacraments. Do you get it now?'

'Not at all!'

'It must be too early in the morning for you. What time is it in Iceland? The text gives you two numbers, ten and seven!'

'Yes, I got that much. But what then?'

'Bjørn, you really are bloody slow! To find the message, you have to look in *The Saga of the Holy Cross* using combinations of the numbers ten and seven.'

'Combinations of ten and seven?'

Snorri Sturluson's last saga is the least known and the least recognised. The saga was written as fairy tale, a fable, and many academics question whether it was Snorri who wrote it at all. The story is about the mysterious Viking king, Bård, who goes on a voyage to the Holy Land and steals the cross of Jesus. When he gets back to Norway, he plants the cross, which soon becomes a forest of crosses. He then describes how Norway is overrun by crusaders, Knights Templar, members of the Order of Hospitallers and the Pope's soldiers. It is thought that Snorri wrote *The Saga of the Holy Cross* in 1239, shortly after he had visited Norway for the second and last time. He fled the power struggle between Earl Skule and the *Birkebeiner* king, Håkon Håkonsson. That was how they lived – and died – in those days.

Combinations of ten and seven . . .

'And the other text?' I asked.

'Just as impenetrable. I've decoded it, but I haven't had time to analyse and interpret it yet. The text must have been written for readers who have references that we don't.'

He read out his preliminary translation:

'Honourable GUARDIANS
Who read these secret words

You alone shall know that Asim's sacred rune rose
And the hidden mystic runes of the church cross
Will lead you to the holy tomb
And the holiest of them all
Lies in the first chamber.

'Honourable GUARDIANS
Who interpret the mysteries of the symbols
You alone shall find the rune stone
In the last grave of the rune rose
Where Bishop Rudolf lies.

'Honourable GUARDIANS
Who know the hidden story
You alone shall know that the rune stone
Will lead you to the mystic symbols of
The runes, harmony, the altarpiece.'

5

'I am a terrible person!'

Sira Magnus was still half asleep. He was sitting by the kitchen window drinking coffee when I came bursting in with Terje's translations. He looked terrible. As so many of us do, Sira Magnus had succumbed to melancholy and self-pity. From experience, I know that nothing can be rushed when you are in this frame of mind. I poured myself some of the freshly made coffee, which was full of grit, and sat down at the kitchen table.

'Listen,' I said, popping a sugar lump in my mouth, 'what you are calling theft is no more' than a temporary loan of the parchments. All in the name of science.'

His sigh was as heavy as Judgement Day.

'Magnus, I will go into the manuscript institute tomorrow and personally register the discovery. They will understand. And then this burden will be lifted from your heart.'

'Do you really believe that the merciful gift of forgiveness knows no bounds?'

'My friend . . .'

'You don't know me as well as you think. There's more. I . . .'

'Tell me, then. It can't be that bad!'

'We have to give the codex to the manuscript institute.'

'Of course. When you and I are finished with it. I will talk to them. Then the institute and the Good Lord can draw a line under what you have done.'

'Bjørn . . . I've got people coming. Tomorrow . . .'

'What do you mean?'

'I got carried away, talked too much.'

'Who's coming?'

'Experts. From the Schimmer Institute. They want to study the parchments.'

'You told the Schimmer Institute?'

During all the excitement surrounding the discovery of the Shrine of Sacred Secrets in a field by Værne cloisters in Østfold, I had had some doings with the Schimmer Institute. It was one of the world's leading theological research centres, and lay in a stony desert in the Middle East.

'I can't bear to explain. Not just now. They're sending some people.'

'Then we'd better get a move on. You must not let them have the codex!'

'They just want to look at it.'

'That's what they *say*. They will offer you a fortune for it.'

He started to say something, but then just shook his head.

'I've got some news that will cheer you up.' I held up the page with Terje's translation of the text which he had decoded for us in the course of the night. I then read the text out to him. And I pointed to the reference to *The Saga of the Holy Cross*.

'Well, I'll be damned,' he exclaimed. He gulped down the last of his coffee and spat out the grit. 'Come on! We've got work to do!'

Terje's translation of the coded text had galvanised Sira Magnus's spirit to the extent that I had to run to keep up with him as he strode from the rectory to Snorrastofa. He unlocked a door in one of the side corridors and we went through the church and down to the museum in the basement.

The original manuscript of *The Saga of the Holy Cross* was displayed in a glass case over by the far wall. Sira Magnus opened the case and took out the manuscript. 'Snorri wrote this saga just after he had defied King Håkon and fled from the Norwegians, home to Iceland,' he said.

'The text is disputed.'

'Everything Snorri wrote is disputed. The events he describes took place centuries ago. Maybe we have read his stories in the wrong way. Could Snorri have been trying to tell us something – without saying it directly?'

Sira Magnus carried the book over to an oblong table, where we bent over the manuscript. He pointed at three symbols: ankh, *tiwaz* and the cross. 'The same symbols that appear in the codex. And do you see that text in the margin? The small addendums to the side of the main text? The same handwriting as in the Snorri Codex! The main text, the initials and the illuminations are no doubt the work of scribes. But could it be Snorri who wrote the addendums in the margin? As a rule, they are omitted when a manuscript is copied. Those making the copy often thought that any writing in the margin was just scribblings and doodles.'

39

6

Sira Magnus and I sat for the whole day and far into the evening going through the original of *The Saga of the Holy Cross*. We worked our way methodically through it, letter by letter, character by character. If there is one thing that scholars have, it is patience. At regular intervals I phoned Terje in Oslo for advice. Every now and then Sira Magnus would exclaim with delight over some beautifully formed letter or a striking alliteration.

'Look!' he shouted suddenly. 'The text in the margin here mentions Thordur the Stammerer.'

'Who?'

'Snorri's nephew. He gathered all Iceland's chieftains together and became so powerful that King Håkon had to summon him to Norway, where he drank himself to death.'

In another addendum, there was a reference to *the holy cave*. The rest of the sentence had been scraped away with so much force that the leather was almost translucent.

The holy cave?

7

It was nearly nine o'clock by the time we finally worked out the code.

As usual, Terje was right. The numbers ten and seven were the code key. Starting with the first letter and then extracting every tenth letter from the main text and substituting it with the seventh letter down in the Latin alphabet, using the Caesar method, we revealed the following message:

The number of the beast
Shows the way

Along the rock face
From Lögberg
To Skjaldbreiður.

Voice from the Grave

1

'So it was you who found Sira Magnus dead?'

The chief superintendent from Borgarnes looks as though he was reared on rotten fishballs and too much cod-liver oil that was out of date. Everything about him, his eyes, hair, skin and voice, is grey and colourless. He is sitting behind his tidy desk with a framed photograph of Mrs and Junior Chief Superintendent and a poodle that I bet is called Bonzo. He taps a biro impatiently on a form in front of him.

'Yes,' I reply.

'Full name?'

'Bjørn Beltø.'

'Norwegian?'

'Yes.'

'What year were you born?'

'1968.'

'Profession?'

'Archaeologist. Associate professor at the University of Oslo.'

'What were you doing at Snorrastofa?'

'I was working with Sira Magnus on a research project.'

'Why are you certain that his death is due to murder?'

'Because I found him lying dead in the hot spring.'

'He might have taken a turn.'

The chief superintendent is reluctant to accept that

God's kind servant at Reykholt has been killed. Reykholt is not a big place. The few people who live there are peaceful and pious. Only tourists and academics search out the secluded outpost with a beautiful church and museum and the remains of Snorri's farm.

'They stole something,' I say.

He studies my face, which is as white as chalk. My eyes have a red sheen behind my thick glasses. I'm short sighted and nervous. I'm a nuisance for the chief superintendent. I can see that he does not *want* Sira Magnus to have been killed. A murder would be too much to deal with.

'What did they steal?' he asks.

'An ancient manuscript.'

'You mean to say that Sira Magnus was murdered for a manuscript?'

'Not just any old manuscript. It was the *Codex Snorri*.'

'What is that?'

'A collection of parchments with texts dating from the eleventh to the thirteenth centuries.'

Silence.

'Written by Snorri?' A muscle twitches in the chief superintendent's eyebrow.

'A long story.'

A seagull swoops past the window outside, then belly-flops to the ground and looks around for something to eat.

'As far as I am aware, Snorri's manuscripts are kept in the Icelandic manuscript collection at the Árni Magnússon Institute in Reykjavik,' the chief superintendent ventures.

'Not all of them. Some. There are other manuscripts in Copenhagen, Uppsala, Utrecht.'

'And one in Reykholt, in Sira Magnus's house?'

'He discovered it just over a week ago.'

'And was the finding reported?'

'Today. That was why I went into Reykjavik. Before I found him dead.'

'Who do you think stole the manuscript?'

'The same people who killed him.'

'Why did they steal it?'

'To sell it, I presume. A manuscript written by Snorri would be very valuable for collectors.'

'I see.'

I think to myself that it is a good thing that the police from Reykjavik are also on their way. The chief superintendent from Borgarnes obviously does not want to get involved with a murder and the disappearance of a national treasure.

'This research project you were working on . . .' he begins.

'It's quite complicated.'

'Try me all the same.'

'We were working on a theory that Snorri left behind secret directions in his texts.'

'Secret directions?'

'Codes. Maps. Sacred geometry.'

'Uh-huh.'

He does not have the faintest idea what I am talking about.

'We think,' I explain, 'that Snorri knew that our forebears built important landmarks – churches, cloisters, farms and fortresses – according to a sacred geometric order based on Pythagorean and Neoplatonic philosophy and mathematics.' It sounds as if what little sense I may have had has got lost somewhere between my brain and my tongue. 'Our ancestors used these ancient sciences for everything from drawing up maps to the construction of Viking ships and stave churches.'

A veil of disbelief has fallen over the chief superintendent's eyes. He stops writing. Perhaps it is just as well.

There is a lot I don't say. There is a lot I *can't* say. Because I don't know. Because I don't understand. I say nothing about the code that Sira Magnus and I managed to crack yesterday evening. Sometimes it is best to keep some things to yourself.

'I'm not an archaeologist,' says the chief superintendent. 'Nor a historian. And even though I realise that such a discovery might be very exciting for you experts, I find it difficult to understand why someone would be prepared to kill for it.'

This time it is I who am silent. Because exactly the same thought has struck me.

I spend the next hour and a half trying to explain to him, though I think what I say actually confuses him more than clarifies anything. His questions are all over the place. He doesn't understand much of it. But then, neither do I.

Halfway through the interrogation, a detective arrives from *Ríkislögreglustjórinn*, as the police are called here in Iceland. He throws a transparent plastic bag down on the table in front of the chief superintendent. Sira Magnus's glasses, which the chief superintendent's local investigators had not found at the bottom of the hot spring. The chief superintendent is affronted. They go into the next-door office. I can hear their heated discussion through the wall. Then they come back and continue to question me. The detective from the capital sits by the window. He looks at me several times as if he is not sure that I am right in the head. After a while, he asks where I was at the time of Sira Magnus's death. I tell him that I was with Professor Thrainn Sigurdsson at the Árni Magnússon Institute in Reykjavik.

Straight after, I am led out of the room and into a cell. Am I being arrested? I sit in the cell for three-quarters of an

45

hour before they come back. Only now does the detective from Reykjavik shake my hand and introduce himself. When Icelanders say their name, it sounds as if their mouth is full of marbles.

'We just needed to check that you are who you say you are and to verify your story.'

'Did you think that I had drowned Sira Magnus?'

Neither of them replies. Finally, the chief superintendent says: 'My colleague from the *Ríkislögreglustjórinn* felt that we should give you the status of suspect so that you were also allowed the rights of a suspect . . .' The words froth with indignation. The respected chief superintendent – protector of the law, pillar of the local community – has just been steamrollered by a senior officer from the capital. I feel some sympathy for him. The balance of power has shifted. The chief superintendent is now on my side. Two against one.

The questioning continues. I tell even less than the little I know. The chief superintendent and the detective jot down some notes and key words with such a lack of interest that I realise that the police in Borgarnes and the *Ríkislögreglustjórinn* will never manage to tie up all the loose ends that Sira Magnus and I have created.

So I will just have to do it myself.

2

It is evening by the time I get back to Reykholt.

The police have tied yellow plastic tape, with *lögregla* written on it, all around the rectory. The tape flaps in the wind. I stand listening to it for a while. Then I go down to the hot spring.

The police cars have gone. Sira Magnus has been taken to the forensic institute in Reykjavik in the *sjúkrabíllinn*. The pathologists there will cut him up into small pieces to find out what killed him.

But the journalists are keeping watch. They smell blood. A TV reporter from Stod 2 is standing talking into a microphone, bathed in brightness from two camera lights. Journalists and photographers from *Morgunbladid*, *Frettabladid* and *GV* hang around the scene of the crime. Thankfully they don't spot me. They circle the hot spring with impatience and without direction.

And all the while, I see Sira Magnus in front of me. I try to understand it, to find an explanation. Finally, I wander up to the flat in Snorrastofa.

3

I see straight away that someone has been there.

The flat is as tidy as it was when I left it. But I have a sensitive eye. I know exactly where and how I put things down. Like my laptop, for example. My notes. The right sock with a hole in the heel.

Someone has been here and looked around. But they haven't taken anything. Other than my peace of mind.

It may of course have been the police. It's possible that on Iceland they have the right to ransack the flat of the main suspect without mentioning it to him. But I wouldn't rule out the possibility that it might have been Sira Magnus's killers.

I walk around the flat to make sure that I am alone. I close the curtains. I look under the bed and in the cupboards. I check my mobile phone on the bedside table. I have two messages. One is a voicemail and the other is a photograph. Both are from Sira Magnus. The voicemail was left at 13.42, just before he died.

'Hi Bjørn, it's me,' says the voice from the grave. He sounds agitated and surprised. '*Those foreign experts . . . the*

47

ones from the Schimmer Institute . . . They're on their way up from the car park. Quite a gang. I'm going to send you a picture.' He gives a tense laugh. *'You know some of their people – do you recognise any of them? It's just that . . . oh, I don't know. I just wanted you to know. See you later.'*

The picture is not very sharp and was taken through the sitting-room window, looking down towards the car park. There is a four-by-four people carrier in the background. I can make out four people walking up towards the house. One of them is built like a shithouse.

The chief superintendent tells me that it is too late in the evening to do anything with this new information. He will come out first thing tomorrow morning. He asks me to forward the photograph to him in the meantime.

I ask whether the police have searched my flat. 'No. Should we?' he adds with a laugh.

4

The morning sun bathes the landscape in such an intense light that Reykholt looks overexposed. Below the ridges of the volcanic mountains in the distance, steam rises up from geothermal sources in circles on the faint breeze.

I close the door and walk out on to the grass in front of Snorrastofa. It is completely quiet.

I once visited Leonardo da Vinci's childhood home on a Tuscan hillside and I was overwhelmed by the thought that Leonardo had looked over these very same slopes with olive trees and vineyards. I get the same intimate feeling here at Reykholt. The very same peaks filled the horizon when Snorri moved here, when he was twenty-seven years old. He was already a mighty chieftain by then.

A police car swings into the car park. The wheels grind on the gravel. The local chief superintendent has driven all the way from Borgarnes to confiscate my mobile phone and inspect the scene of death more carefully. And possibly also to check whether that suspicious albino Bjørn has gathered together all his Micro Uzi SMG guns and sickle-shaped Arabic daggers and disappeared under cover of night. Or I am just being paranoid? Whatever, he walks towards me, right hand outstretched and an expression on his face that could resemble a smile. We squint at each other in the morning light. He is newly shaven; the skin on his jaw is red and irritated. He asks whether he can borrow my mobile phone in order to analyse and secure the voicemail and picture.

He asks who the experts are. I say that I don't know.

'We'll find them! When you came back from Reykjavik yesterday, did you notice passing cars in particular?'

The drive from Reykjavik to Reykholt takes one and a half hours through a landscape that could easily make you think you were on Mars. Every second car in Iceland is a four-wheel-drive. So why should any one car be different from the others?

'We have a witness statement that confirms what you can see in the picture,' he explains. 'A black Blazer was observed driving away from the scene at high speed yesterday . . .' He checks his notepad. '. . . at fourteen hundred hours. A car rental company in Reykjavik had rented a Blazer out to some foreigners. We have two men waiting there now, for when they return the car.'

'Foreigners?'

'Arabs. From the Emirates, according to their passports.' Short pause. 'Can you see any reason why Sira Magnus should have any contact with Arabs?'

A lie can be so many things. A distortion of the truth. Not telling the whole truth. I say that I know of no connections between Sira Magnus and the Emirates.

A growing fear twists my intestines. Untrustworthy

employees from the Schimmer Institute. Collectors. Rich eccentrics who would do anything to get their hands on a historical curiosity. But I don't say any of this to the chief superintendent. He wouldn't understand. I barely understand it myself.

When the chief superintendent leaves, I ring a contact at the Schimmer Institute. I explain what has happened and ask who they sent. He claims that they have not sent anyone.

'We would send Professor Osman, Professor Rohl, Professor Dunhill, Professor Silbermann, Professor Finkelstein, Professor Phillips and definitely Professor Friedman to study such a remarkable find. But first of all we would have tried to convince Sira Magnus to bring the codex with him here to the Institute.'

5

I drive back to Reykjavik at midday. The road passes abandoned farms and sheep pens and thermal steam plants. The volcanic mountains look as if they are just waiting to explode. Every now and then, the road makes a peculiar swerve, no doubt to avoid a fairy knoll. Road construction workers in Iceland have enormous respect for the invisible *huldufolket*, their fairies and elves, who live in the rocks out in the wilderness. When an Icelandic engineer has drawn a straight road through a stone that undoubtedly houses a fairy family, the construction workers avoid total catastrophe by laying the road round the stone.

I keep seeing mysterious cars in the rear-view mirror. Black Blazers. But it could just be some Icelandic guy out for a drive. In his black Blazer. Or perhaps those bloody fairies are playing games with me.

The black Blazer in the rear-view mirror overtakes me and is a dark blue Volkwagen Touareg.

*

Everyone has their demons.

I haven't named mine. But I know them, just as you know yours. They lie there asleep inside, somewhere between your intestines, liver and kidneys, and all the half-digested food that helps you to function, and then suddenly one night they show their ugly faces.

I have never had a problem with alcohol. But I munch my way through antidepressants as though they were fruit pastilles. The happy pill, that's what they call it, but they don't make you happy, they just help to keep the claws of anxiety at bay. Don't get me wrong. I'm not mad. But sometimes my nerves get a bit frayed. Battling with nerves is no worse than having diabetes or cystitis. But people look at you differently. They take a step back. *I see. Nerves?* They give a sympathetic and slightly tense smile. As if you have a meat cleaver hidden up your sleeve and your head is full of evil, screaming voices.

I've been sectioned a couple of times. And that was definitely to my benefit. I don't call it a psychiatric ward. That sounds so cold. But I don't call it the madhouse or sanatorium either. I just say nerve clinic. My own little cuckoo's nest. And there we mature nicely, enclosed in our angst as if under a cheese bell, under strict supervision and in controlled conditions.

That is part of who I am too.

I can be an awkward bugger. I know. I have problems doing what I'm told. That is probably why I'm not a professor. Authority and rules provoke me. Other people provoke me. Existing provokes me.

I'm not that easy to be with.

I have a half-brother whom I seldom see and a stepfather whom I go to great lengths to avoid. He is my boss at the institute in Oslo.

My mother died last year. Cancer of the lymph glands.

*

My pursuers have disappeared.

After some miles and a toll station, the road widens and the asphalt is new. The motorway into Reykjavik does not swerve around any fairy knolls. The poor invisible fairies who have had their homes destroyed by merciless bull-dozers, thanks to the engineers' self-righteous devotion to the straight line, now roam around in the wilderness, homeless and full of vengeance, making mischief.

So I wave out of the window. I always sympathise with those on the outside.

6

The Árni Magnússon Institute, which houses Iceland's manuscript collection, lies on the edge of the university campus in Reykjavik. Most people shiver when they see the grey façade of a university building. I feel a warm flush of joy: I have come home.

Professor Thrainn Sigurdsson, doctor of philosophy, is sitting hunched over his crowded desk studying a text, moving his lips as if in some silent oath. His name and pon-derous title are engraved on a bronze plate that is threaten-ing to fall from his desk. He looks up when I knock on the half-open door, stands up and shakes my hand. 'Well, well,' he says to no one in particular, 'my condolences.'

When the old manuscripts that Árni Magnússon had dedicated his life to collecting were returned to Iceland, the homecoming was celebrated with a national holiday. Just before he died in 1730, Magnússon left the entire collection to the University of Copenhagen in his will. It was not until 1970 that Iceland got the manuscripts back. The event was broadcast live. Workers and children took the day off. Housewives, labourers, students and down-and-outs all flocked to the harbour when the ship carrying the manu-scripts, *Den Arnamagnæanske Samling*, arrived back in

Reykjavik. Icelanders know how to look after what is theirs.

'Is there a connection?' Thrainn asks.

The papers have written reams about the murder, but the police have not said anything about the missing manuscript.

'They stole the codex,' I tell him.

'Do you have a copy?'

I shake my head.

We sit for a while and discuss what secrets Snorri might have concealed in the text. I describe how the manuscript switches between Snorri's own writing, which Thrainn is sceptical about, and an even older rune script. I draw the symbols that are repeated here and there in the manuscript. Ankh. *Tiwaz*. The cross. The pentagram.

Together we search for a meaning that we cannot grasp.

'Ankh,' Thrainn says. 'The hieroglyph for the Egyptian word that means life. The symbol for eternal life and rebirth. *Tiwaz*. The rune from the elder futhork, representing the Old Norse god, Tyr. The Latin cross. *Crux ordinaria*. The symbol of Christianity and the martyrdom of Christ. The pentagram. A five-pointed star. An ancient, sacred geometric symbol.'

'Sira Magnus and I played with the theory that Snorri had concealed references and instructions in his sagas.'

'Omissions and changes are normal in facsimile editions and handwritten copies of original manuscripts. And writing in the margins.'

'You mean that part of the text is left out?'

'Or added. There are facsimile editions of Snorri's texts in Uppsala in Sweden. And I'm sure there are unknown paper copies that are based on erroneous medieval versions. If we were to compare the most recent versions and the original, word for word, we might get some new information. But that's quite a job.'

'We don't even know what we're looking for. Sira Magnus and I talked about the possibility of discovering proof of contact between the Viking and Egyptian cultures. Evidence that everything from Viking ships and stave churches to maps and mythology was influenced by the Egyptians.'

Thrainn sits looking out of the window. On the wall beside him is a photograph of a figure, holding his long beard. The beard looks like an upside-down ankh. The eleventh-century bronze figure was found at Eyjafjördur on Iceland in 1815.

'Has it struck you that the whole thing might be a fraud? That someone in the Middle Ages made up the codex in order to fool someone?'

Of course the thought has crossed my mind. Museums all over the world are full of forgeries. I open my bag and place a facsimile of *The Saga of the Holy Cross* on the table.

'You know, many people believe that Snorri had nothing to do with that text,' Thrainn points out.

'It contains a code.'

His eyes hold mine for a second too long.

'And Sira Magnus and I have deciphered it,' I continue.

'A code?'

'I think that there's some kind of holy cave out at Thingvellir.'

Thrainn bursts out laughing. 'A holy cave? At Thingvellir? You don't say . . .'

'And I know roughly where it is.'

'You know what?' His good-natured laughter is still bubbling. 'I don't believe a word of it.'

Time for a *coup de grâce*. I show him the instructions. *The number of the beast shows the way along the rock face from Lögberg to Skjaldbreiður . . .*

'Now you're having me on,' the professor exclaims.

The same evening, I book into Hotel Leifur Eiríksson opposite Hallgrím's Church in Reykjavik. I can hear the drone of a street cleaning machine through the window. Hallgrím's Church is floodlit. The façade looks like the pinnacles of an iceberg adrift on an endless ocean.

I make my way to *Á næstu grösum*, a vegetarian restaurant, to have some soup and a vegetable lasagne.

Later on in the evening, the chief superintendent from Borgarnes phones me. He has the autopsy report.

'Sira Magnus died of a heart attack.'

I remain silent for so long that he asks whether I am still there.

'A heart attack? In the hot spring?'

'He might have fallen in. He had water in his lungs, but not enough to drown him. It was his heart.'

'What was he doing in the hot spring? Fully dressed? And what about the stolen document? What about the black Blazer?'

'We will of course continue to investigate. But a heart attack does not mean a murder case.'

The chief superintendent promises to hand my mobile phone in at the hotel reception in the morning. He doesn't say so, but I can tell that the image and message from Sira Magnus have been reduced to evidence of academic interest.

'What do you think caused the heart attack?' I ask, curtly.

'He may of course have been threatened. But it would be difficult to prove a connection between a heart attack and the reported theft of the codex in a court of justice.'

When a policeman says *reported* it is usually because he doesn't know what is going on. In a way, I can sympathise with him.

*

I sit in my hotel room and try to organise my notes and see the logic in what we have established so far. Could the Arabs be part of a gang that has specialised in tracing and stealing historical cultural treasures for collectors on the black market? There are plenty of stinking-rich sheikhs in the Middle East with vaults full of cultural artefacts that any museum worth its salt would have exhibited in closely guarded cases. There is still a lot that confuses me. I don't have the full picture yet. The dates, chronology and different historical lines are a mess. But I'm too tired to concentrate.

I fall asleep on the bed.

Fully clothed. I have not brushed my teeth or washed under my arms. In my dreams I sense my mother's disapproving angel eyes.

Thingvellir

1

A WALL of lava rises, pitch black, into the sky. The
mountains draw spiky silhouettes against the
clouds that roll in from the west and jets of underground
steam hiss out from the rock. Boulders are stacked into
lava monoliths. Frost swathes the lake in a glittering
mist and covers the bogs in a silver blanket. At the foot
of the great rift wall lies a small wooden church and
a cluster of houses that seem to huddle together for
warmth. The North American and European continents
pull and tear at each end of Iceland, splitting the island at
Thingvellir.

'So,' Thrainn says, with a condescending chuckle, 'where
is your treasure trove?'

Crestfallen, I look at the metre-wide rift. Everyone who
visits Thingvellir is struck by the mystical atmosphere. Two
rift walls run straight through the volcanic landscape where
the Althing, the world's oldest national assembly, was
established under open skies in the year 930. From here, the
lovesigemennene, or law speakers, surveyed the bare lava
formations and tussocks and bushes and windswept trees.
Whenever they attended an assembly, they pitched
their tents on the grass between the river and small
streams.

We look at my handwritten translation of Snorri's
text:

The number of the beast
Marks the way
Along the cliff face
From Lögberg
Towards Skjaldbreiður.

Thrainn nods at a recently constructed wooden platform by one of the boulders. 'Lögberg. The Law Rock. The laws were proclaimed from here and all free men could plead their case. This is where they stood, the great heroes of our history books. Law speakers, such as Snorri, ruled from here, together with the men of the Althing.' Thrainn shades his eyes from the sun with his hand and peers from one side to the other. 'If we look hard enough,' he teases, 'perhaps we'll find a big red X.'

And then he turns away and chuckles again.

Thrainn has gathered together a group of archaeology students to help us look; they are all intrigued by the secrecy, the vows of silence and the prospect of being part of something potentially historical. With spades and crowbars on our shoulders, we march down the path along the black lava cliff, for all the world like the seven dwarves, only there are more of us, and none of us is a dwarf. The sun breaks through the clouds. There are very few tourists here this early in the day. An American tour party glances at us with indifference, no doubt thinking we're some kind of work team that the local authority has scraped together from all the pickpockets who have been sentenced to community service.

Thrainn parks the students where the walkways intersect, then together we carry on up to the Lögberg.

'Skjaldbreiður.' Thrainn points towards a mountain in the distance. Then he says thoughtfully: 'Lögberg . . . Sjaldbreiður . . . the number of the beast . . . 666 in the Book of Revelation. Isn't that a bit, well, obvious?'

'For us, perhaps. But Snorri was writing at a time when only a handful of people could read. And even fewer could decipher codes. In order to recognise a concept like the number of the beast you had to be literate.'

'All the same, you say that Snorri wrote encoded directions . . .'

'. . . Intended for other learned people who knew the key needed to decipher the code. Men who shared Snorri's ideas and values. They knew how to read and interpret a coded text. *The number of the beast* is an obvious reference for us. But Revelations was hardly bedtime reading for the masses in the thirteenth century.'

We start to mark out 666 steps from the *Lögberg*. The students follow us in a line like ducklings. We step over lava rocks and grassy knolls. A flock of birds circles high above our heads. The volcanic peaks graze the clouds.

After four hundred steps we stop. I feel disheartened. 'If there was a cave here, it would surely have been discovered years ago!'

'That depends on how well hidden it is. When Howard Carter discovered Tutankhamen's tomb in the Valley of the Kings, archaeologists had been searching for it for decades.'

After a further two hundred steps, we come face to face with a jagged pillar of lava and have to decide whether to go left or right. We follow the cliff face.

Another sixty-six steps and we are there.

And there is nothing there.

2

The rift wall towers some ten or fifteen metres above us and the base is strewn with boulders and moss-covered scree, and the odd hardy plant pushing through here and there.

Once again I read the directions. The number of the beast, 666, marks the way along the cliff from the law stone, *Lögberg*, to Skjaldbreiður. Thrainn and I look at each other despondently. 'No cave,' I confirm, giving one of the lava stones a good kick.

'Snorri might have used a natural cave in the rock face, and concealed it afterwards,' Thrainn suggests, 'in the same way that the Egyptians blocked the entrances to the kings' tombs with stones, once the burial ceremony was over.'

'Surely the locals would have noticed if a natural cave was concealed?'

'Locals? Look around. Can you imagine anywhere more remote and devoid of people? And no doubt in Snorri's day it was even more desolate, if that's possible. The most powerful Icelanders only came to Thingvellir once a year. No one was likely to raise an eyebrow if the entrance to a cave had been covered by a rock fall since the year before.'

'Would it not be risky to hide something in a cave out here?'

'On the contrary. There has always been something mystical, almost sacred, about Thingvellir. It would have been an obvious choice for Snorri.'

We look at the scree at the base of the cliff wall.

'Do you think the entrance to the cave might be concealed in a ravine or crevice below ground level?' Thrainn asks.

'And then covered with stones?'

We look at the scree again.

3

We start to hump lava together with the students.

One of the first things you learn when studying archaeology is patience. Archaeology is best suited to those who are patient, meticulous and unassuming. After all, there are few high points to be had in the field, and vast amounts of earth and clay and reams of intractable forms for registering and cataloguing finds. Only once every century does someone find a Tutankhamen or a Troy.

After a good hour, we have managed to dig about a metre into the scree. Nothing. The rocks thud on the ground behind us and roll into piles and drifts of lava. Soon we have to form a line, passing the stones from person to person.

We must have moved several tons of stone when suddenly one of the students – a young girl whom I could not help noticing – shouts out. We all stop. Small stones and gravel spray out from under my feet as I run towards her.

In the bared rock face, someone has carved out a rectangular niche, about ten centimetres deep. I brush away the earth and moss. The students gasp.

Three symbols have been chiselled into the stone.

Ankh, *tiwaz* and a cross.

4

We accompany the students back up to the car park and fool them into believing that we will continue the work in the morning. They protest. They want to uncover the cave. Now. They want to know what we have found. Now, not tomorrow. I can understand them. But we don't need them. Their presence and curiosity will only complicate and hamper the work. Thrainn says something about using the rest of the day to take measurements and make preparations for excavating the cave. His professorial clout lends him authority and makes him sound convincing. Somewhat reluctantly, the students drive back to Reykjavik, disappointed. Thrainn and I stay standing where we are until the last minibus has been swallowed by the horizon. Then we run back and carry on moving stones.

*

It takes us a couple of hours to uncover the top of the entrance to the cave. An hour and a half later, we have moved enough stones from the entrance.

Thrainn fastens a nylon rope to a boulder just below the opening and I drop it into the cave. Gripping the rope hard, I wriggle through the hole and lower myself down until my feet hit the uneven ground.

The cave is not particularly big. The sun sends a sliver of light through the hole.

Thrainn lowers himself down more quickly and I catch him with both arms.

We find ourselves in a natural cave in the volcanic rock. It is about four to five metres deep and two or three metres wide. We turn on our headlamps. The beams of light bounce and scrape along the walls. Thrainn nudges me. Something resembling an altar has been built against the west wall, from carefully formed blocks of lava. As the altar is made from the same material as its surroundings, it is well camouflaged against the wall. A heavy, smooth slab rests on top of the oblong lava structure.

We position ourselves on either side of the slab and lift it off. In the cavity under the slab is a blackened chest.

Gently, we lift the chest on to the edge of the hollow altar. I scrape the surface with my fingertips.

'Dust? Soot? Lava?' Thrainn asks.

'None of them.' I rub harder. My first guess was right. The casing is tarnished. 'It's a silver casket,' I tell him.

5

We wrap the silver casket up in a tarpaulin and carry it back to the car park. We use ropes to secure it in the back of Thrainn's Toyota Landcruiser.

We are so excited that we don't say a word.

Thrainn pulls out on to the main road to Reykjavik. It is

dead straight. Not a car in sight. We tear through the lunar landscape at well over a hundred and thirty kilometres an hour. The water of Thingvallavannet glitters to our left and the horizon is broken by a row of volcanic peaks.

The Chevy Blazer is parked at an angle across the road straight over the next ridge.

Two men stand waiting on either side of the car. Both of them in an unnatural position, their hands clasped in front of their groins, as if they were posing for a film poster. In the bright sunlight, I can't make out whether they are holding guns.

Thrainn reacts instantly. 'Hold tight!' Without any hesitation, he swings the Landcruiser off the road. I let out a shout. Thrainn grits his teeth and stares straight ahead in deep concentration, as if an action hero has been lying dormant in him and has now woken joyously to life; a specially trained commando soldier who has pretended to study old Icelandic scripts for the past fifteen years as part of some undercover operation.

In a cloud of dust and sand, we accelerate away from the Blazer and the main road. The wheels thunder against the uneven ground.

I catch a glimpse of the Blazer's headlamps through the swirling dust.

Thrainn steers between the boulders. 'We're driving on the remains of the old road between Reykjavik and Thingvellir,' he shouts.

Even though we have the advantage of driving in front, with a clear view, the Blazer is catching up with us.

'Ring 112,' Thrainn instructs me.

I fumble for my mobile phone. Fortunately there is reception. When the operator finally realises that I am speaking English and not some obscure Icelandic dialect, and he understands that we are being pursued by armed men, he sends a patrol car out to meet us. Even though addresses are hard to come by out here in the wild.

The Blazer is only a few metres behind us. Suddenly it veers out to the right. They intend to cut us off.

I see the rock before the driver in the Blazer does. He doesn't manage to brake or to swing aside. With a metallic crash, the Blazer ploughs over the rock.

And gets stuck.

We continue to drive along the old road for a few kilometres until we meet up with an asphalt side road that leads back to the main road.

The police contact us as we are nearing the university. They ask where we are.

It is understandable that they couldn't find us.

But the fact that they have not found the Blazer is more alarming.

6

We borrow an empty laboratory at the Árni Magnússon Institute. A friend of Thrainn's, who is a curator there, helps us to open the casket.

Wrapped in cotton, which in turn is wrapped in leather, we find a small hardwood box. Lying in the box are six thick parchment scrolls, tied together with a leather thong, protected by several layers of soft material.

With extreme care, we open the first scroll. It is in surprisingly good condition. The parchment scrolls each contain two columns of small, symmetrical symbols. I try to read them, but the symbols are unintelligible to me, if vaguely familiar. Thrainn runs his eye down the tightly written pages. The two columns are written in different languages. The left-hand column appears to be Coptic, the language written and spoken in Egypt from around

200 BC until the twelfth century. The right-hand column is possibly Hebrew.

Thrainn feels one of the scrolls with his fingertips, smells it and studies the letters. 'I would guess that the parchment is a thousand years old, give or take a hundred years.'

He rolls the document up again and puts it back in the box. We carry the casket down the spiral stairs into the basement, where Iceland's oldest and most valuable manuscripts are kept in a secured vault, with a regulated atmosphere. Behind a thick, heavy steel door, the entire written history of the Nordic countries is stored on metre-high shelves, carefully wrapped in paper and placed in flat cardboard boxes.

It is in this solid vault, in the Arní Magnússon Institute, that we hide the chest containing the scrolls from Thingvellir.

7

It turns out to be a long day. Police. Journalists. Researchers. Everyone wants to hear the story, again and again.

In the taxi on the way back to Hotel Leifur Eiríksson, I get a phone call from the chief superintendent in Borgarnes.

They have just received a report of a break-in at the guest apartment at Snorrastofa. It seems likely that the flat was broken into yesterday, soon after I had moved into town. He adds: 'I've spoken to the police in Reykjavik and, given everything that's happened, they're going to send a patrol car over to the hotel in the course of the evening. Just to be on the safe side.'

The taxi stops outside the hotel. I pay. It strikes me that 'just to be on the safe side' has an ominous ring to it.

The Rune Code

I LIKE hotels. You always feel welcome. You're part of a community, but one that never bothers you with unwelcome attention. When you go out, someone comes and makes your bed and tidies your room without complaint. When you let yourself in again, exhausted, everything is clean and tidy and nice.

With a gentle smile, I open the door and enter Room 206.

There are two of them.

Arabs.

One of them is enormous and muscular, and must weigh well over a hundred kilos. His eyes are two black pits. I recognise him. He is the giant from the photograph that Sira Magnus sent me. He has shaved his head, but kept his great moustache. His cheeks and chin are speckled black with stubble.

The other one is short, but stocky and well built, like a coiled spring, with a pained expression on his face, as if he's spent his childhood walking around with a sharp stone in his shoe.

They are both wearing neatly pressed, dark grey suits.

And they are both in my hotel room.

The short one is standing just inside the open door,

about a metre away from me. The giant is sitting in a chair over by the window.

I stand stock still. A dart of fear drills through me and nails me to the wall. A couple of things prevent me from spinning round and legging it out into the hall and down the stairs. One is my knees, which are trembling so much that my whole body shakes. And the other is the gun that the smaller of the two Arabs is pointing straight at me.

Thanks to my super-thick glasses and a childhood fascination with guns, I'm able to identify it as a Glock.

'Please,' I whimper.

The short man pushes the door shut.

I catch a faint whiff of aftershave and cigars.

'Good evening, Mr Beltø,' says the smaller of the two Arabs, in English. His voice is as dry as a desert wind.

My heart is hammering so hard and fast that my ears are ringing. I gasp for breath.

He waves me into the room. I obediently stumble forward a few steps.

'What do you want?' A pathetic and unsuccessful attempt to take control of the situation. My voice is so shaky that it sounds as if I am crying.

The bigger man rubs his face with his hand. His skin is rough. He must have sat outside through one too many sandstorms. His nose casts a shadow.

'Where are they?'

'What?' I try. My mouth is so dry that my tongue sticks to my palate.

The short man waves his gun around and shouts: 'Where are the scrolls?'

Scrolls. Manuscripts.

For a moment I wonder whether I should pretend that I have no idea what they are talking about. But only for a moment. The knowledge of what they can and might do to me has transformed me into a pathetic shaking leaf, a miserable creature cringing with fear.

'I don't have them!'

My voice shakes. My hands shake. My knees shake.

The man in the chair gets up. He is even bigger than I'd imagined. A monolith of muscle. He motions for me to come closer. As soon as I'm close enough, he grabs my shirt and pulls me up to his face. I can smell his stinking breath. He must have eaten something raw and bloody for lunch. I can see the pores in his skin and the bottomless pit in his eyes.

He takes my left hand and forces my little finger back.

'Where are the scrolls?' asks the man with the gun.

Outside the window, Hallgrím's Church soars into the sky, bathed in a supernatural glow. Down on the pavement, people hurry by through the biting wind.

He pushes harder. The pain is unbearable.

'Where?'

I cry out. High and loud. The muscle mountain continues to look at me without batting an eyelid. And pushes my finger back even farther.

By now I am prepared to admit to anything. To tell them where the scrolls are. That I'm the leader of a satanic cult that sacrifices small children. That I'm a member of al-Qaeda. That I'm a double-crossing agent for the CIA, FBI, MI5 and Mossad. But the pain is so intense that I can neither think nor speak.

'Where are the scrolls?'

I've never really thought of myself as being particularly fragile. With a shudder I hear my pinkie snap. It breaks with a sharp, cracking sound, as when you step on a dry branch in the woods. I scream. A flame of pain shoots from my hand up into my head.

He lets go. I grab my left hand, whimpering. My whole arm is burning.

'I'm sorry about what happened to the priest,' the man with the gun says. 'But we won't hesitate' – he looks at me intently to make sure that I understand – 'to mutilate or kill you. We want the scrolls!'

Muscleman puts his great paws round my neck. My Adam's apple bobs up and down over his index finger. He hasn't closed his hands. But still I gag and gasp for breath.

If this were a film, I would make a break for it and leap out of the window. Through the glass. People will do anything to escape danger. But I have always been a wimp. I don't like heights. Or shards of glass. There is something about getting cut and blood and broken arms and legs that I have a problem with.

I have no intention of sacrificing my life for the scrolls from Thingvellir. Just as I'm about to tell them that the scrolls are in the vault at the Arní Magnússon Institute, I look down into the street.

A police car pulls up opposite the hotel.

Something in my eyes must have shown a glimmer of hope. The big Arab turns and looks out of the window. His hands loosen their grip round my neck. I sob and gulp down the air. His friend comes over to the window. The short guy says something that sounds like *mokhabarat*. The big guy answers *shorta*.

Down on the street, two policemen get out of the patrol car. They have all the time in the world.

The Arabs glare at me like two hyenas who have had their prey snatched from under their noses.

I whimper.

Quick as a flash, they tie my wrists to the bed frame and cover my mouth with gaffer tape.

Then they disappear.

2

The police eventually hear my half-strangled cries and storm into the hotel room, but the Arabs have long since vanished down the fire escape and out through the backyard, into one of the quiet streets behind the hotel.

I feel faint. The policemen remove the tape and help me into bed. My pain and fear are in no way proportional to something as minor as having your pinkie broken. But for me, it is more than enough.

The police call for reinforcements. From the bed, I hear police cars and an ambulance slam to a halt outside on the street. Soon the hotel is crawling with officers and detectives. A young locum with a cold stethoscope listens to my heart, which is pounding away. He puts a splint on my sore, swollen finger, which he then tapes to my ring finger. I'm given a sling and some pills for the pain. A female nurse strokes my cheek in sympathy. The detectives question me. I point out the biggest of the Arabs on the mobile phone picture and suggest that the small, solid guy may be one of the fuzzier people in the background. They are so indifferent as they take notes in their spiral-bound notebooks that you might be forgiven for thinking that aggressive Arabs coming to plunder the country of its cultural heritage and breaking the fingers of innocent researchers were regular occurrences on Iceland.

Some hours later I have told them all I know. The ambulance has returned to the hospital without me.

Two policemen stay in the hotel, one outside my door and the other down in reception.

I toss and turn all night. The whole universe has been reduced to one single point of pain: my pinkie.

3

'Bjørn Beltø?'

The woman in the doorway looks uneasily at the police-man then at me, while she clutches an envelope to her chest.

I have just been down to eat breakfast. With my police escort.

'My husband and I are friends of Sira Magnus,' she con-tinues, in a mixture of Danish and Norwegian. Then adds: 'Were. We are parishioners from Reykholt. My husband sings in the church choir. Can I come in?'

She does not seem to be particularly dangerous, but the policeman still studies her from head to toe with his X-ray eyes.

'My husband is waiting in the car,' she tells me when I let her into the room and shut the door. She is obviously not used to being in hotel rooms with strange men. She stays standing in the middle of the floor, the envelope still clutched to her chest. 'The day that Sira Magnus died . . .'

'Yes?'

'He came to see us in the morning. He said that if any-thing should happen to him, we were to give you *this*.' She hands me the envelope, which has been sealed with several layers of Sellotape. 'We were not to go to the police, but to make sure that *you* got it.'

'Thank you.'

'We've been trying to get hold of you.'

'Sorry. I've been very busy.'

'We heard about it on the radio. That you found a cave out at Thingvellir.' She cocks her head as if she is waiting for an explanation.

'Thank you so much. Sira Magnus would be very grateful.'

My silence makes her shrug and repeat that her husband is waiting in the car. I thank her once again and she leaves.

4

I tear open the envelope and pull out the piece of paper.

Forgive me, Sira Magnus, but I can't help it: I burst out laughing. A man unto himself. Unto death.

There are three lines on the page.

Runes.

At first glance, the text looks utterly incomprehensible.

I can actually read runes, but even when I look at it for a second and then third time, the text remains incomprehensible.

At the top of the page is:

G88C3

Under this, he has written the following text:

ᛁᛁᛁ·ᛏᛈᛉᛋᛟᚾᛂᛐ �

ᛗᛟᛈᚲᛉᚦᛏ:ᚾᛋᚲᛈᚦᛒ

ᛋᚷᛖᛖᛁᚦᚦᚾ:ᛈᛋᚲᛟᛋᚾᛏᚲᛘᚾᚷᛋ

I stare at the text for a long time, trying to understand it. But even when I go through it letter by letter, it is still unreadable.

The runic message is in code.

He must have feared that something would happen. He was afraid of what they might do. So he left a message with friends he could trust. This realisation sends a shiver down my spine. Sira Magnus must have realised that his life was in danger.

What was it that he knew and never let on?

When I read the text again, I sense a pattern that is not visible on the surface. He must have replaced letters according to the Caesar method, but by how many letters? And which way?

I phone my friendly code genie and dictate the rune text to him.

'G88C3,' Terje Lønn Erichsen mumbles. 'That must be the key.'

A flash of recognition. 'G88! The official registration number for the Kylver Stone,' I exclaim. The Kylver Stone was found in a tomb on Kylver Farm on Gotland in 1903. A piece of limestone with the *elder futhork* on it, the earliest runes. We transcribe the runes' sound values and come up with the following incomprehensible text:

iii.ndgëo.hÞd

rëtwpgdt: uëp dÞb

sgëëiÞwu: dëp oëutpëhgs

'We're getting there,' Terje assures me. 'This code isn't particularly advanced. It might just be a simple Caesar three.'

It might be. By applying the Caesar three rule, and then translating it into English, we come up with the following text:

www.gmail.com

Username: your mother

Password: my passion

'Voila!' Terje crowed. 'A ready-made email account.'

Magnus, you old fox . . .

I thank Terje for his help, log on to the Internet and Gmail on my laptop, then write in my mother's name and Magnus's passion, which is not Snorri as you might easily assume, but foie gras, which for my purposes has to be written as a single word in order to be a password.

There is one email waiting for me in my inbox.

Subject: *To Bjørn*

The message is short: '*Shit happens. Good luck, Bjørn. I'm with you all the way. Don't judge me too harshly. Your friend, Magnus.*'

I open the attachment.

For a few seconds the world stops turning.

Sira Magnus has sent me a scanned and digitalised version of the Snorri Codex.

5

I stay in Iceland for a few more days.

The whole time, I am escorted by two uniformed police, who by virtue of their presence prevent me from doing any of the things I should really do.

Thrainn and I are interviewed by the papers and TV channels about the discovery of the cave and the silver casket with the manuscripts that everyone now calls the Thingvellir Scrolls. The name is not coincidental. In 1947, a goatherd in Quram found some scrolls in a cave by the Dead Sea. Over the course of the next decade, goatherds, Bedouins and archaeologists found no less than eight hundred and fifty scrolls containing old Jewish biblical texts. These manuscripts have gone down in history as the Dead Sea Scrolls.

I have forwarded a copy of the Snorri Codex to Thrainn. For safety's sake, I ask him not to tell anyone that we have a copy. You never know.

The Thingvellir Scrolls are securely stored in the massive vault in the basement of the Árni Magnússon Institute. The Arabs will not be able to open the steel door, not even with dynamite, Semtex and flame cutters.

Thrainn recruits three specialists – two linguists and one historian – to translate the text.

I decide to go back to Norway. The police have no objections. They are happy about it. They drive me out to the airport at the crack of dawn and make sure that I get safely on board the plane.

I don't see them standing there waving as the plane takes off, but I imagine that is what they are doing. And heaving a sigh of relief to be rid of me.

The Pentagram

1

SOMEONE HAS been in my flat.

I live in a block of flats: two bedrooms, a sitting room and a kitchen. Far too big for a hermit like me, but the view over Oslo is superb.

For me, home is sacred. When the door closes, I shut out the world. Problems at work, annoying colleagues, pushy women, unscrupulous murderers.

So my feet feel like two lead weights as I stand on the mat in my hallway. I carefully remove the key from the lock and close the door behind me. I put my suitcase down on the hand-knotted rug that I bought in a bazaar in Istanbul.

The door to my study is ajar. I remember closing it before I went to Iceland. I always close the doors before I leave the flat. In case there is a fire or a leak.

I hold my breath. Are they still here?

My eyes sweep over the hallway.

Somewhere in the building, a door opens. I jump. *Get a grip, Bjørn!* Of course they're not here. They're in Iceland. They can't be in Norway and Iceland at the same time.

In my mind's eye, I see Sira Magnus's dead eyes. And the two Arabs in the hotel room in Reykjavik.

The silence oozes and swells. What should I do? Run away? Stay where I am? Call the police? 'Are the burglars in the flat?' they'll ask. 'I don't know,' I'll reply. 'Has the door been forced open?' 'No,' will be my answer, 'I just have a feeling.' Then the emergency operator will sigh and ask me to ring the central switchboard if I discover any signs of a break-in or if anything has been stolen.

I push open the door to my study.

I had expected to step into an office that had been ransacked. But everything is in perfect order. Just as I left it.

Almost.

The left side of my keyboard has been pushed a centimetre or two in from the edge of the desk, whereas I always leave it parallel.

The sitting room is tidy. But they have put *Iceland's Bell* by Laxness back to the right of Nabokov's *Lolita*, not to the left. In my CD collection, I see that Pink Floyd's *Wish You Were Here* has been put back next to *Ummagumma*. The crossword on the small glass table in the corner between the sofas – where six down has still not been solved – has been turned upside down. My crossword pen is lying at an angle across it, not parallel with the bottom.

They have looked in the bedroom and the kitchen and the small, overflowing cupboard. I don't know whether they found what they were looking for. I don't even know what they were looking for.

When I have unpacked my suitcase and put the washing machine on, I take a can of beer from the fridge and collapse into the sofa.

The telephone rings before I have a chance to open the beer. Thrainn. He tells me that his house has been broken into, and so has the institute. Fortunately, they found nothing. They haven't even tried to get into the vault.

I ask him to contact the police and add that it is probably best that we don't say any more in case the line is tapped.

I fiddle around for a while before I manage to open the

can. Because I bite my nails, it's difficult to get my finger under the aluminium ring. We all have our problems.

With a shaking hand, I raise the can to my mouth and drink.

I'm not a hero. But I am obstinate. And I think to myself that I've had enough now.

I phone the police. They are not going to believe a word. I am transferred to the central switchboard. I stammer out my story about everything that happened on Iceland – about Sira Magnus, about the Arabs, about the archaeological finds. I say that I think someone has been in my flat. As I listen to myself, I can just imagine the person on the other end ticking the box in the logbook that says 'psychiatric case'.

Then the policeman says something unexpected: 'Jesus,' he exclaims.

Maybe he has heard about me. Maybe he is impressed by my title and all the references to Snorri. Even a policeman might yearn for a little adventure and drama in daily life.

'We'll send a man round,' he says firmly.

2

The man they send round is plump, dressed in a knee-length skirt and a tight-fitting sweater that doesn't exactly hide the weight of her breasts.

At first I think she's a door-to-door salesman. Then I notice that it says POLICE on the ID card hanging on a lanyard round her neck.

Her name is Ragnhild and she is a detective inspector. I make some instant coffee and we sit down in the sitting room. I tell her about everything that happened in Iceland and the reasons why I think someone has broken into my flat. She neither laughs nor rolls her eyes. When I have finished, she examines the door frames and locks. I say that they are more professional than that. One by one, I show her the signs of the break-in: the keyboard, the books, the CDs, the crossword and crossword pen. She smiles inscrutably and says that I am a very observant gentleman.

Later, two police technicians arrive to go over the flat with their brushes and small plastic bags in which they gather all the evidence.

The police are in my flat for a couple of hours. They find no evidence. By the time the technicians leave and Ragnhild gets up to say goodbye, we are none the wiser.

'As I'm sure you understand, there is not enough evidence for us to put you under police protection,' she says. 'But – take care.' She gives me a card with a series of telephone numbers. Then she writes down a mobile phone number with a biro. 'My private number. Just in case . . . well, you know.'

When Ragnhild has left, I lock the door. The main lock and the security chain. I have a drink from the can. The beer is flat and warm.

The phone rings. This time no one says anything. But I do hear someone breathing. They hang up.

Someone is checking to see whether I'm at home.

I throw only the most necessary clothes and toiletries into a bag and run down to the car. There are those who would hesitate to call Bolla a car. I have never felt the need to show off with big cars. Bolla is a Citroën 2CV. A tin can with a sewing-machine engine. Full of soul and charm and synthetic oil.

In my trusty Bolla, I flee my flat. No one follows me. Which is a good thing, as Bolla doesn't go that fast. But I'm sure they are watching me. They know where I am. I can't see them, but they can undoubtedly see me.

The head of my department at university, Professor Trygve Arntzen, is an unbearable shit. That I know for sure. He has been my stepfather for over twenty-five years.

When Mother died, any fragile bonds of forced politeness and strained tolerance vanished.

The professor took over Mother, to put it nicely, when my father fell to his death from a mountain ledge that the professor had insisted he should climb on to. I was twelve. If nothing else, I learnt that it was fatally dangerous to challenge gravity. Some years ago I found out that Father had tried to kill the professor, because he was having an affair with Mother. Instead it was Father who became the victim of the abseiling accident. As Sira Magnus said: *Shit happens*.

I know the professor's peculiarities. Such as the fact that he is always at work early. He says that he gets so much done before the rest of the world wakes up. I myself have slept in the car all night. In the car park. Watched by a surveillance camera.

The professor is already in his office when I knock on the door. The look on his face is similar to one he might have if someone had squeezed lemon into his mouth.

'Bjørn? I thought you were in Iceland?'

'Correct, I *was*.'

I dutifully tell him about the highlights of the trip, which he must already have read about days ago. I keep quiet about anything that might be viewed as breaking with formalities. Professor Arntzen is a stickler for rules who would try the patience of a saint. But I manage to interest him enough to let me continue working on 'the project' for the time being. He looks daggers at me and asks me to report to him regularly, so he knows where I am with my work.

Right.

4

Cicero once said that loneliness is not a burden for someone who is engrossed in study. I am always engrossed in my studies, but that doesn't make my longings any easier to deal with. They just become easier to repress.

I have locked the door to my tiny university office, where I sit squashed between a bulging filing cabinet and bookshelves full of wisdom. I roll my pencil between my fingers and stare out of the window, then at the computer screen. I'm desperately trying to work out what Sira Magnus knew, and realised, and why he was so afraid of the supposed experts. Did he know that they didn't represent the Schimmer Institute? Who had he spoken to? What made him scan the whole Snorri Codex, page by page, and then create a rune code to lead me to it?

I have printed the codex out on shiny high-quality paper. Hidden in between the rows of runes and Latin letters, symbols and maps, there are obviously more messages and clues. Parts of the text are encrypted, but many of the paragraphs are legible.

What was the secret that made Snorri handwrite a text for posterity?

The first three pages are written in runes on a darker, older parchment than the rest. The runes were a Germanic alphabet that spread and developed throughout northern Europe in the first century AD. The spread of Christianity meant that the runes were gradually replaced by the Latin alphabet, but for several hundred years, runes and letters were used side by side.

Symbol by symbol, word by word, I translate the runes. The text appears to be a cross between a set of rules, an oath and instructions, and opens as follows:

> Beware, reader, of the mystic runes. The torments of Duat, Helheim and Hell await those who decipher the mysteries of the runes without leave. Turn aside this parchment of the Gods.
>
> For thus it is: In the mystery of the Gods, we protect the Holy Secret. The power of the runes hides the prophecy behind a veil of signs.
>
> Chosen are you who guard the mystery with your honour and your life. Your sacred helpers, Osiris, Odin and the White Christ follow and protect you. Praise be to thee, Amon!

The next verse, which is written in runes but has obviously been translated from Egyptian, is even stranger:

> ~ The Key ~
> Courtiers of the Royal Court accompany
> The Osiris King Tut-ankh-Amon westwards.
> They proclaim: O King! Come in peace!
> O God! Protector of this land!

The key?

The rune texts are followed by several pages written two hundred years later by Snorri himself, in Latin letters, with maps and drawings. Some of it is written in code, and some of it in legible text:

> Kings and earls, chieftains and knights, skalds and initiated men are united in the Holy Circle, the circle of the GUARDIANS of the Sacred Secret.
>
> Only the chosen and initiated shall interpret the hidden words and hidden signs.

I picture Snorri sitting in the writing room in Reykholt. The scriptorium is lit only by the tallow candles standing on the sloping desks and oil lamps hanging from the ceiling and on the walls. He must have dismissed his scribes so he could be on his own. In front of him, he has the stretched white, soft vellum. The quill is stripped and cut. Then he starts to write, with an even hand that follows the faintly marked lines. He draws a pentagram in the middle of the page, also known as a devil's star; and in Snorri's day, people believed that you could protect yourself from the demons that plague you and disturb your sleep by carving the star on your door.

Even in a modern office, with a computer, telephone, fax and a magnetic paper-clip holder, I can feel the power of the pentagram. For five thousand years, the five-pointed star has shone brightly in the occult sky. The Egyptians drew a circle round the star, *duat*, which pointed to the underworld, the next life. The Arabs used it in magic and rituals. The Pythagoreans believed that the pentagram was an expression of mathematical perfection, as the golden ratio 1.618 is concealed in the lines of the pentagram. For Jews, it symbolises the Five Books of Moses, or the Pentateuch. For Christians, the symbol represents both black magic and the five wounds of Christ. And, if you turn it round so the single point faces down, you have a satanist symbol, the devil's star.

On the fifth page, I find a map of southern Norway, from Trondheim down. The map is not particularly good. Maps in Snorri's day were based on measurement by eye and guesswork. The first known map of the Nordic countries is the Nancy map from 1427, drawn by the Dane Claudius Clavus, who lived in Rome for a number of years and fraternised with the Pope's cardinals and secretaries. Someone, however, had drawn a map of Østlandet several hundred years before him – copied from an even older rune scroll.

I sit and study the text and runes for hours and hours. I translate the rune text and Snorri's text. I struggle with the codes. I know that a message might be concealed in these pages – instructions, maybe in a code that I haven't even discovered yet. I examine the map of Norway and the symbols.

But I find no meaning.

After lunch – two slices of bread with Gouda cheese, a piece of raw turnip, a carrot and a cup of tea – I phone the chief superintendent in Borgarnes to find out whether there is any news. There is. The suspects have been caught on CCTV at a petrol station in Saubær. The pictures are now being sent to Interpol. The Norwegian police have received a copy. But he tells me that the Arabs have sunk into the sand, ha ha. Then he is serious again and tells me just enough about the investigation for me to feel that I am being kept informed without knowing anything at all.

As soon as I put the phone down, Ragnhild from Oslo Police calls. She has just received the pictures from Iceland and asks me whether I can identify the suspects. She has sent me a copy by email and will hold while I open the mail and attachment.

The images from the CCTV are black and white, but sharp and clear.

I recognise the two men who visited me in my hotel room in Reykjavik. The small, slimy one. And the giant of a man who broke my finger.

'That's them,' I say.

'We'll get them. Now that we've got a picture, we've got something to work on.'

I ask her to wait a moment. Under her email is another, unopened message:

From: < sender unknown> Sent: <date unknown>
To: bjorn.belto@khm.uio.no

84

Cc:

Subject: Bjørn Beltø – read this!

Dear Bjørn Beltø,

You don't know who I am. But now I 'know' you. I apologise for any pain or fear that my men may have caused you. I have asked them to do a job, and I can't follow them up on every detail.

Your friend in Iceland, Sira Magnus, found a codex that my men have now secured. But you also managed to discover a copy of the manuscript that the press, in their limitless creativity, have chosen to call the Thingvellir Scrolls.

I am willing to go to great lengths – and I repeat, great lengths – to secure this manuscript, whether it is still in Iceland, or in your possession now, in Norway.

I don't like to make threats. But you are forcing me to use methods that I would rather have avoided.

Therefore I ask you: please give the Thingvellir Scrolls to my men. Your cooperation will be richly rewarded. And by 'richly', I mean with more money than you can imagine. You could live the rest of your life in luxury, without having to worry.

If you choose not to do as I ask, your fate will no longer be in my hands. My men have very clear instructions. I do not wish to harm you, but nothing is of greater importance to me than securing the copy of the manuscript from Thingvellir. I have given my men permission to do everything necessary. I will refrain from going into details.

My throat fills with sand and putty.

I have never received a written threat before in my life. This is my first.

I read it out to Ragnhild in a stammering, whining voice.

She asks me to do two things: to print out a copy and to forward the email to her.

I press Print. Nothing happens. I press the mouse again in irritation. Several times.

Nothing.

Just as I'm in the process of forwarding the email, the screen starts to flicker. The email disintegrates in front of my eyes, as if every pixel has suddenly let go of its neighbour and is moving away in absolute chaos.

In the end, the mail is gone.

'It's disappeared,' I say.

'That's not possible.'

I look in the Outlook inbox. The email is still at the top. I click on it and immediately the whole line disappears.

'Check in Deleted Items.'

Nothing.

She tells me that what I have just described is technically impossible. An email can't just disappear from the receiver's computer. The text must have been a passable attachment that would be picked up by the anti-virus program.

'Was it an X-attachment?'

'It was a completely normal email.'

'Someone must have hacked into your computer and installed a spy program.'

'Have they been here? *Here?*'

'If they have the software to make Outlook mails disappear, they have considerable data expertise. In which case they could easily have sent you an email – even one that ended up in your spam file and was then deleted – that would automatically install a hidden program.'

'It didn't say who the email was from.'

'It's easy to manipulate and change the sender's address and date. Theoretically, it should be possible to find out which server the mail was sent from, but there are also smart solutions here, such as hacking into a poorly secured server and sending mails from there.'

Ragnhild asks me to write down what the email said, as far as possible, word for word.

Half an hour later, she arrives with a police technician to take my computer away. But I doubt that they will find anything.

5

Late in the afternoon, I unlock my office door to leave. I am anxious. I have hidden the printout of the Snorri document in a transparent plastic bag under my shirt. The plastic is sticking to my chest.

I hurry along the endless corridor, down the stairs to the basement and then out into daylight, at the back of the institute. The sun feels like red-hot needles in my eyes. I clip my sunglasses on to the frame of my ordinary glasses. The air smells of late summer.

I take the metro from Blindern down to the city centre, and then walk to the multi-storey car park where I have left Bolla.

He is sitting on some steps opposite the entrance, pretending to read a paper. But the whole time he is actually watching the glass doors, which open and close automatically.

What really alarms me is that there are so many entrances to the car park; if they have someone watching one entrance, they must also be watching the others. How many of them are there?

I disappear round the corner and leave Bolla where she is – alone and surrounded by the enemy – on level P2.

Who are they? Could Sira Magnus have contacted collectors on the black market? Rich foreigners who are happy to go to great lengths to get hold of curiosities via the back door. But to go as far as killing? For an old parchment scroll?

Or, for the information concealed in the text.

I take the tram down to Skillebekk and hide in an entrance-way down a side street.

Terje Lønn Erichsen arrives a good thirty minutes later. In his shoulder bag – the same one he has had since we were at university together – he has a tin lunch box, a thermos from his school days, and a copy of one of the tabloids to read on the tram. His shoulders are lopsided as he saunters down the street. Terje has small teeth and big ears, and a bald patch which he compensates for with otherwise long, curly hair and an impressive beard.

He stops when he sees me and grins. 'Bjørn! Trouble with the ladies?'

We specialise in irony and have developed our own language where even the cruellest insults are well meant. Terje knows perfectly well that I, like him, have been nowhere near a woman for years.

I stay the night with Terje. He thinks that having to hide someone who is on the run from mysterious pursuers is exciting.

I assume that he probably thinks I'm imagining things. But that's fine. Both for him and me.

6

Ever since I was a boy, I have been drawn to witches.

A strange attraction, to be fair. My desires have never followed the well-trodden path of reason. Initially, when I was very young, witches frightened me to death. They wore black capes and had long noses and warts sprouting hair. They cooked stinking brews in large cauldrons and flew through the dark on broomsticks with an evil, screeching cackle. As I got older and my hormones somewhat gingerly broke out of their shell, I understood intuitively that witches also possessed a subtle erotic attraction that made me go weak at the knees.

Though I was just as terrified.

Which was why I stand on Adelheid af Geierstam's doormat, swallowing and gasping for air.

'Bjørn Beltø?' she asks and cocks her head.

'Adelheid?'

'Come in, come in!'

Adelheid af Geierstam fits my expectations of what a genuine Wicca witch should look like. She is enchanting in a sensual and subtle way. Her lips are narrow and moist, her eyes icy blue and burning with veiled promises.

She lives in Lillehammer, in a big, old, draughty wooden house with flaking white paint and a garden full of forgotten apple trees, overgrown redcurrant bushes and compost heaps that have long since been left to themselves.

She guides me from the porch into the hall, where I hang my coat on a peg. She asks about my train journey. Dressed in flowing garments that almost hide her figure, she floats down the hall in front of me then turns into a large room full of bongo drums, hanging zebra skins, wooden masks, spears, an antelope head and a woven dreamcatcher resplendent with ostrich feathers and lions' claws.

Adelheid offers me some herbal tea in a big, ceramic mug.

'I'm so glad you've come. It really is about time! The established sciences have never had any understanding of sacred geometry! You must be the first professor who has come to see me.'

Instead of pointing out that I am in fact a humble associate professor and do not really represent anyone other than myself, I take a sip of my herbal tea, which tastes like a stewed brew of grass and contaminated perennials.

Adelheid has written four controversial books about the history of sacred geometry and its influence on the locations of Nordic monasteries, churches, burial grounds and castles.

'There are examples of sacred geometry all over Norway. But many scientists view the discipline as mere superstition.' Her voice is warm. When she puts her hand on mine, her stone bead bracelet and jewellery jingle and jangle. I am not unaffected by the unexpected contact with her skin.

She continues before I manage to ask a question.

'Along the coast of Norway, from Rogaland to Nordfjord, sixty stone crosses show the influence of the Celts and the Christianisation of Norway in the period to around 1000. Holy Olav reaped the benefit of this Celtic influence. Do you really believe that the stone crosses, some of which are three to four metres high, were positioned arbitrarily?'

'I've never really thought about it.'

'Is it a coincidence that if you draw a line from Utstein Abbey near Stavanger to Tønsberg, and then up to Trondheim, the lines form a ninety-degree angle?'

'Ah.'

'And is it a coincidence that the Cistercian Order built Lyse Abbey in 1146, the Sancta Mariae Abbey on Hovedøya in the Oslo Fjord in 1147, Munkeby in Trondheim in 1180 and Tautra on the Trondheim Fjord in 1207?'

'Hardly.'

'And is it then a coincidence that the distance from the Augustinian abbey at Utstein to Oslo is the same as from Lyse Abbey to Oslo? Is it a coincidence that it is exactly two hundred and seventy-five kilometres from Halsnøy Abbey, established by the Augustinians in 1163, to Tønsberg Fortress, as it is from Tønsberg to Utstein?'

'Wow.'

'All ancient, holy places in Norway accord with a mathematical logic that shows that our ancestors were inspired by and learnt a lot from the Greeks and Egyptians. And is it perhaps just coincidence that the religiously significant towns of Bergen, Trondheim, Hamar and Tønsberg are all situated on the points of a pentagram on the old medieval map?'

A shiver runs down my spine. I feel ice cold. I still have not told her why I am there. And yet she has pre-empted one of my questions.

'I don't want to sound alarmist or melodramatic,' I say, 'but a priest in Iceland has been killed because of what I'm about to show you.'

I put the copy of the Snorri Codex down in front of her.

'Is this the Thingvellir Scrolls?'

'No, this text led us to the cave in Thingvellir. Snorri wrote the part that is written in Latin letters. The runes were presumably written a couple of hundred years earlier. The maps and the magic symbols were drawn some time between 1050 and 1250.'

We allow a few seconds for the words to sink in.

She looks through the pages with reverence and studies the maps and symbols. 'The ankh! The pentagram! This is amazing!'

I give her a summary of the rune text and explain that the text and maps probably hide some instructions.

I leaf through. 'Here is a map of southern Norway. Even though it doesn't quite correspond with modern geography, I don't understand how anyone was able to draw such a precise map several hundred years before cartography became an established science.'

'Have you put a pentagram over the map?'

I look up at her before looking back down at the map.

'The pentagram and the map belong together,' she says. 'You have to base yourself on the holy places of the day. Bjørgvin, Nidaros, Hamar and Tunsberg.'

As she speaks, she marks each place with a dot, and then she draws a line from Bergen to Trondheim. From Bergen to Hamar, where Nicholas Breakspear, who later became Pope Adrian IV, established a diocese in the 1150s. Then from Trondheim to Tønsberg, Norway's oldest town and the medieval centre of power.

'Now we're only missing two lines,' she says, 'and then we have a pentagram.'

'But there are no religious centres in the north-west.' I point to the missing coordinate, which appears to be somewhere near Stadlandet.

'Don't say that. There are several mysterious caves in the area, like Dollstein Cave. A colleague of mine, Harald Sommerfeldt Boehlke, who is a scholar, has studied the cave and the stories connected to it. The opening of the cave faces the sea, sixty metres up the mountainside on the west of Sandsøy in Møre and Romsdal county. Legend has it that King Arthur was once in that part of the country and that there is treasure hidden in the cave. From the opening, a tunnel leads into a huge chamber. There are five such chambers or caves, linked by narrow tunnels. The cave measures a hundred and eighty metres, but in the olden days it was believed that the tunnels ran under the sea to Scotland. The crusader Ragnvald Kalle Kollson, Earl of Orkney, who was named after Holy Olav's foster son, Ragnvald Bruseson of Orkney, visited the cave in 1127 to try to find a treasure that was supposed to be hidden there.'

Adelheid draws the two last lines, and as if by magic, a pentagram appears on the map of Norway.

In secret, someone with an esoteric understanding of the magic of numbers, geography and geometry has laid the basis for what became Nidaros Cathedral, Hamar Cathedral, Tønsberg Fortress and a sanctuary in the Bergen area.

'Few people know that a great number of sanctuaries throughout the Nordic countries are situated according to a hermetic, mathematical order,' Adelheid tells me. She goes over to the bookshelf, pulls out a book and turns to a page that shows an aerial photograph of the burial mounds in

Gamle Uppsala in Sweden. 'Can you see how the mounds and surrounding churches and castles are situated in relation to circles and angles?' She illustrates with a red nail-varnished finger.

In another book, she shows me a map of Bornholm, the Danish island in the Baltic Sea. 'If you superimpose a pentagram on the island, you can see that the crusaders' round churches, fortifications and sanctuaries are all situated on the lines of the pentagram.'

She pulls out yet another book. 'The Icelanders, Einar Pálsson and Einar Birgisson, have documented how big farms, churches and important places were situated and built in accordance with sacred geometric principles from the time that Iceland was settled. Imagine a circle that symbolises the horizon and the heavenly zodiac. The spokes of the circle were defined by the movements of the sun, and together formed a cosmic map that shows that the Icelanders must have been familiar with Egyptian cosmology.'

I drink some more herbal tea, which is starting to get cold.

She takes several more books from the bookshelf. 'You can find the same patterns and mysteries here in Norway. The research of Bodvar Schjelderup and Harald Sommerfeldt Boehlke, who have both written fascinating books about their findings, documents how widespread sacred geometry was in Norwegian history. Remember, the Vikings were not simply bloodthirsty warriors. They were people of deep faith with enquiring minds. They valued harmony. Just look at the shape of their ships. And the runes. When the Vikings wanted to establish important landmarks, they adhered to a geometry of sacred lines and forms.'

'But, at the end of the day, it's just a jumble of lines and coordinates,' I say, and point at the map.

'I would assume that more detailed directions for the place are concealed in the text. Perhaps encrypted.'

Crestfallen, I stare at the text. I have gone through it so many times that I cannot believe that there are hidden codes there that I have failed to detect. But of course I am wrong.

7

On the train, on my way back to Oslo, I discover that I have eight missed calls and four voicemails on my mobile phone, which I have left in silent mode. I do not want to become hostage to my mobile phone.

All the missed calls are from the same person. Ragnhild.

When I call her, I hear her sigh with relief: 'Bjørn! Where *have* you been?'

'Has anything happened?'

'I have to speak to you. Immediately. Where are you? We'll come and pick you up!'

Back in Oslo, Ragnhild is waiting for me at the police HQ in Grønland, with a worried look on her face.

'We've identified one of the Arabs,' she says, and holds up the picture from the Icelandic CCTV, pointing to the largest man.

'That's the one who broke my finger.'

'Interpol has an entire library dedicated to him. His full name is Hassan ibn Abi Hakim.'

'Hassan . . .'

She pushes a pile of pictures of Hassan over to my side of the desk. He is dressed in military uniform in several of them. In others, he is dressed in expensive suits that were clearly tailor made to fit his enormous frame.

In one black-and-white photo, he is lording it up in front of a mass grave, with a wide grin on his face.

'Iraqis.' Ragnhild passes me a translation of an Interpol report. 'This is a so-called I-24/7 from Interpol Criminal Data Access Management System.'

****INTERPOL****
****Internal radiogram****

Radiogram no.: 7562   Date submitted: 2007-11-17 14:13:48
From station: Lyon   Sender no: SN   Date sent: 171107
Time sent: 14:13:48   Priority: URGENT   Receiver zone: OSLO
From: 'I-247-G° 14'   To: 'NORWAY'
Subject: Our ref: 1711/07 GD/VG/OKK

INTELLIGENCE MESSAGE No. 26/11 REGARDING Hassan ibn Abi Hakim

Subject's name: Hassan ibn Abi Hakkim
Nicknames: Unknown
DOB: Unknown
Year of birth: 1963
Resident: Unknown

From 1985 to 2003, Hassan ibn Abi Hakim was an officer in Saddam Hussain's army, first in the Republican Guard, and then from 1992 in Saddam's special unit, the Iraqi Special Republican Guard.

Subject specialized in and led several *dirty* operations.

In the period 1986–1989, he was involved in Iraq's *al-Anfal* campaign. Thousands of Kurdish villages were attacked and several thousand Kurds were massacred, using chemical weapons, among other things.

Subject was one of the commanding officers responsible for the poison gas attack on Halabja, which killed around 5,000 people.

According to the CIA, the subject was a key figure in *al-Anfal*.

MI5 estimates that he personally liquidated between 3,000 and 4,000 people during his time as an officer in the Republican Guards.

Since 2003, the subject has made a living as an 'independent military consultant', based in Abu Dhabi. In practice, he is suspected of operating as a mercenary/contract killer.

According to French intelligence, La Direction Générale de la Sécurité Extérieure, the subject has worked exclusively for an unidentified employer in Saudi Arabia from 2006.

Israel's intelligence service, Ha-Mosad le-Modi'in u-le-Tafkidim Meyuhadim (Mossad), has, despite repeated infiltration and tactical work, been unsuccessful in confirming the identity of his employer as Sheikh Ibrahim al-Jamil ibn Zakiyy ibn Abdulaziz al Filastini.

·'Well, at least we know who he is,' I say.

I have a tendency to hide my fear beneath a veneer of assumed indifference. The information terrifies me, but it would never occur to me to capitulate. Quite the opposite, in fact; I feel a definite need to defeat him. To defeat the invincible. To defeat the executioner named Hassan. I am extremely stubborn. A man with any sense would know when to bow out. But me? Oh no. Deep inside lives a hunchbacked nerd who is hell bent on finding the answer, someone who would take apart a clock in order to solve the mystery of time. If at all possible, I am even more curious and stubborn than I am frightened. To give up now would be an insult to the memory of Sira Magnus.

The look on Ragnhild's face reminds me a bit of my mother, from when I was a child. 'My dear Bjørn, please be careful,' she says.

The police provide me with a panic alarm.

I will have my very own private bodyguard over the coming days, a policeman with an earpiece, sunglasses and a keen eye for potential assassins in the bushes.

I also get my PC back. The programs that Hassan and his men managed to install in some way or another have equally magically disappeared or been swallowed up by other programs. The only thing the police have managed to uncover is a dialler that is connected to a proxy server in the Caribbean, which in turn communicates with a server in Abu Dhabi.

8

I swap offices at the university with a colleague who is on holiday. My bodyguard sits on a chair out in the corridor reading the tabloids and getting bored while he waits for the remains of the Republican Guard.

I ring Thrainn in Iceland.

I detect from his voice that something is bothering him. He flounders for words that will not put him in an unfavourable light when he confesses that he thinks he is being watched. Someone is following him, looking through his papers when he goes out on an errand, creeping around his house when he is not at home. His strained laughter when he says this only strengthens the impression that he thinks I won't believe him.

I tell him about Hassan. About the policeman sitting outside in the corridor protecting me. About everything that has happened since I returned to Norway. Then I tell him to call the police and explain to them how serious this is.

'They're after us, Thrainn,' I say.

It sounds as if he's trying to swallow an egg. 'I have for a long time hoped that it was purely my imagination.'

'Are the Thingvellir Scrolls safe?'

'Yes, we've moved them to . . .'

'Stop! Don't tell me.'

'But . . .'

'The phone might be tapped.'

He is silent. For a long time.

We eventually agree that I should call him on one of his colleagues' phones, from another phone in the university.

On a secure line, Thrainn tells me that the researchers at the Árni Magnússon Institute have taken the Thingvellir Scrolls to a laboratory connected to a manuscript exhibition in an arts centre in Reykjavik, where they are pretending to work on the preparation of a folio of the fifteenth century Flatey Book, *Codex Flatöiensis*.

In a voice trembling with satisfaction, Thrainn also admits that he set up a cover operation. Four PhD students who have been sworn to secrecy, in a slightly exaggerated way, are working on a copy of the eighteenth-century

Heimskringla in the main laboratory in the Árni Magnússon Institute. The crooks will no doubt think they are working on the Thingvellir Scrolls.

'Have your researchers discovered anything yet?' I ask.

'It seems to be a transcript of the Bible.'

'What do you mean, *seems to be*?'

'Well . . .' He pauses. 'The language used in one of the columns is Coptic. The other is written in an old-fashioned form of Hebrew, which is called classical or biblical Hebrew. The Coptic translation runs in parallel with the original Hebrew text. The Hebrew Bible, the Tanakh and the Old Testament were written in the same language. It's not dramatically different from modern Hebrew, but the grammar varies slightly and the style is more archaic.'

'But *is* it a biblical transcript?'

'The translators are confused. It must be an alternative manuscript version. Parts of the text are a copy of the Five Books of Moses. Other parts are unknown, but we haven't got that far with the translation. We've done some sample translations of various extracts from the document.'

'And?'

'Well, to be honest, I'm not entirely sure what to make of it. It might all just be nonsense. Maybe some joker, a sceptical monk or scribe, has played around with rewriting the Bible. And even if the text is an approximate translation of the Books of Moses, I don't really know how to interpret it.'

'Why?'

'If the transcript had been a thousand years older, then we would have had an international sensation in our hands. The Septuagint – a pre-Christian translation of the Old Testament – was written in Alexandria in Eygpt, about one to three hundred years before Christ. *Codex Vaticanus*, one of the oldest preserved Bible manuscripts in the world, originates from the fourth century. The *Codex Sinaiticus* version of the Bible was copied between AD 330 and 350.

Vulgata, the Roman Catholic Church's first authorised Bible translation into Latin, was written around AD 400. The Thingvellir Scrolls were copied in the Viking Age, Bjørn. To be fair, a copy of the Bible from the eleventh century would be of academic interest, but not much more than that. It's the sort of thing that you and I would spend years studying, but remember, it's a transcript of something that was already over a thousand years old when it was copied. That might be exciting for a scholar, but not for many other people.' He pauses for a second. 'Which makes it even harder to understand why Snorri hid this copy in a cave at Thingvellir.'

'The question is, which original was it copied from?'

'We'll never find out.'

I tell him about my visit to Adelheid. We discuss sacred geometry for a while. The discussion moves on to Egypt and the ancient Egyptian sciences and mythological pseudo-sciences. The connections do not make it any less confusing. What on earth does Egypt have to do with the history of the Vikings or Snorri? When I think about Egypt, I picture Cleopatra in the shadow of the pyramids. But by the time Cleopatra seduced her way into world history, the pyramids at Giza were already 2,500 years old and Egypt was a crumbling superpower. The Egyptians had established their nation five thousand years earlier, and the first three thousand were ruled by pharaohs who have long since been forgotten, and others whose names still live on our lips, such as Wazner, Iry-Hor, Qa'a, Hotepsekhemwy, Khaba, Cheops, Mentuhotep, Kamose, Amenhotep, Thutmose, Hatshepsut, Ramses, Seti, Xerxes . . . the leaders and demigods of their age. But the Egypt of the pharaohs disappeared just before the birth of Jesus. Julius Caesar's adopted son, Octavius, invaded Egypt thirty years before Christ was born. Cleopatra took her own life. The last pharaoh of Egypt, Cleopatra's seventeen-year-old son Caesarion, was executed in the same year. And after that, the country was ruled by foreigners. In the mid-600s, the Arabs invaded Egypt and took over from the Byzantines and Persians. Egypt was an Islamic caliphate in the Viking Age.

9

Over the next few days, I search through Snorri's text, trying to find the instructions that Adelheid hinted at. But I find nothing.

My bodyguard is withdrawn; the official reasons are 'resources' and 'threat evaluation', but it is more likely that the poor man was about to die of boredom.

I sneak out of Terje's flat in the morning, and slip into my temporary office via basements, forgotten staircases and corridors on different storeys.

I hear clicking sounds on the phone line and receive spam that I am convinced is installing spy programs in my computer that will reveal everything that I have stored on my PC and what I ate for breakfast. I get unintelligible text messages on my mobile phone from telephone numbers that do not exist and that no doubt send GPS signals to one of the crooks' satellites.

Without much success, I try to forget my pursuers and concentrate on my work.

Terje and Adelheid have helped me to understand what it is I am looking for. They have explained to me how I should look. Apart from that, it is a matter of patience and imagination.

I spend the greater part of the day studying combinations of letters, and reading the text vertically, horizontally, diagonally and backwards.

And I know that the answer is hidden somewhere in the thousands of letters and symbols.

10

I find the answer early on Monday morning.

The raindrops are running down the office window in curving streams. My brain feels like wet cotton wool.

And it is in this state of numbness that I discover it.

There is a confusing passage in Snorri's text – in terms of typography and content – which includes the Greek letters alpha and omega, which are written in red ink and extra large. The Greek characters A and Ω start and finish a paragraph with a legible, but otherwise meaningless, text. Alpha and omega also mean the beginning and end. So if the characters A and Ω represent the beginning and end of a message, then I have to search within the defined text.

When I read the first and last letters of the lines *downwards* from top to bottom, I suddenly discover two place names: one under the A in the left-hand margin and one above the Ω in the right-hand margin.

When translated from Old Norse, the first part of the puzzle is:

A	R
D	Ø
Ø	Y
S	K
O	E
K	N
O	E
R	S
S	Ω

Under the A, taking the first letter of each line, I get *Døso* and *kors*.

In the same way, I get *Røykenes* from the last letters of each line above the Ω.

I look it up in a reference book. Døso is a place in Os in Hordaland, three miles south of Bergen. The name is derived from *dys*, the Norwegian word for a small cairn or pile of stones, which in turn refers to the fifteen-hundred-year-old burial mounds in the area. Røykenes is the name of the place at the end of a path used by monks, some kilometres north of Døso.

Path used by monks?

Excited, I look at a map of the local area.

I make a mark at Døso and a mark at Røykenes and draw a vertical line.

Kors, or cross . . .

Does Snorri mean that I should draw a cross, using Døso and Røykenes as my starting points?

I draw the horizontal line of the cross. The right end finishes somewhere in a forest.

The left end hits . . . Lyse Abbey.

I sit there staring for a few seconds.

The pentagram isn't pointing to a sacred place in Bergen, but at Lyse Abbey!

Lyse Abbey is a Cistercian monastery from the

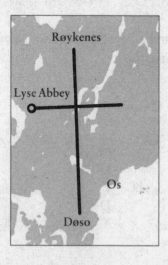

1100s which is swathed in mystery. The monastery was closed in 1536, but the ruins are still a popular tourist attraction, as it lies in particularly beautiful surroundings. Here the monks practised moderation, peace and devotion, and gave thanks for the blessings of the source.

Lyse Abbey . . .

Of course!

Full of anticipation, I carry on searching in the labyrinth of letters. Now that I have cracked it, things start to move more quickly. Some of the letters are bolder than others and make it easier to find new words that are hidden among and behind the words and sentences. For example, in the line *ouR king, we Can diE for yoU, Valhalla'S NOrns are spinning* I pick out the word *source*.

Between the R and the S in the two vertical lines, I find the word *sinister* written backwards. *Sinister* is Latin for *left*. I also find the words *Salomos segl* (Solomon's seal or the pentagram) and *obelisk* (stone pillar) between the letters S and K. I read *øst møter nord* (east meets west) backwards. But the most striking thing is that, in two places, I discover the name of Holy Olav, or *Olav den hellige*, as it says in the original text.

Translated and adapted to modern Norwegian, the text diagram looks like this:

<u>A</u>						R
DRON		RETØM				TSØ
Ø						Y
SALOMOS		SEGL				OBELISK
OLAV		DEN				HELLIGE
K I L	D	E		V	A N	N
OLAV		DEN				HELLIGE
R	E	T	S	I		N I S
S						<u>Ω</u>

I sit there, my eyes darting back and forth over the mixture of letters and words. Snorri could of course have been playing around. But it is equally possible, in theory, that I have actually found the directions to the legendary grave of Holy Olav.

Many people believe that Holy Olav, the Viking king who Christianised Norway and died in the Battle of Stiklestad in 1030, is buried in Nidaros Cathedral in Trondheim.

But he isn't.

When the Battle of Stiklestad was over and Olav lay with the blood draining from his wounds, Torgils Hålmasson, a farmer, and his son, Grim, searched the battlefield for the king's body. They had promised Olav before the battle that, if the king should fall, they would look after his body. They found him and wrapped the corpse in linen and laid it in a coffin which they then hid under the boards of a boat. They rowed south to Nidaros (modern-day Trondheim) and went up the river some way, where they hid the king's body in a shack. The farmer later buried King Olav in a wooden coffin in a sandbank by the Nid river just up from the market town. In the months that followed, the locals told many a tale of mysterious doings, wonders, miracles and signs. Bishop Grimkjel was called from Lake Mjøsa. A year and five days after the Battle of Stiklestad, the farmer Torgils showed where he had buried the body. Under the supervision of the bishop and the government, the coffin was dug up. King Olav looked as though he were sleeping. His nails, hair and beard had grown. His cheeks were red. According to the poet Snorri, a sweet fragrance rose from the coffin. The corpse was laid out in honour in the Klemens Church and was then later transferred to a new coffin which was covered in expensive cloth and called the Olav Reliquary. Two further caskets were made later. The first one was covered in gold, silver and precious stones. It was two metres long and eighty centimetres wide and high, with a curved bottom and a lid on the top. The smaller wooden coffin was then placed inside. The lid looked like a roof with a ridge and Viking dragon's head, and was closed with hinges and locks. Then yet another outer casing was made for the two older caskets.

No one knows where the Olav Reliquary is.

Some people believe that the casket, or the remains of it, is hidden in the ground under Nidaros Cathedral. Others claim that the casket was plastered into the walls of the fort at Steinvikholmen, just outside Trondheim. Historians believe that the reliquary was destroyed in 1537, as it was left behind when Archbishop Olav Engelbrektsson fled Steinvikholmen after the Reformation. Everything that was of any value was taken to Copenhagen and melted down. In September 1540, the Danish king's treasurer, Jochum Bech, wrote out a receipt for ninety-five kilos of silver, one hundred and seventy crystals mounted in silver and eleven precious stones that had fallen off when the casket was broken up.

The Olav Reliquary was promoted from the realms of history to legend.

11

Before I leave the office, I phone Ragnhild, to let her know that I am going away for a few days.

'Where are you going?' she asks.

'The phone is bound to be tapped.'

'The police have to know where you are, Bjørn.'

'And Hassan would like to know too.'

'Send me a text, then.'

'We'll see.'

'Don't do anything stupid.'

I make a false promise.

If I do actually manage to find the grave at Lyse Abbey, I have no intention of involving the Directorate for Cultural Heritage, the university or the police. Technically, I am about to commit a crime. The Cultural Heritage Act is quite particular when it comes to our history. But I don't have either the patience or the time to follow the rules of bureaucracy.

'Is there any news?' I ask.

'Hassan and some of his men came to Oslo the day after you. From Iceland. With false passports, of course. They took the Gardermoen Express into the centre of town. Then vanished. They haven't booked in to any of the hotels.'

'Who was in my flat, then, if they came after me?'

'They must have a cell operating here in Oslo.'

'Could they be staying somewhere privately?'

'Presumably. Maybe with contacts from Saudi Arabia or Iraq.'

'Have you investigated them?'

'There are twenty thousand Iraqis living in Norway, Bjørn, and just under a hundred Saudi Arabians.'

I leave my mobile phone in the office. It is entirely possible that Hassan, like the police, has the equipment necessary to trace my calls and find out where it is.

The Grave

1

IN THE light of the evening sun, the ruins of the abbey look as though they have been frozen in time.

The elegant cloisters, supported by a row of double columns, throw long shadows in the dusk. A layer of lush grass and moss grows along the top of the arcade, and on the crumbling walls and façade.

'Beautiful, isn't it?' Øyvind Skogstad comments.

'A real gem,' I reply, in agreement.

Øyvind is standing with his arms crossed, surveying the ruins; by the look on his face, you might be forgiven for thinking that he had built them himself. He is a research assistant at the Cultural History Collection of Bergen Museum, and I have known him since 2003 when we both attended a conference on religious art and iconography. Øyvind grew up in Os, and spent every summer of his childhood in the area around Lyse Abbey. He thinks that it was the ruins which whetted his interest in history and archaeology. When I called him from a telephone box at the railway station and told him I was in Bergen and needed his assistance at Lyse Abbey, it felt like offering a ten-year-old a free ride at the fair.

'There are many mysteries attached to Lyse Abbey,' he says. Øyvind has a penchant for grandiloquence. He squints at me in the low sunlight, excited and full of expectation. I have promised to tell him why I am there. But not yet.

We are surrounded by towering dark pine trees.

'Tell me about the abbey,' I encourage him; a polite invitation to give me a lecture, which I know I will get, whether I ask for it or not.

'With pleasure!' He strikes the pose of a guide surrounded by curious tourists. 'On the request of Bishop Sigurd of Selja, Lyse Abbey was founded in 1146 by monks from Fountains Abbey in England. It was dedicated to the Holy Virgin,' he lectures, adjusting his round glasses, which are getting steamed up.

'But why here, in the middle of the darkest forest?'

'Look around you, man! The Cistercian Order venerated quiet, calm and contemplation. They were aesthetic, methodical and practical. They wanted to cultivate the soil and to be self-sufficient, and so needed a local water source. The location was perfect.'

'You mentioned mysteries?'

'Bjørn, what do you know about the Knights Templar?'

'Quite a lot,' I admit. People who are interested in the Knights Templar and that sort of thing have an inherent disposition to nerdish behaviour and passionate obsessions. 'The Knights Templar were a medieval, Christian monastic order founded by the Crusaders in 1119 – just a few years after the founding of the Cistercian Order in 1098 – in order to protect European pilgrims on their way to Jerusalem. The King of Jerusalem gave the knights permission to have their headquarters on the Temple Mount, above the ruins of the Temple of Solomon. The Templars planted the seed of what was to become our modern banking system. The order became so wealthy that the knights were massacred by the French king.'

'On Friday the thirteenth, no less.'

'In 1307,' I conclude, to show that I know my stuff. 'There is speculation that the knights were the guardians of a historical secret. Like the body of Christ or the Holy Grail . . .'

'Or, quite simply . . . knowledge. Did you know that there were a number of links between the Knights Templar and the Cistercian Order?'

'Such as?'

'They were sister organisations. About the same age. But one common denominator which is really exciting is Bernard de Clairvaux!'

'Do you mean the saint? St Bernard? The French abbot?'

'At Easter-time in 1146 – the same year that Lyse Abbey was founded – Bernard de Clairvaux preached the Second Crusade. Bernard was one of the Church's most powerful authorities. The voice of conscience, they called him. He was perhaps the most central figure in the establishment of the Cistercian Order. Without him, we would not have been standing here in Lyse Abbey today.'

'And the connection?'

'Bernard was the nephew of one of the founders of the Knights Templar, and became their patron and guardian. Thanks to Bernard de Clairvaux, the Knights Templar were officially endorsed by the Church at the Council of Troyes in 1128. This recognition contributed to the Knights Templar's economic growth and earned them support from the wealthiest families in Europe. In 1139, the order was placed directly under the Pope in a decree issued in Pope Innocent II's papal bull, *Omne Datum Optimum*. Priests who were against Christians fighting with swords were put squarely in their place by Bernard's defence in *De Laude Novae Militae*, where he argued for the paradox of *killing in Christ's name*. Bernard de Clairvaux also formulated what were to be the rules of the Knights Templar.'

History is full of inexplicable connections and coincidences. Why was Lyse Abbey founded here, on the fringes of civilisation, by a monastic order with links to the Knights Templar? Is it as 'by chance' as Værne Abbey in Østfold being transferred from King Sverre to the Johanite Order – who were also known as the Order of Malta, or the Hospitallers – in 1190?

I gaze out over the ruins. The pine trees sough in the breeze from the sea.

Was Holy Olav buried somewhere here at Lyse Abbey by his loyal supporters, who had managed to save the remains of the Christian king with help from the Cistercian Order and the Knights Templar? Was the original Olav Reliquary moved from Nidaros Cathedral before the major building works in the mid-twelfth century? Was it a copy of the Olav Reliquary which the Danes destroyed in the 1500s?

As I look at the ruins and ponder, a hawk sits silently swaying on a branch in the wind.

2

In the evening, once I have told Øyvind everything I know about the Snorri Codex and its links to Lyse Abbey, I tell him about Hassan and my pursuers. The only question he asks is who I think they are working for.

He invites me to stay with him in the empty basement flat in his childhood home, not far from the abbey. We sit here most of the evening studying Snorri's manuscript and books about the abbey that Øyvind has taken with him.

'There's a reference to Solomon's Seal in the text,' I say, and unfold a map. 'A pentagram, in other words.'

'There's not much here that implies a pentagram, Bjørn.'

'The word *obelisk* is written together with the words Solomon's Seal, which might mean a marker on the ground.'

Øyvind looks at me, astonished. 'You're joking? There are actually two standing stones in the area. Historians have never been able to work out what their significance is.'

He marks a point on the map about two hundred metres south of Lyse Abbey, and another to the north-east of the abbey.

'If these are two of the points in a pentagram,' I draw a circle that touches the two points, 'then we should find three more here, here and here.' I draw three more points on the map.

The next morning, we rise with the sun and drive up to the parking place by the abbey. I have borrowed a pair of green wellies from Øyvind, and together we tramp through the tangled terrain of moss-covered rocks, meadows and forest floor.

After searching for half an hour, we find the first standing stone, half hidden by a wild, overgrown thicket at the end of a small wood. The stone has been crudely hewn and is about half a metre tall.

'Local historians have never made any connection between these stones and the abbey,' Øyvind tells me.

We carry on through the woods, wading through grass, over knolls and a stream. Our wellies squelch in the mud. As we get closer to the spot where the next standing stone should be, we slow down and move a couple of metres apart. Step by step we search the ground. When we have undoubtedly gone too far, we extend the distance and circle back on ourselves. Then we turn again, and move farther apart. And so it continues.

I find the standing stone almost by accident. My glasses have steamed up so I have to take them off and, as I'm drying the lenses with the corner of my shirt, I catch the vague contours of an obelisk. I put my glasses on again. The

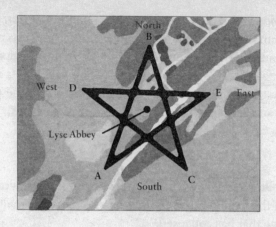

obelisk disappears. I look around, confused. I see tree trunks, bushes, a formation of moss-covered rocks, branches and twigs on the forest floor. I take off my glasses and the shape reappears. This time, I keep my eyes fixed on the stone while I put my glasses back on. I am astonished when I realise that the obelisk is in fact part of a rock face. The people who raised the obelisks have carved on a stone that was already there.

Over the course of the day, we find all five obelisks that have been positioned to form a pentagram around Lyse Abbey.

The next two we as good as stumble over, whereas it takes us well over three hours to uncover the last one. Øyvind marks each stone precisely on a map of the area.

Then we drive back to our local research station in the basement flat of Øyvind's parents' house and fry some fish that we bought fresh from the fjord in Os.

So now we have the standing stones, we have the pentagram, but we don't have the grave.

When we've eaten, Øyvind and I sit down with a bottle of cold beer each.

One of the clues in Snorri's peculiar crossword says *east*

meets north. It strikes me this might be a description of the secret intersection between one of the east–west/north–south axes of the pentagram. But as an instruction it is vague, as there are several points where east meets north. So what we have to do is follow all the lines of the pentagram, and see if the terrain gives us any more clues.

3

The following day, we have barely begun to walk along the first of the five lines, axis A–B, when I discover a small stone building that has collapsed.

The ruins are a short distance away, by the edge of the forest, just where the A–B axis meets the D–C axis on the inner pentagon, partially hidden by branches and growth.

'Nothing important,' Øyvind states.

'The position is striking.'

'A dead end. It looks like a well house that has collapsed, but the Directorate for Cultural Heritage believes that it might even just be a superstructure.'

'Well?'

I grab Øyvind and pull him towards me.

'What is it, man?' Øyvind exclaims. 'Calm down! The Cistercians were obsessed with being able to get fresh water.'

We step over the roots and rocks.

'The main well was up by the abbey, so this was a reserve, in case the water supply to the abbey ran dry. According to various sources, the reserve well dried up long before the main well.'

'Has it never been investigated?'

'Investigated?' Øyvind shrugs. 'The abbey has been studied and examined. The first excavations took place in 1822, but obviously that was up by the main buildings, not here. There have been several excavations since, but I don't know that the well has ever really been deemed to be part of the abbey ruins. I'm sure it was inspected, at least visually, when the abbey was excavated in 1888. But as I said, it is really too far from the main buildings to be of any interest.'

I smile like the cat that got the cream.

'Bjørn, look around! Can you see any graves?'

I look around. I can't see any graves, but I know better.

'What?' Øyvind mutters when my self-satisfaction becomes too much to bear.

'Øyvind, what are we looking for?'

'A grave. A burial mound. Something that is big enough to contain Holy Olav's coffin. And as he was the King of Norway, and also a saint, if his remains were brought here and buried a hundred years after his death, we'd be looking for something quite grand. This . . .' He points to the ruins. '. . . is a pile of stones!'

'A well.'

'OK. So what? Hundreds of years ago it was . . .' Then I see on his face that it is obviously dawning on him. 'A well,' he repeats to himself, and he looks over at me.

4

I take a series of pictures with a digital camera so we can leave the stones as they were for posterity.

We collect our work gloves from the car and set to moving the stones. We work with great care, but this does not detract from the fact that I am ruining yet another historical site.

Bjørn Beltø. Historical vandal.

If we were to follow protocol, we would have to apply for permission to open the well, which *might* then perhaps be granted. In a year or two. Neither the Cultural Heritage Act nor its champions are prepared to make it easy for treasure hunters to do things quickly. My colleagues would, with some justification, condemn me.

I suddenly stop, straighten up and say to Øyvind: 'When this is over, I will take full responsibility. You haven't been here. You haven't helped me. You know nothing about this.'

Øyvind looks down. Of course he wants to share the honour with me, but then he would also risk his career.

I don't give a damn.

Fortunately the weather has turned cold and damp, so that the few tourists who are around do no more than hurry around the ruins. We are left to work in peace for the whole day. By the time dusk falls, we have managed to roll and move several tons of moss-covered stones to reveal a surface of rounded stones that have been cast together to form a solid base.

5

We are back before dawn. Øyvind and I work with head-lamps, which we switch off as soon as the first strips of light appear above the trees to the east.

With the help of crowbars, sledgehammers, hammers and chisels, we manage to loosen all the stones in the base. We have to get through three layers of stone. Under it we find some rotten wooden beams, which presumably were the lath-work for the masons who laid the stone floor.

Finally, around midday, we have cleared a big enough opening.

To prevent any accidents – such as both of us getting stuck at the bottom of a well – Øyvind waits at the top while I tie a rope under my arms and lower myself down the well shaft. My headlamp illuminates the rounded walls, which are stone lined and covered in moss. The stones are huge and neatly hewn. Given that this is a reserve well, the monks and builders have gone to an awful lot of trouble.

The well has a radius of about a metre and is five or six metres deep. My wellies sink into a layer of mud. I call up to Øyvind that I've reached the bottom, then I focus my headlamp on the damp, moss-green walls.

Nothing.

I had not really expected to find a burial chamber at the bottom of the well, but I had expected to find *something*.

With my gloves, I start to brush the moss from the walls. After some time, I discover that one of the stones is much lighter than the others. Marble? Soapstone?

I move closer so the light on the stone is stronger. It is full of lines and marks. I lean in even closer.

At first it is difficult to see what the lines represent. I brush away more moss and rub the stone with my glove. Then I see it.

Three symbols have been carved along the top of the stone.

Ankh, *tiwaz* and a cross.

Øyvind sends down a bottle of water so I can wash away the moss, dirt and earth. With trembling hands, I clean the stone. But I don't find any more symbols or letters. I take some pictures of the three symbols and call to Øyvind to help me up.

Excited, we race back to the flat. We discuss for a long time what we should do. There is no doubt that the entrance to the grave is hidden by the well. Should we involve our superiors? Should we let the Directorate for Cultural Heritage know?

The answer is, of course, yes.

But not yet.

We both know that we will lose any remnant of control if we involve more people. An excavation would take all winter and spring. And I don't have time to wait.

6

In the evening, we put on an album by Supertramp and discuss the possible links between the Vikings and ancient Egypt.

'Of course, nothing is documented, but it's not so improbable that the Vikings went down the Nile,' Øyvind comments. 'After all, they were sailors by nature. They sailed, rowed and pulled their boats over thousands of kilometres through Russia, down to the Black Sea and the Caspian Sea.'

'But Egypt?'

'The Vikings made raids all along the shores of the Mediterranean, even North Africa. Why would they not go to Egypt?'

He has a point. Sigurd Jorsalfar, the Crusader, got his name because he went on a crusade all the way to Miklagard and Jerusalem. And then there is the story of Harald Hardråde, Holy Olav's half-brother. As a fifteen-year-old, he survived the battle at Stiklestad and then fled south to Byzantium. Here he was made an officer in the Byzantine court, had an affair with the emperor's wife and fought in a number of battles, not least in North Africa. According to Snorri, he captured over eight African towns. Snorri writes that Harald was in Africa for many years, where he acquired chattels, gold and treasures. His ships were laden when they returned.

'As early as 800, the Vikings sailed as far south as the Mediterranean and Africa,' Øyvind continues. 'These raids are described in the sagas and by Arab chroniclers.'

'But never to Egypt.'

'What a stickler you are! The Vikings were warriors who were frightened of nothing or no one. Why on earth should they be frightened to sail up the Nile? In 844, an expedition of longships and several thousand men made the journey to northern Spain, then travelled along the coast of what is now Portugal, and attacked Lisbon, Cadiz and several towns up the rivers in southern Spain. They sailed up the Guadalquivir river all the way to Seville. A dangerous and daring manoeuvre! They wreaked havoc in the city for a week. They killed and raped and burned and robbed; they destroyed the great city walls and torched the mosques. The Muslim emir, Abd al-Rahman, had to send his elite forces down from Cordoba so that the Moors could regain control. The Vikings retreated south and attacked the North African caliphate before sailing home again with their bounty. Fifteen years later an even bigger Viking fleet returned. This foray lasted for three years and, according to those who survived, was led by the Viking kings Håstein and Bjørn Ironside. With over sixty long-ships and thousands of Vikings, they plundered their way down the Rhone Valley, then attacked Galicia, what is now Portugal, Andalusia and North Africa. They sailed north along the east coast of the Spanish peninsula, passed Majorca, and then followed the Ebro river north as far as the Basque country. Take a look at the map! The Ebro twists and turns for hundreds of kilometres from the coast all the way to Pamplona. There they kidnapped King Garcia Iñigues. When they left, they had with them seventy thousand gold coins. They carried on north along the Spanish and French coasts, to Provence and Italy, where they attacked Pisa. They then conquered the town of Luna, which they thought was Rome. There were rich pickings, and the Viking chieftains became very wealthy indeed. This wealth then tempted others to carry out the same enterprise. A hundred years later, they were at it again. A fleet of around a hundred ships, carrying just under ten thousand men, plundered Galicia and León, deep in Christian northern Spain, and they wreaked havoc in Santiago de Compostela and Catoira. Bjørn, do you really believe that warriors such as these were scared of the Nile?'

Before going to bed, I ring Thrainn in Iceland. He says that he has been trying to get hold of me. Three unknown men broke into the main laboratory at the Árni Magnússon Institute and attacked the four PhD students who were acting as a decoy. All four were threatened, gagged and tied to a radiator. The crooks then made off with the sixteenth-century copy of Heimskringla.

'Presumably they thought it was the Thingvellir Scrolls.'

'Thrainn, the scrolls aren't safe in Reykjavik.'

'I've realised that.'

'Sooner or later someone will work out where you've hidden them.'

His breathing is laboured.

'I'm going to make a call,' I tell him.

'Who to?'

'I know someone who can help us.'

7

Early the next morning, we return with more equipment: several lengths of thicker rope, a battery-powered hammer drill with three batteries, chisels, sledgehammers, torches and overalls.

We attach two ropes to a big tree and then lower ourselves down. The stone wall seems to be as solid as a rock face. But with the help of the drill and chisels, we manage to work loose the white stone with the three symbols on it. There is another stone wall behind it. But now that we have removed one stone, it is easier to wedge loose the one underneath. Soon we have a hole in the wall that is about a square metre wide. Then we get to work on the second wall behind. An hour, two broken drill pieces and three batteries later, the final stone gives way. With the help of sledgehammers and crowbars we then push the stones inwards so that they fall into the chamber behind the well shaft.

We are through.

A blast of pungent, stagnant air streams out through the hole and whistles up the well like a genie set loose after hundreds of years of imprisonment. 'Well, at least there is some form of ventilation down here,' Øyvind remarks.

I shine a torch into the chamber. An empty room with stone walls.

'Can you see anything?' Øyvind asks.

'Nothing.'

'Come on, then!' No one can nag like someone from Bergen.

I crawl in first, with Øyvind immediately behind me.

What I had thought was a room proves to be the end of an arched tunnel, with stone walls, just like the well shaft. The tunnel is about two metres in diameter, so we can stand upright. Step by step we wade forward through the mud and water. The air is raw. The beams from our torches bounce around in the dark. The walls are covered in green slime and roots. The odd spider curls up in a ball when the light hits it.

After about five minutes, we come to an internal chamber, where the tunnel opens out by two to three metres in height and width. It carries on straight ahead, but some granite stairs lead up to the left from an ornamented stone landing.

'Presumably the way up to a well shaft or concealed entrance,' Øyvind says.

We decide to investigate the tunnel further, before checking the stairs.

*

The tunnel stops at a solid stone wall.

'We must be directly underneath Lyse Abbey now,' Øyvind estimates. 'Perhaps this was an escape route.'

We left all the equipment at the bottom of the well, so we turn around and go back to the chamber where the stairs were, without even testing the wall.

The chamber is about halfway along the tunnel. In which case, it must be at roughly the intersection of the inner pentagon corresponding to where the well is on the pentagram.

We climb the stairs. At the top we meet another wall. Again. There's something about me and walls.

The stairs have taken us up to a narrow platform, a kind of antechamber that ends in a solid construction of stones as big as building blocks, which have been mortared together with perfect precision. Five wide by ten high.

In the torchlight, we see a row of Egyptian hieroglyphs and two rows of Nordic runes. And above it all: ankh, *tiwaz* and a cross.

We run back to the well and gather up the sledgehammers, then race back to the antechamber.

In order to avoid damaging the ornamentation, we work on the bottom right-hand corner of the wall. We use a chisel first. The stone is porous. When the chisel finally breaks through into thin air, we hammer loose the first stone. Then we make an opening two stones high and two stones wide, which is big enough for us to crawl through.

8

I stand there staring, speechless and in awe.

The burial chamber has five walls and a vaulted ceiling that is supported by five stone pillars. There is a plinth in the middle of the room, about a metre and a half high.

On the plinth is a stone coffin.

The burial chamber! I can hardly believe it. We have found the burial chamber!

'Incredible!' I stammer.

We stand by the wall that blocked the entrance. The beams from our headlamps sweep backwards and forwards through the chamber's dark.

The chamber is shaped like a pentagon, the five-sided shape that is made by the intersecting lines of a pentagram. The pillars are positioned in the corners of the room at the five points of intersection.

The chamber is freezing cold and is filled with the damp raw smell from the tunnel below. The walls, floor and ceiling are surprisingly dry. A few stones have fallen down on to the floor, but otherwise it looks as if the burial chamber is more or less as it was left some eight or nine hundred years ago.

One step at a time, we make our way over to the coffin. On the stone lid, carved in runes, it says: HIR:HUILIR: SIRA:RUTOLFR.

ᚼᛁᚱ᛬ᚼᚢᛁᛚᛁᚱ᛬ᛁᚱᛅ᛬ᚱᚢᛏᛅᛚᚠᚱ

Here lies Sira Rudolf, I translate in my head.

And at the bottom of the lid it says: RUTOLFR:BISKUB.

ᚱᚢᛏᛅᛚᚠᚱ᛬ᛒᛁᛙᚢᛒ

'Bishop Rudolf,' I whisper, in an attempt to respect the peace of the burial chamber that has already been violated. 'One of the bishops who followed King Olav to Norway from England, before the country was Christianised.'

'So it's not Holy Olav?'

'No.'

I am too overwhelmed by the discovery and the wonderful sight to feel disappointed. Of course, I still wish it had been the Olav Reliquary and not a stone coffin that awaited us on the plinth.

Øyvind and I each grab an end of the coffin lid and push it carefully to one side.

The skeleton is dressed in a red bishop's cope with a decayed ermine collar. His knuckles are bent around a crozier, and his skull is crowned with a mitre, that oblong, pointy hat that bishops wear.

Bishop Rudolf . . .

Quite unexpectedly, I feel tears in my eyes.

'Bjørn?' Øyvind nudges my arm.

With his headlamp, he points to the wall to the left of us. At first all I can see is the glare from the light, but then I see four ceramic pots.

'Oh my sweet Lord,' Øyvind moans.

Each of the pots is overflowing with jewellery, and Egyptian figurines in gold and alabaster. Cats, amulets, scarabs, the jackal-headed god, Anubis, mythical animals, cobras . . . The light from the torches twinkles on deep red gems. Øyvind picks up a statue of the bird-headed Horus.

'Put it down,' I urge him. 'We should leave as much as possible untouched for when our colleagues come to inspect it.'

He laughs. '*You're* a fine one to talk!'

Behind the dust on the walls we find inscriptions and drawings of runes and Egyptian hieroglyphs. The tomb is decorated with a mixture of Old Norse and ancient Egyptian symbols. We study the wall inscriptions in the dark chamber for a long time.

At the foot-end of the plinth, I discover a marble inlay which is covered in hundreds of characters.

A rune stone.

Using a knife, I lever it loose from the plinth's embrace and brush it clean. I then lay it gently on the floor. The edges of the rune stone are studded with jewels.

I can see three symbols along the top.

'Ankh, *tiwaz* and a cross,' Øyvind mumbles.

I focus my headlamp on the characters and translate from Old Norse.

Holy art thou, Saint Olav, our good King

Finally, a text that it is possible to read.

'I'll take this with me!'

I can tell from the beam of light that is shining straight on to my face that Øyvind is looking at me.

'We have to report what we've found,' he says eventually.

'Of course. But we don't need to say anything about the rune stone.'

'They'll notice that it's not there, sooner or later.'

'I'll give it back, obviously. When I'm finished with it. They might think that pillagers have raided the tomb.'

'Which they have.'

INTERMEZZO

Bård's Tale (I)

ＱↃↄ↑ ✝

'[They] trampled the holy places with polluted steps,
dug up the altars and seized all the treasures of the
holy church. They killed some of the brothers, took
some away with them in fetters.'
SIMEON OF DURHAM, *History of the Kings*

'The barbarians came at daybreak, when Amon-Ra's
breath coloured the skies red. I [. . .] stared at the
strange ships that came sailing down the river;
elegant longboats with great sails and snapping
dragon mouths raised on their prows.'
ASIM, EGYPTIAN HIGH PRIEST OF THE AMON-RA
· CULT

At NIGHT, *on the hard bunk of his monk's cell, he dreamt often of his youth when he sailed with King Olav on Viking raids. Half asleep, he pulled the damp homespun blankets around him as his memories rose up in pictures and smells and sounds that filled the chill darkness of the cell. Sometimes, when he could not sleep, he would drag himself over to the window opening and listen to the breathing of the vast sea and the waves breaking on the rocks. Chilled to the bone and almost blind, he stood in the draught and longed for the old days. His sight was so weak that he no longer needed to close his eyes to conjure up the fleet of Viking ships as . . .*

EXTRACT FROM BÅRD'S TALE

. . . they ploughed through the waves in a cloud of spray. I stood at the prow of the longship, *Sea Eagle*, together with King Olav, cheering and shouting in the wind. I dried the salt water from my face with my arm. The king laughed and whooped.

The *Sea Eagle* was the king's ship, an elegant boat with carved dragonheads raised on the prow and stern. We called her *drakkar*, the dragon ship. Nimble-fingered wood carvers at home in Norway had crafted terrifying dragons, foul snakes and grotesque sea monsters on both posts. The mast was tall and straight. The sail caught the wind and propelled us over the water like an arrow shot straight from a bow. Olav and I turned away from the wind and looked out over the ship. Many of the men were dozing in the heat from the sun. Some were playing dice, others were telling of daring deeds and bloody battles. One of the navigators was marking our position on a parchment chart. Then he cut a mark on the crescent-shaped gauge of the sun compass. Olav used his fingers to whistle to the helmsman, indicating to him to swing a touch to the east. Then he nodded to Rane, whom his mother had sent to guard him when we set sail so many years ago. Olav grabbed me by the hair and gave me a shake as he said: 'I see you like the open sea, Bård.' I spat over the railing and replied: 'Who does not, my king?'

We were the same age, Olav and I. We called him King, though he did not rule a country. The strong, salty blood of the Vikings ran in his warrior's veins. Olav Haraldsson was of royal lineage; his great grandfather was Harald Fair Hair and his father was Harald Grenske, the philandering king of Vestfold who was burnt to death by Sigrid the Haughty from Sweden, when she tired of the Viking's sexual advances. When Harald Grenske was killed in a house fire in Sweden, Åsta, his mother, was already carrying Olav in her belly, and the man she then wed, Sigurd Syr, was his opposite: whereas Harald had been a Viking through and through, aggressive and ready to fight, Sigurd was a peace-loving, thoughtful and enterprising farmer who preferred to tend to his land and animals, and shunned battle. But young Olav was his father's son and as a young lad would look at his stepfather, the farmer, and mock him behind his mother's back.

With my hand on the smooth carvings of the hull, I stared ashore at the foreign land they called al-Andalus, which was ruled by Muslims. What violent resistance awaited us? Let them come, I thought boldly. I feared no one. From the time that we set sail from Norway, first for Denmark and then east, our raids had been smiled on by the gods. We were invincible. We fought and plundered for a long time in Sweden and the countries and islands around the Baltic, before we sailed back to Denmark, where we joined the fleet of the chieftain, Thorkell the Tall, brother of Earl Sigvald the Jomsviking. The two Viking chieftains, Olav and Thorkell, sailed together along the coast of Jutland, where we defeated a huge army. Our victories in the Baltic, Denmark and the Netherlands made us bold. Together with Thorkell the Tall and his men, we crossed the Channel. In England, we joined forces with a great Danish army, and it was autumn when we set up camp outside London. King Ethelred was fearful. He paid Olav and Thorkell forty-eight thousand pounds to spare his kingdom. We loaded our ships with over eleven million silver coins. What riches! Every single coin would buy us a cow or a slave. Olav and Thorkell then parted ways. Thorkell switched allegiances and entered the service of King Ethelred, and Olav and his fleet sailed on to France.

'Bård,' the king said. 'I had a strange dream last night.'

Outside, golden sand dust swirled in the sun and wind.

The people who hurried down the narrow whitewashed streets were wrapped in wide garments to protect them from the biting southerly desert wind. I looked over at my lord. Olav was lying in bed, his head and shoulders against the stone wall. I was sitting on a rickety wooden chair, drinking sour wine from a clay mug that dirtied my palm. The sun shone in through an opening high up in the wall. Olav sat up in bed. 'It was perhaps a god who spoke to me in my dream,' he said. 'Which god?' I wished to know. I worshipped Odin and the gods of our forefathers. On our journey through Europe we had heard talk of other gods, in particular one they called the White Christ. He was able to turn water into wine, they said, to transform one loaf into many. He also healed the sick and could walk on water, though for what reason I was unsure. But I could not understand this White Christ. Was he a god or a person? How could his father, a god, plant his seed in a mortal woman without lying with her? And would not a god's human son be a demigod?

The king, who had noted that I had forgotten we were two in the room, coughed and continued: 'In my dream, a man came to me, the kind of man you notice because he has fire in his eyes, and he said to me that I should return home to become King of Norway for ever.' The king cocked his head and waited to hear what I thought of this prospect. 'Who was the man?' I asked. I did not want to go home yet. I was yearning to sail eastwards, through the straits of Norvasund, which separated Europe from the Great Serkland, the desert land to the south, and on across the sea to the Land of the Jews, where the White Christ had lived a thousand summers ago. The king smiled, as if he understood my thoughts, and replied: 'I did not know him, yet I answered him truthfully: "I will go home! And I will rule Norway! But not yet."'

Relieved, I raised my mug of wine. 'Bård,' the king said, 'I will now confide in you where we are bound.' 'The Land of the Jews?' I asked. He shook his head. 'We are bound for the Great Blue Land,' the king told me. 'A desert land they call Egypt.' 'I have never heard of such a land,' I replied. The king told me it was a country thousands of years old, with streets lined with gold and precious jewels, protected by forgotten gods, divided by foreign rulers and tribes, and split in two by a river called the Nile. 'Why are we going to this land?' I asked. 'We are going to find a treasure,' the king answered. 'A treasure?' I repeated, and felt my heart leap with joy. 'A treasure,' the king said once more, 'hidden in the cliffs behind a temple, hidden in a tomb behind a tomb.'

I did not understand much. The king said it was sufficient that he himself understood. 'How do you come to know this?' I asked. And the king explained:

One of his forefathers, Håkon the Good, son of Harald Fair Hair, was fostered by King Athelstan of England. King Athelstan had many friends. His court often received relics and manuscripts from ancient Rome, such as the swords of the first Christian Roman emperor, Constantine the Great, and the lance of Charlemagne. These shipments included objects and manuscripts from Mark Antony, who had a child with Queen Cleopatra after Caesar's death. Among the manuscripts was a papyrus script and a map. The directions would lead to a tomb filled with the most precious treasures, holy scriptures and a sleeping god. No one at the court paid heed to the Egyptian manuscript. But Håkon was curious. With the help of learned monks at the court, he drew a copy of the map and translated the directions in the manuscript into Anglo-Saxon. Still no one took heed of the content. As one of the monks sneered: 'There is enough treasure of that kind in *A Thousand and One Nights*.' Håkon took the translation with him when, together with the Bishop of Glastonbury, he returned to Christianise Norway. It is said that at that time, Håkon spoke Anglo-Saxon like an Englishman, but had as good as forgotten his mother tongue. For reasons that are unknown, Håkon's interest in the ancient Egyptian directions waned. The monks' copy became a curiosity in Håkon's family. King Olav himself was eight when his mother, Åsta, showed him the Anglo-Saxon parchment with a map of the river that leads to the treasure. I asked the king: 'And this copy and map, do you have them with you?' Olav nodded and said: 'I think it is time to discover if there is any truth to the tale. And if any in my family is able to do that, it is I!'

That very same evening, in one of the many narrow

alleyways around the harbour of Cadiz, we came upon a man who was unlike any other we had seen before. His skin was black with a bluish hue; he was small in stature with carefully groomed hair and wore an outfit that resembled more that of a woman. A blue man. The man and his company refused to step aside for Olav, who was surly and ill tempered after his afternoon nap. Olav's retainer struck several of the men in the blue man's company with his sword, before they yielded and begged for mercy. Olav drew his sword to strike down the defiant blue man, who fell to his knees and begged for his life in his own incomprehensible tongue. One of his servants spoke in Latin, and a learned man in our company translated his words thereafter into Norwegian. When Olav understood the blue man was an Egyptian, an unmistakable glow lit his eyes. The king said: 'He knows the desert land. He speaks their tongue. He can help us.' So Olav spared the blue man's life and instead cast him in irons.

The following day we set sail for the land they call Egypt. The blue man was chained to the mainmast. For several days we sailed first south, then east. With favourable winds from the north, we were soon engulfed by the heat.

The sun blazed, the air was warm and heavy, and most of us had thrown off our clothes. Our shoulders and backs burned red hot in the heat. Men stood on the boats and stared at the shore. Ahead, on a small island outside a town the blue man called Alexandria, a lighthouse rose up so gigantic that we could not believe our own eyes. The tower was made of white stone and soared straight into the sky. How high it was, was hard to guess. The memory still fills me with awe. I tried to count all the windows, but lost sight with every wave. At the base of the tower was a low, square fort. The foot of the tower rose up from a courtyard that was wider and longer than any house I had seen. And atop the building that already reached the heavens was another, narrower, eight-sided tower, and on top of that, still one more tower, round and thin. Far up on the very top was a mirror that flashed and twinkled in the rays of the sun. Olav, too, who was not oft impressed, stared at the building with open mouth. 'A great beacon, indeed,' I heard him mumble to himself.

When we reached the western estuary of the River Nile, a short distance from the lighthouse, the wind picked up. The Egyptians sent boats out to bump us, but their square vessels were such that they could not come properly alongside. We stood ready with raised swords, spears and axes. The spear bearers hit the deck rhythmically with their spears. No one dared board our longships. Olav laughed, full of scorn. But the blue man warned: these attacks that barely scratched us were poorly organised and led by foolhardy commanders of peripheral outposts and customs points. Soon we would meet the true warriors.

The warriors of the Fatimid caliphate awaited us in a bay to the north of the twin garrison towns of Fustat and al-Qhira that flanked the fortified Ibn Tulun Mosque. We steered our longships, *Sea Eagle* and *Odin's Raven*, alongside the largest of the Egyptians' boats. With a mighty roar, we boarded the ship from both sides.

The Egyptian warriors were smaller than us. Though they had been trained to fight, most men lacked courage and passion. As we cut our way on to the battleship, many chose to jump into the water and swim to the shore. We steered our ships into the banks and stormed ashore. Our enemy was better organised and disciplined on firm ground. On Olav's command we ran towards them, roaring and yelling, like a savage army of berserks and warriors from Valhalla. They threw down their bows and arrows and pulled their swords and double-headed spears.

The air trembled with shouts and yells and the sweet stench of blood. The Egyptian army was in the throes of organising its retreat. When fighting man to man, they were drained of the courage they derived from fighting together. To a man they had no heart for it. They fought as though it were a duty. We lost several hundred men in this first battle.

Once the Egyptian forces had retreated in a dust cloud of dishonour, we continued our voyage up the river. Soon we met another army, first on the water, then on land. The pattern repeated itself: after a short battle the Egyptians were defeated. We could continue our journey.

For days we sailed south up the River Nile. This lengthy waterway gave life and food to people who lived in houses built from stone, clay and reeds. The river twisted and turned like a serpent through a desert of sand, stone and cliffs. Olav was much impressed by the detail and correctness of the map. Every bend in the river was included in the monks' copy of the Egyptian original. The oarsmen, who preferred the open seas and high winds, moaned and complained. No sooner had they pulled to the left, than they had to turn to the right. Again and again. On occasion the ships ran aground on sandbanks. Here and there we had to force our way through thick algae. Thousands of people thronged on the banks. Small children ran shouting along the shore. We met many merchant ships that silently made way for our fleet.

We sailed day and night. In the evening we would lie on our backs on the deck and watch the twinkling stars as we ate sun-ripened fruits that we took from the shores. The crescent moon was parallel with the water. A strange sight. The air was thick with insects and sounds and desert scents.

The fleet reached the palace at the break of day. The detailed descriptions from the old parchments were as written yesterday. The entrance to the side canal was guarded by two stone jackals. The great temple lay in the shadow of the cliff edge. Olav's gaze moved from the shore, farther on to the palace and up the cliff wall. 'Well, well,' he said, 'so we are here at last.' I stood beside him and looked at the map with its ornate drawings. Everything looked exactly as it did on the page. 'Where are the people?' I asked. 'They are sleeping,' Olav answered. I argued that there must be guards. Olav said: 'The guardians of the temple and the priests are the guards. They have no need for more. No one knows of this tomb. Two thousand five hundred years have passed since the burial.' 'Which is a long time,' I agreed.

We moored by the riverbank and went on foot to the temple. We were wrapped in a cloud of dust and sand. I walked with Olav along the flagstone path that led to the temple. Suddenly a thin Egyptian stood in our way. He boldly met the king's eyes. Olav gave an assured grin. 'Move, blue man!' said the king. But the Egyptian did not move, which was to his honour. The expression on his face and his dress immediately told me that he was in all likelihood a priest or holy man. 'Move!' Olav said once more. I said to the king that it was improbable that the foreigner spoke our language. 'Then I am certain he will understand *this*,' Olav said, and drew his sword. The small blue man did not move. Olav prodded him with the sword. A thread of blood ran from the wound and dripped into the sand. He did not tremble. But his eyes flashed. The Egyptian uttered something that we could not comprehend and fell to his knees. To my ears the words sounded like an oath. Olav unexpectedly pulled back his sword and put it in its sheath. 'We'll take him with us!' he said, looking down at the kneeling Egyptian. 'He may be useful,' the king said to himself, more than us – I think.

On the brow of a nearby hill, a group of men with weapons had gathered. Olav waved to the men behind, instructing them to meet these men who had been sent to defend their land.

Together with Olav and his hand-picked group of men, I entered the empty temple, which smelt of incense. The floor was covered in mosaics. The walls were decorated with gods. Behind the altar, the entrance to the tomb was hidden by a tapestry. We pulled the tapestry down and overturned the altar. The tomb had been walled up and sealed with mysterious animal figures and symbols that bore no resemblance to the runes or letters. Olav had picked six of the strongest men in the fleet to knock down the wall. But still it took time. When the opening was large enough for us to clamber through, we descended the narrow steps. The air was thick and warm and reeked of mould and stone. In the dark, we lit the torches we had taken from the temple. The tunnel at the bottom of the stairs led to the first burial chamber. Olav was the first man in. I followed.

Our torches lit up the room. A coffin stood in the middle of the floor, surrounded by wooden statues and four ceramic pots, full of jewellery and precious stones. 'Well, that is something,' I said to the king. Again, the walls were covered with gods and symbols. The very thought that the burial chamber had stood like this for thousands of years made me dizzy. Or perhaps it was the heat and the heavy air. We called on a group of porters to take the pots down to the ships. Olav was impatient. With a pointed stone, he drew on the wall where the strong men should ram it through. Again they set to with their mallets. The noise felt like spears in my ear. The trapped echo rumbled and tumbled backwards and forwards. Then we were through, and we went down yet more steps to the second burial chamber. It was as the first. Just as big, just as warm. And here, once again, a coffin stood in the middle of the floor. There were four red ceramic pots full of treasure. The king studied the old Egyptian map and marked where he thought the entrance to the third and final chamber would be.

The last wall was more solid than the two first, and appeared much as the rest of the chamber. But Olav knew what hid behind the stones. The men set to work once more. 'Knock it down,' said the king. The men hit the wall as hard as they could. Slowly the iron ate its way into the stone with resounding thuds. Small chips of stone flew off. The sweat poured from the exhausted men's brows. They worked two and two, hammering at the wall until finally it gave way and collapsed. 'That is how it should be done,' said the king.

Behind the wall, an even narrower, deeper and steeper staircase awaited. 'If it continues,' Olav said, 'we are headed straight for Hell.' No one laughed. With torches aloft we descended the stairs. At the bottom, another tunnel led farther into the ground. After a hundred paces or so, the tunnel widened. We passed through a colonnade. And then finally we were there.

The innermost chamber was bursting with treasure. Sapphires, emeralds and diamonds. Candlesticks and torch holders of pure gold. Cats in black alabaster, birds in polished stone, great beetles that were either cast or carved. We found ceramic pots full of parchment scrolls. 'We have your kinsman, Håkon the Good, to thank for all this,' I said. The king answered with a smile: 'So I do resemble someone in my family, after all.' All around us, the men gathered everything that was of value. The stone and plaster statues were left behind. The porters got empty fish boxes from the ships and filled them with treasure. The weight of our trophies and the heat bothered none now that we had found the treasure. The men cheered and laughed. The steps were so narrow that they had to work together as it was not possible to pass on the stairs. When all the jewellery and gems had been taken, Olav ordered that they take a decorated casket that contained six pots with papyrus manuscript scrolls. I could not understand what he would do with manuscripts in a language he could not understand. But King Olav loved manuscripts and a good story. And there was no doubt that the casket was made of gold.

In the middle of the chamber, between four carved pillars, was a large stone coffin. With great effort, we managed to push aside the heavy lid. Inside we found a quartz sarcophagus. And inside the sarcophagus lay another coffin, covered in dust. And inside that was a coffin made of cypress wood, inlaid with coloured glass and precious stones. We lifted the cypress coffin out on to the floor and opened it. Inside there was a gold cast of a dead man, and inside this, the corpse wrapped in linen. 'The sleeping god,' Olav said. I did not think that the odd figure looked much like a god, but I have always imagined powerful gods such as Odin and Loki. We placed the gold casket and the mummy back in the cypress coffin. 'We shall take him with us,' Olav said. I protested. After all, we had now amassed more gold and treasures than on any other raid. The idea of disturbing a foreign god – albeit a small and sleeping one – unnerved me. But Olav was not to be swayed. He claimed he had dreamt of finding a sleeping god, and this god would stay with him for ever. 'Very well, my lord,' I said. I knew that the king would not be dissuaded from this notion. We looked around the burial chamber. 'I wish that when my days are done, I could rest for eternity like this,' Olav said. I answered peevishly that his eternal sleep would no doubt be disturbed by tomb raiders such as us.

Then Olav did something most strange. He took off his necklace, a heavy golden chain with a pendant of the rune *tiwaz*. The symbol of the warrior Tyr that gave Olav strength and courage in battle. He placed the chain in the empty sarcophagus. I wished to ask why, but refrained. Not a word was said. We breathed in the humid air. The king's chain lay coiled in the sarcophagus, for all the world like a golden serpent. Then we left the chamber and went out into the scorching morning sun.

In the early morning light, when he had eaten a bowl of porridge and drunk a glass of water, he sat down at his desk. The ink had a metallic smell that he both loved and hated.

Though he could barely remember what he had talked of with the monks the day before, the memories from his times with King Olav were still vivid and alive with overwhelming detail. He remembered the swarms of flies that hovered over the pools of blood, the smell of the salty ocean and the smoke that smarted in his eyes when they set light to the towns and villages. The terrified screams still rang in his ears, and he remembered the sight of the horizon, which swallowed the clouds. But he had forgotten what he ate last night.

And now Olav was a warrior in Valhalla, or perhaps one of the White Christ's angels, he thought to himself, and I am destined to wander round in Helheim, the icy underworld of the dead, as a moss-covered corpse.

PART II

The Hidden Sign

☥ ↑ †

'Odin was burnt, and at his pile there was great
splendour.'
SNORRI

'Let him that hath understanding count the number
of the beast, for it is the number of a man, and the
number is six hundred three score and six.'
REVELATION 13: 18

'I owe everything to Egypt, Egypt is everything to me.'
JEAN-FRANÇOIS CHAMPOLLION

The Rune Stone

1

I PUT my suitcase with the rune stone in it down with a thump that echoes and bounces off the corridor walls. Then I fumble around for my keys, which jangle against each other.

It is a risk coming home, but I have been in Bergen for a week now and I desperately need some clean clothes. And a couple of books that I had started to read. And the tube of cream for the eczema in my groin.

The main lock – an old-fashioned mortise, which does not lock by itself – opens with a click.

I put the long key into the security lock that a door-to-door salesman managed to palm off on me, resorting to persistence, flattery and veiled threats about the nameless terrors that might visit me in my home if I did not secure it with an extra lock. I turn the key. It rattles and clicks. Out of habit, I leave the keys in the lock as I open the door. The hall light is on. This time they have closed all the doors behind them. A circle of light escapes through the keyhole in the sitting-room door.

They are in there.

Fear starts to burn in my diaphragm. I hold my breath. I sense Hassan with my entire being. Or the smell of his after-shave and cigar, mixed with a pungent sweat. Trembling, I rest my hand on the door frame. I look down the hall. No one. But I know that they are there.

My heart is hammering so hard that it feels as if it wants to break free from my body and take the lift back down to the ground floor.

I think to myself that either they have a copy of my keys, or a picklock that is so sophisticated that it can unlock even the security lock that the salesman had assured me was impossible.

Bjørn, you're being paranoid!

I think I hear a noise from the sitting room. The sound of shoes on linoleum. But it might just be my imagination.

The rune stone is in a black Samsonite suitcase with a coded lock which I bought in Bergen, wrapped in damp towels, shirts and dirty underpants. No one knows about it. Not even the Directorate for Cultural Heritage. Only Øyvind and me.

'Pull yourself together, Bjørn,' I say to myself. 'There's no one here. They haven't been waiting for you in your flat, the whole time that you've been in Bergen. They don't know that you came back on the train this morning. You're being irrational. You're panicking for no reason. Bjørn,' I say in my sternest voice, 'get a grip!'

The light in the keyhole goes out.

In 1905, Albert Einstein proved that time is relative. He was right. The seconds and minutes in a dentist's chair or in front of a firing squad pass at a different speed from those spent on the beach.

The sitting room door opens.

I stop breathing.

Hassan's eyes seem even colder and more unfeeling now that I know who he is. He is wearing a dark suit with well-pressed trouser legs. White shirt. Tie. He has a gun in his hand. A Glock.

We are about three to four metres apart. He fills the doorway to the sitting room. I'm still standing with my feet on the mat.

Another head pops out from behind Hassan. I don't know what he is called, but I recognise him from the hotel room in Iceland.

As I still have my hand on the door handle, I react quick as a flash.

I slam the front door shut, turn the key in the security lock, grab the suitcase with the rune stone in it and run back to the lift.

If you want to escape from a wild animal, you have to outwit it. So I send the lift down to the ground floor. Without me. And I bolt out to the stairs and run up a flight.

I press the alarm that I have to the police.

My pounding heart fills my mouth.

Hassan manages to open the door after about thirty seconds. They storm down the corridor below me. They don't wait for the lift. They burst out on to the stairs and thunder down like a landslide.

I catch my breath as I stand and wait.

The first patrol car arrives about five to six minutes later. And a second car, with Ragnhild in it, a couple of minutes after that.

Hassan has disappeared. He has vanished into thin air in one of the villa-lined streets near by.

2

My friend Terje picks me up from the police HQ a couple of hours later.

There is no sign of the thugs. But we take several detours

all the same, at a speed that could cost Terje a month's modest wages and several points on his driving licence.

I tell him about everything that happened in Bergen. But he has already read about most of it in the papers. The discovery of the burial chamber at Lyse Abbey has become a bit of a tricky question for cultural heritage bureaucracy. At first, people were wildly excited. *An untouched burial chamber? From the twelfth century? In a well at Lyse Abbey?* Then it dawned on them all that I had excavated the tomb on my own and had not followed formal procedures. I had not applied for permission. I had not informed anyone. On the contrary, I had broken in like a true tomb raider. A vandal! The Directorate for Cultural Heritage and the most irascible professors want to report me to the police. But fortunately the Minister of Culture got involved, and more than anything, he wants to avoid a scandal. They have shown me some mercy, so I have narrowly avoided losing my job, though I have been suspended until the inquiry has finished studying all aspects of the case. Which is fair enough. I have broken every rule in the book. And I haven't even told them about the rune stone that I took from the chamber.

That night, I sleep on the sofa in Terje's sitting room. My mobile phone, which I picked up from the university, rings several times. Number unknown. I don't answer. It is not likely that they will be able to trace my mobile phone here in the centre of town.

Terje, in his infinite kindness – and possibly also in order to protect his flat from being the target of a potential bazooka attack – lends me his family summer house at Spro on Nesodden, which is half an hour by ferry from the centre of Oslo. Practically impossible to find even for anyone prepared to go to any lengths to get the rune stone. Such as killing me, for example.

3

It's raining. The raindrops slither and trickle down the window. The Oslo Fjord is cold and dark, and I have lit the black wood-burning stove.

The rune stone is hidden out in the woods, wrapped in a traditional Norwegian sweater and tarpaulin, then stuffed into a hockey bag that I have left in a natural hollow between two boulders, which I then covered with stones.

In front of me on the desk, which looks out over the fjord and the islands, I have a full-scale photo of the rune stone. A friend at the Geological Institute has looked at the jewels that are set in the stone and they, alone, are worth millions.

Apart from Øyvind, Terje and the geologist, no one knows that the rune stone exists. Though obviously the workers busying themselves in the tomb will soon start to wonder why there is an empty niche in the marble base.

I have no difficulty in understanding the stone.

The Old Norse text is written in runes. But not encrypted. I translate the five verses word for word. The text is a religious homage to Holy Olav, with references to Old Norse, Egyptian and Christian mythology. According to the person who carved the runes, Odin, Osiris and the White Christ entered into a pact at the dawn of time, pledging that their people would live together in peace and harmony. Right.

In my translation of the Old Norse runes, the introduction reads:

So holy are you Saint Olav our good king
You employ Christ's sword with faith and without mercy
A fearless king holy saint honour be to you
Rest you so eternally in God's sight White
Christ Osiris Odin you king of kings.

The text is just as enigmatic as most rune texts. As I am slow, it takes me two days to find the hidden thread running through it. The key is carved on the right corner of the rune stone: an upside-down U followed by two vertical lines: ∩||. For a long time I think that it is some kind of magic spell. But then I realise it is quite simply the Egyptian number 12.

I play with the number in different directions and combinations. Eventually I manage to solve the puzzle. If you count twelve letters in from the left-hand margin and then read down, the name of a place appears:

So holy are yoU Saint Olav our good king
You employ ChRist's sword with faith and without mercy
A fearless kiNg holy saint honour be to you
Rest you so etErnally in God's sight White
Christ OsiriS Odin you king of kings

Urnes.

Urnes stave church in the county of Sogn and Fjordane was built around 1130 and is Norway's oldest preserved stave church. The construction of Lyse Abbey started in 1146, sixteen years later.

That may of course be a coincidence. But there may equally be a connection.

A considerable number of churches and abbeys were built all over Norway in the 1100s. The country had recently been Christianised and was eager to worship its new god.

The raindrops slide down the windowpane. Behind them, slightly out of focus owing to condensation on the glass, a sailing boat defies the wind. I have a tendency to identify with anything. An abandoned, crumpled ice-cream wrapper. The last potato left on the plate. A cunning elf on an Icelandic plateau. Or a sailing boat, stubbornly thrusting its way forward against the wind and waves.

Late in the evening, as I sit watching a cargo ship pitching its way south down the fjord, I hear a celestial fanfare of bassoons and harps. In other words, the mobile phone that I have borrowed from Terje. I have only given the number to my most trusted confidants.

I recognise Øyvind's number on the display screen. He tells me that they have excavated the northern end of the tunnel, where we turned at the wall. From there, the archaeologists went on to find a part of the cellar under Lyse Abbey that had not been discovered before. At first they thought that it was perhaps a granary that had been filled in, but then today they realised that the large room must have been a pool.

'A pool?'

'Not only that. The water from the pool would flood the entire tunnel.'

'A water trap!'

Øyvind describes a mechanism that the monks at Lyse Abbey had to open and close an underwater hatch, so they could regulate the water level in the tunnel between the pool and the well. In this way, they could seal off the burial chamber with water – and, if necessary, drown any intruders.

'So that is why the burial chamber lay above the tunnel,' I exclaim.

'Perfectly protected. In those days, the tunnel was full of water. The tomb itself was safe and dry, several metres above the water.'

'Do you think the monks had any idea of what they were protecting?'

'Only a very few. There are elusive hints in some of the abbey manuscripts from the fourteenth and fifteenth centuries that they are protecting some sacred secret. But historians, and possibly even the monks themselves, have always thought that it was a religious metaphor. Knowledge of the burial chamber must have been lost over the centuries. The last three abbots certainly seemed to have no idea of its existence. It seems unlikely that the monks who left the abbey when it was abandoned in 1536 knew anything about the chamber, which was, after all, the very reason for which it had been built in the first place.'

'So the rune stone and the bishop's remains were left in peace.'

'Man, it's just incredible!'

'This, my dear Øyvind, is just the beginning.'

He falls quiet. 'The beginning?'

'The burial chamber at Lyse Abbey is the first of five sacred places.'

'Five?'

'Each point of the pentagram marks a tomb.'

'So there are four more?'

'Lyse Abbey isn't even the most important one. Otherwise we would have found Holy Olav there, and not Bishop Rudolf. No one would kill Sira Magnus and attack me for the sake of a rune stone and a bishop's tomb. There must be more out there, something else . . .'

'More? What do you mean, more? And *out there*? What are you talking about?'

'I know *where*, but I just don't know *what*.'

'And what do you mean by that?'

'I think I've stumbled on another clue.'

'Another one? Bjørn, don't we have enough loose ends as it is?'

'The rune stone refers to a place that has nothing whatsoever to do with the pentagram.'

'Heaven help us . . .'

'Øyvind, what do you say to coming with me on another trip?'

I dutifully ring Ragnhild to say that I'm going away for a few days.

    'Bjørn . . .'

    'I've got my alarm with me!'

    'Look what happened the last time!'

    'I found the tomb!'

    'And you were suspended.'

    She sounds just like my mother.

The Stave Churches

1

URNES STAVE church sits serenely on a hill over-
looking the Luster Fjord at the end of the Sogne
Fjord and is surrounded by majestic mountains that tower
up from the long, narrow fjord. The tower and roof cast
sharp shadows over the graveyard. The water below is like
a mirror and cold. Somewhere a dog barks.

Like most stave churches, Urnes church has roof upon
roof below a tower that points straight up to the heavens.
The timber is tarred and coarse. The carvings, which originally came from the remains of two earlier churches that
stood on the site, were made in the final throes of the
Viking age. They twist and turn in great, thin loops, curves
and circles.

'Bjørn!'

In the dark interior, the smell of old timber blends
with the sharp resinous scent of pitch tar. There is an
edge of suppressed anticipation in Øyvind's whisper. He
is peering at the carvings on one of the staves – a pillar
or column – and picking at a familiar motif. In between
the elegant swirls, some lines have been scratched into the
wood, and I recognise three symbols: ankh, *tiwaz* and the
cross.

We wave over Vibeke Wiik from the Society for the
Preservation of Norwegian Ancient Monuments. We
have not said a word about what we are looking for – the

truth is we barely know ourselves – but the very idea that Urnes might have anything to do with the discovery of the tomb at Lyse Abbey makes Vibeke and the Society more than willing to help. She let us in and showed us round, before leaving us to our own devices, while she did her own thing over by the altar. Øyvind and I have been studying the inscriptions, carvings and decorations for hours.

'Oh, that,' she says, somewhat embarrassed, when we ask about the symbols. 'Our curators reckon that the person who carved those symbols there was trying to draw strength from different religions. Not everyone was solid in their Christian faith. In fact, this rather odd combination of symbols appears in several wood carvings from the period to the sixteenth century.'

With renewed enthusiasm, Øyvind and I start to study the carvings around the symbols in minute detail. Norwegian stave churches contain a wealth of runic inscriptions. The symbols indicate that the carver has left a clue. A clue that was supposed to be found. Not just by anyone, but by those who had the secret knowledge.

Hidden in the myriad animal figures, mythological symbols and runes, we find words like *Holy Olav* and *the king's reliquary* and an inscription which, when translated, says: *We who guard the Holy One.* In several places we come across the number 50 written in modern characters and the Roman number L. We read the phrase *Hail the wise blue man*, which must refer to an Egyptian or a North African, and a reference to *the Pope's retainer* and *the Holy Cult of Amon-Ra's worthy GUARDIANS.* I don't know what to think. I have never heard anything about papal retainers or Egyptian religious cults in Norway. But if nothing else, the Egyptian references correspond with the references to Egypt in the Snorri Codex.

'Boys?' Vibeke's voice calls to us from one of the

church's four corners. 'I have just had a thought – it wasn't by any chance this crypt that you were looking for, was it?'

She opens a hatch in the floor and hooks it back to the wall. The odour of mould, earth and groundwater rises up from below. I turn on my torch and shine it down into the dark, stone-lined room under the church floor.

I look at her askance. 'A crypt? Weren't tombs like this always located by the chancel, in front of the altar or to the east of the nave?'

'This tomb was in fact only discovered when the church was renovated in the seventeenth century,' she explains. 'They had to break up large parts of the floor, because the timberwork was starting to rot. The crypt was concealed in such an intricate way that they then had to break up the whole floor in order to get to it. The original floor had not been laid in the usual way. When the church was built, someone had put down an ingenious construction of timber beams and cog wheels that could open an enormous lock by moving a beam right over by the altar into a new position. Unfortunately it all ended up in the bonfire. The little we know about the locking mechanism is based on two manuscripts that have been kept here in the community.'

'The stone lining is also an anachronism, isn't it?'

'Normally graves were shallow and the bodies were laid on birch bark. A tomb like this was most unusual.'

'What was in the crypt?'

'That's the odd thing. It was empty. Completely empty.'

Øyvind, Vibeke and I climb down into the narrow, low tomb. But there is nothing to see. Everything has been removed. There is not even an inscription on any of the stones in the walls and floor.

We continue our investigation the following day. It is a chilly morning. Øyvind and I are both wearing thick, washed-out woolly cardigans. Vibeke hovers around us like a helpful genie that someone has let out of a bottle. Around midday, we eat the packed lunch that we made at the hotel on the other side of the fjord. We share our sandwiches with Vibeke, who has a large thermos of coffee with her, which is something that Øyvind and I had not thought about.

A couple of hours later I find the hatch.

It is perfectly camouflaged. It is not entirely by accident that I find the small door on the back of the capital of one of the solid staves that go from floor to ceiling, but it is still a stroke of luck. It is about four metres up from the floor, and the pulpit was built right underneath it in 1690.

At first glance, the door looks like a joint in the ornamental frame that has been carved into the wood. I knock on the stave to determine whether it sounds hollow. It is not easy to say. Then my focus returns to the joint, and I follow the rectangular line in the carving, centimetre by centimetre. I call Øyvind and Vibeke over. They come bounding up into the pulpit, but they don't spot the opening until I mark it out with my finger.

'My goodness,' Vibeke says. 'And I thought we knew every square metre of this church.'

Using the tip of my finger and Øyvind's Leatherman knife, I try to prise open the hatch, but it has been cut into the pillar with perfect precision. It will not budge. Øyvind and Vibeke try to help, but Vibeke can't even get her long, red nails properly into the crack.

'Maybe it's been glued shut,' she suggests.

'Then we'll have to use a keyhole saw. Or drill it open,' I joke.

Vibeke gives me a look that tells me that certain things

are not to be joked about.

'We could just saw through the whole stave,' Øyvind cackles. He is not as sensitive as I am when it comes to unspoken language.

We spend an hour trying to find a way to open the hatch. We are just about to give up when Øyvind discovers a clever locking mechanism.

In a framed square on the other side of the stave, there are three carved, ornamental flowers, and the crowns turn out to be wooden pegs. By twisting and turning the swollen pegs – and carefully prising them out with the smallest blade on Øyvind's Leatherman knife – we finally manage to get them out. 'I'm going to get into *so* much trouble,' Vibeke says, sighing, but her eyes are radiating enthusiasm.

For a while we wonder what to do with three holes that are too small for our fingers. I stick a biro in and feel that I am pushing at something inside the pillar. But nothing happens. Only when we each put a pen into the three holes at the same time is the internal weight mechanism released. Something rattles. The mechanism opens an internal lock and suddenly the hatch opens without any resistance.

I shine my torch into the cavity. Inside I see – a piece of wood?

I gingerly put my hand in. I am concerned that whoever made the lock might also have made a contraption for chopping off the hands of thieves.

I grab hold of the piece of wood, count to ten in my head, and then pull it out hastily.

My hand is intact. And in it, I am holding a rune stick.

Vibeke is euphoric. On behalf of the Society for the Preservation of Norwegian Ancient Monuments, Sogn and Fjordane County Council, the Directorate for Cultural Heritage and Our Lord, she wants to take the stick immediately, thank you very much. But using our charm, Øyvind and I manage to persuade her to let us borrow the rune stick so we can study it. We promise to return it undamaged and in perfect condition so that it can be exhibited in a glass case for the benefit of the tourist board, the mayor and hordes of cruise-ship passengers.

The rune stick is, not unexpectedly, completely incomprehensible. But by trying out various Caesar combinations, we discover that all the runes have to be substituted with those five places to the right. Once the text has been decoded and translated, it reads:

> The sacred
> instructions
> were hidden at Urnes
> for 50 years
>
> The Pope's retainer
> came too close
>
> The sacred cult
> of Amon-Ra
> worthy GUARDIANS
> who know the runes'
> sonorous secret
>
> B
> -SELF-
> R
> G

Yet another reference to the Pope's retainer and the Egyptian sun god, Amon-Ra. In Ancient Egypt, Amon and Ra were originally two gods who eventually fused into one.

The man who carved the runes over eight hundred

years ago must have been certain that the encrypted message would be incomprehensible to anyone who might, against all odds, find the rune stick. At the time, most people were unfamiliar with rebuses and coded texts. Only the learned and literate were able to understand the meaning of the mysterious runes. Those who knew what they were looking for, and who understood where and how to find the information, would certainly manage to make sense of the confusion of symbols.

It takes us fifteen seconds to work out the cross of runes. The horizontal characters, -SELF-, are back to front and make up the syllable FLES, and the vertical characters form the word BERG.

Flesberg.

3

Flesberg stave church was built towards the end of the 1100s on a hillside in Numedal in Buskerud. There is a dry stone wall around the church, beyond which it is surrounded by old farms and gentle hills covered in pine forests. In 1732, the priest complained about the condition of the church, 'which has stood here since the time of the Catholics', and thus managed to have the church renovated and converted into a cruciform church. No one knows what happened to the remains of the old church, as in those days timber was reused, or put on the fire.

Somewhat despondent, Øyvind and I realise that the chances of finding any traces from the 1100s are minimal.

The priest shows us around. Like most priests, he takes great pride in his church. But there is not much left from the Middle Ages. The baptismal font, a couple of stone crosses, a row of pews with chip carving, and three of the walls in the nave. The portal is decorated with carved lions and dragons, snakes and vines.

Even after searching for hours, we find no hidden cavities, no runes in the carvings and no codes in the painted decorations.

'I don't know if it's of any significance,' the priest tells us after a coffee break, 'but one of the bells is from the days when the church was new.'

Something jolts inside me. 'A sonorous secret . . .' I say to myself.

Øyvind and the priest look at me in surprise.

'A what?' Øyvind asks.

'The inscription on the rune stick! It mentioned Amon-Ra's worthy GUARDIANS who know the runes' sonorous secret.'

'The rune stick?' The priest is confused. 'Amon-Ra?'

'Of course!' Øyvind exclaims.

With great excitement, we race up the worn stairs to the top of the tower. We are completely out of breath when we tumble into the belfry. The priest opens two of the vents to let in some light.

We can immediately see which of the church bells is oldest. It is not hard. The rune inscription snakes around the lower part of the bell. The inscription is worn, but still legible. Many old church bells are decorated with rune inscriptions that are written backwards as a form of spell or oath. But in this case it doesn't even help to read it backwards. As we make feeble attempts to understand the text, the priest gives us a patronising smile and says that the text has no meaning.

'People have tried to interpret it for centuries, but no one has managed to understand the runes. They are purely ornamental.'

Øyvind photographs the runes, and I write down the text, rune by rune, in a notebook.

Øyvind comes with me in the hire car back to Nesodden. Over the next few days, we try to decipher the runes. But we don't manage to break the code. The mysterious runes are not only written in code but are also twig runes.

The secret behind twig runes is the division into three families, or *ættir*. The rune masters made up a grid that would look something like this:

	1	2	3	4	5	6
3	F	U	TH	O	R	K
2	H	N	I	A	S	
1	T	B	M	L	Y	

Each twig rune thus belonged to one of the *ættir*, which were numbered from bottom to top, in order to confuse. The rune also had a horizontal number within each *ætt*.

In this system, the rune A had a value of 24 (the fourth character in the second *ætt*), whereas B had a value of 12 (the second character in the first *ætt*).

The value of the rune was then shown in branches, so that A – that is, 24 – had two branches (*ættir*) on the left of the stave and four on the right:

An F would have three branches on the left and one on the right, whereas Y would have one left-hand branch and five right-hand branches.

To me, logic and women are much the same – impossible

to fully understand, in other words. Even though I know the principles behind the mystery of the runes, I still don't get it. So we ask Terje Lønn Erichsen to help, once again.

He is not hard to persuade. Equipped with my notes and the photographs of the church bell, he throws himself over the inscription like Champollion faced with the Rosetta Stone.

First of all, he breaks the text down into separate components, in a way that neither Øyvind nor I had thought of. Then he analyses the word structure. In this way, he discovers that the text is comprised of two sections that are repeated three times, plus five single words that are only used once.

The rune master has combined normal runes and twig runes and the text has been written back to front.

'Let's see if the rune wheel can help,' Terje says. He has made a copy of the rune wheel in Bergen Museum. Rune wheels have fascinated and confounded scholars since one was found in Gol stave church, which was dismantled and subsequently rebuilt in the Norwegian Folk Museum in Oslo in 1882. It is a primitive encryption system – a predecessor of Wheatstone's Playfair cipher – and consists of a wooden disc with two inlaid, concentric discs of different diameters, with the elder and younger futhork on them. By turning the discs, various characters meet in different combinations.

But no matter how Terje turns the wheel, it does not help us to decode the text.

Only when he applies a Caesar 8 to the normal runes, and then removes every second character, does Terje finally manage to derive some meaning from part of the text: *SGNIR LLEB EHT*, which is *THE BELL RINGS* written backwards.

It takes him longer to work out the twig runes. They

defy him, but, like me, Terje is stubborn, single minded and persistent, and he eventually manages to break the code. The rune master has consistently manipulated the number of twigs on the right and left of the stave according to an ingenious pattern. The words *SRAEY YTFIF* appear three times, which is *FIFTY YEARS* backwards.

What we are left with then is three words – of five, eight and three characters – which have all been subject to even more encryption. But now that Terje has understood the rune master's code, he manages to conjure up the three names, by trying out various Caesar combinations on backward text. The three names are: *URNES FLESBERG LOM*.

So, the fully deciphered rune inscription on the church bell reads as follows:

THE BELL RINGS

URNES FIFTY YEARS FLESBERG FIFTY YEARS LOM
FIFTY YEARS

5

Before Øyvind and I carry on to Lom, I phone Ragnhild.

She sounds a bit frustrated. She has nothing new to tell me. And I don't tell her where I am going. She asks where I have been. I don't want to tell her that either. I can be difficult too. I have got it into my head that, theoretically, someone might be listening in via lasers, implants or geostationary satellites. But I keep that to myself – so I won't be sent back to the clinic.

'The less you know, the better it is for us both,' I tell her.

'I don't understand your reasoning.'

'The less you understand, the easier it is for you to imagine how I'm feeling.'

'Bjørn, what you are saying makes no sense.'

She sounds like Mother again.

'Are you there?' she asks, after a while.

'Yes . . .'

'Don't forget that the police are here to help you. *I* am here to help you.'

There is so much I would like to tell her – for example, that I am sceptical of authority, organisations, doctors and psychologists, and officials or anyone else who thinks that they are above the rest of us. But I say nothing. The words trip over themselves somewhere between my brain and my tongue. She wouldn't understand. Ragnhild is one of society's obedient and loyal cogs.

I ask whether the investigation has been scaled back. She assures me that the case is still high priority, but her assurances are half hearted. She says they have no leads. They don't know where to look, where to start unravelling the plot. Like me, the police have seen no sign of Hassan and his men for days. Most people would feel a sense of relief. It makes me nervous. The most dangerous predator is the one you can't see.

I know that they are out there. Somewhere.

And they are looking for me.

6

Lom stave church is a dark silhouette against the Lomseggen Ridge. The carved dragonheads snap at a sprinkling of clouds that drift over the Jotunheimen Mountains. This big stave church – the main church in the parish – was built towards the end of the twelfth century, on the foundations of an even older church.

Over the next four days, Øyvind and I investigate every nook and cranny of the church, with great help from the priest, the sexton and various people from the Society for the Preservation of Norwegian Ancient Monuments.

I tell our trusty helpers that if anything gets out about what we are looking for, Lom will lose its innocence. The area will be infested with journalists from Oslo and worse. TV companies will broadcast live, illuminating Lom Church in a harsh light. This threat makes them promise loyally and obediently to not say a word.

Every morning, we leave the hotel trembling with anticipation that today, today will be the day when we finally find a clue. Every evening we return exhausted and disappointed.

The church has undergone numerous renovations and extensions. The original wood panelling has been removed. During the Reformation, all traces of Catholic heresy were removed; pictures of saints, the altarpiece, cabinets, textiles and holy vessels were taken away, burnt or thrown in the river.

The place is, however, crawling with rune inscriptions. But there are no hidden codes. There are inscriptions carved by the construction workers and declarations of love, full of romance and desire. The church has even kept a letter in runes about a love triangle, where Hårvard hoped to lure Gudny away from Kolbein. But there is nothing to indicate that the Nordic Guardians have left any messages behind.

Towards the end of the fourth day, the priest tells us that our colleagues are on their way.

Colleagues?

I look over at Øyvind. Neither of us has asked any colleagues to come.

The priest realises that something is wrong. 'They said that they had the equipment that you asked for and wanted to make sure that you hadn't left.'

Hassan . . .

How did he know where we were? Bolla is parked in a

multi-storey car park in Oslo and I left my mobile phone at home.

I remind the priest of the fate of his colleague at Reykholt and advise him to ring the local police. Immediately. We say a hasty thank-you and leave. I call Ragnhild in Oslo from a petrol station, and ask her to warn the police in Lom, just in case the priest has not taken me seriously. I call him later to find out what has happened. His voice is shaky. The police have been there for some time and reinforcements are on their way from Ringebu. 'What have you done?' he asks. I don't answer.

Øyvind and I drive back to Bergen, where we part company.

7

Sometimes, the answer to a question is so obvious that it is impossible to see it.

If you want to hide a book, just put it in a bookshelf. If you want to smuggle a rare stamp out of a country, stick it on an envelope and send it through the post.

'Bjørn? It's me!' Øyvind shouts loudly, as if to compensate for the distance between Bergen and Oslo.

The winter cold has cast a grey-blue pallor over the Oslo Fjord and islands. I am in a bad mood. I detest failure. I feel useless. Whenever I fail at something, my world is filled with thunderclouds.

I hold the phone to my ear with my shoulder. My friend on the other end is breathless and agitated.

'Are you there? Bjørn? Hello?'

'I was just thinking . . .'

'Thinking? Bjørn, listen! We were in the wrong church!'

Down on the fjord, a passenger boat sails past in the mist, looking for all the world like Las Vegas on water.

'There was another stave church in Lom!' Øyvind pauses to hear my reaction.

The cold air is electric. The steady throb of the ship's engine makes the glass in the windows vibrate and rattle in a moment of complete harmony. Then the noise dies away and the bulging hull of the ferry to Denmark slips out of my sight and mind.

'Another stave church? Øyvind . . .'

In the white foaming wake of the ship, it dawns on me.

Another stave church . . .

Legend has it that when Olav Haraldsson passed through Gubrandsdal in 1021, on his great mission to Christianise the whole country, he persuaded Torgeir Gamle of Garmo in Lom to be baptised and to build a church in praise of Our Lord. Torgeir did as the Christian king ordered. He built a church that stood for one hundred and eighty years, the predecessor of Garmo stave church, which was pulled down in 1880. Pulled down . . . which is why Øyvind and I hadn't thought of it.

'The Sandvig Collections!' I exclaim.

'Exactly!'

Forty years after Garmo stave church on Torgeir Gamle's site had been pulled down, it was rebuilt in Maihaugen Open Air Museum in Lillehammer.

8

A föhn wind blows merrily down the mountainside as I stand outside Garmo stave church, admiring the building with its dragonheads and elegant spire.

The Sandvig Collections, or Maihaugen, as it is commonly known, opened in 1904. Anders Sandvig had collected old objects, buildings and farms for over twenty years, and these were then rebuilt and exhibited in the museum grounds. When Garmo stave church had been taken down, parts of the building were auctioned off. So, together with Trond Eklestuen, Sandvig set about gathering as much of it as he could find. The stave church was rebuilt with some of its original parts, and some that came from other buildings and churches.

The craftsmen and curators responsible for reconstructing the church in the 1920s were very good at recognising what was original. Thus it takes me no longer than four hours to search the church.

In a rather modest and dark part of the church, I come across a wall panel with a faded painting of Holy Olav. The Christian king is kneeling, draped in red velvet, and holding aloft a cross.

I find the symbols ankh, *tiwaz* and cross on the broad, carved frame, as well as extensive rows of Latin letters and Old Norse runes.

A new riddle.

9

The coded text from the wall panel in Garmo stave church is long and convoluted. I sit in my hidey-hole on Nesodden for two days, playing with different character combinations, but get absolutely nowhere.

I know, thanks more to a kind of a spiritual radar and reflex than anything else, that my pursuers are near, that they are out there somewhere. In the boats that glide by down on the fjord. In the helicopters that constantly swoop over the house. In the cars that pass on the main road at the top of the driveway. With the men fishing down on the quay where the Nesodden ferry used to dock.

But they don't know where I am hiding.

I thought I had got to grips with cracking codes, but I obviously haven't. On the third day, I call Terje, who takes some unearned days off in lieu and comes out to help me. We try with various Caesar combinations, but there seems to be no system in the runes. Terje is confused. He says that something is wrong, even though we can't read the text. The structure of the characters is not right.

'This is just a mish-mash of random runes,' Terje says.

Then, on the fourth day, we discover the solution. That is, Terje discovers it. I have more than enough on my plate trying to understand what he is talking about.

A handful of runes appears in the writing with a far greater frequency than is normal in any European language. In modern script, for example, E – or any character that replaces E in a code – will appear far more frequently than the rarer M. All languages have this kind of mathematical regularity.

The problem with the Garmo text is that some characters are repeated with such an absurd frequency that Terje starts to wonder whether they have been included just to confuse the reader. Not only would this make the code difficult to decipher, but it would also explain the overuse and frequency of certain runes.

I suggest that we can try removing every second or third character.

To my astonishment, Terje thinks that is a good idea.

We throw ourselves into the task with renewed enthusiasm.

Once we have identified the dummy characters, which are six runes repeated in a kind of loop, we still have a text that is incomprehensible, but at least now we can start to try to crack the code.

The key is the same as for several of the previous codes, but even more complex.

The code master has first used the Caesar method – substituting for each character another, later character – and then written the words backwards. And in order to spice things up a bit, he has given each word an individual Caesar code.

Letter by letter, we are able to identify the Old Norse words *dylja*, *páfi*, *líkami*, *texti*, *hir* and *heilagr*. But they still don't make sense. The joker who made up the code has written the words in the wrong order. But then we discover that there is a logical pattern here too: word number one has been swapped with word number ten, word number two with word number nine, etc.

Finally, we have understood the logic, and now it is just a matter of time and patience. Eventually we manage to translate the text:

Inge the GUARDIAN carved these runes
200 summers after the death of Holy Olav

The Roman Pope's retainer, the knights of St John and
    Jerusalem's
Knights Templar have gathered for battle

The sacred tomb is hidden as Asim instructed
Our lips are sealed

The sacred scripts and the sleeping god are brought to
    safety
They are with our Guardian kinsmen in the land where
    the sun goes down

Njål the GUARDIAN carved these runes
250 summers after the death of Holy Olav

The magic of ankh and the holy rune Tiwaz, and the
    power of the cross
Protect Olav's Cave and the way thereto

See in the Bible of Lars where the sun rises.

Unless Inge, the carver of the runes, was making it all up, there must have been a massive military operation in Norway, which involved soldiers from the Vatican, the Order of Malta and the Knights Templar, around 1230 – a hundred years after Urnes stave church and fifty years after Flesberg stave church were built. If, as the text indicates, such a powerful army really did come to Norway, they must have been looking for something more valuable than the Olav Reliquary.

Something from Egypt?

What is the connection? 1230?

In 1230, Gregory IX was Pope. He was an authoritarian advocate who excommunicated Emperor Frederick II and who fought vigorously for papal power, in a secular as well as a religious context. Gregory IX sent many heretics to the stake. In one of his bulls of excommunication, it says: 'I pour God's wrath on the barbarians of *Noruega*, who desecrate the holiest of holy.'

The Grand Master of the Knights Templar until 1230 was Pedro de Montaigu. He was appointed at a ceremony on the Nile in the middle of the disastrous Fifth Crusade. The Crusaders hoped to win back Jerusalem and the Holy Land by conquering Muslim Egypt. One of the Crusaders who distinguished himself in the war with Egypt was the Grand Master of the Hospitallers, Pierre Guérin de Montaigu. He died in 1230.

But what was the connection?

'The sacred scripts and the sleeping god are brought to safety they are with our Guardian kinsman in the land where the sun goes down . . .'

The kinsman had to be Snorri on Iceland. But were *the sacred scripts* the Snorri Codex? It didn't seem likely. It was more feasible that they might be the Thingvellir Scrolls. And what was it about the manuscripts which made them sacred? And who the hell was the sleeping god?

The inscription prompted more questions than answers.

And then fifty years later, a guardian by the name of Njål made an addendum. The runes say that Olav's Cave and instructions for how to get to it are protected by the magic of ankh, the holy rune *tiwaz* and the power of the cross. And how is that supposed to be interpreted? And how can we search for *where the sun rises*, which is obviously somewhere in the east? Who is Lars? And how am I going to find his Bible?

The ambiguity of the text confuses me. It appears to contain two different sets of instructions that lead to two different places. The sacred scripts and the god were looked after by Snorri. Whereas the Olav Reliquary – and possibly more – is still in this country. *Where the sun rises . . .*

Terje and I exchange bloodshot looks.

'Where is the clue that tells the way to the next stave church?' I ask.

'The guardians who these messages were intended for were not likely to know much more than us. So the text must contain all the information we need.'

We continue to search, but no matter how much we twist and turn the sentences, we find no hidden words in the text. Around midnight, Terje falls asleep on the sofa. I stay sitting up, chewing my pencil, making futile notes in a notebook. What power does a cross have? A symbolic power, obviously. A religious power. Is there any connection between the symbols ankh, *tiwaz* and the cross and the place where the sun rises?

1030 . . . 1130 . . . 1180 . . . 1230 . . . 1280 . . .

What is the connection between these years?

And so my thoughts keep churning.

A couple of hours later, I wake up with a start.

There is a strong northerly wind blowing which makes

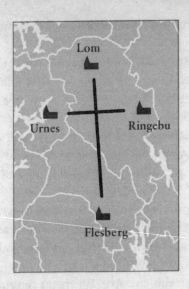

the windowpanes rattle. Whether I have been dreaming or half asleep, I'm not sure, but an idea has come to me.

In my thick woolly socks, I pad over to the bookshelf, where there is an atlas from 1952. Then I go back over to the table by the window and turn to a map of southern Norway. A thought is chasing around my head. Terje is snoring over in the sofa.

See where the sun rises.

In the east, that is.

The power of the cross.

Urnes, Flesberg, Lom.

I mark each point with a pen.

The fourth point should be in the east, where the sun rises. I look at the map and let out an involuntary gasp.

The power of the cross.

See where the sun rises.

Ringebu!

I sit there, holding my breath. In the course of a century, the Guardians have built four stave churches.

Urnes. Flesberg. Lom (Garmo). Ringebu.

If you draw two lines between the four points, you get a cross.

The Christian cross. *Crux ordinaria*.

The power of the cross.

10

Early next morning, I take the ferry into Oslo.

I have already phoned and woken the priest at Ringebu stave church. Once he had rubbed the sleep from his eyes, cleared the irritation from his voice and realised that I was looking for an archaeological sensation in *his* church, he transformed into my loyal helper.

I take a taxi from the ferry up to the university to pick up some equipment. Excessive caution that stems from my paranoia makes me ask the taxi driver to take all the detours and side streets that I know of between the university and the multi-storey car park where Bolla has been patiently waiting. Hiring cars gets very expensive in the long run.

I check the entrances to the car park one by one. They have stopped their surveillance. Which in itself is suspicious.

I take the lift to level P2. Before daring to go out to the parking bays, I put my bag between the doors to make sure I can beat a hasty retreat. I look around. Nothing. No one standing behind the pillars watching. No one sitting waiting in a parked car, hiding behind a newspaper.

There is no one else on level P2.

Very suspicious.

I pick up the bag and tiptoe, stooping as low as I can, along the wall. I feel like a character from a cartoon strip. I approach Bolla with caution.

I can't see anyone.

I have a torch and work gloves with me. I carefully and

methodically check behind the bumpers, around the mud-guards and under the car.

I find a GPS transmitter behind the left front mudguard. It is about the size of a matchbox and is so well attached that I need to use considerable force to get it off. They have covered the red, blinking light with black tape.

Smart.

But I am not fooled into stopping.

I find another GPS transmitter attached to a pump in the engine.

Satisfied now, I attach one GPS transmitter to a silver Mercedes and the other to a blue Peugeot that are parked on either side of Bolla.

Then I pay a small fortune to get the barrier to open, and head north towards Ringebu in Oppland.

11

The great stave church with a red spire dominates the hillside behind Ringebu, near an old pagan site of worship, where they also used to hold 'thing' assemblies in the old days.

The priest comes down to meet me while I'm parking Bolla. He must have been standing waiting for me. We shake hands. I apologise for waking him so early. He tells me that it is decades since he has been woken with such exciting news.

Sigmund Skarnes, the priest, is a plump and amiable man in his early sixties. He takes me into the church and with great delight shows me around. Ringebu stave church was built around 1220 and bears witness to how reluctant the Norwegians were to let go of their Old Norse gods and embrace the salvation of Christ. At the very top of the main staves, just under the ceiling, you can still see the remains of paintings of the Old Norse gods.

One of the oldest artefacts from the original church is a statue of St Lawrence, which miraculously survived the total destruction of any image of saints during the Reformation. The beautiful wooden sculpture, which stands to the left of the chancel, holding a red Bible, is so feminine that at first I think it is a woman.

The grey, soapstone baptismal font is also from the old days. A darker stone rings the top of the font.

When Sigmund Skarnes has finished showing me around, I ask whether it would be possible for me to have a look around by myself, and to study all the beauty. I tell him, somewhat diffusely, that I am looking for a hidden message that the men who built the church may have left. Skarnes retires to his room to write his Sunday sermon.

I collect the bag of equipment from the car. Digital camera, laptop, magnifying glass and powerful torch. Slowly and methodically, I work my way around the church. I study the St Lawrence statue particularly well, as it would be natural to use such a relic for hidden messages and symbols. But I do not find anything. I examine the statue and the pedestal on which it stands. I look at the red Bible, as the Bible was in fact mentioned in the last message.

Sigmund Skarnes pops in to see if everything is all right. 'Ah, so you're interested in St Lars, I see.'

'It's a beautiful statue,' I reply before his words sink in. 'What did you call him?'

'Well, he's really called St Lawrence. He was a treasurer of the church and deacon in Rome in the second century. According to legend, the poor man was martyred on a gridiron for sharing out the church's wealth among the poor. That's the way things can go! His skull is apparently still kept in the Vatican.'

'Did you say Lars?'

'That is what he was called around here. St Lars.'

See in the Bible of Lars where the sun rises . . .

The text from Garmo is referring to St Lawrence!

Once the priest has retired to the vestry and his sermon again, I circle St Lars. I photograph the statue from every angle with my digital camera, with and without flash and with different light settings. I take close-ups of his face, his tunic, the red cloth that hangs from his left hand, and the Bible.

See in the Bible of Lars . . .

I transfer the pictures to my laptop in a dark corner of the church. I then download them on to PhotoManipulator Pro and start to study the motifs. The computer program makes it possible to change negative into positive, to simulate ultraviolet light, to adjust the contrast, size, number of pixels, colour values, and to distort the colours, perspective and angles of light. Archaeologists and art conservationists use the software to fade out colours so that they can see the original brush marks under the layers of restored colour.

The pictures of the Bible are a digital treasure trove.

Under eight layers of different types of paint, I see the outline of some symbols that are so faint that they must have been more or less invisible to the naked eye when they were drawn. I have no idea what sort of ink was used – it could be anything from distilled honey or onion juice with processed vinegar or urine – but the result was invisible writing that they could paint over. To make the letters visible again, they would have to warm up the text or paint over it with some kind of developing agent (for example, the water used to boil red cabbage combined with certain chemicals can make vinegar writing visible). Or, nowadays, manipulation with the help of advanced computer software.

'Are you getting anywhere?' the priest calls over from the vestry door.

'This will take some time.'

I don't like lying to a priest in the house of the Lord, but then it is not entirely untrue either. And I don't see any reason why I should tell him that I have just discovered an ankh, *tiwaz* and cross followed by a short text.

12

The guest house where I am staying is down in the centre of Ringebu. The room is simple, but then I don't have many demands. Someone has moved some of my things. Not much. But enough for me to notice. I wonder whether Hassan knows that I'm here, but then dismiss the thought.

I spend the rest of the evening deciphering the coded text that was hidden under the paint. Once you have cracked the code master's technique – displacing characters in a given pattern and adding random characters to cause confusion – it is more a question of patience than intelligence.

At twenty-seven minutes past eleven exactly, I have unravelled the text:

> Just as the Virgin Mary held Jesus in her lap
> The belly holds the casket
> Praise be to Thomas!

I sit still for a long time.

I can't hold back my laughter.

Those Guardians of old have hidden their message inside a statue that serves as a guide.

13

The rising sun shines down from the pale morning sky. Sigmund Skarnes, the priest, smiles kindly at me as he comes up the path. He gives the toolbox and equipment at my feet a double-take, and turns to me with exaggerated concern: 'Are you thinking of pulling my church to pieces?'

'I've found out where the message is!'

He looks at me with great excitement and curiosity.

'Inside St Lawrence,' I tell him.

'Are you sure? *Inside* the statue? As far as I know, it's solid.'

We let ourselves into the church and turn on the light. The air inside is cold and damp. The sunlight comes in at an angle from the cross-shaped windows high up on the walls. Skarnes shivers. While he lights the candles on the altar and in the tall, wrought-iron candlesticks, I carry my toolbox and equipment down the aisle and put them on the floor in front of St Lawrence. Chisels, screwdrivers, hammers, a bottle of white spirit, a torch, a knife and a fine saw blade.

I turn on the torch and look to see how the statue is fastened to the wooden pedestal. Old things are often fragile and I don't want to do any more damage than is necessary.

I spend about an hour examining the statue. Using a cotton bud and white spirit, I carefully remove the stubborn paint and glue between the statue and the pedestal. Somewhere behind me, the priest is talking to the verger about a wedding, in quiet voices, as though not to disturb me.

A draught of air rushes along the floor when the door is opened and people come into the church.

'Good morning,' Sigmund Skarnes says, and goes to meet them. 'I'm afraid that the church is not open to the public today.'

I shine the torch into the gap that I have created between the wooden statue and the pedestal.

One of the visitors says something.

Skarnes asks them where they are from.

A deep voice replies: 'Far away.'

14

Hassan.

The air drains from my lungs, the blood from my heart, the strength from my muscles. I gasp and grab hold of the wooden pedestal.

Hassan is standing between the rows of pews with four men I have not seen before.

'Bjørn?' The priest wrinkles his brow. 'Is something wrong?' He looks from me to Hassan and back. 'Who are they?'

I stumble towards the altar.

'Bjørn!' Sigmund Skarnes implores, in a priestly voice. He wants an explanation, right now, and it had better be good.

One of Hassan's men drags the verger over to a pew. She struggles to break free. 'Excuse me!' she protests with indignation. She gets a slap on the face. He doesn't hit her hard, but it shuts her up. A trickle of blood runs from her nose and pools on her upper lip before dripping down on to her white blouse, just by the black name badge. They push her down on to the pew.

The priest looks at Hassan, confused and alarmed. 'What do you think you are doing?' he asks no one in particular.

One of Hassan's men lights up a cigarette. Sigmund Skarnes is about to say that it is strictly forbidden to smoke in the old wooden church, goodness gracious, surely they must realise that – but I see from his face that he appreciates that nothing a rural priest might say will make this man put out his cigarette.

Hassan's footsteps echo as he strides down the aisle. He shoves the priest in front of him. I watch every step. He stops a couple of metres away from me.

'Where are the Thingvellir Scrolls?'

His voice is full of gravel, but his tone is not threatening. He is simply asking a question and expects an answer. He is used to people obeying him.

'I don't have them.'

'But you can tell me where they are!'

'They were in Iceland. But I don't know where they are now.'

'I see. And how is your little finger?'

His voice sounds just as I imagine the voice of the dead might sound, muttering in the catacombs.

I try to disguise a shudder. I can't swallow. One of the henchmen laughs. I don't know whether he is laughing at Hassan's question or my reaction.

Hassan takes my left hand in his. Tenderly, like a father. I had the splint on my pinkie removed a week ago. The doctor said the break had healed nicely.

Hassan grips my pinkie once again and gives it a squeeze. I groan, partly from pain and partly from fright. He lets go, unexpectedly.

Two of his men tie my wrists to the round pillar by the chancel.

My knees turn to jelly.

'Bjørn? What are they doing to you?' the priest exclaims in horror.

I have lost my voice.

Hassan looks at the statue of St Lawrence with curiosity.

'Does that have another copy in it?'

Another copy? I suddenly realise that he thinks that the wooden statue contains another transcript of the Thingvellir Scrolls.

The thought hadn't even occurred to me.

'I don't think so.'

'Where are the Thingvellir Scrolls?'

I find it hard to breathe. The smell of Hassan's aftershave

blends with the smell of wood and tar. Outside the church, in another universe, a train blows its whistle down in the valley.

'You've got ten fingers,' Hassan states.

I immediately look at my white hands. My nails are in a terrible state. I have bitten them since I was a boy. I instinctively clench my fists to protect them.

'And I have plenty of time,' he adds. 'So where are they?'

'The scrolls are safe. I'm sorry, you won't be able to steal them.'

I try to make it sound like dry information, a straight-forward statement, but I actually sound like a whining, snivelling coward.

'That is not what I asked.'

He nods to two of his men. This is it, I think to myself. My lungs have ceased to function. I am about to faint. Just as well. Turn me off, I think. Turn off the lights and pull out the plug.

I envisage them breaking my fingers, one by one. First my pinkie, then my ring finger, then the middle finger, then the index and finally the thumb.

And then they'll start on the right hand.

I feel sick with fear. Please let me faint, I pray. I don't care how embarrassing it is. Just let me lose consciousness and wake up when the danger is over and Hassan has stuffed Ringebu stave church in his pocket and driven off.

The men position themselves in front of St Lawrence and examine the statue, talking to each other in low voices.

The priest is confused. He glances over at me. I shake my head.

Hassan tries to rock the statue. One of the men takes a chisel out of the toolbox.

'Now just a minute!' the priest exclaims.

183

He has realised, just as I have, what they intend to do.

One of the Arabs forces the chisel in between St Lawrence and the wooden pedestal and starts to pry.

Sigmund Skarnes takes a few steps towards the man who is about to destroy the eight-hundred-year-old treasure.

Hassan hits him. Swiftly and unexpectedly. His fist connects with the priest's temple. The punch is so hard that he twists round and falls, banging his head on the pew-end. There is a crunching sound. He drops to the floor and lies there, motionless.

Unperturbed, the others concentrate on prying St Lawrence loose from his pedestal. The wood splinters. I feel the statue's silent scream in the pit of my stomach. The smallest of the men hands the statue over to Hassan. He holds it up in front of him, like a trophy.

Now it's my turn, I think. They're going to break my fingers now, one by one.

But they are even more brutal than that.

One of them takes the bottle of white spirit over to the nine-hundred-year-old baptismal font and pours it in. Another man drags the weeping verger over.

'You're forcing us to baptise her,' Hassan says.

Baptise her?

One of the thugs grabs hold of the struggling verger's hair and pushes her face down into the white spirit. She fights against it, screaming and gurgling.

'Where are the Thingvellir Scrolls?' Hassan asks.

I realise with a shock that they are prepared to let her suffer the same fate as Sira Magnus in Snorri's hot spring. Only worse. At least it was spring water which drowned Sira Magnus. If the verger gets white spirit in her lungs, she will develop a fatal, chemical pneumonia. That is, if they don't let her drown first.

'Wait!' I shout. 'I'll tell you . . .'

With dripping wet hair, the verger grabs the metal bowl in the font in a panic and throws it to the floor. A shower of white spirit sprays over the candles and falls on the man who is smoking. He goes up like a torch.

My heart jumps.

With a horrifying scream, the man lurches into the aisle, where he falls down and curls up in a ball. Hassan and the three others throw their jackets over him in a desperate attempt to put out the flames. He roars with panic and pain.

I scream for help. The flames lick the floor, catching the runner, then leaping up the pillars. The fire starts to eat at the dry woodwork.

My hands are still tied.

Just then, the automatic fire alarm and sprinkler go off.

Hassan straightens up. He looks at me. As if all this is my fault. He is holding St Lawrence under his arm.

I tug at the rope holding me to the pillar in desperation. The water from the sprinkler drips off Hassan's huge frame.

He seems to be considering whether to draw his pistol and wreak his revenge right now. Either that or he is visualising me being left to the flames and dying a painful death by burning.

The fire alarm is deafening. One of the men shouts something at Hassan. He answers. They hurry towards the door, dragging their burnt colleague with them.

'Help!' I scream.

All around me, fire and water are fighting to win the upper hand. The flames engulf the pew where most of the white spirit fell. The water from the sprinkler makes the fire crackle. Each time I breathe in, the smoke makes me cough.

Still crying, coughing and gasping for breath, the verger cuts the ropes around my wrists. 'What's happening? What's happening?' she sobs.

We take the unconscious priest by the arms and drag his heavy body down the aisle, out of the church and down the stone steps. When we are a safe distance from the burning church, we lay him out on the withered grass between the gravestones. Smoke belches out from the main entrance.

A black Mercedes GL four-by-four spins out of the parking place. I catch a glimpse of St Lawrence through the back window, wedged between the man with burns and Hassan.

The priest has stopped breathing.

His eyes are half open, staring into the eternity that he has devoted his life to understanding. A thin trickle of blood runs from his eyes and nose.

The verger and I desperately try to breathe life into his lungs and to jump-start his heart.

But we are not able to do it.

The verger's face crumbles again.

I close the priest's eyes with my fingertips.

Through the screeching of the alarm, we hear the sirens of the fire engines howl their way up from the valley.

'I'm so sorry,' I whisper, and burst into silent tears.

The Mission

1

SOMETIMES PEOPLE from your past catch up with you unexpectedly – when it is not welcome.

Ghosts disguise themselves in flesh and blood, and reappear as people you have made every effort to forget.

They say that you cannot escape from your past. You can try to forget. You can try to hide. But they will always find you. Always.

2

The marble façade of the headquarters of the Society of International Sciences graces Whitehall, in the heart of London, with its presence, much like a Greek temple or an emperor's palace in Ancient Rome. Wide amber granite steps sweep up to double doors of flaming birch wood behind seven massive pillars.

The Society was established in 1900 to coordinate all research in one common knowledge bank, a kind of CIA for science, and they now keep in touch with universities and research establishments throughout the world.

The reception area of the SIS feels like a museum for the initiated. Everyone speaks in a hushed voice. Gigantic oil paintings with motifs from antiquity and the Middle Ages hang above the highly varnished mahogany panelling: druids at Stonehenge; Moses parting the Red Sea; the assassination of Caesar; Jesus on the cross; Mary Magdalene nursing a baby; the Knights Templar at Solomon's Temple; King Arthur's knights of the Round Table raising the Holy Grail to a full moon.

Diane and Professor Llyleworth are waiting for me behind a dark red meranti reception desk.

'Bjorn,' Diane says quietly, giving me a quick hug. 'It's been a long time.'

Some years ago, we were in love. Or perhaps I should say, we were lovers. For a few blissful weeks I thought I had finally found the woman in my life. I remember one night at her flat in a London skyscraper, and making sweet love at my grandmother's place by the Oslo Fjord. Then suddenly she flicked me out of her life, like an irritating fly. It is a while now since I first noticed the exclusive gold ring on her left ring finger. Neither of us has ever said a word about the fact that she once whispered *Bjorn* (she never said my name right) into my ear as her long, deep red nails tore at my skin and soul.

Professor Llyleworth holds out his hand. 'Delighted to see you again,' he says, formally, crushing my hand ever so slightly.

Again . . . I have tried to forget the last time we met. We had found a gold casket in the ruin of an octagon at Værne Abbey, which had been the seat of the Hospitallers. The Shrine of Sacred Secrets. Professor Llyleworth was sent by the SIS to excavate the site and secure the casket and, wherever he could, to put a spanner in the works of my life. Llyleworth gives a strained laugh when I remind him that I stole the casket back from him on behalf of Norwegian cultural heritage. At the time, Diane was a willing and helpful secretary at the SIS. It later transpired that she was the daughter of Michael MacMullin, the Grand Master of the ancient order that had pursued me when I was protecting the valuable contents of the casket. Diane, the professor and I became increasingly enmeshed in a web of mutual distrust. When it was all over, there was a bit of a to-do. The casket contained a hitherto unknown gospel. But they managed to keep even that quiet.

I personally sank deep into a quagmire of depression and delusion. They sent me back to my nerve clinic, where I closed down and gave myself up to darkness and self-pity.

Some months later, I brushed the dirt off my clothes and soul and staggered back to reality.

3

And yet it was Professor Llyleworth that I called when Thrainn and I needed to hide the Thingvellir Scrolls. The SIS sent a plane to Iceland. Thrainn's translators and researchers are now working with specialists from the SIS at a secret location, somewhere in the London area. I don't want to know where. It is safest that way.

Professor Llyleworth had managed to get hold of me by phone at the police station in Ringebu, earlier that afternoon. The fire in the church had been put out. Thanks to the sprinkler and the fire brigade, the damage could be repaired. How did the SIS know where I was? I wondered. The professor said that we had to talk and I asked why. 'I'll tell you when you get here,' was his reply. 'Get here?' I exclaimed. 'There's a plane waiting for you at Gardermoen Airport,' the professor said.

That is how the SIS operates.

When I was done with the police in Ringebu, I drove back to Oslo. The police accompanied me up to my flat, where I had a shower and put some clothes and my passport in a holdall. I also put in the rune stick from Urnes in a flute case, as I needed help with dating it.

Ragnhild drove me to Gardermoen. On the way, I told her about everything that had happened. She thought that going abroad for a few days might be a good idea.

I flew from Gardermoen to London in the SIS's Gulfstream jet. It was dark by the time we landed. A limousine was waiting to take me from Heathrow to Whitehall.

4

'What did they manage to take from Ringebu?' Professor Llyleworth asks.

'A wooden statue of St Lawrence.'

We are sitting in a meeting room behind reception, in three comfortable chairs, in front of a screen that unfurls as soon as Diane touches the remote control.

'Can you tell me what the Thingvellir Scrolls are?' I ask.

Professor Llyleworth folds his hands. 'A copy of a biblical manuscript.'

'What makes it so exceptional?'

'That's what we are trying to establish.'

'How did it end up with Snorri on Iceland?'

'We don't know,' Diane replies.

'I find that difficult to believe.'

'We have some theories,' Professor Llyleworth admits.

'Let me hear them!'

'Let's start at the beginning.'

Always a good place to start.

Diane turns on the projector. A portrait appears on the screen in a cascade of light.

'Stuart Dunhill,' Diane says. 'A leading archaeologist in the 1970s.'

Professor Llyleworth takes over: 'In 1977, he found a hitherto undiscovered tomb in the cliffs behind the Amon-Ra temple near Luxor, the old Thebes, in Egypt. The entrance to the tomb had been walled up, camouflaged and hidden behind an altar.'

The portrait on the screen is replaced by an Egyptian mural, framed by hieroglyphics.

'This photograph was taken in the tomb that Stuart Dunhill found,' Diane says.

'The mural is dated to around 1015,' Professor Llyleworth explains.

'But the Egyptians no longer used hieroglyphs then,' I object. 'They wrote in Coptic or Arabic. Or Greek, for that matter.'

'Correct,' Professor Llyleworth says. 'But this was a sacred script, not meant for mortal eyes. A prayer to the gods. It is said that hieroglyphics are far more powerful in such instances.' I detect a smile. 'Which is why they used the old symbols.'

'The tomb,' Diane continues, showing a series of pictures from the burial chamber, 'is thousands of years old. It actually contains three chambers. An outer chamber which is purely a mask for an inner chamber. But, and this is the exciting bit, there was yet another tomb in the hidden inner chamber, which was even better camouflaged than the middle and outer chambers.'

'Who was buried there?'

'We don't know,' Professor Llyleworth replies. 'The hieroglyphs – and we're talking about texts that are thousands of years old – talk about the deceased as the Apostate, the Condemned and the Holy One.'

'It seems,' Diane adds, 'that the mummy was a person of royal descent who was condemned to death, but then later worshipped.' She clicks on to some photographs of various statues and reliefs. 'The most recent hieroglyphs are two and a half thousand years younger than the oldest ones.'

'What does it say there?'

Diane zooms in on the hieroglyphs. 'It took quite a long

time to interpret them. The problem is that they don't really make much sense.'

The professor says: 'The tomb was found by Stuart Dunhill in 1977, but as the mummy and any treasure that was there had been stolen by tomb raiders, the discovery didn't attract much attention internationally.'

'The tomb is some way up the cliffs by the Nile, to the north of the Valley of the Kings.' Diane clicks on to a picture that has been taken on the banks of the Nile. I see the barren cliffs rising up against the blue sky. A temple has been built up on a plateau. 'A thousand years ago, there was a side canal that ran from the Nile past the temple,' she explains.

'The strange thing is,' the professor says, 'that the hiero-glyphic messages say the temple and tomb were attacked a century after the birth of Christ, according to the Egyptian calendar used at the time. They were attacked – and now I quote from the inscriptions on the wall – by *the barbarians from the wild countries of the North.*'

'Does that make you think of anything?' Diane asks.

'The Vikings?'

'That was the conclusion that Stuart Dunhill also came to,' Professor Llyleworth confirms. 'Unfortunately, he not only suffered stiff opposition from his peers, he was ridi-culed. Discredited, with his reputation in tatters. The archaeological establishment managed to destroy him as a professional and as a human being.'

'Of course, we know that there is no proof that the Vikings went up the Nile,' Diane continues. 'Not even Snorri, who could be pretty creative when embellishing the sagas, so much as mentions any Viking expeditions to Egypt. One would think that an archaeologist who discov-ered such a tomb would be admired and respected. But for Dunhill, it was the beginning of the end. Instead of writing about the find and documenting the empirical basis of his theories in academic publications, he sold the story to the *National Geographic* magazine. He vigorously maintained that Norwegian Vikings had invaded Egypt.'

'Stuart did everything wrong,' Professor Llyleworth tells me. 'He thought he would be hailed as a modern Howard Carter, but he drew too many hasty conclusions, based on material that was speculative, to say the least. His colleagues who studied the hieroglyphics came to completely different conclusions. For example, they interpreted the *barbarians from the wild countries in the North* as being soldiers from the Byzantine Empire.'

'As a result of the fiasco, he increasingly sought solace in alcohol,' Diane says. 'And that was his downfall.'

'Is he dead?'

'That's a matter of opinion.'

'He drinks,' Professor Llyleworth says. 'He has lived and, to a limited extent, worked at the Schimmer Institute since 1979.'

'Paradoxically, there have been more and more indications in the past twenty-five years that corroborate Stuart's theory that the Vikings sailed up the Nile. It now seems entirely feasible. Your own discovery confirms the theory,' Diane adds, and clicks on to a photograph from Lyse Abbey.

The photographs give me goose bumps. I had no idea that there were representatives from the SIS among the researchers who took over from me at the tomb. But of course there were. The SIS is everywhere.

'Who is behind the death of Sira Magnus and the priest at Ringebu?' I ask.

'We don't know. But we have our suspicions,' Professor Llyleworth tells me.

'After the discovery of the tomb in 1977, there were so many rumours about what the inscriptions on the walls revealed,' Diane says. 'Lots of international collectors competed to get as much information as possible, such as precise transcriptions, or pictures, of the writing on the walls.'

'When she says competed, she means *bought*,' Professor Llyleworth elaborates. 'For vast sums of money.'

'One of the most dedicated collectors who surfaced around this time was a previously unknown sheikh. A mysterious multibillionaire. Sheikh Ibrahim al-Jamil ibn Zakiyy ibn Abdulaziz al Filastini. I don't know that anyone has ever met him. We don't even have a photograph of him. He has one of the world's largest collections of antique reliquaries. Lots of people believe that he has a complete version of *Codex Sinaiticus*, a handwritten copy of the Greek Bible, which is spread all over the world. There are three hundred and forty-seven books in the British Library, twelve books and fourteen fragments in St Catherine's Abbey, forty-three books in the Leipzig University Library and three books in the National Library of Russia in St Petersburg.'

'And possibly one complete and undamaged copy with Sheikh Ibrahim,' Professor Llyleworth adds.

'The sheikh has collectors, antiquarians, librarians and researchers working for him all over the world, to keep him informed of any developments in connection with Viking raids to Egypt,' Diane says. 'Why? We don't know. And is it Sheikh Ibrahim's men who are responsible for the deaths at Reykholt and Ringebu? We don't know that either.'

'But it's not unlikely,' Professor Llyleworth concludes. 'We suspect that the sheikh's organisation was responsible for two murders in the 1980s. That was how he secured an Alexandrian copy of *Codex Vaticanus* from the same period, which is reckoned to be one of the oldest existing Bible manuscripts.'

'Copy? I had no idea that there was a copy.'

'There are lots of things that we academics don't know.'

'But you know the theory of parallel universes?' Diane asks.

I look at her, wide eyed.

She laughs. 'There are also two worlds when it comes to historical artefacts. The one that we academics, scientists and researchers move in, and then another commercial world full of collectors, thieves, fences, middlemen and dealers. They will pay any price for the most valuable artefacts. Manuscripts. Paintings and works of art. First editions. Archaeological finds.'

'And the sheikh is one such man?'

'He is the worst.'

'He is a mysterious character who has a network of operators, agents and representatives,' Professor Llyleworth explains. 'He himself is a hermit, who has withdrawn to a palace somewhere in the desert, where he now cultivates his collections, his wealth and his faith.'

'But how did he know about Sira Magnus's manuscript? About my finds?'

'He knows *everything*,' Diane states.

'He has resources that could compete with the intelligence service,' Professor Llyleworth adds. 'And he has no scruples.'

'Why would he be so desperate to get hold of the Thingvellir Scrolls?'

'We haven't got far enough yet with the translation work,' Diane tells me. 'But we assume that the Thingvellir Scrolls include a Hebrew copy and a Coptic translation of a very old original Bible manuscript. Possibly even older than *Codex Vaticanus*, and definitely older that the Septuagint.'

'But what would the sheikh do with the text?'

'Maybe he just wants to *have* it,' Diane suggests.

'To own it,' Professor Llyleworth adds.

Their suggestions sound anything other than plausible.

'Maybe it contains new information, new knowledge,' Professor Llyleworth says.

'We really don't know, Bjorn,' Diane repeats. There was a time when I thought the fact that she couldn't pronounce my name was charming. *Bjorn* . . .

'So, what do we do now? Why did you ask me here?'

Diane and Professor Llyleworth look down.

'The SIS would like to employ you,' Diane says. 'We need you!' She meets my eyes. *We need you* . . .

At the time when the SIS found the Shrine of Sacred Secrets, I was the last person they needed. I was the Norwegian gatekeeper. A pale, cunning pain in the arse for the sophisticated Brits. They wanted the gold casket that contained a manuscript that was thousands of years old and I stood in their way. It wouldn't surprise me if my sheer obstinacy actually impressed them. If you are persistent enough, you find solutions that no one else would think of. I've made quite a name for myself in academic circles. At conferences and seminars, foreign academics nod at me in recognition when they meet me. Bjørn Beltø. The Norwegian archaeologist. The albino who forced the great Michael MacMullin to his knees. But that is a different story.

'We know you, *Bjorn*,' Diane says. 'You are persistent. Determined. Fearless. Irrepressible.'

And also – as she well knows – easily fooled, naive and trusting.

'Don't worry about the money,' Professor Llyleworth assures me. 'You will have an unlimited budget. We will just transfer what you need into your account. And you'll be paid a handsome fee.'

'I don't even know where to start.'

'Start with Stuart Dunhill,' Diane says. 'Go to the Schimmer Institute and talk to him. Then go on to Egypt. Go wherever you like.'

'But . . . what do you want me to do?'

'Find out what happened in Egypt,' Professor Llyleworth states.

'And find out before Sheikh Ibrahim does,' Diane adds.

The Fallen Star

1

S TUART DUNHILL has the wan complexion and watery, evasive eyes of a man who sleeps too much and stays indoors all day, drinking and waiting for dark.

He is sitting in a chair in the farthest corner of the Schimmer Institute library, as if he has found a point in the universe that is as far away from any tormentors or discomfort as possible. There is an unopened copy of *The Times* in his lap.

Once upon a time, he must have been an elegant and good-looking man. He has silver-grey hair that is combed back over his head. His features are distinguished and regular, giving him the look of a fallen aristocrat who has gambled away the family fortune and now lives on the charity of a tired drinking partner. He glances up at me. I recognise something about him, as if we once drank ourselves senseless together at a party, and were so drunk that we then immediately forgot about it.

I sit down in the empty chair beside him. I don't say a word. He is breathing heavily. My very presence makes him uncomfortable.

'I know who you are,' he says. His voice is slightly nasal.

I am too bewildered to answer.

'And I know why you've come.'

Without a word I give him my hand, which is only just paler than his. His handshake is surprisingly firm.

'Apologies that I am so inebriated. Bjørn Beltø.' He pronounces it almost perfectly. '*The* Bjørn Beltø. The archaeologist who found the Shrine of the Sacred Secrets.'

'The SIS found the casket. My job was to look after it.'

'And you certainly did that.'

'I was only doing my job.'

'And now, the Snorri Codex. The Thingvellir Scrolls. A burial chamber under Lyse Abbey. And would you care to chance it and come to the bar with me?'

'With pleasure.'

2

The Schimmer Institute nestles, as if deep in slumber, at the bottom of a valley in an unfriendly desert of stones, surrounded by fig and olive groves. The road from civilisation to the institute is an absolutely straight strip of asphalt that shimmers in the heat from horizon to horizon. The hillsides around the institute are covered with oleanders, boswellia bushes and sandalwood trees. Seven hundred years ago, monks built a monastery in this oasis of quiet. In the early 1970s, the sun-scorched stone building was extended with several thousand square metres of aluminium and reflective glass: libraries, archives, lecture halls and research labs. An accommodation wing. And now theologians and philosophers, linguists and palaeographers, ethnologists, historians and archaeologists all work together in this truly monstrous mixture of old and new. Each and every one a leading world expert in his or her own particular field. In its archives, the institute has parchment and papyrus manuscripts and documents that pre-date Christ. Some of the people restore these ancient texts, others translate. And yet others again interpret them.

Some just sit in the bar and drink.

'The thing that distinguishes an outstanding archaeologist from a mediocre one,' Stuart Dunhill says as he looks at me – distorted – through a glass of gin and tonic, 'is the ability to see logic where others only see chaos. A good archaeologist is a detective. He manages to get into the mind, the thought processes, of the people he is studying. We have to understand how the people we are trying to track thought. You have that ability.' He leans forward and lowers his voice. 'Why do you think the sheikh's men keep letting you get away? I'll tell you why. They know that there is a greater chance that *you* will find what they are after than that *they* will! You are an exceptional archaeologist. You've got balls. You are unique, Bjørn. You have focus, perseverance and talent. That's why you manage to solve everything you set out to do.'

'How do you know who they are?'

'That they work for the sheikh, you mean? That's obvious. He is the only person who is mad enough and rich enough to fund such an operation.'

3

When we meet again later that evening, Stuart Dunhill tells me about his childhood in the upper echelons of Windsor society. He shares with me his deep fascination for ancient history and how his search for information back to the time of Moses led him to the tomb at Luxor in 1977. He was crushed by his colleagues' volleys of laughter when he published his theories on the Viking raids in Egypt in the *National Geographic* magazine. 'But I only have myself to blame,' he says, by now well into his ninth or tenth gin and tonic.

'What happened?'

'I was stupid. I was so fired up by my discoveries that I wanted to share them with the world. Immediately. I thought I had no time to waste. I was young and didn't care that archaeology has its set methods and traditions. That is how it *must* be. I understand that now. I should have published my findings in recognised academic publications. I should have documented and reasoned and organised the material so that my colleagues could go over my theories with a fine-toothed comb. After all, I was launching a new theory. Vikings in Egypt . . . I had credible circumstantial evidence, but it required an open mind. In order to win the experts over to your side, you not only have to argue convincingly against the existing pool of knowledge, you also have to document the validity of the alternative hypothesis. Difficult, very difficult . . . To convince everyone across the field of your theory takes years. Even if you are right.'

'What did the experts say?'

'Well, when the laughter died down, they argued objectively and well against my theories. They said that my interpretation of the hieroglyphics was far too literal. They believed that *the wild countries in the North* were the Byzantine Empire, which was flourishing again and in constant conflict with Egypt. They maintained that the word *barbarian* meant non-Egyptian. They claimed that most Europeans were *pale and fair of skin* compared with the Egyptians, and that *shoulder-length hair and beards* were all the rage in the greater part of Europe. They even dismissed the descriptions and drawings of the Viking longships. Professors from Cairo to London documented how the Egyptians had obviously just drawn stylised ships inspired by the descriptions of Phoenician merchant and warships. They even managed to find alternative solutions to my most evident interpretations. No one believed my theories.'

'How did you end up here?'

'Initially I went on a bender, but luckily the SIS managed

to trace me and hung me out to dry. They finance my research . . .' He raises his glass of gin and tonic. '. . . here at the institute.'

'The SIS?' I exclaim. Neither Professor Llyleworth nor Diane told me that Stuart was on their payroll. That is so typical. They never tell you more than you strictly need to know.

'Do you know Diane?'

I say that I know Diane.

'Great girl. She's looked after me in the past few years.'

'I see . . .'

'You probably think I've just been lounging around drinking.'

'No, no.'

'Don't even try, I can see it in your face. I have in fact done some research. And a considerable share of what the SIS knows about these things, they got from me.'

'Such as?'

'I have traced known and forgotten documents and letters. I've been researching these things for thirty years.'

'These things?'

'We've known about the existence of the documents that are now called the Snorri Codex and the Thingvellir Scrolls for over ten years now. We just didn't know where they were. Not until your friend, Sira Magnus, came across the codex.'

'I thought that both the documents were unknown to historians.'

'Most historians, yes. We have been working quietly away. Archaeologists, historians, linguists and Egyptologists are involved in the project. We've studied the documents that the Vatican has released in recent decades, and we have access to texts in Egyptian museums and archives. We've also looked in the Old Norse archives in Iceland and Norway, but have never let on what we are looking for.'

'Can I see some of your findings?'

'Of course. Tomorrow. Because now, my dear Bjørn, I am pissed.'

The rune stick from Urnes is lying in a flute case in my room. The four hairs that I placed along the edge when I closed the case are still there. I will give the stick to the technical department tomorrow.

I sit in my room and watch TV, trying to repress the thought that they are no doubt here too. My pursuers. Hassan and his men. But they are invisible. They are watching me with a microscopic camera that I can't see. They will hear me breathing when I go to sleep.

4

The archives are in the cellar under the Schimmer Institute library. It is neither dark nor dusty down here. Quite the opposite, in fact, it is spotlessly clean and bright. The documents are stored in endless rows of cabinets that bring to mind the great ancient library in Alexandria.

The Schimmer Institute's archives include ancient clay tablets with cuneiform writing, papyrus scrolls, parchments and manuscripts written on yellowing handmade paper. There are fragments of original biblical texts, decrees signed by emperors such as Tiberius, Vespasian, Hadrian and Caesar. You can find papyrus texts that were possibly read by Cleopatra, military and political reports from the Roman province of Judaea regarding the beginnings of a Jewish revolt led by an agitator by the name of Jesus. There are manuscripts written by the Roman historian Flavius Josephus and the original manuscripts of Paul's first letters to the Corinthians.

All around me are researchers who look like adult versions of the people who always sat nearest the teacher in the classroom, and who lined the walls at school dances. Slight men with thinning hair and round glasses. Tall, thin women with ponytails, whose only focus is the most subtle reasoning of metaphysics. Over in the one of the corners, an old man sits asleep. He has probably spent his entire life documenting a forgotten Jewish sect with close ties to a group of Gnostics who everyone thought had been massacred a century earlier. Talented young women with hijabs and pencil cases and grants from their country's leading educational institutions search for the latest information on the persecution of Cathars. The place is full of Christian theologians, side by side with Orthodox Jews and Muslim scholars. And academics such as Stuart Dunhill and myself.

The alcoholic and the albino.

We sit at one of the reading desks by an aquarium full of colourful fish, which stare at us with half-open mouths. Which is precisely how I feel, sometimes.

Stuart Dunhill carries over a pile of shallow cardboard boxes and a scroll with a handle at both ends. He unrolls this across a long table.

'The Torah! The Jewish name for the Pentateuch. This copy is four hundred years old. Not that old, in other words. The texts were originally written on scrolls like this. They could be up to several metres long. It was only later that they discovered that books were easier to produce and read. The Old Testament was originally a collection of Hebrew religious and historical texts and laws that were collected into a canon about two and a half thousand years ago. The oldest preserved version of the Old Testament is called the Septuagint, which is a Greek-Alexandrian Bible translation that is over two thousand years old, and was put together by Jewish scholars who could speak Greek.'

'Does the original still exist?'

'The Septuagint itself is in the Vatican. But many of the

original texts of the Old Testament have been lost. And we have unfortunately lost all possibility of checking, verifying and disqualifying what is written in the originals that we do have. Or to date important biblical events.'

He opens a box and takes out a copy and a translation of a Coptic parchment.

'We came across this letter when we were given access to some dusty boxes from the Vatican. We were actually looking for a transcript of the Septuagint from Pope Innocent III's day that was supposed to exist. The Schimmer Institute had been asked to do this by the Pope's Cardinal Commission. But we found this letter instead. It was sent from Rouen in 1013 to the Fatimid Caliphate of Egypt. The Fatimids were a Muslim dynasty who governed North Africa from the tenth century until 1171. But the letter never reached its destination. The Pope's intelligence services snapped it up. Here,' he hands me a piece of paper from the box, 'this is an English translation.'

To His Highness, Caliph Al-Hakim bi-Amr Allah
Ruler of God's Command, Absolute Caliph of Egypt

It is with my humblest respect that I, High Priest Asim, great vizier of the Amon-Ra Cult, send these words as a prisoner in foreign lands. By my faith in Allah and loyalty to my life's mission, I am now with THE HOLY ONE, to protect Him and His treasures with whatever humble means I can. I know not where this journey will lead. I write these words from the scriptorium of a Duke Richard II in the town of Rouen, in the duchy of Normandy in France. We are resting here before continuing our journey to the barbarian lands beyond civilisation. I pray that my words will reach Your Highness, Ruler of God's Command, Absolute Caliph of Egypt, Caliph Al-Hakim bi-Amr

Allah, in order that someone can rescue THE HOLY ONE.

In respect,
Asim,
Great Vizier of the Amon-Ra cult

'Asim!' I exclaim – the name from the text I found in Garmo stave church.

'The recipient, Caliph Al-Hakim bi-Amr Allah, was ruler of Egypt at the time. Quite a character,' Stuart tells me. 'Asim refers only to Allah and does not mention the other gods he worships, out of pure fear. The caliph was, with reason, regarded as mad. During his reign, Egyptians were forbidden to eat grapes or play chess. He had determined to destroy as many churches in the world as possible, and it was Caliph Al-Hakim bi-Amr Allah, no less, who destroyed the Church of the Holy Sepulchre in Jerusalem. The year 1013 was a critical year for him. His country was invaded by the Vikings, and this insulting humiliation coincided with the culmination of his persecution of the Christians.'

'But what is this Asim person actually writing about in the letter?'

'Asim was captured by the Vikings. But of course I can't say that in any official capacity.'

He gives me the translation of another manuscript.

. . . farther on to the end of the world, to the frozen chill of the kingdom of death. We travelled from the kingdom of the sun and the fertile banks of the Nile to the barren stony coast of the land of snow. We left behind the beneficence of Amon-Ra, the warm breath of Osiris and submitted to the barbarians' gods. O Gods of my ancestors, give me strength! When I was a child and my nightmares showed me the gates to the kingdom of death – it was always a landscape such as this – cold, desolate and wild – that I thought I could see through the mists of death. We sailed for days . . .

'We assume this was copied from a manuscript fragment that was originally written by Asim. The copy was found with a bundle of letters and manuscripts left behind by the family of Christopher Columbus, of all people.' He opens his hands. 'And there is no point in even asking, because I have *absolutely* no idea.'

He puts some more parchments, copies and transcripts down on the table in front of me, including a transcript of Snorri's *Saga of the Holy Cross*. I read English translations of faded documents recounting the Vatican's hunt, along with the Knights Templar and the Hospitallers, for a holy relic. I read about papal expeditions to Norway in the twelfth and thirteenth centuries and am reminded of the words on the wall panel in Garmo stave church: *The Roman Pope's retainer, the knights of St John and Jerusalem's Knights Templar have gathered for battle. The sacred tomb is hidden as Asim instructed.*

'So what are we to conclude from all this?'

'Is that not obvious?'

'That the Vikings did go to Egypt?'

'More than that – that they got all the way to the Amon-Ra temple, where they raided a tomb and kidnapped a vizier. And then took their loot back to Norway.'

'Without anyone having heard so much as a word about it?'

'Throughout the course of history, many things have happened that we know nothing about.'

'A Viking raid down the Nile? That would have been mentioned in Snorri's sagas and the Egyptian annals at least.'

Stuart Dunhill shakes his head. 'Not necessarily. If King

Olav decided that the trip down the Nile should be kept secret, neither the skalds nor Snorri would have any sources. Remember, Snorri lived several hundred years after the events he wrote about. The Viking age was the age of skalds. Very little was written down. Snorri relied on oral traditions and written sources of varying reliability. And Snorri based both fact and fiction on these meagre foundations.'

'How could they keep something like that a secret? A fleet of Viking ships sailing down the Nile?'

'Vikings didn't leave behind much written heritage. They didn't write letters. Individuals may have told the tales of their adventures in inns and round the fire at sacrificial feasts, and a local skald may have composed an exciting poem about their feats. But that is very different from a history book. Remember, the Vikings had no relationship with Egypt. For them, Egypt was just another faraway exotic, hot country. Like the Holy Land and Byzantium. The Nile was a river just like any other river, be it the Seine or the Volga. The West only developed its fascination for Ancient Egypt in the nineteenth century. The Vikings didn't give a damn.'

'But they went to Egypt all the same?'

'Some Viking expeditions followed the trade routes east along the North African coast from Gibraltar to Alexandria in Egypt. Another important trade route went from Byzantium south to Jerusalem and then carried on southwest to Africa. Think of Harald Fair Hair's attacks on North Africa. Lots of Vikings went to Egypt, of course they did, but they were thought to be Byzantine soldiers or northern tradesmen. It is a well-known fact that the Vikings traded with the Arabs. Considerable numbers of Arabic coins have been found at known Norwegian trading centres and in Viking graves. And the white falcon that could be caught in Greenland was very popular with Arab sheikhs.'

'And what do the Egyptian sources say? Do they talk about a Viking raid on Luxor?'

'They never attacked Luxor. The Amon-Ra temple is to the north of Luxor, on the "dead" side of the Nile, and for the local people, the temple was shrouded in mystery and legends. A military attack on the temple would be of far less significance than if they had carried on sailing south to the Karnak temple or Hatshepsut's mortuary temple.'

'A defeat would have been humiliating for the army.'

'The humiliation was absolute. The Vikings faced greatest resistance in the north, from the twin garrison towns of Fustat and al-Qahira, today's Cairo, in other words. The mad Caliph Al-Hakim bi-Amr Allah must have felt so disgraced by his failure with regard to the enemy that he forbade anyone ever to talk about the defeat. The Egyptians have always omitted unfavourable events and unpopular rulers from their history. Those in power have from time immemorial manipulated the pages of history. Even the names of the most revered kings were dismissed if they fell into disgrace. Powerful men vanished from the national memory and history. Their names were erased. Memorials crushed. Temples and statues were destroyed or dedicated to a new ruler. The best example of this is the great prophet from the Bible.'

'You mean Moses?'

'If the depiction of Moses in the Bible is correct, he must have had enormous influence in society. The Egyptians could hardly have remained indifferent to Moses, whether they regarded him as prophet, sorcerer, freedom fighter, agitator or traitor. But what was said in Egypt about Moses when he was alive and after?'

'Not a great deal.'

'Exactly. Moses has been more or less erased from history.'

'And what is your conclusion?'

'Either he didn't exist, or he fell out of grace with his peers.'

'And where do all these premises and hypotheses lead?'

'What could have been so important that the high priest, Asim, who had dedicated his life to protecting this holy relic, would write a letter to the caliph of his country?'

'A splinter from the holy cross?' I joke.

'Or something even more sacred?'

'More sacred?' Then I twig. 'Please, Stuart, spare me yet another Holy Grail myth!'

To my surprise, he bursts out laughing. 'The Holy Grail? Bjørn, Bjørn, Bjørn . . . The Holy Grail is a medieval myth. No, think about it. Asim's sect had a sacred task: to protect the tomb and its contents. The treasure. The mummy. The scriptures. Everything that was in the tomb. According to Egyptian sources, Asim was the high priest from 999 until he disappeared from history, fourteen years later. He was a respected and learned high priest who had mastered many languages and sciences. He was an astrologer and sooth-sayer, a magician and interpreter of dreams. At the time, the Amon-Ra cult was already over two thousand years old; it later combined the Egyptian gods with Judaism, Christianity and Islam. They had many gods, but even in the first century the sect saw the old Egyptian gods as being the most important. Jahweh was one of many. The priests lived in the temple and the entrance to the tomb was concealed. At the time, Al-Hakim bi-Amr Allah was the caliph of Egypt. He disappeared mysteriously in 1021, but half the Druze sect still worships Al-Hakim bi-Amr Allah as their Mahdi, who will return again to redeem the world and Islam.' Dunhill pauses for a moment, before continuing: 'What does all this tell you?'

'Not a lot.'

'I'll let you in on a secret. Do you know what I was looking for when I found the tomb in 1977?'

I shake my head.

'I was looking for something of enormous religious value. Something that was hidden with a mummy and the most valuable treasures.' He closed his eyes. 'Something that the Vikings stole by accident, because it was together with all the gold and precious stones.'

'What was that?'

'Something that could possibly throw new light on the history of the Bible. If we are to believe the Jewish scriptures, such as the Mishnah, a holy relic was hidden in a tomb in *a desolate valley under the prow of a hill*, such as the Valley of the Kings . . .'

'You can't say what you were looking for?'

'Bjørn, don't you laugh at me too.'

'I'm not laughing.'

'I have often played with the thought that the Vikings stole the Ark of the Covenant!'

His eyes become glazed.

Well, well, that's all we needed. The Ark of the Covenant. Anyone who has ever dreamt of finding the Ark of the Covenant has long since drunk themselves to death or madness.

The Ark of the Covenant was a portable reliquary. The Bible describes it as being a casket two and a half metres long, which is covered in gold both inside and out, and decorated with two cherubs. Temple servants carried it with great solemnity with the help of two wooden poles that were fed through two gold rings on either side. The Ark contained, among other things, the stone tablets on which the Ten Commandments were written and accompanied the Tabernacle during the Exodus and was later moved to Solomon's Temple in Jerusalem, but then vanished from history when the temple was destroyed 586 years before the birth of Christ. Some people believe that Nebuchadnezzar II stole the Ark. Others believe that it was hidden under Solomon's Temple and that it was the Ark of the Covenant, and not the Holy Grail, which the Knights Templar dedicated their lives to protecting. Some are convinced that the Ark of the Covenant was taken to Ethiopia, where it remains to this day.

And some, like Stuart, believe that the Ark was hidden in or somewhere near the Valley of the Kings.

And some of the most contrary among us believe that it didn't exist at all.

5

The bar looks like something the Schimmer Institute might have stolen from the Waldorf Astoria. The pianist is playing a potpourri of Elton John hits. Stuart Dunhill has snapped his fingers for a waiter, who comes over with two ice-cold gin and tonics. We raise our glasses. We sit there for a couple of hours discussing stories about Ancient Egyptian gods and pre-Christian mythology. By then we are both tipsy and in need of some fresh air.

In the silence of the desert, the pianist's notes play in my head like a musical echo. *Goodbye Yellow Brick Road* . . . It is chilly and dark. We amble over the asphalt car park and up into a grove of fig and olive trees. I think about the last time I was here. The moon shone through the trees, as though from a Japanese paper lantern. Tonight the heavens and stars are hidden behind a layer of thin clouds. Between the trees that have been scored by centuries of animal claws, Stuart's voice sounds insignificant.

'What we can see is the faint outline of a historical riddle. Many people have, separately, managed to uncover a tiny sliver of the mystery. The Knights Templar, the Hospitallers. The Crusaders. The Vatican. All those mysterious orders and fraternities and societies that we love to hear about. What was it that they knew? What were they hiding? What were they trying to find? They probably all had their own little slice of the truth. And that was enough for them.'

'Did they ever find what they were looking for?'

Stuart Dunhill closes his eyes and then answers. 'I doubt that they had any idea of what they were looking for. They each were guardians of a small portion of the truth. Only when all these fragments can be put together will we be able to understand the whole truth. And that is the problem. Everyone has fiercely guarded their little slice. No one has shared the knowledge.'

We stare out into the darkness in silence, thinking the same thought.

'But enough about me,' Stuart exclaims. 'What about you? Tell me about what you have found in Norway.'

I tell him the whole story. I start with the murder of Sira Magnus and the stolen Snorri Codex. I tell him about the Thingvellir Scrolls that we found in the cave in Iceland. About Hassan and the men who are pursuing me, and who probably work for Sheikh Ibrahim. About Sira Magnus's rune code that led me to an email address and a copy of the stolen document. I tell him about the hidden codes in Snorri's text and how I managed to crack them, with the help of my imagination and good friends. How Øyvind and I managed to find the tomb under Lyse Abbey. About the rune stone that I have in my possession. About my hiding place, and the code on the rune stone that led me to Urnes and then on to Flesberg, Lom, Garmo and Ringebu. I have copies of the texts that I have managed to decipher so far in my pocket. I show them to him. He reads them in the dim light from the institute and I can hear from his breathing how excited he is. I tell him about the murder of the priest at Ringebu stave church and the wooden statue that they stole and my journeys to the SIS and the Schimmer Institute.

'That's quite a story,' he says. 'The manuscripts that you found on Iceland, the Thingvellir Scrolls, I hope they're in a safe place.'

'Of course.'

'In Norway? Or in Iceland?'

'We're trying to get them translated.'

'You've got good people helping you?'

'The best.'

'Strictly speaking, the best people are here at the Schimmer Institute.'

'OK. The next best.'

'You should really get the parchments sent here, for the best conservation, treatment and translation.'

'They're in good hands. And for the moment, I don't know that it would be safe to bring them here. It wouldn't surprise me if the sheikh actually *owns* the Schimmer Institute. Sira Magnus phoned here when he found the codex.'

Stuart is quiet for a moment before picking up the thread. 'You and your friends have come farther than anyone else. You have discovered codes where others have only seen text. And not only that, you've also managed to crack the codes!'

'But we still haven't found the most important tomb. And we've lost the last clue. It was in the statue of St Lawrence.'

Despite the dark, I catch Stuart Dunhill's vague smile. 'You are competing with the world's leading academics and a mysterious billionaire. But you've got flair and intuition and a stubborn streak that not many have. I admire you, Bjørn. Really. I admire you.'

My cheeks feel warm.

Stuart continues: 'If the tomb is ever found, and the riddle is solved, it will be you who does it. And I'm not the only one who thinks that.'

6

I spend the whole of the next day in the Schimmer Institute archives, where I borrow shallow cardboard boxes full of documents, parchments, scrolls and fragments of papyrus. The archivist conscientiously registers everything that I carry over to my reading desk.

With the care and precision of a neurosurgeon, I study the texts and search back in history. I find a clever thesis from the nineteenth century that draws parallels between the mysterious sixteenth-century Voynich Manuscript (a 272-page document written in unknown script in an incomprehensible language) and an equally cryptic manuscript written by Leonardo da Vinci in the Biblioteca Ambrosiana in Milan. I find letters, accounts and letters of credit, testimonials and appendices, instructions, charters and notes, deeds of conveyance and circulars. An English translation is attached to most of the documents. I have silk gloves on, and at regular intervals a curator comes over to my desk to check that I'm not making papier-mâché of these irreplaceable treasures.

And yet I discover absolutely nothing that indicates that anyone – with the exception of the high priest Asim – has written anything that might confirm that the Vikings raided Egypt in 1013. And if such a document had existed, Stuart would no doubt have discovered it years ago.

7

Stuart Dunhill and I have agreed to eat dinner at six o'clock. So while I wait, I wander over to the technical department to see if they have discovered anything new about the rune stick. For example, how old it is, or what sort of wood it is. If there is anything inside it.

The technical department was built in 1985 as a separate

wing of the Schimmer Institute and has all kinds of workshops and special equipment. They can do everything here, from Carbon 14 dating to restoring artefacts and putting together documents that arrive at the laboratories in a thousand small pieces. Specialists in white coats and overalls, some with surgical masks and protective glasses, sit bent over their workbenches and machines.

A female lab technician in green plastic overalls shows me to the Technical-Historical Department for Wooden, Paper and Papyrus Artefacts. I pop my head into a workshop where two Jews with kippas are working on a Torah that has been rolled out on an aluminium table that is several metres long. In the next workshop, there is a group of experts restoring an intricately made coffin. Then I open the door to a cleaners' cupboard, followed by an office where an indignant woman behind a desk full of files and forms asks whether I am in the habit of not knocking.

The third workshop is empty.

Except for Lars.

St Lawrence.

The wooden statue that was stolen from Ringebu stave church.

St Lawrence is secured to a workbench with straps and clamps, as though they want to prevent him from getting to his feet and running off into the desert.

It is not the air conditioning which chills me to the bone. I can't understand what the statue is doing here – at the Schimmer Institute. Sheikh Ibrahim must have the institute eating out of his hand. Which means that I am, at the very least, being watched and, at worst, am in danger.

I stand in the doorway for a few seconds, staring at St Lawrence. Then, in a moment of madness, I step into the workshop. The statue looks remarkably unfamiliar, lying there on the workbench, surrounded by electric keyhole saws and drills. Despite the arsenal of alarming instruments, they have obviously treated it with great care. There are pieces of protective felt under the straps and clamps and the blades and drill pieces are of the finest, thinnest type. There is an X-ray hanging on a light box on the wall. Surprised, I stand in front of it and study the image. The X-ray of St Lawrence shows that there are no cavities or hollows where a message could be hidden. It is obvious that the technicians have stopped halfway through the work, abandoning their tools when they saw the X-ray.

St Lawrence is solid wood.

There is nothing inside.

I look from the X-ray to the statue and back, perplexed. The text in the Bible was absolutely clear. *Just as the Virgin Mary held Jesus in her lap, the belly holds the casket. Praise be to Thomas!*

So why was there nothing in the statue?

I notice a surveillance camera on the ceiling. I wonder whether anyone is watching Bjørn the Albino standing there with his mouth hanging open.

I leave the workshop, closing the door behind me, and take a few moments to compose myself. Just then, two technicians, a man and a woman, come round the corner.

They both stop.

'Hello,' says the woman.

'Can we help you?' says the man.

Technicians prefer it when we academics stay in the library.

With a dry mouth, I explain that I am looking for the workshop where they are examining a rune stick from Norway.

'Rune stick? Workshop Fourteen.'

I thank them and carry on down the corridor.

The rune stick is lying in a transparent plastic bag in a locked glass case in an empty workshop, which is called Woodwork

Laboratory XIV. I break the glass with my elbow and put the rune stick in my pocket.

The red light on the surveillance camera blinks at me from the ceiling.

Breathless, I hurry back the way I came. The alarm will go off at any moment. A siren will start to wail and a voice will boom over the loudspeakers: 'Stop! Thief!'

But nothing happens.

Whenever I meet someone, I slow down. I look back through the double swing-doors as I burst out of the technical department. I run through the conference suite and into the large, open reception area.

I can just imagine Hassan standing there, with a platoon kneeling beside him, rifles aimed straight at my heart.

But no one pays any attention to me. The receptionist carries on as normal. Some people are watching TV, others are chatting. Someone is on the phone. There are people reading newspapers.

No one looks up.

No one shouts: 'That's him!'

8

Stuart Dunhill lives in a suite in the accommodation block. I rap on his door. When he opens it, he raises an eyebrow in surprise: 'What? Already?' He is just getting ready for dinner. His face is covered in shaving cream and his white shirt is open.

I force my way past him and shut the door. 'They're here.'

'Who is here?'

'The sheikh. Hassan. I don't know. I just saw St Lawrence – in one of the workshops.'

'Saint who?'

'St Lawrence! The wooden statue!'

'Here?'

'I've come straight from the workshop. I was looking for the rune stick.'

'Have you asked anyone about . . .?'

'Are you crazy? The Schimmer Institute is obviously involved.'

'The institute? That's going a bit too far. This is a respectable, professional institute. They would never steal historical artefacts, let alone kill anyone.'

'So what is St Lawrence doing here?'

'I'm sure there is a perfectly good explanation. Let's go and tell the management about it. Straight away.'

'No!'

'Consider it. Maybe one of their employees is dishonest. Maybe they've been tricked. Maybe someone has brought the statue here without telling the institute where it's from and how they got it.'

'I don't dare trust them.'

'Hundreds of academics and researchers work here. The institute is not in league with a bunch of bandits. You took the rune stick with you yourself. The institute can't be held responsible if you have stolen it from a museum.'

'I have to leave.'

'Bjørn, you are in the middle of the desert!'

'I can't stay. Sorry!'

'Bjørn!'

Just then the phone rings. Stuart answers. Listens. Then puts the phone down. The receiver is covered in shaving foam.

'I'm coming with you!'

'With me?'

He swiftly takes out a pile of underwear, socks and shirts from the chest of drawers and puts them in a suitcase.

'Who was that who called? What did they say?'

Stuart stops. 'It was the SIS.'

'Professor Llyleworth?'

'They asked me to look after you.'

'Look after me?'

'And I will do my best.'

'Has something happened? Does the SIS know that I found the statue?'

'I doubt it. But Sheikh Ibrahim knows that you are here. The SIS just found out that the sheikh's men are on their way. To the institute. And they are not corrupt academics.' Stuart looks at me. 'He's sent Hassan.'

Before we leave, I put my mobile in a padded envelope and send it to my office at the university. I don't know whether it is my GSM card or an untrustworthy employee at the institute who lets them know where I am all the time.

But Hassan is not that easily fooled. He won't follow the post van. All I can do to get a bit of a head start is to create a bit of confusion in the sheikh's high-tech spying ranks.

9

We drive through the desert in a Mitsubishi Outlander; I don't know whether it belongs to Stuart or whether he has stolen it.

The sky is dark, clear and full of stars. The desert is interminable. The front lights illuminate two deep grooves which could, with a bit of goodwill, be called a track. The female voice on the satnav that is sitting on the dashboard tells us to turn right after three hundred yards. She seems to think that we are on a motorway.

'Where should I go?' I ask.

'Away!'

'Where away?'

'As this is how things have turned out, I'd like to show you something.'

'Which means?'

'That we should go to the only place where we have something to do.'

'Which is?'

'Good God! For someone so intelligent, you really are a bit slow!'

'Where?'

'Egypt!'

10

For hours and hours we drive through the dense darkness of the desert until the night dissolves on the horizon.

As he drives, Stuart lectures me with the enthusiasm of a teacher who has finally found a student who has no way of escaping. Or perhaps that is just his way of staying awake. With one hand on the wheel and the other gesticulating wildly in the air between us, he tells me about the patriarchs of the Old Testament and how the development of the Egyptian state influenced their tribal culture.

'The Patriarchs were a nomadic people, goatherds,' he says as he keeps his eyes on the dawning day. 'Jews, Christians and Muslims all worship the same Patriarch: Abraham. He had one son, Ishmael, one of the great Muslim prophets, with a servant girl, Hagar. With his wife, Sara, he had another, Isaac, one of the forefathers of Moses and the Jews. When Abraham died, Sara banished her stepson, Ishmael, thus splitting the Semite race into Arabs and Jews. And they have argued ever since.'

As the sun rises and the sharp light floods the desert landscape, Stuart tells me how the tribal cultures fused and different civilisations emerged. The car tyres smack on the uneven ground.

'The Old Testament stems from a time when the ancient tribes formed organised national cultures. The authors of the Old Testament took their material from the cultures in the region that functioned well, such as the Babylonians and the Egyptians. Learned Egyptian texts were copied straight into the language of Solomon. Just look at King David's administration, with all its ministers and fancy titles. Nothing more than a copy of the Egyptian state hierarchy.'

I turn on the air conditioning. The heat is starting to beat down on the car roof. There is a warm cool bag on the back seat, with bottles of water in it. I take out two bottles and hand one to Stuart. The water is lukewarm, but I still drink the whole bottle in one go.

Stuart struggles to unscrew the top. 'Storytelling was central to the Patriarchs' tribal cultural tradition, a kind of oral history. In Egypt, on the other hand, it became more usual to write down the best stories.' He puts the bottle to his mouth and drinks greedily. Then he burps and mumbles: 'Excuse me.'

Outside the car, all I can see is endless desert.

'Are you tired?' I ask.

But he is not.

'When the British archaeologist Layard found the ruins of the Assyrian king Ashurnasirpal II's palace in Iraq, they also discovered cuneiform tablets from the Assyrian occupation of Babylon. In their story of the Creation – a forerunner of what we know from the Bible – the first person, a man, was created in a garden of paradise. A woman was made from his rib.' Stuart coughs and drinks some more water. 'The man and woman were later expelled from Paradise. They were disobedient to their god.' He drinks the rest of the water. 'Even Noah's flood stems from Babylonian mythology. The three-thousand-six-hundred-year-old epic poem about Gilgamesh tells of a god who instructs a man to prepare for a flood. The man saves himself, his family and many species of animal on board an ark, which then runs aground on a high mountain.'

I turn the air conditioning on full.

'The Tower of Babel,' Stuart continues. 'The Assyrian king Esarhaddron built a tower in Babylon, dedicated to the god Marduk, that was to reach to the heavens. What do you think happened? Gravity won. The tower collapsed.'

'But Stuart, doesn't all this just confirm the stories of the Bible?'

'You could interpret it like that. Or you could be difficult and say that the creators of the Old Testament didn't even have the imagination to make up their own stories.'

'The Tanakh consists of more than these examples.'

My arguments just provoke him. 'Substantial, key parts of the Holy Scriptures have been stitched together from the myths and stories of even older cultures . . .'

'All right.'

'. . . cleverly interwoven with the creation of a new religion that focuses on a new and absolute god.'

Neither of us says anything for a while.

'Even the life of Moses has a precursor. In Babylonian mythology, King Sargon of Akkad's mother sent him down a river in a reed basket when she was trying to hide him. Luckily he was found, and adopted.' Stuart drums the steering wheel with his fingers. 'That's how original the most important story in the Old Testament is.'

There are forms of life that thrive even in the hellish heat of the desert. Hairy, colourful caterpillars. Donkeys. And the Rose of Jericho; in wet weather it is flat and green, but as soon as the ground dries up again, it rolls into a ball in defiance of the elements. I can relate to the plant. If the drought lasts, it pulls up its roots and rolls through the desert. It is blown on the wind until it finds another wet place to settle.

Very few people think that it is an attractive plant, but most people find it amusing.

A bit like me.

11

We eventually come to a town on the border where we buy a visa for Egypt. Then we cross the border and drive south down the Sinai Peninsula, along the Akaba Bay to Sharm el Sheikh. From here, we take a ferry over the Red Sea to Hurghada and then head south again to Port Safaga, where we join an escorted convoy of tourists west through the desert to Luxor.

Stuart confides in me that he hopes that our research will lead to a breakthrough in his own research.

'Vindication! Call it what you like! Revenge! Professional credibility! You have no idea how much that would mean to me, to be able to show, with your help, that my theories are right. That the Vikings *have* been in Egypt.'

To my horror, a tear rolls down his cheek. Embarrassed, I sit and stare out of the window.

'I think,' Stuart says, 'that the Thingvellir Scrolls will have something in them that will show that I am right. That I've been right for all these years.'

In ancient Thebes, the Karnak Temple and the Luxor Temple were connected by a paved avenue, where the pharaohs walked around in dusty sandals, hatching military strategies before going home to the palace to eat dates and sully their sisters.

And to this day, the two temples, with their sanctuaries and obelisks and sphinxes and gigantic statues, still cast long shadows on the ground above the river.

When we book into the Winter Palace on the main street, Corniche el Nile, the sun is setting in the west on the other side of the Nile. The cliffs glow in the red light of dusk, making the temples and tombs worthy of dead pharaohs, queens and princes.

Slightly more exotic than arriving at Brandbu on a grey, wet day!

The Forgotten Town

EGYPT

1

T HE VALLEY of the Kings lies in an eternal slumber between the cliffs on the west bank of the Nile, the Theban Necropolis.

The eternal genius loci (or spirit of the place) that pervades the barren valley is the same feeling of imperishability invoked by the Forum Romanum in Rome and the Acropolis in Athens – a sense of the passing of time and the slow waves of history. Great kings lie in their hidden tombs in the cliffs. Ramses. Seti. Thutmose. Amenhotep. Tutankhamen. More than sixty burial chambers were carved into the rock over the course of five hundred years.

The wind whistles down the valley.

Along with hundreds of other tourists, Stuart and I enter the valley on a mini-train that is pulled by a snorting tractor. The dust sticks to my skin. The cliffs tower up into the sky.

The tomb that Stuart wants to show me is high up in a narrow cleft. The entrance is to the north and the inner chamber faces east, in a pattern that symbolises the underworld.

We breathe heavily as we climb the long, steep steps that lead up to the modest and once well-hidden entrance. An attendant takes our tickets and lets us into the tunnel. The air is so humid and warm that I start to tug at the neck of my T-shirt.

'One of the first things a king did was to start working on his tomb,' Stuart says. 'It took hundreds of labourers decades to make these tombs. First came the stone cutters, who did the hard work. Then came the decorators with their brushes and the priests with their blessings.'

On the way down the narrow steps we have to squeeze sideways past tourists who are on their way up. I try to repress any feelings of claustrophobia. The air is terribly heavy. In fact, when tomb raiders and archaeologists opened up the tombs, the air that had been closed in for centuries could be dangerous. The author of Sherlock Holmes, Arthur Conan Doyle, even suggested that spores of deadly mould were left in the chambers to punish any intruders.

I don't know whether it is conscious or not, but I breathe only through my nose.

With every step we go back hundreds – no, thousands – of years. In order to prevent any wear from the millions of tourists' shoes, the authorities have installed wooden walkways. The long queue goes steadily deeper into the mountain. I am finding it hard to breathe. The air doesn't seem to reach my lungs. But I don't say anything to Stuart – nobody wants to be a wimp.

The ceiling is blue and full of yellow painted stars. The vestibule is dominated by two massive pillars and is decorated with images of 741 deities. A staircase takes you several storeys farther down to the oval burial chamber with two pillars and four side rooms.

I hear the enthusiastic murmurings of the tourists. If there are so many of us down here, surely we will use up all the oxygen? Someone bumps into me. I stumble into the view of a tourist taking a photograph of the mural. I smile apologetically and pull at the tight neckline of my T-shirt.

'Is anything wrong, Bjørn?' Stuart asks.

'No,' I gasp.

The walls of the burial chamber are decorated like a huge papyrus scroll which contains the entire text of the Book of Amduat, or the afterlife. There are passages from the Litanies of Re and a motif that shows the deceased in the company of a goddess. The mummy of Pharaoh Thutmose III was laid to rest here nearly 3,500 years ago. He was the seventh pharaoh in Egypt's eighteenth dynasty and is recognised as one of Egypt's greatest kings. He ruled for half a century, until his death around 1425 BC. The tomb was discovered by the French Egyptologist Victor Loret, in 1898. The mummy of Thutmose III was found seventeen years earlier, stored with fifty other mummies, in the Deir el-Bahri Cave in the cliffs by the Temple of Hatshepsut.

I prod Stuart's arm. 'The air in here is not very good,' I say. 'Have we seen enough?'

2

We leave the Valley of the Kings and follow the cliffs north along the Nile. I roll down the window and fill my lungs with greedy gulps of air. Stuart asks whether I'm trying to catch flies. I remind him that I am a vegetarian.

Soon he stops by a wall with barbed wire on top, behind which is an impressive building complex in the cliff face.

'This is the temple of the Amon-Ra cult,' Stuart says. 'This is where the Vikings came.'

He opens an unlocked gate and parks in the shade of a tree.

'There was once a canal down there,' he points to a plain that lies between the cliffs and the Nile, 'which has been filled in by the farmers.' He turns to face the temple again. 'And this is where the high priest Asim presided.'

Two gigantic statues of the gods Amon-Ra and Osiris guard the broad steps up to a square in front of the temple. We walk along the sandy path that leads up to it.

'The sect called themselves the Humble Servants of His Holiness, the Sun-God Amon-Ra, and the Guardians of the Holy Covenant, but we know it as the Amon-Ra cult. The cult existed up until the 1200s. By then, the reliquary that the sect was supposed to be guarding – and which the Vikings stole – had been gone for two hundred years. Even the most dedicated high priests must have felt that it was a waste of time to look after something that had been lost a long time ago.'

'The Ark of the Covenant?'

'That would certainly be something,' he says in a surprisingly weak voice. 'But maybe it was something else altogether.'

We look at the stone statues and the temple. I try to imagine what life would have been like here, a thousand or two thousand years ago. Or even three thousand years ago.

Then I turn to face the Nile and try to imagine the fleet of Viking ships.

'Exactly,' Stuart the mind-reader says.

Neither the temple nor the tomb is open to the public, but Stuart has a permit from the Egyptian authorities and the attendant who is sitting dozing at the gate is appeased by an Egyptian fifty-pound note. We enter the temple. Stuart leads the way to the main hall. Behind what was once the altar, I see the broken entrance to the burial chambers.

I take a deep breath before we go in.

It is dark, and Stuart and I turn on our torches. We have to go down a lot of steps and then along a tunnel before we come to the first chamber. Our torch beams sweep over the murals and inscriptions.

'This was where I found the most recent paintings and hieroglyphics – the ones that depicted the attack a thousand years ago,' Stuart says.

He shows me the paintings.

Longships.

Long-haired, bearded barbarians with blue eyes.

Swords, axes and shields.

Dragonheads.

'Vikings . . .' I murmur.

'I thought the same. Vikings! Not soldiers and ships from bloody Byzantium! Vikings! And the bastards all laughed at me.'

We go down some more stairs into the second burial chamber. As we are the only ones in the tunnel, I know that I can run up and get some fresh air, which makes it easier to keep my claustrophobia in check. Just.

At the back of the second chamber we see the remains of what would once have been the end wall. We step through the hole in the wall and go down the narrow, steep steps and then carry on along the tunnel.

At the end, we come to the final burial chamber.

The holiest of the holy.

Empty chambers, empty coffers.

An empty sarcophagus . . .

Here, in the innermost chamber, a disgraced dignitary had been laid to rest, someone who was later referred to as THE HOLY ONE.

Who was he? Why did they take such care to hide him?

What treasures did they leave with him in the burial chamber?

What inscriptions?

What reliquaries?

And why did they guard him for two and a half thousand years?

'We think,' Stuart interrupts my thoughts, 'that the scrolls that you found in the cave at Thingvellir were a copy and translation of an original manuscript that was kept here.'

Stuart shows me murals, inscriptions and cartouches in the empty tomb which only really make sense once he has patiently explained them to me. Our torches eventually start to flicker, so we make our way back to the entrance.

The fresh air feels like a caress on my cheeks.

We pass the attendant, who has now fallen asleep, and walk back to the car in silence, each deep in his own thoughts.

Before starting the engine, Stuart says that he wants to take me to a town that does not exist, to talk to a man who does not exist.

3

The Coptic monastery of St Mark is built of sandstone around a lush garden with running water and happy plants. It still looks exactly as it must have done around nineteen hundred years ago when the monks put down the final stone and brushed the sand from their hands.

A gilded ankh dominates the roof.

Stuart comes to a halt in a cloud of dust, which then skitters across the parking place like an irascible and rebellious miniature desert storm.

The monastery is in the Forgotten Town, which lies in a valley in the desert some way out of Luxor. You won't find the Forgotten Town on any map, and on the rare occasion that it is mentioned in tourist brochures, it is often in quaint phrases such as 'the ruins of a desert town that refuses to die'. Officially, the town does not exist. The Egyptian authorities have refused to acknowledge its existence since the fifteenth century, as a result of a dispute between the monks, a Bedouin tribe and the central authorities about the ownership of a spring, which was essential to the town's survival. When the authorities gave up their fight with the stubborn desert dwellers in 1481 – after all, the blasted desert town and monastery lay far away in a windswept hole of heat and sand and farting camels – they removed the town from all official papers and registers. And to this day, no one has thought of bringing the town back into the real world. The authorities in Egypt can bear grudges for a long time. The town, which was originally called something that has long since been forgotten, has no schools, no town hall, no police, no health service. Children who grow up here are bussed into Qena, where the school registers them as homeless. The best description of the local doctor would be medicine man. On the rare occasion that he is in doubt, he drives his patients to hospital on the back of the town's lorry, as school doctors, as he so scornfully calls them over his hookah in the café, have better equipment than he for carrying out brain surgery and cornea transplants. And also, because his hands have an unfortunate tendency to shake a lot.

St Mark lies on the outskirts of this oasis, this non-existent collection of stone and clay houses, forgotten and ignored by the local and central authorities and the rest of the world.

4

The monastery gate opens.

Out comes a man who looks as though he has lived and worked at St Mark from around the time the monastery was built. His face reminds me of a sun-dried, wrinkled raisin. And he has a turban, no less, wrapped round his head. He shuffles towards us in his raffia sandals with a toothless grin and shakes our hands. He has a small cross tattooed on the inside of his forearm. He says his name in Arabic, which sounds like a landslide of arbitrary consonants, and even though Stuart has repeatedly told me his name in the car, I can't get it to stick in my mind. So I just call him the monk.

He invites us into the desert monastery and shows us around the dormitories, the refectories, the study, the church and the monastery's well-kept garden. To my surprise, he speaks perfect English. He studied at Cambridge, where he later lectured for years.

'Even though we are very different,' the monk says with a hint of affection in his voice, 'Stuart and I have a shared history. I was his supervisor in Egyptology at the University of Cambridge.'

I look at his sunburnt, sandblasted face in astonishment, and find it hard to imagine the monk as a professor at Cambridge. But then again, there are plenty of people who find it hard to imagine that I am an associate professor at the University of Oslo.

He tells me that the Coptic Orthodox Church was established in Egypt by Mark the Evangelist, some years after Christ had been crucified. The Coptic Christians were the first organised believers. The monks at St Mark's Rest were adamant that Mark himself had helped to build the monastery. The head of the Coptic Church is still called the Pope of Alexandria and Patriarch of all Africa on the See of St Mark, and the early Coptic Church used the ankh symbol, the *ansate*, as its cross.

When the Egyptian Christians were driven from the towns in the third century, they fled out into the desert. Here they built their monasteries. Several hundred monasteries were established in the mountainous desert of Egypt, in fragile buildings and sheltered caves. From here, the monastic movement spread to the rest of the Christian world.

The monk tells me that the church's holiest relic is a thorn from the crown of Christ, which rests on a red silk cloth in a gold casket. And in a chased silver casket, they have eight pages of what is supposedly part of the original text of the Gospel of Mark and a Coptic fragment of the Gospel of John.

5

'God is dead.'

We are sitting on a wooden bench in the shade of the arcade that runs around the garden, drinking cold water from plastic bottles.

The monk kicks the ground with his sandal. An expression of pain passes over his face.

'Dead?' I ask.

'Osiris,' he says, and puts one finger in the air. 'Odin.' Another finger in the air. 'Zeus. Ptah. Bacchus. Thor. Pan. Poseidon. Cupid. Ashtoreth.' He has run out of fingers now, but continues all the same. 'Bellona. Isis. Jupiter. Anubis. Balder. Nebo. Loki. Amon-Ra. Aphrodite. Baal. Ahijah. Freya. Hades. Mulu-hursang. Njord. Llaw Gyffes. Mu-ul-lil. Frigg. Venus. Set, the greatest ruler of the Nile Valley. I could carry on for ten minutes or more. What do all these gods have in common? They have ruled the lives of millions of God-fearing believers. Their names have caused men to tremble with fear and women to lower their heads in prayer. The masses have worshipped them. We have built temples in their honour. Slaves have laboured to construct buildings so we can praise them. Civilisations have blossomed and fallen in their names. Battles have been fought. Generations of priests and monks have dedicated their lives to understanding them, interpreting them, making sacrifices to them, worshipping them.'

A breath of wind blows a ball of straw down the path in the garden.

'And now?' he asks. 'We don't believe in them any more. Now they are all dead. Not all of them are forgotten. But no one believes in them any longer. No one worships them. And if they ever existed, they now pass their sacred lives in boring oblivion. As gods, they are dead.'

The breeze that passes through the arcade sounds like a sigh.

'I think,' the monk continues, 'that God is also dead. The god we knew as Jahve. Jehova. Elohim. Our Lord. He has many names. And so the signs of his death are many. The prophesies of the Bible have been fulfilled. God is dead. Nietzsche was right.'

'How do you know that?'

He gives a sad, toothless smile. 'Look around! Does the world bear the hallmarks of a living, active God? Is there anything about our existence that indicates that a loving God watches over us?'

'I'm not a believer.'

'How can you live in this world without believing?'

'Why should I believe in a god?'

'Jesus is the way, the truth and life.'

'That's just a platitude. Why is your belief more true than Buddhism or Hinduism? What makes your God more powerful than Brahman? Jews and Christians, Muslims and Sikhs – they all believe so sincerely in *their* god, *their* interpretation, *their* truth. Are they all right? Or are none of them right? Your God condemns all the others. So tell me, who is right? Which of the world religions is more true than the others? And which Christian belief is favoured by your God and Jesus? That of the Catholics? The Mormons? The Jehovah's Witnesses? Protestants? Baptists? Pentacostalists? Or the Adventists?'

'Bjørn . . .'

'Why should *I* believe in a god who rules over the entire world, but who, for some reason, chooses a nomadic tribe in the Middle East as his people, above all others? What about the indigenous people on Hawaii? The Inuits? The Aboriginals? Why does your God sit up there in his heavens, clutching this small tribe close to his heart, whereas others haven't even heard of him?'

'The ways of Our Lord are mysterious.'

'The ways of Our Lord are completely irrational. I can understand that the Israelites believed in him two or three thousand years ago, but the fact that people still swear by this superstitious nonsense is beyond me.'

'The words of a fool.'

'You said yourself that the heart of your God has stopped beating.'

'A god dies slowly, Bjørn. He does not die overnight. Based on various signs and interpretations of the Bible, and our understanding of the prophecies and prayers, it is our conclusion – and I grant you it is only an assumption – that God started to die at some point in the twelfth century, but His final passing was towards the end of the nineteenth century. God has been dead for over a hundred years, but we just haven't managed to accept it.'

'You are a monk. Who do you worship if your god is dead?'

'Do you stop loving your mother and father simply because they are dead? We worship the memory of God. Of Jesus. Of the values they stood for, and all that they taught us.'

'So what does it mean? If you are right. Who has taken over? Are there other gods waiting to take over where God stopped?'

'We don't know. Not yet. The Gnostics, a Christian sect who were branded heretics by the Catholic-Orthodox church that prevailed in the battle of the teachings, never accepted that our God is omnipotent and absolute. There were many others who believed that Jahve was an inferior and power-crazed god whose creations – the world and people – were actual proof of his incompetence. A more powerful god, the true god, ruled over Jahve and the other minor rival gods. This true god was above all the trivialities here on earth. Well, neither the Jewish rabbis nor the Christian fathers could accept such a distorted teaching. The God of the Old Testament had, after all, ordered us to worship Him and Him alone. Hmm. But what if the Gnostics were right? What if the Jahve of the Old Testament was a power-crazed god – an aeon – who was obsessed with the trivialities of how we should worship him? What if Jahve was just one of many gods? Suppose there is a creator, a true God, who no religion has yet managed to capture in their divine delusion? Hundreds of years may pass before this new god becomes strong enough to appear before us humans and to find prophets who humanity will listen to and worship. You are a child of godlessness, of secularity, of indifference to eternity and all that is sacred. And as such, your atheist attitude is a result of God's absence in the world.'

We sit in silence for a while, shaded from the desert sun. When we have finished the water and burped discreetly into our hands, the monk shows us down into an earthen cellar under the monastery. We pass through several rooms before coming to an iron door, which leads into a room that is lit by a flickering neon light.

The monk opens a metal filing cabinet and pulls out a drawer full of coins. He gives me a handful. I look at them. To my surprise, I see that the silver pennies have an unknown Norwegian royal seal on them.

'How did they get here?' I ask.

'They were made here.'

'I've read quite a bit about numismatics at the university. As far as I can remember, Olav Tryggvason made the first Norwegian coins in around 995. The legend on the coins was *ONLAFREXNORmannorum*, which means *Olav King of the Norwegians*. There was a picture of the king with a sceptre on the front, and a cross with the letters *CRVX* on the back. It was assumed that the coin maker had come from England.'

'Old Norse merchants also had coins made here in Egypt, or to be more precise, in the village of Misr, south of Alexandria on the banks of the Nile.'

'Archaeologists have assumed that the Arabic coins found in Norway had come north with merchants who had traded with the Byzantine Empire. The Arabic coins were also widely used as an international currency. I didn't know that the Vikings had actually minted coins here.'

'For a short period.'

'There's more,' Stuart says, and gives the monk a nod in the direction of an even more solid-looking cabinet. 'And in return, I hope that you will show me the Thingvellir Scrolls.'

'Soon . . .'

The monk opens the cabinet and pulls out a wooden case. In it lies a piece of gold jewellery. He hands me the chain, which lies heavy in my hand. The pendant is the rune *tiwaz*.

'A piece of Viking jewellery,' Stuart says. 'Can you guess where it was found?'

I can't.

'The chain was found in the empty sarcophagus in the innermost burial chamber at the Amon-Ra temple,' the monk says.

6

That evening, straight after supper, I phone Professor Llyleworth at the SIS from a telephone box several streets away from the hotel.

The connection is terrible and the noise from the street makes it impossible to hold a conversation. But I manage to explain to him that I have escaped from the

Schimmer Institute and that all is well. His questions drown in the cacophony of mopeds and buses and vegetable sellers offering juicy melons and the muezzins' disharmonious calls to prayer booming out from the minarets.

On the way back, I am unintentionally drawn into a score of bazaars and small shops where, as a result of a serious of unfortunate cultural and linguistic misunderstandings, I manage to acquire a considerable collection of stone scarabs, cat statues, mummy reliefs, castes of Anubis, miniature sarcophagi and mummies, as well as a papyrus poster of the Sphinx at sunset and a bottle of Nubian Nights essential perfume that beautiful women cannot resist.

Outside the hotel, I spot the tourist who was taking photos at the tomb of Thutmose. He is standing watching out for someone – maybe his charming wife who has the credit card and is not afraid to use it. When he sees me, he gives me a flustered smile. Either because he recognises me, but can't remember where from, or because I was not supposed to see him.

7

Early the next morning, Stuart and I walk to the Luxor Museum, which lies a few blocks from the hotel.

Stuart phoned the museum the previous evening and made an appointment with the director, an acquaintance and colleague he has kept in touch with over the years.

On the way there, Stuart again tries to persuade me to show him the Thingvellir Scrolls. I say surely he understands that I don't have them with me.

'But you know where they are,' he persists. 'We could go there.'

Even though I understand that it is difficult for him to

curb his professional curiosity, this constant nagging is starting to get on my nerves.

The director of the museum looks like a good-natured gorilla. He has a great beard and bushy eyebrows; hair even grows through the collar of his shirt.

'Stuart!' he growls, giving his old colleague a bear hug.

They look at each other, laughing in disbelief, like old war comrades who have survived the trenches.

'He was my assistant when I excavated the Amon-Ra burial chamber,' Stuart explains.

'Assistant?' The director roars with laughter. 'I was your slave!'

The museum is already quite full. I look around for the tourist who was taking snapshots at the tomb, but he is not there. They have of course replaced him with someone else.

'Only a few people know about a collection of papyrus, parchment and paper documents that we have archived in the basement here, and even fewer can be bothered to look at it,' the director tells me. To Stuart, he adds: 'That's where I keep the documents.'

Stuart winks at me.

'Documents?' I ask.

Just at that moment we pass a statue in a glass case that stops me in my tracks.

The wooden sculpture is about forty centimetres tall and is of a man or a god, who is holding his long beard with both hands. According to the sign on the case, the statue is 3,200 years old and is covered in black pitch, the colour of the god Osiris, and was found in a tomb in the Valley of the Kings. The statue is alarmingly like one that Thrainn has a picture of in his office in Reykjavik; the thousand-year-old bronze statue that was found by Eyjafjördur in the north of Iceland in 1815. Where did the Eyjafjördur statue come from? Did it originate from Egypt? And if it was an Icelandic Viking who had made the Eyjafjördur statue in the tenth century, where did he get his inspiration from? Could he have been on board one of Olav's longships?

I hurry down the stairs into the cellar after Stuart and the museum director.

'According to legend, the high priest of the Amon-Ra cult, Asim, was taken by the heavenly gods early one morning in 1013.' The director laughs, and gives Stuart a nod. 'Why the renewed interest in Asim? After thirty years?'

'We are working on a theory. We've come across some manuscript fragments that may have been written by him.'

'Manuscript fragments? Written by Asim? How exciting! I would be very interested to see them!'

'I'll send you copies.'

'Thank you, my friend. Thank you.'

The director unlocks the door to the archive room and turns off the alarm. He takes two laminated A4 sheets out of a steel cabinet. One is an Egyptian and English translation of a text that was originally written on papyrus. The other is a photograph of the original document, which is now in a museum in Cairo.

'This text was written by our friend Mr Asim. It's a section from a description of the burial of a pharaoh, more like a journalistic report than a religious blessing, based on a papyrus document from the New Kingdom, hieroglyphs and murals. Unfortunately the beginning and end are missing.'

. . . since dawn, people had been gathering by the river along the funeral route. The masses chanted in homage to Amon-Ra. His tomb on the other side of the Nile, the side of the dead, had stood ready for nearly a decade.

Only those who made the tomb knew where it was. And now the pharaoh had been dead for seventy days. Osiris was waiting. The professional mourners wailed and threw dust on themselves and the spectators, waving their arms in the air. The Muu dancers, dressed in loincloths and feather headdresses, moved to the rhythm of the drums. The funerary boat waited by the bank at the palace, with the mummy in a gold coffin. The crowd murmured as the boat carrying the wailing and grieving relatives pushed off from the quay. The funerary boat followed. The gilded coffin lay under a decorative roof, held up by four carved pillars. The rowers stood upright. The other boats in the procession then cast off, with the priests, the officers, the courtiers, official representatives, dancers and servants, who had with them all the treasures. These were to be placed in the grave and would follow the deceased on his journey to the afterlife, where he would live on as a god. The crowd stretched down the banks of the Nile, and flocked together behind the rows of guards as they watched the boats cross the river. The unsanctioned were not able to follow the procession over to the side of the dead. The king's final resting place was secret. On the west bank, the coffin was lifted on to a bier, which was also shaped like a boat, and this was then placed on a sled. Palace officials had the honour of pulling the sled that bore the pharaoh. Behind them came another sled with the Canopic jars that contained the viscera of the king. The closest relatives of the deceased walked beside the coffin. And the servants carrying the treasures that the pharaoh was to have with him in his new existence, and the Book of the Dead with the magic formulas and instructions needed to guide the deceased on his journey through the underworld, followed behind the second sled. The sleds made slow progress, owing to the heat and their weight, from the river over the plain and up the hillside to the tomb. The monotone beating of the drums echoed around the cliffs . . .

'There isn't any more,' the museum director says when he sees that I have finished reading.

Then he turns to Stuart. 'The other document is a letter from 1300, from a prefect at the Vatican Archives to the Egyptian vizier.'

He puts a laminated document down in front of us.

'The vizier had obviously sent an enquiry to the Vatican regarding the existence of letters or documents from Asim. The vizier must have had powerful connections, as the Vatican prefect, who might easily have overlooked any request for access to what was, after all, the Pope's archives – not least from a vizier in a Muslim country – has conscientiously sent a reply.'

I try to read the Latin text.

'Basically, the prefect acknowledges the existence of three documents written by Asim,' the director tells us. 'The oldest document is a letter from the high priest to His Highness, Caliph al-Hakim bi-Amr Allah, Ruler of God's Command, Absolute Caliph of Egypt . . .'

'We have a copy of that letter at the institute,' Stuart interrupts.

'. . . and the second document is a copy of an unknown original that describes an attack on the temple and tomb by heathen barbarians, and the third is a copy of a fragment from a travelogue – possible from the same text – which describes the voyage to, I quote, the outposts of civilisation.'

Stuart turns to me with a half-smile. 'The outposts of civilisation . . .'

'He must mean Norway.'

'Heathen barbarians . . .' Stuart's voice is thick. 'They

would not have described Byzantine soldiers like that. He was talking about Vikings!'

'That means that there are three documents written by Asim in the Vatican Archives.'

'Then,' Stuart says, 'we should go there and see if we can find them!'

The Antiquarian

1

A STONE'S throw from the throngs of tourists on Piazza Navona in a narrow, cobbled passage leading from a quiet backstreet down to a busy main road, between a picture-framer and a milliner, is an antiquarian bookshop which, according to the sign over the window, is simply called The Antiquary. Maps of Rome mistakenly show that the passage, which curves so much that you can't see from one end to the other, is a dead end. The locals use the passage as a short cut down to Via del Governo Vecchio, whereas any tourist who happens upon it might think that they have stumbled into the past. The shops in the tiny, tucked-away street look as if they have barely been visited since the days of Emperor Nero and that time, in some strange way, has stood still. The dusty books that are displayed in the windows are past bestsellers that have long since been forgotten. At night, the seemingly dead pages of the half-open books flutter like thin ghosts on the draught from the air conditioning. Outside the entrance, where the opening hours are written in calligraphic script on a yellowing piece of paper (the ink of the swirling letters seems to fade as you look at it), are the remains of an ancient black bicycle, which has been padlocked to a pipe.

Stuart Dunhill straightens his blazer. 'Shall we go in?'

On the way from the hotel, he has told me all about the man we are about to meet. Luigi Fiacchini is a legend in illegal antiquarian circles. He knows everyone of any importance in the business: antiquarians, librarians, publishers, scholars, book dealers and collectors. He deals with honest and respectable people and shady charlatans: bibliophile women and men from Milan and Florence, Vienna and Paris, Hamburg and London, St Petersburg and Moscow, Oslo and Stockholm, Copenhagen, Helsinki and Reykjavik, New York City and San Francisco, Hong Kong and Singapore, Buenos Aires and Santiago and Rio de Janeiro, Sydney and Cape Town. From his base in Rome, Luigi Fiacchini has negotiated the sale of a number of the world's most expensive books and collections. He was the middleman when Opus Dei bought a third-century copy of the Gospel of Luke, and it is rumoured that it was Luigi who managed to find the handwritten manuscript of Shakespeare's lost play, *Love's Labour Won*, which a collector in the Emirates apparently paid over fifty millions dollars for. He was behind the sale of one of the existing forty folio editions of Shakespeare's collected works, printed seven years after the maestro's death, for 2.8 million pounds. Stuart has heard that Luigi was also involved when Sotheby's of London auctioned one of the world's first printed atlases from 1477, which was based on the work of the third-century geographer Klaudios Ptolemaios, for around 2.5 million kroner.

As we go in, a man passes. Our eyes lock for a tenth of a second, and I get the feeling that I have seen him before. But he shows no sign of recognising me and by the time the hysterical bell rings to announce our arrival in the shop, I have forgotten him.

The shop's modest façade – a window and a door – had led me to assume that the shop was tiny. But it is in fact huge. You first come into a narrow section with books lining all the walls, and a counter with an old-fashioned till. Behind this, the shop opens out and is more reminiscent of a library. Thousands of books fill the labyrinth of bookcases, counters, chests, tables and shelves. The air is thick with the peculiar smell of books: paper and paper dust, bindings, glue and a whiff of sweat from the protagonists who fight their battles between the covers.

Stuart nudges me in the ribs.

I had pictured Luigi Fiacchini as a tall, distinguished Italian count with greying hair and wise eyes. The creature standing with his back to us, muttering *'momento, momento'* while he moves some books and who then makes a bobbing movement as he turns to see who has disturbed him, is short and round shouldered, with thin wispy hair and cloudy eyes that look in opposite directions. The only things missing are a hunchback, scales and a very long tongue.

'Stuart!' he exclaims.

'Luigi!' Stuart replies.

They shake hands with an intensity that indicates that they are both trying very hard to overcome the urge to embrace each other.

Stuart introduces me. Luigi looks at me with the open curiosity that is permissible between freaks.

'Mr Beltø! You certainly created some waves in my world when you impounded the Shrine of Sacred Secrets. Shame that you didn't put it on the market. You could have been a billionaire!'

His laughter sounds like wind rustling through pages, as though it were a sound effect and not an expression of his merriment.

He is much shorter than I am. One eye is covered by a grey film.

'Blind in the left eye, but like a troll, that means that I see even better with the other.'

Luigi had first tried a cigar as a young man, and now he refuses to give up. He claims that he is indirectly related to Leonardo da Vinci. Personally I think he looks like the lost descendant of a Spanish Moor who has taken pleasure in a donkey.

Then he says: '*Momento, momento*, gentlemen,' and runs over to the door, locks it and pulls down the blind.

He shows us around the bookshop with the proud passion of a lover. The shop is organised according to a thematic pattern that I can't quite grasp. He pulls out rare editions – a version of *Le Avventure di Pinocchio* signed by the author, Carlo Collodis, an eighteenth-century illustrated edition of Dante Alighieri's *La Divina Commedia*, a first edition of Machiavelli's *Il Principe*, and a proof of Umberto Eco's *Il nome della rosa* from 1979, with the author's corrections.

Luigi throws up his hands and sucks happily on his cigar: 'I have thousands of the world's best-written books here, and each one of them is begging to be read again.'

Luigi's lives in a flat above the shop. To get there, you go up a spiral staircase that has a thin chain hanging across it, with a sign that says *Riservato*.

The flat is not so very different from the shop. There are books everywhere. He has made space in the middle of the room for a leather chaise longue and a low table, which is piled high with Italian newspapers and magazines.

He gets a pot of coffee from the kitchen.

'As I said to you on the phone,' he says to Stuart as he pours the coffee, 'copies of the fragments of Asim's description of his travels to the country in the north have been coveted objects in the collectors' market since the nineteenth century. We don't know where the copies come from, but some of them have found their way into the Vatican Archives. The copies are incomplete fragments, but it seems that they all come from the same original manuscript, which has presumably been lost.'

'So what you are saying,' I venture, 'is that everything that's in the Vatican is already in circulation?'

'Not at all. The Vatican Archives are inexhaustible. It all depends on how you search and which references help you to look farther. Even though academics and collectors have already combed through the archives, no one has really known what they were trying to find. If you pass over even one single, arbitrary document, you may have overlooked the one and only cross-reference, and so lose the thread that would lead you to your goal. And what's more, it is really only now,' he looks at me again, 'that all these pieces of information are starting to mean anything.'

'What can we hope for?'

'One of the fragments is about an attack on Asim's temple. Another one appears to be some kind of travelogue describing a journey to the ends of civilisation.'

'Outpost,' Stuart corrects.

'Outpost, of course. The Vatican had already established in the 1100s that this outpost was Norway. The problem was that no one knew precisely *where* in Norway.' He looks questioningly at me, and I shrug. 'Another problem has been identifying which documents can be definitively linked to the case.'

'Most seem to be marked.'

'Marked? With what?'

'With three symbols: an Egyptian ankh, the rune *tiwaz* and a cross.'

Luigi looks away. '*Oh, cazzo . . .*' he exclaims. He focuses again. 'I think someone would have discovered Asim's travelogue long ago if the manuscript had been anywhere in the Vatican.'

'We don't necessarily need a complete version,' Stuart says. 'Any lead, big or small, would be helpful.'

'And you're hoping to find that in Archivum Secretum Apostolicum Vaticanum, the Vatican Secret Archive?'

'If they let us in.'

'The archives are not as secret as the name indicates. Some people believe that the word *secretum* derives from the concept separate, rather than secret. The archives were opened for restricted viewing in 1881. You have to apply for permission to visit the archives, but today around fifteen hundred researchers are granted permission every year.'

'A hopeless task. Both getting access and then searching.'

'Oh, don't say that. Several of the archivists belong to my – hmm, now what should we call it? – bibliophile guild. They owe me a few favours. I'll sort out passes for you and get you a dedicated archivist who knows where to look.'

I shake his hand in gratitude.

'Interest in Asim's manuscripts and maps increased when Stuart made his sensational find in 1977,' Luigi continues, 'but academic circles dismissed the issue with the usual arrogance and left it more to private individuals.'

'He means illegal collectors,' Stuart informs me.

'Did you say *maps*?'

'Oh yes, didn't you know that? At least one map exists, which Asim sent to Egypt. It supposedly shows where the mummy and the treasure are hidden. It's possible that there is a copy in the Vatican Archives, I don't know, but it doesn't appear to have helped any treasure hunters.'

'So you deal in maps too?'

'I most certainly do! Wait, wait a moment.' With sudden enthusiasm, he runs down the spiral staircase and comes up again with an armful of paper rolls and document holders that he carefully spreads out on the table in front of us.

'Maps are often just as valuable as handwritten documents. It's all about understanding the world. The glory of the great explorers. Marco Polo. Christopher

Columbus. Vasco da Gama. Hudson. Nansen. Amundsen. Heyerdahl.'

He unfolds a sheet: 'This is a facsimile of Mercator's map of the world from 1569. You can recognise Scandinavia, the northern tip of Scotland, Iceland and parts of Greenland, but much of it is drawn from imagination. Mercator based it on the medieval documentation left by a travelling monk who wrote a book called *Inventio Fortunata* in the fifteenth century, which has unfortunately been lost. The first known written description of Vinland is by the geographer and historian Adam of Bremen, in his book *Descriptio insularum Aquilonis* from around 1075, a whole generation after Leif Eiriksson first saw Vinland. *Pope Urban's map* from 1367 indicates the existence of some big islands – the coast of America – to the west of the Atlantic. The disputed Vinland map, *Mappa Mundi*, is supposedly a map of America. The parchment has been dated to the 1400s, but scientists cannot agree on the age of the ink. A map from Sir Thomas Phillips's collection from 1424 shows details of the east coast of America as far south as Georgia and Florida.'

I groan. 'That's all we need. America! Can't we just stick to our own continent?'

'As you please.'

I take a sip of coffee, which is like tar, and ask whether Luigi is worried about thieves. 'After all,' I say, 'an opportunist could easily steal things here that are worth more than he'd get from raiding a bank.'

'True, true.' Luigi goes over to the banister by the stairs. A button has been installed in the carving on the post. 'I have around fifteen of these spread around the shop. The alarm is connected directly to the police, so they would be here in a matter of minutes. And I've hidden electronic sensors in the most valuable books which will set off an alarm when the thief gets too close to the door.' He knocks on the window out to the passage. 'Bullet-proof glass.

You couldn't even break it with a hammer. You would need explosives if you wanted to get through this window.'

'I understand that you've been in contact with Sheikh Ibrahim?' Stuart ventures, with caution.

Luigi looks up, like an animal sensing danger. 'Anyone of any consequence in the international world of ancient books and manuscripts has been in contact with Sheikh Ibrahim.'

'How well do you know him?'

'No one who says that they know the sheikh well actually knows him.'

'Have you sold anything to him or bought anything from him?'

Luigi looks at me with his one good eye. 'In my business, discretion is the secret of success. To let anything slip about a client, be they a buyer or a seller, would be indiscreet.'

'What we were wondering,' Stuart expands, 'is why the sheikh would be interested in the high priest Asim and the treasure that the Vikings stole? Is it the treasure that he's after? Or the mummy? Or the manuscripts and writings that were stored in the jars?'

'The sheikh has always been interested in antiques and manuscripts.'

'How does he know about the story of Holy Olav and Snorri in the first place?'

'Maybe he read the *National Geographic* in 1977.'

'Can you help us?' Stuart asks.

'I'll check a few things.'

Stuart winks at me. I understand that when Luigi says 'check a few things' he means he will find out.

'But don't think that I'm doing it as a favour,' he adds, with some intensity, apparently having seen our satisfied smiles and wanting to bring us back down to earth.

'Of course not,' Stuart says. 'It would never cross my mind to think that you wanted nothing in return.'

He chuckles. '*Amico*, you know me well. My motive – I might as well tell the truth – my motive is entirely selfish. It seems likely to me that Sheikh Ibrahim's treasure hunt is not some ridiculous search for a measly monk's document from the 1400s. Sheikh Ibrahim smells money, lots of it. And if there's big money involved, I am not against joining the dance around the golden calf.'

2

The reading room in the Archivum Secretum Apostolicum Vaticanum is long and narrow with a domed ceiling that is decorated with frescoes, like a church. The desks are positioned in the middle of the floor, each big enough to seat two or three people, and there are so many desks that I give up counting. The inner wall is two storeys high and lined with books.

A receptionist leads us through several vestibules and rooms with panelled walls, painted ceilings and dark wooden bookshelves. All around us sit supervised researchers, all in their own personal dust cloud.

Tomaso Rossellini is a short, chubby man with nut-brown eyes that twinkle at us inquisitively from behind square, gold-rimmed glasses. He is waiting for us outside his office. 'So, you are friends of Luigi,' he says in a conspiratorial voice, shaking our hands. The hint of a smile tugs at the corners of his mouth.

'Who isn't?' Stuart spars, causing Tomaso to burst out into silent laughter. You have to work for years as an archivist or librarian in order to perfect a laugh that no one can hear. We make some polite comments about the interior and how grateful we are that he has taken time to help us, which he dismisses with an impatient wave of the hand.

'Luigi told me that you are looking for documents and letters that might be linked to a high priest – Asim from the Amon-Ra cult – and to the Norwegian saint Holy Olav. Might I, out of sheer curiosity, ask why?'

'We are trying to document a closer contact between the Old Norse and Egyptian cultures than has previously been acknowledged,' Stuart explains quickly, and vaguely. 'We believe that the Old Norse belief system was influenced by Egyptian gods as well as Germanic and Celtic mythology.'

Tomaso looks at us while the hard disk takes a nanosecond or two to process, categorise and save this information. We are hardly the first people to come here in the hope of proving a hopeless hypothesis.

'I have gathered together some archive references to the people, the topic and other related topics. But for various reasons – *time!* – I have not managed to go through the material myself.' He hands us three sheets of references, in a combination of letters and numbers. 'The oldest references are nine hundred and fifty years old, but there are cross-references from the twelfth century right up until the sixteenth century.'

He explains what we will be able to find ourselves and what will require an archivist, which is the lion's share. 'Our archives include the collections of two hundred and sixty-four popes from the fifth century. And we don't just have religious writings – you can find anything from a reminder from Michelangelo to Henry the Eighth's love letters. But you have to know what you are looking for. The archives are enormous! The tightly packed bookshelves cover a total of eighty-five kilometres. And I must warn you, only a fraction of the texts are translated, at best to Latin.'

'I read Latin, Greek, Coptic, Hebrew, Aramaic and old Italian,' Stuart says, and adds, when he sees our stunned faces: 'Part of my basic education.'

3

Tomaso shows us into the reading room and then down into the archives. The bulk of the references are in the basement, where the rows of shelves disappear into infinity. One of the curators carefully gathers together our requests, and then we carry two cardboard boxes with files, protocols and document holders back up to the reading room.

We make ourselves comfortable and start our search.

Stuart and I sit bent over books with disintegrating glue and dusty documents for hours, sifting through the material, some of which only touches on the periphery of the mystery.

In one document, I come across a cross-reference to a letter to General Master Stephanus Scannabecchi with the key words *Noruega* and *Dollstein*. Stuart reads through a papal bull that Anastasius IV issued just before his death in 1154 which declared Nidaros as the seat of the archdiocese over Oslo, Hamar, Bergen, Stavanger, the Orkneys, the Hebrides, the Faroes and Greenland.

There are abundant references to *Diplomatarium Norvegicum*, a twenty-two-volume collection of over twenty thousand letters from Norway in the Middle Ages, some dating as far back as the eleventh century.

In all this confusion of information, I read a letter dated November 1354, in which King Magnus names Pål Knutsson as the commander for a special expedition to Greenland, to strengthen the position of Christianity there. Then, in a document from 1450, there is a reference to 'the attack on the barbarians in Greenland'; evidently 'some of the barbarians escaped'.

In a pile of writings about St Magnus, I discover the papal bull from Pope Celestin III that proclaims Ragnvald Earl of Orkney a saint in 1197.

More surprising is a reference to a parchment from 1131, where the knight Clemens de'Fieschi, in a letter to Cardinal Bishop Benedictus Secondus – with reference to earlier reports – argues that the same Ragnvald must have got there before him and emptied the cave of its treasures.

Cave? Treasures?

De'Fieschi suggests in the letter that the Vatican should enter into an alliance with the branch of Ragnvald's family that is disloyal to the earl and opposes him.

The information interests me for several reasons.

Ragnvald Earl of Orkney is the same Crusader who, according to Adelheid, went looking for treasure in the Dollstein Cave.

Did he *actually* find the treasure?

What was his role?

Was he a guardian who rescued the mummy, the scrolls and the treasure from the claws of the Vatican – or was he just a treasure hunter?

In 1137, a few years after he had been to Dollstein, Ragnvald started to build St Magnus's Cathedral in Kirkwall on the Orkneys, in honour of his uncle, Magnus, who had suffered a martyr's death. When the cathedral was restored in the early 1900s, the construction workers found the skeletons of Ragnvald and his uncle, Magnus, built into the pillars in the choir.

According to the chronicle, Ragnvald Earl of Orkney was killed by some relatives at Caithness in Scotland in 1158, following a power struggle. De'Fieschi's letter indicates he may have been killed by defectors on behalf of a *congregatio* in the Vatican.

The murder of Ragnvald in 1158 makes me think about the fate of my friend, Sira Magnus.

4

Half an hour later, Stuart finds a document that leaves us both speechless.

The seal on the document is from the Cardinal Commission and has been broken, and there is a fraying silk ribbon round it. In the document, it says that the Vatican has been informed that 'barbarians from the land of snow' have carried out a raid in Egypt and stolen 'a sacred mummy, irreplaceable papyrus scrolls and valuable treasures'.

'Could it be said any clearer?' Stuart's eyes are shining. Right now, I think that the hope of vindication is more important to him than the tomb and the Viking raid.

According to the document, two Egyptian envoys – Caliph al-Mustarshid and an unnamed high priest – had visited the Vatican to present their case. The visit coincided with the translation of a letter written in Coptic by the Egyptian Asim, which had been gathering dust in the Vatican Archives.

The Egyptians' message and the Coptic letter must have made an impression on Pope Innocent II, as later the same year the pope ordered the first delegation to go to Norway, led by the knight Clemens de'Fieschi.

Together with the Cardinal Commission document is a letter that was sent by courier to General Master Scannabecchi in the Vatican – it must be the same letter that we found a reference to earlier – from Clemens de'Fieschi, who boldly signed his report *the Lord's Man-at-Arms*.

To the Right Honourable
General Master Stephanus Scannabecchi
Sancta Sedes & Curia Romana
The Vatican

My lord,

I was ordered, by Cardinal Bishop Benedictus Secundus on behalf of the Holy Father, to lead a group of learned men-at-arms who were to travel to Norway, on the northern edge of civilisation, in order, if possible, to find a sacred papyrus manuscript. Among my men were representatives from the Vatican, the Order of the Knights Templar, the Order of the Knights Hospitaller and entrusted men selected by the Caliph of Egypt. The caliph instructed his envoys to bring home a mummy (embalmed in accordance with heathen Egyptian traditions) and the other contents of the mummy's tomb, ostensibly gold and jewels and art.

Alas, there is much to indicate that the Norwegians knew we were on our way, though I am not able to establish how. They may have been warned, indirectly, by the envoys of the Hospitallers or scouts who were sent in advance by Cardinal Secundus to help us find clues, or by loose-tongued individuals we met along the way in the abbeys and lodgings where we slept, who may have passed on the nature of our enquiries and conversations.

On the advice of several merchants and hunters who had travelled widely in Norway, whom we met in a village in Denmark called Domus Mercatorum, or Kaupmannahafn, we sailed to Ásló, a village on the plains of the gods below the hills, from where we could ride north-west, first through green valleys and then over mighty mountain ranges. This we were advised to do rather than to sail north along the dangerous and wild cliffs of the coast, where waves as tall as houses could rise up from nowhere and a sea monster named Kraken is said to dwell, who is able to sink great ships.

On our arrival in Norway, we were surprised by the severe winter weather, bringing with it much snow and icy winds, and we were forced to spend six months in a Norwegian abbey while we waited for the snow to melt. Two of our men died of illnesses that the winter cold brought with it.

We read and studied the century-old maps and descriptions of the Egyptian Asim, high priest of the Amon-Ra cult, and we thought we had located the whereabouts of a cave named Dollstein on an island on the north-west coast. This seemed to tally well with Asim's descriptions.

I shall, with consideration to my reader's precious time, not describe in any detail what we encountered in the deep, dark forests that lead up to the high peaks we had to cross in order to reach our final destination. Suffice to say that we came across several hostile barbarian tribes, trolls and ogres, and in our confrontations with these, we lost five brave soldiers.

We arrived on the island of Sandsøy late one afternoon and set up camp on some open, flat land where we made a fire and cooked some birds. We had a local man with us who had promised to help in return for a coin and a blessing on behalf of the Holy Father. We could see Dollstein from our camp, far out at the end of the headland on the west side of the island, by the fjord.

At sunrise the following morning, we rode along the water's edge to the mountain. Here we tethered our horses and left men to stand guard.

The mountain was steep, rugged and wet. The cave lies a good couple of hundred strides up, facing out to the open sea, and resembles most a chasm that leads straight to hell. A narrow, steep and slippery tunnel leads deep into the dark.

We had to light our torches and climb carefully over great boulders. The air was ice cold. We finally came to a great cavern. From here we ventured farther in through narrow passages and over some high walls. There were five such caverns, one after the other. Altogether, the cave was many hundred strides deep, but locals believe that the caves stretch endlessly under the sea to Scotland. There are many sagas that tell of a great treasure to be found in the cave. It is said along the coast that two years since, Ragnvald Earl of Orkney had come to the island in search of treasure.

We ventured as far into the cave as was possible. Right Honourable General Master Scannabecchi, it pains me to tell your Excellency that despite our greatest efforts in searching, the cave turned out to be empty.

With my humble respect,
CLEMENS DE'FIESCHI
Our Lord's Man-At-Arms

5

Twenty-five years after this first, unsuccessful expedition, Pope Adrian IV – who had previously visited Norway and Hamar in 1153–54, under his former name of Nicholas Breakspear – appointed a commission to investigate the mystery. The document more than indicates that Breakspear's previous mission in Norway had also been connected to the treasure. Pope Alexander III sent another group of soldiers north in 1180, around the time that Flesberg Church was built. Fifty years later, another group was sent by Pope Gregory IX.

1230 . . . I am reminded of the text in Garmo Church:

The Pope of Rome's retainer, the Knights Hospitaller and Jerusalem's Knights Templar have gathered for battle. The sacred tomb is hidden as Asim instructed.

In a plastic document holder marked with the Roman number LXVII lies the letter that Stuart showed me a copy of at the Schimmer Institute, which the high priest Asim had sent to the Caliph of Egypt from Rouen, but which never got farther than the Vatican.

Our fingers trembling with excitement, we carry on looking through the piles of paper and parchments that diligent monks in the past and meticulous archivists have shrouded in a web of inferences and hidden instructions.

6

Towards the end of the second day, as the golden beams of the afternoon sun come in through the high, deep windows, I find a leather document holder. Even though I do not understand a word of it when I open the dossier, I know intuitively that I have found the two short fragments of Asim's story which were referred to in the letter we discovered in Egypt.

'Coptic,' Stuart confirms. A Latin translation has been attached, and using both documents, Stuart reads the text out loud:

> Holy Osiris, they stink! Like unclean animals – yes, pigs with rotting intestines and badgers with gangrene – they infect the air around them with their bodily odour, the pungency of stale sweat, acrid belching, fermenting intestinal gas, confined feet and unwashed sexual organs. Their clothes reek of old urine and excrement, of sweat, blood and . . .

. . . fearless, crude and brutal. They fight savagely against any enemy. Even with fatal wounds and missing limbs they continue to fight. Courageous men who die in battle are taken to a paradise they call Valhalla by the Valkyries, where the fallen warriors can fight, eat and drink eternally . . .

7

Enthused and confused by the discovery of these ancient texts, I tumble out into the streets of Rome. Stuart has stayed behind at the Vatican to take copies.

The sun is tepid. Mopeds zigzag in and out between the cars that are caught in the impatient afternoon queues. A church clock chimes somewhere and is answered in the distance, loud and clear. In the pavement cafés, tourists and Romans sit at tiny tables with tiny cups of coffee. At the Piazza Venezia, I wander through a flock of pigeons that opens and closes like a zip.

My heart will not stop racing. Might Asim's treasure still be in the Dollstein Cave, as Adelheid said? Or did Ragnvald Earl of Orkney take it with him and hide it somewhere in St Magnus's Cathedral in Kirkwall?

In a parallel street on the other side of the piazza, a police car bullies its way forward with the help of a siren, and somewhere else a car honks its horn, while a bus spews out tourists.

I remember the first time I was in Rome. It took me well over an hour to find the Tarpeian Rock. I spent hours at the Colosseum, where I imagined I could still hear the humming of ancient Roman crowds; I endured the sun beating down as I explored the ruins of the Forum Romanum. Then in the velvety warmth of the evening, I wandered along the pavements – alone – among the happy couples dining in the Travestere district.

I am stopped abruptly by a scooter shooting out of an entranceway, which is then immediately swallowed by the traffic. An indignant pigeon that has found some crumbs of bread refuses to move out the way. I step absent-mindedly into the road. Someone grabs my jacket and hauls me back as an Alfa Romeo slams on the brakes and horn. I turn to thank the stranger who saved me from being knocked down, but he is already running off in the opposite direction.

I phone Ragnhild from a phone box, to see whether there is any more news.

'*There* you are,' she says in a voice that makes it sound as if I'm the one on the run. She tells me that they have found Hassan's hideaway in Oslo: a flat in Frogner that he had bought from an estate agent. With cash. The money was taken from an account in London. When the police broke into the flat, they found weapons and surveillance equipment, but no people.

My head is spinning. I wander back to the hotel on Quirinal Hill.

8

An invitation is waiting for me at the hotel reception – beautifully illuminated calligraphy on handmade paper – requesting the pleasure of my company at a gathering at Luigi's bibliophile gentlemen's club at eight o'clock that evening.

I take the rickety lift up to the fourth floor.

Someone has been in my room. It looks just as it did when the chambermaid and I left it. The bed is made. The wastepaper basket is empty. But the tiny bits of thread that I left in the zip of my sponge bag and between books and papers on the desk are no longer there.

Someone has been looking for something they did not find.

Hassan? Does he know that I am in Rome? Why hasn't he got me, then?

I stand by the window, looking out over the city's mosaic of roofs and church spires and domes. Through the smog, on the other side of the Tiber, I can just make out St Peter's Church. Down on the street, hidden behind a copy of *Corriere della Sera*, a man stands leaning against a lamp-post. There is actually nothing special about him. Which is perhaps what arouses my suspicion.

Satan's Bible

1

LUIGI'S GENTLEMEN'S club meets behind a mahogany door on the second floor of an august apartment building on Via Condotti, close to the Spanish Steps, in an area that looks as if it thinks it is still in the past but can't quite decide which era it belongs to. A fellow of the fraternity or a lackey – I can't tell the difference – lets us in and then disappears. Twenty-three men in dark suits are gathered in the drawing room. Most of them are drinking cognac. The cigar smoke is so thick that it stings my eyes.

'Bjørn! Stuart!'

Luigi breaks out of a circle of gentlemen, puts his cognac down on a shelf in front of a mirror and his cigar in an ashtray, then claps his hands. 'Gentlemen, gentlemen,' he cries. 'Let me introduce Mr Bjørn Beltø. You all know about his great efforts to save the Shrine of Sacred Secrets.'

Scattered applause.

'And Mr Stuart Dunhill, the archaeologist who proved that the Vikings did go to Thebes!'

Stuart gives a gentle bow.

Luigi takes us round and introduces us to his fraternity. We shake hands with each of them. One of his fellow bibliophiles is Tomaso from the Vatican Secret Archives. Another owns one of Italy's largest bookshop chains. Several of them are antiquarians, like Luigi, and others are librarians and authors. There is a publisher there, from Bompiani. The professions of a handful of men are discreetly glossed over and the whispered names immediately evaporate in my pathetic memory.

One of them holds my hand for a long time. 'Bjørn Beltø, so it's you.' I would put him somewhere around sixty or seventy. He is still a good-looking man, toned and with fine features, his long grey hair combed back.

When he lets go of my hand, it is taken over by a fat man with no hair who mumbles that he is an *ammiratore*, which Luigi tells me is an admirer.

'I took the liberty of mentioning to my brothers in an email why you were here,' Luigi says. 'And I am proud to say that our humble network has come across something that may help you in your search. And we hope,' he adds, 'that you will help us in return.'

There is a ceremonious tone to his voice. Glasses are raised by the league of elegant, grey-haired gentlemen.

'Let me present the club. You, and all others who are aware of our exclusive fraternity, know us as a bibliophile gentlemen's club. Which we are. *Naturalement*. But the club was established in 1922 with a specific and occult goal in mind.'

'Occult?'

'That's how most people would see it.'

'Because?'

Luigi raises his cognac glass. 'I'll say it straight: we are looking for Satan's lost Bible.'

The room is so quiet that you can hear the sounds of the city penetrating through the window. A dart of fear stings in my chest.

'Are you satanists?'

Everyone in the room bursts out laughing.

Luigi slaps me on the shoulder. 'No, no, no, my friend. We are not satanists. We do not worship Satan. Our interest is purely academic. We are interested in Satan's role and function in the Bible and in Christian and Jewish mythology.'

'Satan's . . . role?'

'We know that a lost Bible exists, or perhaps it would be more precise to describe it as a collection of writings, from pre-Christian times. These manuscripts were written by the followers of the Devil, and are about his history and vision, in exactly the same way that the Bible is about the lives and precepts of the prophets and Jesus.'

'Wow!'

'The reason for us telling you our secret is that we believe and hope that you are in possession of the manuscript of the so-called Satan's Bible.'

I chew on the name. Satan's Bible sounds like some heathen curse.

'What on earth makes you think that?'

'Deduction, assumption, guesswork. A version of the Bible was taken from Mesopotamia to Egypt five hundred years before Christ, where it subsequently followed a holy man to the grave. It may have been the manuscript that your Viking ancestors took with them.'

'And the mummy is the Devil himself, then?'

Again, a wave of jolly laughter rolls around the room.

'What makes you presume that this satanic manuscript was in the tomb at the Amon-Ra sect's temple?' I ask.

'When you mentioned the three symbols ankh, *tiwaz* and cross, it got me thinking. I remembered that I had come across the same combination of symbols before. But I couldn't remember where and when. So I asked my brothers.'

One of the oldest men, Marcello Castiglione, takes a step forward as he pulls a piece of paper from his inner pocket.

'This is a photostat copy of a diary entry that Bartolomeo Columbus, Christopher's brother, wrote on one of their voyages in the Caribbean,' he stammers in otherwise perfect English.

He hands me the sheet, which is covered with elegant writing, full of loops and flourishes.

'It is not likely that you will understand much of it, but I would draw your attention to this . . .' He points to the middle of the page:

'Huh!' I exclaim.

I don't know whether *huh* means the same in Italian, but I can see by their smiles that they are amused by my open-mouthed astonishment.

'You say this was written by Christopher Columbus's brother?'

Marcello Castiglione nods solemnly.

'Why did Columbus draw these symbols?'

'No one knows,' Luigi answers. 'He described the combination of symbols as *the Guardians' Seal*.'

'In the diary, Bartolomeo Columbus refers to a sealed letter he was asked to take back to Europe,' Marcello Castiglione continues. 'He doesn't say who it was on the newly discovered Caribbean island who sent the letter, but he does say who the letter was addressed to.' He makes a dramatic pause. '*Archbishop Erik Valkendorf of Nidaros in the Kingdom of Norway.*'

I swallow a gasp.

'We know from other sources,' Luigi picks up the story, 'that Columbus diligently took the letter back to Europe with him, first to Lisbon and Vale de Paraiso in Portugal, then on to Spain. He gave the letter to a Spanish bishop who was obviously not that interested in playing postman, not even for a Norwegian colleague. The suspicious bishop must have broken the seal and then, having read the contents, been so alarmed that he handed the letter over to a representative of the Spanish Inquisition, which was under the Spanish king and not the Vatican. However, the letter is mentioned in the Vatican Archives register in 1503, that is under Pope Julius II. Fifty years later, the Pope's inquisition was given the title the Supreme Sacred Congregation of the Roman and Universal Inquisition, and this congregation of learned priests classified the letter as a sorcerer's letter, a secret magic letter, and therefore heretical.'

'The Inquisition still exists today, albeit in a more merciful and milder form,' Tomaso adds. 'Today it is called the Congregation for the Doctrine of the Faith, and is part of the Roman Catholic Church's central administration.'

'So we wonder,' continues Marcello Castiglione, 'what it was in that letter that not only scared the bishop so much that he failed to deliver the letter to its rightful recipient, but that also made the Inquisition take it so seriously.'

'Does the letter still exist?'

'Yes. Well, no. That's to say, maybe. But we don't know where,' Luigi admits.

'It would seem that it was stolen from the Vatican Archives some time between 1820 and 1825,' Marcello Castiglione explains.

'The suspect was a wealthy Jewish theologian who lived in Prague,' Luigi says. 'He had dedicated his life to collecting religious writings and was fascinated by material about Satan. We suspect that he may have bribed a subordinate working in the archive to steal the document. All the same, it is hard to understand why an apparently incomprehensible letter from the sixteenth-century Caribbean, addressed to a Norwegian bishop, would interest a collector who specialised in manuscripts and documents from the Middle East.'

'What happened to his collection?'

'Before he died in 1842, he donated everything – four thousand, six hundred letters, documents and manuscripts – to a trust that was administered by his son, Jacob. In 1934, everything was confiscated by the well-known German industrialist and Nazi Maximilian von Lewinski. And after that, no one knows what happened to the collection. Many fear that it was lost when the von Lewinski residence in Dresden was bombed and destroyed in February 1945.'

'*Satan's Bible*,' I mutter to myself, still in the dark.

Marcello Castiglione adopts the posture of a priest talking to a group of non-believers. 'Different faiths have very different images of Satan. The name Satan comes from the Hebrew for adversary or accuser. Satan was the treasured archangel, Lucifer, who fell from grace and was cast out of Heaven by God.'

'He is God's tool,' Luigi adds. 'Just as Judas was a tool for Jesus. Some people see the Devil as a symbolic representative of evil. For others, he is a physical and animal-like creature with hoofs and horns.'

'Some, like the Jews, believe that he surrounds himself with a profusion of demons,' Marcello Castiglione says. His voice and slightly commanding tone remind me of a preacher in a country chapel. 'The Jews have two types of demons, the hairy, satyr-like *se'irim* and the snake-like *shedim*. Demons are not quite so physical in the Christian tradition. They are more often seen to be evil spirits. In the 1500s, Johann Weyer – the author of the demon catalogue *Pseudomonarchia Daemonum* – calculated that there were 7,405,926 demons, divided into 1,111 legions of 6,666 members each.'

Then Luigi takes over: 'The head of all this devilry,

Satan, has been a controversial figure through the centuries. Who is he, really? Satan does not play a key role in the Bible, whereas the Mormon text, *Pearl of Great Price*, describes a meeting between Moses, God and Satan. According to the Mormons, this chapter was originally part of the Bible.'

'In both the Old and the New Testaments, God used Satan as a tool to put man to the test,' Marcello Castiglione says.

'When the unknown versions of Genesis and Exodus were discovered in the Dead Sea Scrolls in 1947, theologians learned that *the Day that the Lord creates Light, he also creates Light and Dark Angels*,' Luigi quotes.

'You see?' Marcello Castiglione asks. 'God created the evil angels. And you might well wonder why.'

'Just as our image of God has changed, so has the concept of Satan. In the Jewish Old Testament, God is strict and reprimanding,' Luigi explains. 'Then in the time leading up to the birth of Jesus, this image changes. God becomes merciful. Many people believe that the God of the New Testament is far gentler, and there is more room for forgiveness and tolerance.'

'At the same time, people's understanding of Satan changed,' Marcello Castiglione picks up the thread. 'He became an antigod. The polar opposite of God.'

'But Satan is still not lord over his own domain,' Luigi continues. 'Hell does not belong to Satan. In the Bible it says that Satan and his angels were *sent* to the sea of flames when they were thrown out of Heaven. So Hell existed before Satan. It was only later that people started to think that Satan was the ruler of Hell.'

'Our image of Satan – as the Devil, who is half-creature, half-man, with horns and hoofs – does not originate from the Bible,' Marcello Castiglione concludes. 'It was invented during the Middle Ages.'

'Why?'

'No one was afraid of him!' Marcello Castiglione bursts out laughing. 'Satan frightened no one. And the Church need a terrifying devil to chasten the people. They needed a terrible troll.'

'One of the contributors was a monk at the Saint-Germain Abbey in Auxerre in France,' Luigi says. 'In the eleventh century, Rodulfus Glaber depicted Satan as a small man with a tortured face, an abnormally protruding mouth, a goat's beard and hairy, pointed ears. His teeth were like a dog's canine teeth, his head was pointed and he had a hunchback.'

'More and more witnesses came forward,' Marcello Castiglione tells us. 'Satan's appearance became increasingly animalistic, and less and less human. They gave him horns, hoofs and wings. Oh, and by the way, do you know why angels have wings? It was the artists who gave angels wings, in order to explain to ordinary people how they got from Heaven to earth.'

'Just imagine,' Luigi muses with a dream-like expression on his face, 'if we actually did find Satan's Bible! Just imagine if the story of Lucifer reveals the Devil's true self. The archangel who dared to question the way God played with people. The angel who stood up to God.'

'Why do you think that what we found in Iceland is this "Bible"?'

'Deduction,' says Marcello Castiglione.

'And maths,' adds Luigi.

'Maths?'

'The way in which Columbus combined the three symbols ankh, *tiwaz* and cross to make up a grid of nine symbols is hardly coincidental.'

On a piece of paper, Marcello writes down:

> **Ankh.** *Tiwaz.* **Cross.**
> *Tiwaz.* **Cross. Ankh.**
> **Cross. Ankh.** *Tiwaz.*

'If we substitute each symbol with a numerical value,' Marcello Castiglione explains, 'the number one represents holy unity. The number two represents the duality of existence, two-sidedness. Man and Woman. Yin and Yang. Life and Death. And the number three has many religious connotations: from the Holy Trinity to the Three Wise Men who came bearing gifts for Jesus – too many to mention, really. So one, two and three are our most fundamental numbers. What we do is we replace Bartolomeo's symbol combinations with numbers. Ankh equals one, *tiwaz* equals two and the cross equals three. So, using numbers instead of words, we get:

$$1. \ 2. \ 3.$$
$$2. \ 3. \ 1.$$
$$3. \ 1. \ 2.$$

'And I'm supposed to make an association between these numbers and Satan?' I ask.

'Try!' Marcello Castiglione exclaims. 'We find the connection in the Bible, in the original Greek manuscript of the Revelation of John. In numerical form, it is χξς and in writing εξακόσιοι εξήκοντα εξ. And in Latin letters: *hexakosioi hexékonta hex.*'

'Aha. And in our Western numbers?'

'Do you mean in *Arabic* numbers?' Luigi grins. 'Simple. Add them up.'

Marcello writes up the grid again.

$$1. \ 2. \ 3. = 6$$
$$2. \ 3. \ 1. = 6$$
$$3. \ 1. \ 2. = 6$$
$$= 6 \ \ 6 \ \ 6$$

'Six six six!' I shout. 'The number of the beast!'

'Horizontally and vertically,' says Marcello Castiglione.

'Even in Roman numbers, six six six is a magic number,' Luigi says, and writes on his palm:

DCLXVI

'If you write down every symbol used for Roman numbers between one and five hundred, you get:

IVXLCD

Which, if you look closer, is DCLXVI backwards.'

'Six six six. The number of the beast from Revelation,' Marcello Castiglione repeats.

'The number of the Antichrist,' Luigi says.

And part of the hidden instruction in Snorri's Codex in Iceland, I think. But I say nothing.

It is late by the time we leave the gentlemen's club and walk back to the hotel in silence.

When I eventually manage to fall asleep, I am tortured by a terrifying dream that I cannot remember anything about the next morning.

But my bedclothes are wet with sweat.

2

Once I have showered and shaved, I ring Thrainn and ask him whether there is anything in the text to indicate that it might be – here I hesitate and cough – Satan's Bible that his colleagues are in the process of translating.

'Satan's Bible?' he repeats, laughing. Then, after a long pause, as if he wants to give me the chance to say that I am joking, he answers: 'To be perfectly honest, I had no idea that Satan's Bible existed.'

'It's a theory . . .'

'Whatever, there is nothing to indicate that the manuscript contains any devilry.' He gives a short laugh. 'But there is still a lot of work to do. We can't rule anything out until the whole manuscript has been translated.'

I then go for a walk in the Roman morning, whistling one of the tunes from *Les Misérables*. The pavements gleam like silver in the light drizzle. The city is just up, warm from sleep, and slow.

Last night, before we left the gentlemen's club, Luigi asked me to drop by his shop on my way to the Vatican. He had something he wanted to show me. Discreetly.

Stuart has already gone to the Vatican's not-quite-so-Secret Archives. His calm, British and slightly intoxicated gentleman's manners have been replaced by excitement and restless enthusiasm. He knows that we will soon be able to document that the Vikings penetrated into Egypt and that he will be able to write a detailed, empirical article and publish it in a reputable academic periodical. Vengeance is mine, says the Lord. *Mihi vindicta, ego retribuam, dicit Dominus.* I don't think that he would worry about pulverising his opponents on behalf of himself and the Lord.

3

The bell tinkles cheerfully as I enter the bookshop.

'*Momento, momento!*'

Luigi rolls round the corner with tired, blinking eyes and a napkin that is obviously not finished with breakfast yet.

He welcomes me with a firm handshake. 'Come, my friend, come!' He locks the door and invites me upstairs. 'Thank you for a lovely evening. I hope we didn't frighten you?'

The beautiful aria, '*Je crois entendre encore*', from Bizet's opera *The Pearl Fishers*, pours out of the loudspeakers. Luigi sits down on the sofa. With a contented sigh, he leans back. 'Beautiful, isn't it?' It takes a moment or two before I realise that he is talking about the opera duet. Tears well up in his good eye. 'Only music and women can make you feel this good.'

I imagine the kind of women that Luigi might attract.

'You wanted to show me something,' I prompt.

He turns towards me, and I feel as if he is staring at me with his blind eye.

'Last time you were here, you asked why Sheikh Ibrahim was interested in Asim,' he starts. 'I've been doing a bit of research. It seems that, during the war, one of the Vatican's trusted employees was actually selling copies and originals from the Vatican Archives. This dishonest servant had no doubt hoped to earn himself a small fortune, but he was of course caught, and the greater part of the material was traced and returned to the archives. However, unauthorised copies of the material continued to circulate among collectors and academics, and these documents – or, rather, copies – were eventually compiled into a collection that was called *The Vatican Papers*. The collection comprises copies of individual evangelical text fragments, some controversial Gnostic texts, several papal bulls about orthodoxy, and a collection of Egyptian texts, largely Coptic, which possibly included some of Asim's documents. *The Vatican Papers* quickly acquired an air of mystery in antiquarian circles. The collection disappeared in the 1950s, but then reappeared again at an illegal auction in Buenos Aires in 1974 – three years before your friend, Stuart, made his sensational discovery in Egypt. The whole collection was sold for one and a half million dollars. And can you guess who bought it?'

'The sheikh?'

'Correct. Sheikh Ibrahim.'

'Thank you, Luigi!' I get up to leave. I am impatient to get on with our search in the Vatican Archives. And to tell the truth, this information about the sheikh was no great surprise.

'But there's more . . .' Luigi lowers his voice. 'After our meeting in the club last night, one of the members held me back. He confided in me that he was in possession of a document fragment that is pretty badly damaged, but two of the symbols, ankh and *tiwaz*, are visible just by the torn edge. He doesn't know what the document is about. He bought the fragment, which was part of a collection that representatives of the Vatican seized in Greenland around 1450, at an illegal auction in Santiago in 1987.'

'Greenland?'

'Greenland.'

Luigi goes over to the bookshelves, takes out a version of Niccolò di Bernando dei Machiavelli's *De Principatibus* from 1532. He has hidden the document fragment in the middle of the book.

'My contact wondered if you would be interested in buying it.'

He was right when he said that the fragment was badly damaged, but I can still clearly see the ankh and the *tiwaz*. The paper has been ripped where the cross would have been.

'It's called the Skáholt fragment,' Luigi tells me.

The text is in Old Norse, and fully legible. It is a list from the Bishop of Skáholt of the gifts that the Icelandic bishop gave to the Norwegian Church in 1250.

'How did it end up in Iceland?'

'No one knows.'

According to the fragment, one of the gifts that the bishop sent was two carved wooden statues. An Icelandic woodcarver had been commissioned to make them by Thordur the Stammerer, Snorri's nephew.

The list describes one as St Lawrence Thomas and the other as St Lawrence Didymus.

I feel an electric shock go through my body.

Thomas was one of Jesus's twelve disciples. His full name was Judas Thomas Didymus.

Thomas means twins in Aramaic, and Didymus means twins in Greek.

I am speechless.

So two statues of St Lawrence were made! Somewhere in the world, there is a statue identical to the St Lawrence from Ringebu stave church. The whole thing was camouflaged in the annals by giving St Lawrence the double name of Thomas – *twin*! The hidden text under the paint on the Bible said:

> Just as the Virgin Mary held Jesus in her lap
> The belly holds the casket
> Praise be to Thomas!

The last sentence was a clever message to the Guardians that the casket is in the belly of the statue's twin.

'My contact suggested twenty-five thousand euros,' Luigi says.

My thoughts are already elsewhere. Luigi misinterprets my silence. 'I apologise. The demands of a seller. In our business, we are not academics or idealists who help each other. We are dealers. My colleague believes that you, or whoever you are working for, might be willing to pay that much.' He hesitates. 'If you're not interested, he will offer the fragment to Sheikh Ibrahim.' When he meets my eyes, he adds: '*Business.*'

I don't let on that I have already read and interpreted the text. Instead I say, truthfully, that twenty-five thousand euros is so much money that I would like to walk round the block while I confer with my employer.

Luigi lights a fat cigar, as if he were already celebrating a done deal.

<h1 style="text-align:center">4</h1>

I open the shop door, *ting-a-ling*, and go out into the narrow passage, down to Via del Governo Vecchio, where I find a phone box. First of all, I ring Øyvind. I quickly fill him in on the latest developments and ask him to find St Lawrence's double. 'Look everywhere! Churches, museums, castles, stately homes!'

Then I dial Professor Llyleworth's mobile phone number. He answers after three rings. I can hear him apologising and leaving a meeting. 'Bjørn! What's happened? Why did you just disappear from the Schimmer Institute? And what on earth are you doing in Egypt? I barely understood a word of what you said the last time you phoned.'

'I'm in Rome.'

I repeat everything that I had tried to convey through the cacophony of noise in Luxor – that we had fled the Schimmer Institute after the SIS had alerted Stuart that Sheikh Ibrahim's men were on their way, and about the journey through the desert to Egypt and then on to Rome.

Silence.

'Professor?'

'Is Stuart with you now?'

There was something about his voice.

'He's at the Vatican, looking through the archives. I am visiting an antiquarian who wants twenty-five thousand euros for a text fragment that says that St Lawrence has a doppelgänger, a twin. Do you think. . .'

'Bjørn, listen to me. And listen carefully.'

'Yes.'

'The SIS did not ring Stuart Dunhill.'

A bus rumbles by in a cloud of black diesel fumes.

'We never warned Stuart that Sheikh Ibrahim had sent his people to the Schimmer Institute.'

'But . . .'

'All this is news to us. We know nothing about the movements of Sheikh Ibrahim and his men.'

'Maybe someone else . . .'

'Diane and I are the only ones who have contact with Stuart. No one else. I would have known if Diane had rung.'

Something cold slithers over me. A pedestrian bumps into me with an irritated grunt.

'Bjørn, are you there?'

'Yes?'

'Did you hear what I said?'

'But . . .'

'Neither Diane nor I have phoned Stuart Dunhill!'

'Why would he lie?'

Professor Llyleworth sighs. 'We should have warned you. Some people at the Schimmer Institute suspected that Stuart Dunhill was maybe working for Sheikh Ibrahim.'

'Jesus!'

'The SIS has never believed the rumour. There was never anything to substantiate it. They had no proof. Nothing! It was basically just a vague feeling that something wasn't quite right. The SIS chose to support him. To back him up. We deemed the rumour to be a malicious hangover from the seventies. . .'

'. . . and you sent me straight into his arms.'

'Bjørn, if we had known . . .' He stops. 'You have to leave Rome. As quickly as possible. If Stuart is working with the sheikh, you can be certain that Hassan and the others are there waiting. Somewhere behind the scenes. Even if you can't see them.'

'They are here. I know that they're here.'

'You have to leave!'

'Why are they letting me just carry on doing my own thing? Why is Stuart pretending that we're partners?'

'Because they're using you. Stuart was being so ingratiating because he wanted you to share everything you know and find out with him. They are just using you. Leave, Bjørn! Take the express train to Milan and catch a plane from there. I'm sure they're watching the airports in Rome.'

'The text fragment. Twenty-five thousand euros. What should I do?'

'Buy it! And then get the hell out of Rome. Do you hear?'

The Patient (I)

1

THE SHOP is empty.

'Luigi?'

He doesn't answer.

I call again, impatiently. 'Luigi?'

My eyes steal along the elegant book spines, in the way
that men like me look at women.

A sound.

'Luigi? Are you upstairs?'

2

Luigi is still sitting on the sofa up in the flat. At first glance it
looks as though he is dozing and his head has fallen back. His
cigar is lying in his lap and has gone out.

'Luigi?'

Then I realise that half of the back of his head is
missing.

The floor behind the sofa is splattered with something
that was once Luigi.

I gasp and stagger back.

The human body loses much of its divine mystery when,
for whatever reason, there is a hole in it. When the brain is
revealed by a bullet wound, it is hard to imagine that the
yellowish-grey mush once held thoughts about the universe,
love for a woman and delight over *Je crois entendre encore*.

On a saucer in front of him, beside Machiavelli's twisted masterpiece, the document fragment has been reduced to ash.

My knees are shaking.

Hassan.

Hassan has been here.

I can just see it. The henchmen must have come into the shop, *ting-a-ling*, just after I left to make my phone calls. Luigi probably shouted '*momento*' before coming down to meet them. *Si, signori?* Then he saw that they had guns and that they had locked the door. They forced him back up the spiral staircase and on to the sofa, threatening him. *Sit down, you bloody Quasimodo!* Hassan had asked what *Bjorn Belto* wanted. Or maybe whether that confounded *Belto* had tried to sell Luigi the Thingvellir Scrolls. Luigi had shaken his head. He must have realised where all this would end. He had coolly and calmly taken a final puff on his cigar, before placing the lit end on the fragile document, which must have flared up like dry cigarette paper.

Luigi must have known that the Skáholt fragment was important, and his final act in this world was to ensure that it did not fall into the hands of the sheikh.

'Mr Belto.'

I freeze. I am so utterly rigid that a doctor would probably diagnose paralysis. My feet are each standing in a bucket of lead. I know that I should turn round. But I can't. It feels as if my body has been cast in fast-drying, reinforced concrete.

Finally the paralysis lets go of me. I creak as I turn towards the voice.

There are two of them. They are sitting on a divan that is half hidden by the dining table, which is full of precarious piles of books.

They have been waiting for me.

I have not seen them before. Arabs. Both dressed in elegant suits. Both of them have the smug look of men who have an advantage. They are both leaning back, comfortably.

The sheikh's musketeers.

'The boss is starting to lose patience,' one of them says in broken English. *The boss.*

'He wants the manuscript,' says the other.

'Now!'

I am so frightened that I play dumb quite naturally. 'Manuscript?'

'The Thingvellir Scrolls,' says the first one.

'How much was Luigi Fiacchini prepared to pay?'

'There's been a misunderstanding . . .'

'Where are they?'

Just then I realise that I am still standing by the banister where the alarm button is installed in the post.

'*Where?*'

My hand slides along the carving until I feel the button under my fingertip.

'I don't have them here,' I say, as I press the alarm.

I thought it would be a silent alarm. One that alerted the police discreetly. But no. Only now do I realise why Luigi hadn't dared to press the alarm.

A siren starts to howl. Down on the ground floor there is a tremendous rattling.

The two Arabs jump to their feet. Fortunately neither of them realises that it was me who set off the alarm.

'Hurry,' one shouts, and pushes me down the spiral staircase. Too fast. They push me in front of them, my feet and the steps out of synch; I am being swallowed by the stairs, something is going to happen. The moment that I see that a grille has come down in front of the door, I lose my footing.

I try to keep myself standing, but fall awkwardly. A flash of pain hurtles through me as my foot hits the floor at a strange angle.

The bone breaks.

I scream with pain, horror and fear.

The Arabs impatiently lift me up by the jacket and haul me along with them. Like a sack of potatoes they pull me across the floor. I try to get up using my good leg.

Everything goes black.

I come round again almost immediately. The Arabs are pulling at the grille in front of the door, talking in loud voices.

Then suddenly they are outside. Two policemen. They must have parked up on the street, as the passage is too narrow for cars. None of us has heard the siren because of the howling alarm.

They look at us in astonishment. At me lying on the floor. At the two Arabs, who have each drawn a gun.

And then they disappear again.

A moment later, the infernal alarm stops. But now Rome is full of sirens.

I whimper. I can't stop myself.

3

For artists and printers, black is a colour. For physicists, it represents the *absence* of colour. It is said that we humans experience pain differently and that men could never cope with the pain of giving birth. I would have to agree. We can barely cope with a cold.

My leg is aching. It feels as if someone has driven an icicle through my foot, right up to my hip. I cry like a baby. I lose consciousness for short, blissful periods, but am pulled back by the pain and waves of nausea.

Outside, I can see policemen in commando uniforms. Some of them are watching us in mirrors on long, angled arms. The Arabs are having a heated discussion. They grab me by the arm and the legs of my trousers and lift me up. The pain is unbearable.

4

When I come to again, I am lying on Luigi's leather sofa, upstairs in the flat. A hungry jackal is gnawing at my leg.

Luigi has vanished. They have probably carried his body into the bedroom.

They have considerately put a pile of cushions under my broken leg. So they have at least a drop of decency in their unscrupulous bodies.

The telephone rings. They let it ring. For a long time.

In the end, one of them picks it up. *'Na'am!'* he roars into the receiver. He listens. 'We have a hostage,' he shouts, 'and we demand free passage to Leonardo da Vinci airport.' He listens again. His face darkens. He calls on a whole host of angry demons in Arabic and throws down the phone.

I disappear into the soothing fog of unconsciousness.

5

I open my eyes. My mouth is dry as the desert.

How much time has passed? Minutes? Hours? A stab of pain jolts up from my broken leg.

'Water,' I stammer. 'Water. Please.'

The Arabs are indifferent. Neither of them lifts a finger to get me water.

I cough. My tongue sticks to the roof of my mouth.

'Please, I'm thirsty!'
'Quiet!'
'Water, please!'
'Shut up!'

6

I groan.

I am on board a ship that is heaving through the waves. Up and down, up and down . . . The sea is a never-ending, rolling wave. I have been covered by a clammy, damp blanket that stinks of wet wool. My mouth tastes of rancid fat. Up and down, up and down . . . Pain and nausea are intertwined. Every shudder in the break brings up sweet, cloying sick. The bone-ends grind against each other. The ship lurches. Someone is sticking things into my leg; cutting, pinching, sawing, burning with a sharp intensity that is overwhelmed by a rounder, denser ache. My leg is pounding, exploding. The nerve endings all the way up to my thigh are on fire. My pulse is sharp and angry. My stomach convulses. Up and down, up and down . . .

One of the Arabs is talking on a mobile phone. I imagine that he's talking to Hassan. I'm glad he is not here. He would not have rested my leg on soft cushions. Quite the opposite, he would have clasped his great hands around the break and squeezed.

I retch.

The Arab hangs up. He says something to the other man. They look at me. Then straight away the mobile phone rings again. This time the other man answers. He is agitated. Short, angry outbursts replace questions and complaints. I think. I don't understand a word.

Then the phone rings. The police, I think. This time they don't answer.

7

My leg has ballooned. The swelling presses against the fabric of my trousers. Every cell, every fibre of my muscles, every bone, is pulsating. I am thirsty. I am sweating and shivering.

I think: God help me, it's agony, such incredible pain, such fucking unbelievable pain.

Dark.
Light.
Dark.

I slip into a semi-conscious state where the only thing that means anything is the pain.

How much time has passed? I have no idea, I have no notion of time: seconds, minutes and hours weave together into a meaningless web.

As I doze the oxygen is sucked out of the room. I am an astronaut floating around in space with empty oxygen tanks. I struggle wildly with the cable that is slipping out of my hand as I drift away from the spaceship.

Then: nothing.

8

I come to again with the feeling that some great weight is pressing me down into the sofa. I open my eyes. I rasp and gasp for air. My nose and mouth are full of fine sand and mortar. My lungs are being squeezed together by two tight steel bands. My tongue and mouth are stuck together.

I retch. Nothing comes up. Nothing other than dry sounds like those from a dying soldier.

'Water,' I rattle, 'water, water, water.'

But either they don't understand, or they don't care.

*

My mouth is wide open. It's easier to breathe.

Dark. Light. Dark . . .

9

The dark is shattered by sound.

Voices.

I open my eyes.

The Arab is speaking on his mobile phone. He's shouting.

Angry.

Trapped.

10

They have wrapped a white towel round the break.

And pulled it tight with a clothes hanger.

I feel dizzy. For one terrible moment I see that the towel is soaked in blood. An open wound, I think. I squint uneasily at the towel. It is white again. Not a spot of blood.

So I must have imagined it, I think, relieved, and lose consciousness again.

11

'He's dying,' the Arab shouts.

I open my eyes.

The Arab is on the phone again. He is looking at me as he speaks.

He's dying?

His words – in Arabic – bounce around in my head. I can't understand what he is saying. I don't speak Arabic. *He's dying*? I must have been dreaming.

You can't die of a broken leg, can you?

Water.
Water, please.
Please.
Water.

But they give me nothing.

12

Sounds filter in from outside, from another reality.
　　Boots running on cobblestones.
　　Electronic calling systems.
　　Growling police dogs.
　　Short, barking commands.

Water. Please.
　　Shut up! You just shut up!

Bård's Tale (II)

♀ ↑ †

'I say unto you, that likewise joy shall be in heaven
over one sinner that repenteth, more than over ninety
and nine just persons, which need no repentance.'
GOSPEL ACCORDING TO LUKE 15: 7

'But after thy hardness and impenitent heart
treasurest up unto thyself wrath against the day of
wrath and revelation of the righteous judgment of God.'
ROMANS 2: 5

W<small>HEN THE</small> westerly wind was blowing its worst, it could blow out the candle on the rickety desk that the monks had given him. One of the desk legs was slightly shorter than the rest. Or the three others were too long, he could never decide. Some weeks ago, he had wedged a piece of wood under the short leg, but the monks must have removed it when they swept the floor. The old man sat with his elbow on the desk and his chin in his hand. His eyes were half closed. From where he was sitting, he could hear the chanting in the cathedral in Rouen, clear as a bell. The priest's voice rose and fell . . .

EXTRACT FROM BÅRD'S TALE

. . . rolling slowly in waves like the great ocean or a field of corn in Norway in the late summer breeze. The echo lingered beneath the vaulted ceiling. The sun shone in through the window in shimmering, slanting columns. The priest fell silent. Someone coughed. Then, somewhere farther back in the church, the choir took over. The gentle beauty of their song was sensual. None of us understood the words and yet we were able to understand. I cannot explain. I drank in the unfamiliar smell of incense, sweet and acrid at once. A boy's high voice filled the church. The notes touched me deep inside. I remembered the boy whose head I had chopped off with one blow, the blood gushing forth.

The men around me had cheered and laughed. But here in the church in Rouen, it was hard to feel that pride again.

King Olav sat quietly on the hard wooden bench. He sat with his head bent in his hands, for a long time. The evening before he had confided in me that he missed his mother, Åsta. It was now many years since he last had seen her. Was she still alive? Had she given birth to more children? Olav was but a boy when he embraced his mother farewell and went on his first expedition. Now he was a fully grown man. A king. As we walked back from the church, Olav was distant and deep in thought. Several times I tried to strike up a conversation, but he only gave short answers and was uninterested. Without a word he retired to his room. To contemplate, he said. I remained in the hall, and watched him retreat before making my way to the duke's library. My father had taught me to read and write runes, and many of the parchments in the duke's collection were Old Norse. Song and written text have always given me great joy.

As always, the Egyptian Asim was in the library. We called him the Wise Man. Asim filled me with unease. Though I had fought many a battle with men who were bigger and stronger than he, I understood that the small Egyptian was ten times more dangerous. He had the wisdom of many gods and the magic of a sorcerer. This much I had learned as I became acquainted with him on board the *Sea Eagle* on our voyage from Egypt to Rouen.

Asim looked up. He was sitting bent over a desk with a quill in his hand. To his left, a scroll of the material they call papyrus, and in front a shining white, new parchment that he now filled with writing. 'You been to church?' he asked. The smell of incense still clung to my clothes. In the short time that he had been our prisoner, he had learnt our language. On the ship, he had spent much time with the coxswains and learnt the ways of navigation and seamanship.

He knew the stars in the sky to the smallest twinkle and had pointed to the *leiðarstjarna*, the Pole Star, which had another name in his language. 'The church is a beautiful temple,' Asim said. 'What are you writing?' I asked and nodded at the parchment scroll. Asim beckoned me. I hesitated before sitting down on the stool beside him. Asim said: 'Your king has granted me permission to copy the text that THE HOLY ONE took with him to the grave.' 'Do you really understand those strange, old symbols?' I asked. Asim laughed. 'I speak many languages,' he said. 'When I was five, I not only spoke my mother tongue, but also Hebrew and Aramaic. I later learnt Greek and Latin and many other tongues. And now I am learning your language! Young man,' Asim put his hand on my shoulder, 'without language you are nothing. With language, the world is yours.'

The mummy and the coffin were placed in a chapel close to Rouen. Ten of Olav's retainers watched the chapel day and night. Many of the Vikings had returned home in their ships, laden with treasure. Others stayed in Rouen with the king. Each morning, Asim made the long walk from the duke's palace to the chapel to see that all was well. The treasures and riches from the tomb were still stored in the holds on our ships in the harbour, well wrapped and guarded. But not even the most greedy and stupid robber in Normandy would dare steal from us – even had they known what treasures were hidden on board. The king was secretive. The relic had a holy power so great that no others must know of our raid or what we took with us. No verses were to be composed. I reminded him that our men might become loose-tongued when they drank in the inns and kept the company of women, but Olav was not concerned. 'Men will always brag,' said the king. 'No one believes a sailor. But verses and sagas have greater powers. They live longer. No one must know where we have been and what we have stolen.' And so it was.

The weeks passed. The king sat for hours and hours in the company of Duke Richard. The duke had been baptised and worshipped the White Christ. Olav too started to seek this new god. For those of us close to him, it was a sad time. The proud Viking in him was forced to retreat. The Olav that we knew from the battlefield struggled in vain to be set free. The king had long dialogues with the duke, and the archbishop and monks in the abbeys and seminaries. They talked of the Almighty God, and his son, Jesus Christ, of Christian justice and the holy book they called the Bible. It was during this time that my interest in verse and song was awakened. While Olav was being saved by the duke, I was inspired by Asim and the art of storytelling. Olav was so wrapped up in his new faith that the White Christ overshadowed his devotion to his squire and friend. King Olav was baptised in the name of White Christ. Richard's own bishop, his brother Robert, gave the king the sacraments. Asim and I watched the ceremony from the first bench. Olav wished that I too should be baptised, but I hesitated and said that I was not ready.

The day we departed from Rouen, King Olav and Duke Richard stood for a long time on the quay, holding one another by the hand as they talked. In parting, the king went down on one knee and kissed the duke's hand. Thousands of Normans had gathered on the banks of the Seine to see the Viking fleet pass when we caught the wind and sailed for the sea. The sea . . . I could not hold back my laughter when I saw Asim's sorry, seasick face. 'This is not weather,' I told him, 'just a good breeze to stretch the sails that have lain idle so long.' If he found this hard to stomach, then he should have been with us on the Norwegian Sea in the autumn storms.

The longship pitched down into the troughs between the waves with a thump that made the timbers creak. The spray rose high in the air and then fell on us again, freezing cold. The salt water ran off the dragonhead on the prow. The men cheered with glee. Again I had to smile. They were so glad finally to be at sea once more! The long, dark spell spent in Rouen had started to fray more nerves than just mine, and out here in the waves and wind, we finally felt we were alive again.

In England, we entered the service of King Ethelred and once more joined forces with Thorkell the Tall. King Sweyn Forkbeard and his Danish army had taken land from King Ethelred, who had massacred Danes who were settled there. We spent two summers fighting in England, before Olav sold a small share of his bounty, richly rewarded his remaining men and granted them furlough. Some settled in England as wealthy men. Others sailed home in their Viking ships. Two to three hundred of the most loyal warriors remained with the king as his retainers. Olav sold the *Sea Eagle* to buy two merchant ships and in the autumn we sailed north. The two merchant ships were laden with gold, silver, precious stones and the treasures from Egypt. After a tremendous storm that blew for a day and night, Olav and I once more stood at the prow of our ship, but this time we looked north. The ships lurched through the rough seas. They were shorter and broader than our longships and lay heavier in the water. We would soon see Norway on the horizon. It was hard to believe. We had been gone many years.

Olav had persuaded four bishops to accompany him to Norway to support his mission to Christianise the country: Grimkell, Sigurd, Rudolf and Bernhard. They came now in a group to speak with the king. 'My lord King,' said Bishop Grimkell, in a deep bow, casting his eye at me. Some moments passed before Olav understood his intent. Then he spoke: 'Bishop Grimkell, Bård is my confidant. All that I hear, he can hear too.' 'As my lord wishes,' replied the bishop, and then related that they had spoken with Asim in a language called Latin. 'He is,' the bishop said, 'a high priest in his own land.' Olav said that he knew this to be true. The bishop then recounted that Asim claimed that the mummy was a sleeping god. 'An idol?' the king wanted to know, full of fear, as he was intent on following the ten commandments that Duke Richard had taught him. Bishop Grimkell raised a hand to stop him. 'To the contrary, your Highness,' he said. 'Asim has told us of the sect that has guarded the mummy for two and a half centuries, and we do not believe that Asim knows who the mummy truly is.' 'And do you?' the king enquired. 'My lord, we believe so.' The wind caught the king's long, fair hair and teased it. 'So, who is he, then?' King Olav asked . . .

He was a friend of the shadows. In the cool shadows of late summer, he would wrap himself in his woollen cape, making himself invisible to the monks who hurried by, busy with their many tasks. He would sit without moving for a long, long time – hidden in the shadows – while he cast his mind back to the years of his youth, so long ago; those years free from worry spent in the company of the king, when death was a promise but not yet a threat. When the sun's journey across the sky drove him from his sanctuary of shadows, and the sunlight plagued his eyes like a shower of sand, he would seek a new spot in the shadows or return to his cell, where he would bend over his manuscript on the desk and listen to the waves crashing against the cliffs and breaking on the rocky shore below.

PART III

Journey to Vinland

♀ ↑ †

'Too near to the nose said the peasant, when his eye
was knocked out.'

SNORRI

'When I am dead, then bury me in the sepulchre
wherein the man of God is buried; lay my bones
beside his bones.'

I KINGS 13: 31

'For him a golden shrine is made,
For him whose heart was ne'er afraid.'

SKALDIC VERSE

The Patient (II)

1

DAWN.

A trickle of light filters through the curtains into Luigi's flat.

The pain is dull and unending.

With half-open eyes I look at my hand, which is quivering and shaking.

The two Arabs are dozing. One is sitting in a chair beside me, and the other is lying on the divan.

They have talked on the phone all night. In Arabic on their mobile phones and in English on the landline.

The Arab on the divan starts to snore.

I fall asleep or faint. It is hard to tell.

Outside, a new day dawns over Rome.

2

The explosion is so powerful that it overturns the sofa.

The pressure sprays a shower of glass splinters into the flat. The sofa protects me. My leg feels as if someone has twisted it round a couple of times.

The police enter the flat through the smashed window. They must have used ladders or ropes. I can't see them from where I am lying, semi-conscious behind the sofa. But I can hear deep voices shouting 'Polizia!' There is a series of shots.

I don't move.

One of the Arabs screams something or other. I don't know what. But from his voice I can tell that he is giving himself up. The police throw themselves over him. His gun and his head hit the floor. The police shout commands in Italian.

At that moment, three policemen in full commando gear look over the edge of the overturned sofa. They are wearing helmets, visors, bullet-proof jackets and holding machine guns with lights on them. '*Ostaggio!*' one of them shouts. '*Via liberal!*' shouts another. One of them kneels down beside me. '*Dottore!*' he roars. '*Immediatamente!*'

The main entrance downstairs is blown in by another explosion. The grating is pulled off. I hear steps thumping up the spiral staircase. Luigi's flat is full of people. Several policemen. Ambulance personnel in red high-visibility jackets. Two doctors.

The doctors talk to me in English. Where does it hurt? What have they done to me? What is my name? When was I born? When they have the answers, they give me an injection of some kind of painkiller and intravenous fluid.

The claws of pain start to ease off. The medicine wraps me in a euphoric feeling of well-being. In my head I listen to '*Je crois entendre encore*' by Bizet.

When they have stabilised the break and got me on to a stretcher, I see the two Arabs.

One is standing with his back to me, in handcuffs.

The other is lying dead in a pool of blood.

They have a bit of trouble getting the stretcher down the spiral stairs. They manage to lift it over the banisters and tack their way down. Safely down, they open up the trolley with wheels, roll me out of the bookshop and down the passage to where all the emergency vehicles are waiting. A flock of doves takes wing. A gust of wind hurtles down the narrow alley. Somewhere near by a church bell strikes.

3

I spend the next twenty-four hours recuperating in hospital, in a comfortable, drug-induced haze. The doctors have put a cast on my leg. Fortunately, the break is not as serious as the pain had led me to believe.

There are two armed policemen in the corridor outside my room.

A swarm of identical and humourless whippersnappers from the *polizia* come to question me. They all look exactly the same. They are all called the same. They ask the same questions. It seems that every single department in the police and intelligence service has to send their own detective inspector, who comes equipped with an interpreter, video recorder and an astonishing lack of understanding as to why something so indescribably tedious as old parchments and rustling paper documents could be worth killing for.

I tell them what I know.

4

Professor Llyleworth comes to visit the next day. He looks like some rich uncle who has travelled all the way from his estate in the British countryside, in his coat and hat.

It takes me a couple of hours to tell him about everything that has happened since the SIS sent me to the Schimmer Institute. When I mention the Lewinski Collection, his face lights up. He tells me that he has just employed a lady who will be able to help me. Laura Kocherhans is a historian and academic with a PhD from

Yale. Before she was headhunted by the SIS for the head office in London, where she now has the title Chief Manuscript Researcher, she was deemed to be the best manuscript detective in the Library of Congress in Washington, DC.

When Professor Llyleworth has gone, I sleep for a couple of hours. I am woken by the mobile phone that the professor left for me.

Laura Kocherhans' voice sounds slightly nasal on the phone, in an American way, but has a soft resonance that is both vulnerable and charming.

'Of course we can find the Lewinski Collection,' she says after we have spoken for some time.

'How can you be so sure?'

'The problem with people who never find what they are looking for is that they never look hard enough!'

A woman after my own heart.

Laura tells me that scholars do not have a complete overview of all the private collections in the world, which undoubtedly contain unknown manuscripts of great cultural and historical value.

'How do you search for a collection that has disappeared?'

'In the same way that *you* search for things, I assume. With intelligence and imagination. And, if necessary, bribes,' she adds, with a delightful laugh.

'Where are you going to begin?'

'Dresden. And then the state archives in Berlin.'

I stay in bed, resting my leg for a few more days.

When they send me home, it is with two crutches that I have to pay for, and my leg in plaster.

The Monks' Island

NORWAY

1

BANKS OF fog blow in from the sea and roll across the rugged terrain. It is hard to imagine that the sun is actually shining somewhere high above us. Through the swirling fog, I catch a glimpse of a square stone tower sticking defiantly up from the ruins of an abbey.

Holding on to my crutches, I stand outside the temporary barracks that have been positioned between the abbey and the jetty. Some weeks have passed now since I limped off the plane from Italy. My broken leg is almost healed and my suspension has been lifted. The investigating committee concluded – with a great deal of reservation and under considerable political pressure, it has to be said – that my misdemeanour in excavating the tomb at Lyse Abbey would not cost me my job.

We have been working on the preparations for a full excavation both day and night for two weeks now. The people of Selje and the local construction workers who put together the barracks think that we are restoring the ruins of St Alban's Church.

Norwegian, Swedish, Danish, English, French, Italian and German archaeologists, historians and geologists scurry between the tents and the barracks. The project is jointly financed by the Ministry of Culture and Church Affairs and the SIS. There are nearly a hundred specialists involved.

I have seen neither hide nor hair of Hassan and the sheikh's men. But naturally, that does not mean that they are not watching. They say that even the faint movement of a butterfly's wings can generate a hurricane. And in line with this charming postulate from chaos theory, once we had learned that there were two wooden statues, thanks to the detail in the Skáholt fragment that Luigi burnt before he was killed, everything fell into place.

Øyvind managed to find St Lawrence Thomas's identical twin, Didymus, after carefully searching through a handful of archives, registers and glossy picture books. The wooden statue has stood patiently waiting in Borgund stave church in Lærdal for 725 years. The congregation at Borgund were given the wooden statue of Didymus by their fellow Christians at Ringebu in 1280.

The front of the statue slotted on to the back and was locked in place by eight wooden pegs under his tunic and up his sleeves. In the hollow of his belly, we found a casket covered in runes:

> Eirik the GUARDIAN hid this casket in Urnes Church
> 100 summers after the Death of Holy Olav.
>
> Bård the GUARDIAN moved the casket to Flesberg
> 150 summers after the Death of Holy Olav.
>
> Vegard the GUARDIAN took the casket to Lom
> 200 summers after the Death of Holy Olav.
>
> Sigurd the GUARDIAN hid the casket in St Lawrence
>   Didymus' belly
> And moved the statue from Ringebu Church to Borgund
>   Church
> 250 summers after the Death of Holy Olav.

In the casket was a coded document that Øyvind and Terje deciphered with the help of a copy of the rune wheel.

Ragnvald the GUARDIAN wrote these secret words
as ordered by Asim
five summers after King Olav's return

Seek the tomb in the depths of the cave
where the Holy Virgin and martyrs
drifted ashore and received God's mercy

Here rest the remains of the HOLY ONE
from eternity to eternity

Trym the GUARDIAN wrote these words
25 summers after the Death of Holy Olav

The Wiseman Asim
lies in peace with St Olav
by the side of the HOLY ONE
and guards him for all eternity.

St Sunniva's Cave.
Not the Dollstein Cave, as everyone thought.
The burial chamber is at the far end of St Sunniva's Cave on the island of Selja in outer Nord Fjord, in the county of Sogn and Fjordane – the bishop's see for the Gulating assembly until 1170.

I hear birds crying in the mist. That is, I certainly hope that it is birds. There is activity all around me. Electronic signals bleep and peep in the walkie-talkies. Several policemen are stationed around the island. Their presence affords a certain security in the event that Hassan is sitting hiding behind a boulder. Following the murder of the priest at Ringebu and events in Rome, the police have given the case high priority. The Norwegian, Icelandic and Italian police are now working together closely through Interpol. Ragnhild is leading the Norwegian investigation.

The abbey is situated on a piece of flat ground at the base of a steep mountainside, and is very exposed to the weather. It once resembled a medieval castle, with solid walls and a tower. The Benedictine abbey was founded in the twelfth century, but even before then, there was a smaller, wooden cloister here. The ruins of St Sunniva Church cling to the mountainside like an eagle's eyrie, about fifty metres up, and just above them is the entrance to the cave, which once served as a simple chapel to St Michael.

St Sunniva's Cave . . .

St Sunniva was an Irish princess who had to flee a heathen suitor who wanted to invade her country and life, towards the end of the tenth century. Together with a handful of God-fearing men, women and children, Sunniva cast off in three boats without rudders, sails or oars. They drifted on the wind and sea currents over to Selja, where they took refuge in the caves. The pagan idol worshippers on the mainland viewed the strangers with suspicion. Håkon Jarl sent armed men out to the island to fight what he believed were warriors. Sunniva and her companions ran and hid in the cave and prayed to God for salvation. And, according to the myth, God buried Sunniva beneath a rock fall, rather than stopping her attackers. That's the way it goes. In the years that followed, farmers and sailors witnessed a strange light shining from the cave. When King Olav Tryggvasson and Bishop Sigurd went to the island of miracles, they found Sunniva's body intact in the cave, along with other sweet-smelling bones, skulls and skeletons. And it was the island of Selja where King Olav Haraldsson first landed some years later, when he returned to Christianise Norway, his home country.

St Sunniva's Cave . . .

Was the story of St Sunniva made up to mask the fact that there is a tomb at the back of the cave?

2

The fog lifts around midday.

I am sitting in one of the project management huts, studying the latest photographs of the excavation site. The cave has been damaged by rock falls and landslides. We have removed several tons of stones from behind the stone altar, to reveal a vertical wall made from roughly hewn rocks and mortar. In the middle of the wall, an arched doorway has been filled in with smaller rocks.

We are going to break through this sealed entrance tomorrow at eleven o'clock sharp.

I hear footsteps approaching and put the pictures down. She appears, framed by the light in a heavenly glow, for all the world like a goddess who has descended to us common mortals with the promise of eternal life in Paradise. But it is only Astrid, bringing me a cucumber-and-tomato sandwich. 'Are you excited?' she asks. She is a professor and works at the Antiquities Collection. She is also one of the country's leading experts in Norwegian abbey ruins.

I feel a tingling inside.

3

The alarm starts to shriek.

I am suddenly wide awake and sit bolt upright in my camp bed. The remnants of a strange dream that I can't quite remember still linger. I fumble for my glasses before turning on the light. It is half past two in the morning.

Outside, there is a lot of shouting and barking.

I get dressed quickly, grab my crutches and hobble out into the night. All the outside lights were automatically turned on when the alarm went off. The site is bathed in mist and a woolly light. The air is cold and damp. Waves break on the shore.

I hump my way over to the office hut, as quickly as I can on crutches. Several people have already gathered and are talking excitedly with two of the hired security staff, who relate that a third security guard is lying unconscious on the steep, narrow stone steps that lead up to the cave.

Someone manages finally to turn off the alarm.

In the same instant, a motorboat roars off.

Over the next hour or so we manage to piece together what has happened, but that does not make things any clearer.

Someone has forced their way into the cave. The sledge-hammers that they left behind indicate that they intended to break through the doorway and into the burial chamber that we assume is behind it.

The security guard who ran up to check was knocked to the ground.

He comes to, befuddled, as we carry him down to the barracks, where we clean and dress a cut on his forehead. He can vaguely remember being hit. But he doesn't know who they were.

The next morning, three colleagues are missing.

Michael Rennes-Leigh from the School of Archaeology at Oxford University, Paul-Henri de Chenonceau from the Institut de Papyrologie at the Sorbonne and Paolo Baigenti from the University of Rome have disappeared.

I didn't know any of them particularly well. They largely kept themselves to themselves. None of their specific responsibilities would require them to be in the cave. And certainly not in the middle of the night. With sledgehammers. All three have somehow managed to infiltrate the excavation. And presumably, they all work for the sheikh.

According to the local police, the boat they escaped in is now moored in Selje. And the hire car has gone.

When we check with the universities to which they are

affiliated, it transpires that they are all recently appointed fellows. And their research posts are all financed by the same foundation in Abu Dhabi in the United Arab Emirates.

4

We start to knock through the wall at eleven o'clock.

The cave is damp and cold. In frozen anticipation, we form a semicircle around the musclemen who are going to break down the wall. A flock of journalists and a TV crew are waiting outside in the drizzle.

The wall is thick and solid and not very cooperative. But eventually a stone is loosened, and then one more. We lever out the smaller stones with a crowbar, to make the opening big enough. Someone puts a working light through.

When I was little, I used to tear at the wrapping paper on my Christmas presents with my small, pale fingers, my body tingling with anticipation that *this* present would be better, more surprising, than any other gift I had ever received.

When I crawl through the opening and hold up the lamp in front of me to illuminate the darkness, I am finally rewarded.

Astrid pushes my crutches through behind me. Everything is quiet. I stand up and brush the dirt from my knees. I find myself, breathless, at the top of some steps.

Nothing, absolutely nothing, has prepared us for what is waiting behind the wall.

The Cave

1

IN THE dim light I get an idea of the size of the tomb. Two rows of granite columns cast shadows on the walls. A beard of moss and roots is pushing through a crack in the rock. A slight rush of air brushes my skin.

Centuries of darkness are pierced by the beams of the torches of those following behind me.

The chamber is full of Egyptian treasures.

Under the layers of dirt, dust and cobwebs lie splendid antiques. Chests, urns, caskets. Gold, silver and precious stones. Candlesticks. Dishes. Oil lamps. Decorated wall panels. Ornaments. Sceptres. Polished jewels. Diamonds. Rubies. Sapphires. Emeralds.

Statues of Egyptian gods and pharaohs stand lined up as if waiting patiently, in a side room. I recognise several of them. Anubis. Thutmose. Amenhotep. Ramses. Horus. Akhenaten. Thoth.

I am overwhelmed. The tears well up.

Someone slaps me on the shoulder. I bite my lip as I lay my hand on the pillar by the stairs. The smoothed surface is ice cold. I am so moved that I stay where I am, leaning on my crutches, staring into the room. Astrid crawls through the opening in the wall behind me. 'Oh my dear God!' Just like me, she stays standing where she is with her mouth open, looking into the dimly lit room.

For a thousand years, this burial chamber has remained hidden behind tons of granite, behind a wall so thick that it was almost part of the mountain.

2

With the utmost care, I put my crutches down in front of me and descend the stairs step by step. The others follow with their work lamps and torches and exclamations.

There are two plinths in the middle of the pentangular room, carved from the rock.

One of them is empty.

On the other stands the Olav Reliquary – Holy Olav's coffin.

Without a word I turn and exchange looks with Astrid. Her lips are trembling.

I approach the reliquary with great reverence. Numerous diversionary tactics have ensured that the coffin has been left in peace for nearly a thousand years. I stop. Holding both my crutches in one hand, I carefully wipe away some of the thick layer of dust.

A few of us lift off the outer casket, which is bottomless and protects the silver coffin.

The silver fixtures on the outer wooden casing are black with age, under the layers of dust. Under the casing, the silver is bedecked with gold and jewels.

The silhouette is exactly as I remember it from the drawings in history books. The coffin is two metres long and about one metre high and wide. The lid is shaped like a roof; the gables are extended with a dragonhead at each end.

So I just stand there admiring the Olav Reliquary.

When the coffin has been cleaned and restored, it

will be world famous. Pictures of it will flicker across TV screens in the USA and Australia, Japan and Burkina Faso. It will grace the front pages of *Newsweek* and *El País*. The Olav Reliquary that contains the remains of a sanctified Viking king is an archaeological sensation.

More and more colleagues come in behind us. They all talk in hushed voices, as you do in a church.

'The Ark of the Covenant!' someone gasps.

'Leave it out!' I bark. 'It's the Olav Reliquary!'

Someone bursts out in excited laughter.

My eyes move from the Olav Reliquary to the empty stone plinth beside it.

The mummy's plinth? Where is the coffin?

I limp into one of the side rooms. Here there are two smaller coffins lying on a single plinth.

The name *Barðr* has been carved in runes on the lid of one of the coffins. On the other is the name *Asim*.

Asim . . .

I take a step back, overwhelmed.

Asim, the Egyptian . . . The high priest of the Amon-Ra cult. So it is all true. Snorri's references. Stuart's theories. Our wild guesses. Everything we have suspected, but not known for certain.

Everything is true.

A while later, we push the stone lids of the coffins to one side. In each coffin there is a skeleton in the remains of rotted strips of linen. Someone has tried to embalm and mummify the two bodies.

There are even more urns and pots with gold jewellery, precious stones and decorative artefacts lining the walls of the side room.

3

The floodlights bathe the burial chamber in an intense, white light.

Only now do I see that the walls and ceiling are decorated. Behind the layers of dust, I can make out inscriptions written in hieroglyphics, runes and Roman letters. I see faded murals of Egyptian, Christian and Old Norse gods, figures and symbols – a holy blend of mythology, astrology and religion. Jesus looking up to the almighty Odin from a cross, shaped like an ankh. The Midgard Serpent twisting round the earth, which contains a pentagram. Amon-Ra enthroned at the gates to the underworld, where Satan towers in all his majesty. Yggdrasil, the world tree, casts its shadow over the Pyramid of Cheops. Moses parting a turbulent sea with the help of the sword Mimung. The fantastic decorations weave together the Old Norse belief system with Christianity, Judaism, Egyptian mythology and a dash of astrology.

It is possible to read some of the texts. They talk of a sleeping god, of Moses and Holy Olav, of the language of the stars and the journey to the end of the world.

4

For well over a week, I work in the burial chamber from early morning until late at night.

We take photographs, make films and copies of the murals. We measure the cave. We draw it from various perspectives. We register and mark each artefact, each pot, each stone.

I happily dedicate myself to this archaeological work and try to forget that there are men called Hassan and Sheikh Ibrahim al-Jamil ibn Zakiyy ibn Abdulaziz al Filastini in the world. The island and the cave are being guarded round the clock by the local police and a private security company.

Scholars, journalists and TV crews from all over the world come to visit the tomb. We take them in, in groups, every afternoon. As I am wont to spend rainy Sundays in the company of the National Geographic Channel, I am particularly helpful when a crew from the American TV channel comes. They are going to make an hour-long documentary. CNN broadcast live from the entrance to the cave. The Italian channel Rai is planning a programme with the working title *The Grave in the Grotto*, and the Arabic TV channel al-Jazeera is coming tomorrow.

Late one evening I get a phone call from Ragnhild. She has just received a report that one of Hassan's men was arrested during yet another break-in at Thrainn's house. The crook had rented a house at Raudavatn in Reykjavik through a Saudi property management agency in Paris. Three lawyers from London have been sent to support Iceland's most prestigious law firm.

I try to ring Thrainn, but get no reply.

5

We transport the Olav Reliquary from Selja to Bergen by helicopter. The van that takes it from Flesland Airport into a workshop at the University of Bergen is given a police escort.

It takes two days to dismantle the casket.

Under the outer casing is the jewel-bedecked silver casket that Olav's son, Magnus Olavsson, made for his father. The lid and sides are inlaid with gold. Some of the panels are reliefs with religious motifs. The whole thing is decorated with jewels and polished crystals.

With the greatest care, we loosen the hinges and clasps

that keep the roof-shaped lid attached to the silver casket. The four men carefully lift the lid off. The four walls are held together with hinges.

Inside is the original wooden coffin.

The wood is covered with cloth that has long since rotted, whereas the wood itself is solid and hard. The lid has been nailed to the coffin with sixty-six copper nails.

We take them out one by one, so that the lid can be eased off and removed.

Holy Olav's body has been mummified.

The mummy is partially covered with an embroidered cloth. He is resting with his hands crossed over his chest. In his hands, the king is holding a gold sceptre. It is formed into an ankh at one end and the rune *tiwaz* at the other. And around midway along the staff, there is a crossbar.

Ankh, *tiwaz* and the cross.

For several minutes we stand in silence looking at the remains of the holy king. Outside, the wind has picked up and the leaves on the trees rustle in the gusts.

The Lewinski Collection

THERE IS a knock on the office door.

I am back in Oslo. I have spent several days going through reports from the various professional bodies working on the excavation of the cave and the remains.

I throw an irritated glance at the door, and sit tight in the hope that whoever it is will go away.

The Guardians moved the Egyptian mummy from the cave at Selja, as they were frightened that the Vatican envoys might find it, possibly to a temporary hiding place in a stave church, and then on to Iceland. Here the mummy was guarded by Snorri, and then Thordur the Stammerer. But we don't know who took over the responsibility when Thordur was summoned to the king in Norway. Why was the coffin moved? And where to? And why did they leave the treasure and the Olav Reliquary behind in the cave?

There is another knock on the door. Harder this time.

I have cocooned my persecution paranoia in confident indifference. I have won. The sheikh has lost. The legions of killers, spies and hidden pursuers have gone back home with Hassan, disappointed and with their tails between their legs. Cut down to size by a Norwegian associate professor of archaeology. For days now I have nurtured my delight in this with shameless smugness.

'Bjørn?' The door opens. 'It's me!'

Thrainn.

I embrace him with a touch more enthusiasm than a doctor of philosophy might expect from a lowly associate professor.

'I've been trying to call you,' he says.

'Sorry. I turned my mobile off. It was ringing constantly. What are you doing here?'

'I've got something with me that I think might be useful. Then I'm going to go up to Selja to have a look at this cave with my own eyes. You only get to experience this sort of thing once in a lifetime, if that.'

He has a large folder under his arm.

'A translation of the Bible manuscript?'

He shakes his head. 'They're still working on that. Very confusing. Parts of the text coincide with other old Bible versions and others don't at all. They haven't ruled out the possibility that it is a kind of "pirate" version, where some nitwit of a monk has added his own things to a copy of an existing Bible text.'

He opens the folder and takes out some enlarged photographs of a manuscript. 'I've had the interesting pages photographed to scale. Great quality! You can even see the unevenness in the density of the ink.'

'What is it?'

'The Flatey Book, otherwise known as *Codex Flatöiensis*. The largest, most beautiful and perhaps most important medieval manuscript from Iceland. Two hundred and fifty pages, illuminated and illustrated, on the finest vellum. The text was started in 1387 by . . .'

'Thrainn, why have you brought a copy with you?'

'Because the *Codex Flatöiensis* contains more than the other manuscripts. You'll find most of the Kings' Sagas here, such as the saga of Olaf Tryggvason and Holy Olav, but also other historical information. For instance, the Flatey Book contains various versions of the saga of Holy

Olav. Previously, historians believed Snorri's version to be the most accurate, but now we actually rely more on the Flatey Book. What I wanted to show you was this . . .' Thrainn leafs through the book. He stops. 'Here. *Grænlendinga Saga*. The saga of the Greenlanders.'

He points at the manuscript. In the margin, there are three beautifully illuminated symbols: ankh, *tiwaz* and the cross.

'This text in the margin has never been included in any of the copies or translations of the Flatey Book that were made later. It's the same with most manuscripts. If you go back to the original, you'll always find text that has been forgotten or overlooked.'

'What does it say?'

'Not very much. It's obvious that they didn't want any Tom, Dick or Harry to understand it. In summary, the text in the margin says that the Guardians moved the treasure to safety in Greenland in 1350.'

I don't say anything. The treasure must be the mummy and the manuscript scrolls.

Is there yet another burial chamber, in Greenland?

'At the end of the 900s, Greenland was colonised by Erik the Red, who was on the run, having been outlawed in both Norway and Iceland. The Norse colony thrived for several hundred years, in fragile harmony with the native Inuits, but the situation gradually deteriorated. The last Norwegian merchant ship left Greenland in 1368 and the last Christian bishop there died ten years later. According to the saga, the Norse colony disappeared during the first half of the fifteenth century. Some people believe those who remained there were taken prisoner by pirates and sold as slaves. Others think that they sailed south to the Canaries, where they established a tall, fair-haired, blue-eyed Guanches tribe. Some believe that they gradually sailed home to Iceland and Norway. Some think they just died out. And some think that they sailed on to Vinland in the west . . .'

'That would explain all the other references to Greenland that we've come across,' I say.

'There's a reference here to the Black Death. In 1350, the Icelanders were terrified of the plague that had ravaged Norway and Europe. The Black Death never actually made it to Iceland, but you can imagine the panic.'

'So, it was fear of the plague that made the Guardians flee to Greenland.'

'It would seem so.'

'And the rest of the treasure is still there?'

'Oh no!'

Thrainn takes out some other photographs. 'Something has been added here in the margin, in the Icelandic *Skáholtsbók* from the fifteenth century. The text seems to indicate that the treasure was protected by a Norse settlement on Greenland for a hundred years, until around 1450, when some settlers were massacred. Archaeological finds of skeletons, weapons and equipment at the site could indicate that the attackers came from southern Europe. Perhaps the Vatican. But look here . . .' He points at a paragraph. '. . . It says here that a group escaped and sailed to the country over the horizon, which is an interesting formulation. It appears in several other texts from the period, and is then referring to Vinland, the new strange country in the west.'

'In 1450?'

'It was another fifty years before Columbus stumbled on the Caribbean islands.'

'I found a reference to fighting on Greenland in 1450 in the Vatican. As far as I can remember, it also said that some of the barbarians – who may have been the Norwegian and Icelandic Guardians – managed to escape. And fifty years later, Christopher Columbus's brother was given a letter by an unknown group of people on the island of Hispaniola to take back to Europe. The Guardians.'

'Do you have the letter?'

'We're looking for it.'

'The waters around Norway, Scotland, Iceland and Greenland were visited by several southern European expeditions in this period. The Pope's men were very familiar with the waters following expeditions in the 1360s. Christopher Columbus was actually up here in the north, but only as an ordinary sailor, barely a hundred years later. Perhaps it was here that he got the idea to sail to the country in the west.'

'So the mummy was taken from Iceland to Greenland, and a hundred years later was transported from Greenland to a Norse colony in Vinland.'

'It would appear so.'

2

I have an appointment with the doctor at two o'clock, to take the plaster cast off. My leg feels as light as a feather without it. But I'm scared that someone might bash into it. I'm very wary of pain. My doctor says that I'm a wimp. I don't know whether she is teasing me or whether she means it.

Laura – the SIS researcher who is looking for the lost collection of Maximilian von Lewinski – phones me that afternoon. I can hear from her voice how excited she is.

'I'm calling from Berlin. From the national archives!'

'What have you found?'

'I think I've finally managed to trace the collection!'

'Wow! In Berlin?'

'No, no. But it was here that I discovered the lead. I've been in Bonn, Stuttgart, Paris, Warsaw . . .'

'Tell me everything!'

'Maximilian von Lewinski's respect for the collection must have been so great that he didn't dare to take any risks whatsoever. He was a high-ranking officer in the Wehrmacht. He must have realised that there would be a war. So I thought – if I was Maximilian von Lewinski, what would I do? What would you have done, Bjørn?'

'I would have secured the collection, moved it somewhere safe.'

'And where was the safest place in the 1930s, do you think?'

'Well, a country that wouldn't be affected by the war?'

'And that means . . .'

'Quite a lot of countries . . .'

'But one would be natural in this context.'

'The USA?'

'The von Lewinski dynasty already had a head in the USA, in the form of Maximilian's brother, Uwe, who had emigrated to the USA in 1924. He settled in Chicago, where he was head of the von Lewinksi empire's American manufacturing company, Lewinski Steel Corporation.'

'Have you found any connections?'

'You bet. Nazi Germany was a thoroughly regulated society. Even people like Lewinski, who sat at the top, had to go through all the paperwork if they wanted to send anything of any value out of Germany. And that was how I found a reference to the collection. I've spent the last four days in Das Bundesarchiv, the German national archives. In the customs registers from 1935, which ironically survived because they were moved into a bomb-proof vault long before the war, I found reference to the export documents for Maximilian von Lewinski's book collection, which was sent out of the country in 1935, along with his art collection and various other family inheritance pieces. To Chicago!'

'To his brother?'

'Right. Maximilian sent his art and book collections to

his brother, Uwe. Even though it says nothing specific about historical letters and manuscripts, my guess is that Maximilian von Lewinski hid his collection in his extensive library.'

'Without anyone discovering?'

'Not that strange. A couple of thousand documents don't take up that much room. Particularly not when they have been distributed in tens of thousands of beautiful books packed in solid tea chests stuffed with wood shavings and newspapers.'

'Does the collection still exist?'

'It not only still exists – I've discovered where it is. And you won't believe it!'

'Where?'

'Right in front of our noses.'

'Where?'

'Maximilian died in the war. His brother, Uwe, never shared his interest in art and books. For over sixty years, Maximilian von Lewinski's unique collection stood in boxes in Uwe Lewinski's house. Unopened! Even when Maximilian died, Uwe didn't bother to open the boxes. He just moved them up into the loft. Uwe von Lewinski died in 1962, and his son, Albert, was killed in a plane crash a year later. He had no children. So his inheritors – legions of nephews, nieces and cousins – took a quick look in the boxes of old books and donated the whole collection to – are you sitting down? – the Library of Congress!'

As we put down the phone I hear two clicks in the receiver.

Suddenly I hear Laura's voice: '. . . *of old books and donated . . .*' before the ring tone takes over.

The Hunt

1

I<small>T IS</small> night when I land in America.

Washington, DC, is an infinite sea of light. Streets and buildings flicker and twinkle. From the window of the aeroplane, I see the red and white stripes from millions of car headlights that die out like shooting stars.

Laura Kocherhans is waiting for me at Arrivals. I had no idea that she was so sweet. And she, on her part, has obviously not been warned that I am an albino. To most women, I look like something that has been left too long in the bath. So our first meeting is an embarrassing, somewhat clumsy confusion of hugs and crutches.

Outside the airport, the humid dark smells of exhaust and drizzle, and a hint of Laura's perfume. We stand in the taxi queue for ten minutes, and are then driven to the hotel along an eight-lane motorway, under rows and rows of green signs.

The hotel is an oasis in the night.

A bellboy carries my suitcase from reception up to Room 3534. Laura has already checked in to the room next door.

We agree to have a quick drink in the hotel bar once I have showered and unpacked. Laura is sitting waiting when I come out of the lift. What a vision! In a closed-off

325

and unclear part of my brain, I think that a woman could hardly be more genetically perfect. I lean my crutches against the bar and hump myself up on to the bar stool beside her. Several people look at us in disbelief. Beauty and the Beast. I order a gin and tonic. It is the only drink I can remember the name of; Laura is drinking something red with a parasol in it. She tells me that we have an appointment at the Library of Congress first thing the following morning.

One of the men in the bar keeps staring at me. No doubt he is wondering why on earth Laura is with a shabby paleface like me. Or he is one of the sheikh's agents who has been sent to keep an eye on me.

I clear my throat and ask Laura whether she felt . . . well . . . that she was being followed when she was looking for the Lewinski Collection.

She laughs. 'I'm afraid my life is not that dramatic.'

Her laughter makes me tingle.

'You haven't seen anyone in several places? No one has followed you with their gaze? More than would be normal,' I add cockily.

'No, unfortunately.' She giggles. 'Well, actually, maybe the IT guy at the national archives in Berlin. Not really my type.'

The man who is watching us looks Arabic. He definitely needs a shave. When he meets my eye for a fourth time, he finishes his drink and leaves.

Laura and I soon run out of things to say. We take the lift back up to the third floor. As we walk down the corridor, I play with the thought that we are lovers on our way to bed.

Midway between Room 3532 and 3534, Laura says goodnight and gives me a hug.

I stand for some minutes looking out of the window in my room. Then I lie down between the tightly tucked sheets. I feel like a letter that has been stuffed into an envelope that is too small.

It takes a few hours before I fall asleep.

2

When Laura worked at the Library of Congress, she had a trusted position in the Rare Books and Special Collections Division. One of her responsibilities was to support the project to complete and catalogue the Kislak Collection, a historical-cultural collection comprising more than four thousand rare books, maps, documents, letters, pictures and artefacts from American history.

In some countries, the public do not have access to historical collections. The opposite is true in America. The Library of Congress boasts no less than twenty-two reading rooms for researchers, students and those who are interested.

Laura helps me through the security check – where my crutches are for a few nerve-racking moments deemed to be potential murder weapons – and registration at the James Madison Building.

From here, she leads me through an underground tunnel to the reading room – a copy of Independence Hall in Philadelphia, where the American Declaration of Independence was signed – in the Thomas Jefferson Building.

Along the way, she greets and is greeted by old colleagues. Delighted, they call out each other's names, embrace and look each other up and down. Some throw me a questioning glance, as if they wonder who on earth she has dragged in. Laura introduces me as one of Europe's most famous archaeologists. Personally, I feel more like something that has escaped from a display case.

I am used to people's looks. My skin, my hair, everything

is white. When I was little, children used to call me *Isbjørn*, which is Norwegian for polar bear. Adults are more considerate. But I can see everything that is unsaid in their eyes, in that look.

We would normally have to fill in an order form for the books and manuscripts that we want to take out. But the Lewinski Collection is so new that it has not even been catalogued yet. So Laura has made an appointment with the curator, Miranda Cartwright.

Miranda is tall and plump with flaming red hair. She is the sort of woman who is always kind and considerate and full of laughter and witticisms.

Like me, she is used to people looking at her.

She is used to the silences and broken promises. She is used to being overlooked and forgotten, to standing on the sidelines while other children happily sing and play. They say we grow out of it. But of course we don't. Miranda has never told anyone that she cries herself to sleep. She has never said that she has sat in the bath, naked, with the water running and a razor ready to make that one short cut that will set her free. I recognise myself in her. She is just like me; a piece of human flotsam that floats among the seaweed under the jetty. She disguises her self-loathing with a veneer of forced jollity. She is of course extremely observant. We sensitive souls are practically mind-readers. So, when she shakes my hand, her smile is different, full of warmth and genuine empathy. With an almost impercept- ible nod she acknowledges that she knows that I have had a painful childhood, and that I struggle with my self-image as much as she does.

'So, welcome to Washington,' she says with a smile that only I can understand the depths of.

Miranda tells us that the Library received the Lewinski Collection early the previous summer, but that the cataloguing and indexing only began at Easter. The greater part of the collection is original works from the fifteenth to the eighteenth centuries, but that it also contains manuscripts, letters and books from the Middle Ages.

I ask whether Miranda is familiar with a letter from the early 1500s that Bartolomeo Columbus took with him to Europe from the Caribbean. 'There are probably three symbols somewhere on the page: ankh, *tiwaz* and a cross. You won't be able to read the text or understand it, as it is written in code.'

'Fascinating,' Miranda says. 'But unfortunately, no. I'm afraid that's the sort of thing most of us only dream about.'

3

We open the wooden boxes that contain Maximilian von Lewinski's stolen collection; the books have been packed carefully and covered with shavings and crumpled newspapers that declare that Germany is preparing for a victorious future.

We look through thick, heavy books that smell of dust and forgotten thoughts.

We search the folios and leather-bound works with exotic place names and dates on the colophon page.

We go through fragile protocols and palaeographs – old works from the very earliest days of printing – books of sermons, catalogues, maps, letters and encyclopedias.

But we do not find the letter from the Guardians.

When we are finished at the Library of Congress, Laura takes a taxi back to the hotel, and Miranda goes home to loneliness.

I, on the other hand, have been summoned by the FBI.

It is something that was arranged by Ragnhild. When I called her from Gardermoen Airport to tell her that I was going to the USA, she insisted that I should get protection from the American police.

When I was little, I used to sit inside and play chess with myself while the other children played outside in the street. Sometimes I managed to persuade another one of the playground hermits to play with me, lonely boys like me, rejected by the popular masses. I always won, which is why I stopped asking them. Or why they stopped coming. Chess requires the ability to think several moves ahead – even though you do not know how your opponent will react. As every chess player knows, an uncertain opponent will become unfocused.

The FBI agent who interviews me is sceptical and stressed. He has a pile of faxes with him from Interpol. He reads about the three murders. The hostage drama in Rome. He keeps looking over at me, irritated, as if he can't quite work out why a short-sighted albino from Norway has suddenly become his problem.

I watch him when he is not looking. His Adam's apple bounces from his collarbone to his chin every time he swallows.

Finally I say the magic words: 'They are probably Islamist terrorists.'

The express movement of his Adam's apple tells me that I have hit the bull's-eye. He types the information into his computer. The words will lie ticking like a time bomb in his database.

Somewhat reluctantly, he provides me with a personal alarm, which consists of a GPS transmitter and a panic button. The agent explains how it works, but he talks so fast that I can't quite make out whether the alarm goes to the FBI, the United States Marshals Service or the Washington Metropolitan Police. But I feel certain that someone will come very quickly should I press the button.

Laura and I go out for a meal that evening, in one of the hipper vegetarian restaurants in Washington, DC. The waiter is obviously rehearsing for a role as a granite statue. Laura is fascinated by the idea of vegetables that are pretending to be meat. She says that they taste amusing. I choose an asparagus dish that is not pretending to be anything other than lightly boiled asparagus. We drink wine from California and a fancy bottle of mineral water.

Through the window, I see a black car with dark windows parked on the other side of the road. I get it into my head that there is someone sitting inside watching us with binoculars and telescopes. Maybe they are even taking pictures of us. So I smile and wave. Laura asks who I am flirting with. 'My own reflection,' I reply.

The car is still there when we leave the restaurant an hour later.

We walk through the buzzing activity on the street. Laura has slipped her arm through mine. We have drunk so much wine that she starts to tell me about her last boyfriend. He was called Robbie. And he was not ready to commit. The break-up was one of the reasons why she accepted the job with the SIS and moved to London.

At regular intervals I look over my shoulder to see whether the car is following us.

It isn't.

They are smarter than that.

4

The next day, we continue our search for the letter.

In the middle of an alphabetically arranged collection of texts about the arrest of Christopher Columbus, I come across a series of papers about Norse settlements in North America. The most important work is about Helge and Anne Stine Ingstad's discovery of Viking dwellings in L'Anse aux Meadows in Newfoundland. But I also read about controversial rune stones, stone towers that are similar to the old Norse round churches, the discovery of a coin from Olav Kyrre's day near an indigenous Indian dwelling in *Norumbega*, or Norway. In the 1500s, the cartographers Abraham Ortelius and Gerardus Mercator showed that *Norumbega* got its name from the Viking colonies there. When Giovanni da Verrazano explored and mapped the east coast from Florida to Newfoundland, he wrote about *Normanvilla*, or Norwegian land, in the area roughly around where New York is now.

Long before Columbus sailed to the Caribbean, Norsemen had settled along the southern parts of the American east coast.

Laura and Miranda work more slowly than I do. While I look through the books, they register and catalogue each item. They type in all the available information about the books and manuscripts on a special program on the Library of Congress's computer network.

At the end of the day, Laura and I take a taxi back to the hotel. My mouth tastes as if I have been eating newspaper. I am so tired and empty headed that I don't even bother to tell Laura that I think we are being followed. She would only laugh at me. I never see anyone when I turn round. They are too professional for that. But I know that they are there.

5

We find the letter on the third day.

The parchment lies pressed between pages 343 and 344 of a seventeenth-century Spanish book about the discovery of America, together with an envelope addressed to Archbishop Erik Valkendorf of Nidaros in the Kingdom of Norway.

Under the three symbols of ankh, *tiwaz* and cross is a familiar combination of runes and letters. I am in no doubt that it was written by the same order of Guardians who encrypted the codes in the stave churches some three hundred and fifty years earlier.

I whistle to Laura. She opens her mouth in a silent gasp.

For a second, I consider stealing it. After all, it does belong with everything else that we have found. But then I immediately dismiss the thought. Even I have boundaries. It is the *content*, not the parchment itself, which I need.

I take several close-up photos of the parchment and runes with my digital camera, before waving Miranda over.

'I've found it.'

'Oh my God! The parchment?'

'It's encrypted. The document proves once and for all that descendants of the Vikings were living on the American continent when Columbus drifted over on the wind.'

'Can you understand any of the text?' Laura asks.

'Not a sausage.'

Miranda trots off with the parchment in a cardboard box and a glow in her cheeks.

6

Fear arises from love, said the Dominican monk Thomas Aquinas. I, for my part, would say that fear of pain and death come higher up on the list.

As Laura and I leave the Library of Congress, we are greeted by a chilling gust of wind. I spot them through the cloud of dust that swirls up.

On the sunburnt savannahs of Africa, gazelle develop tunnel vision when a lion is attacking. I know how they feel. I manage to single out four characters. Four men. Four men who leave their posts with a sauntering ease. Like heat-seeking missiles, they close in on their target. From each side.

'Walk faster!' I say to Laura, even though I am already struggling to keep up with her. I hold tight on to my crutches. So I have something I can hit them with.

They are about ten to fifteen metres away. Hassan is not one of them. But they are big. They are Arabs. And they are dressed in suits.

'Laura . . .'

She slows down.

'Run, Laura, run!'

Laura rolls her eyes. 'Bjørn! For goodness' sake!'

I have to stop to put my hand in my jacket pocket. My fingers close around the panic alarm.

Laura looks around demonstratively to convince herself and me that I am imagining things. She tells me that I've seen too many action films.

She doesn't even notice them.

They move towards us like invisible chameleons, in their elegant suits, white shirts and knotted ties.

I press the panic button.

'Run!' I whisper again.

'Don't be silly.'

They are five metres away. I tighten my hold on both my crutches, though I realise that a hollow light-metal crutch is a pathetic weapon.

'Brrr, it's cold,' Laura says, pulling her coat tighter around her.

Only when one of the men is alongside us and taps us with his hidden weapon does she realise that even the paranoid can be right.

Her face stiffens and then cracks.

'Please come with us,' one of the men says in an accent that sounds like a parody of a villain.

My heart is hammering so hard that I have a ringing in my ears.

What would they do if I shouted for help? Would they shoot me?

Two of them grab me by the arms. The other two hold Laura with more respect.

An untrained eye would not be able to see that we were being kidnapped.

The men guide us down towards Independence Avenue. They are so subtle, so well trained, that a witness might just believe that it was undercover arrest. If they noticed anything at all.

A black van with darkened windows brakes in front of us. Laura and I are pushed into the back seat. Two of the men sit in front with the driver, and two get in the back with Laura and me.

The van speeds off.

They do not say a word as we drive across town.

I try to ask who they are. And what they are doing. As if I had any doubt. But I don't get an answer. They don't even tell me to be quiet.

They all freeze when a police car with sirens blaring pulls up alongside us at a junction. But then it speeds past and on down the avenue.

My body is shaking. Laura's breathing is shallow.

The driver weaves in and out of the heavy traffic. After a while, the van swerves abruptly to the right and down into the underground car park of a hotel.

Laura and I are led to a lift that takes us up to the second floor. The driver puts a keycard into the lock. The light shows green. We go in.

7

Hassan is sitting in a wing chair, waiting.

Even when he is sitting down, he is enormous. And threatening.

My knees are trembling. Lord knows what Hassan might do when he is tired and impatient.

He looks at me as though he is my therapist and I have arrived at an inconvenient time.

Two of the men frisk us. When they find the panic alarm, they throw it down without looking at it. They think it is a mobile phone.

Two of them then take Laura over to the sofa. I am about to limp after them in a feeble attempt to protect her, but one of the henchmen holds me back.

Laura is about to cry. She looks over at me with frightened eyes.

'Miss Kocherhans,' Hassan says. 'I am delighted that you found the opportunity to visit us.'

Laura bursts into tears.

8

The room is part of the largest suite I have ever been in. I count three closed doors leading from the lounge into adjoining rooms.

Two of the brutes grab me by the arms while a third takes my crutches.

They half-lead, half-drag me into one of the other rooms.

In to Stuart Dunhill.

Stuart commands the gorillas out of the room with a mere look.

Silence.

'Nice to see you again, Bjørn.'

He shows me over to a seating arrangement by the window. I lean my crutches against a velvet armchair and sink down into the sofa.

'Apologies that I left Rome without saying goodbye.' I try to make my voice sound cool, but it actually sounds as if I'm about to start crying. 'I couldn't be sure that I wasn't on the same list as Luigi.'

'You have to believe me when I say that I liked Luigi.'

'Not enough not to kill him.'

'Not me, Bjørn, not me. I am just a small fish swimming with the sharks. Luigi . . . he was starting to take liberties. He got greedy. You know how it is. He was double-dealing. Luigi knew the risk he was taking, challenging the sheikh like that. He was bold, and lost. He had already promised the manuscript fragment that he tried to sell to you to the sheikh. There were other things too. He had cheated the sheikh on a couple of occasions. The sheikh lost all patience with him. And then he got the idea that you and Luigi were negotiating a price for the Thingvellir Scrolls.'

'That's crazy.'

'You know that. I know that. But the sheikh is suspicious by nature.'

'So you admit that you work for him?'

'Sheikh Ibrahim . . .'

The answer hangs in the air between us.

'At the end of the seventies, the sheikh and the SIS were the only ones who supported me. When everyone else just laughed and no one wanted to work with me or publish my work, I was losing it fast and Sheikh Ibrahim rescued me. Together with the SIS, he helped me to get the research post at the Schimmer Institute.'

Through the thin curtain and window, I see people working in an open-plan office on the other side of the street.

Where have the police got to?

'I was given a kind of professional asylum,' Stuart continues. 'An alcoholic joke of an archaeologist who happened to stumble upon one of the greatest mysteries of archaeological history, and had been made a laughing stock.'

'It wasn't so by accident. You know what you were looking for.'

'Most of what I have told you is true. Believe me. If the truth be told, I have actually protected you from . . . them.'

'Tell me about him. Who is this man who is pursuing me?'

'Sheikh Ibrahim . . . Where to start? Some see him as a religious leader, others as a philosopher. A fanatic. No one knows him. He's from the Emirates, where he owns valuable oilfields. He is incredibly rich and a very complex person. His interest in old manuscripts is not just to do with collecting and investment. He also believes that the Jews and the Christians have to acknowledge Muhammad not just as a prophet, but as the one true prophet. The sheikh is a living paradox. Deeply religious, but also a monomaniac when it comes to power and wealth. He has the world's largest private collection of antique art. His library is vast. He is calculating and cynical, but also donates millions of dollars to various causes from animal clinics in Canada to schools in Somalia. He is intelligent, well read and thoughtful. But also the ruthless head of financial organisations that own a number of multinational companies. The sheikh is without scruples. He will stop at nothing to get what he wants. And he employs men whom he knows have balls.'

'Murderers.'

Stuart nods thoughtfully.

'And you.'

'And men like me . . .'

'What does he have in his library?'

'The sheikh's library contains a unique collection of manuscripts. Early copies of the Bible and the Koran. He owns one of the originals of the Book of the Song of Solomon. Solomon is also a prophet in Islam.'

'How did he come across Snorri? Sira Magnus? Me?'

'Since the start of the seventies, the sheikh has hoovered up all legal and illegal manuscripts, letters, parchments, maps and documents on the collectors' market. And that is how he came across a copy of a fragment from the so-called Vatican Papers of the Coptic translation that Asim tried to send to the caliph in Egypt when he was in Normandy with Duke Richard, but the Vatican requisitioned it and stored it away in some archive, without having any idea of what it was about.'

'A different manuscript from the one we found at Thingvellir?'

'A different version, yes. The sheikh had the text translated and became obsessed with finding the original. When he heard about my discovery in Egypt, he immediately saw a connection.'

'What is the original manuscript that you're talking about?'

'Have you really not grasped that yet? Asim copied the papyrus manuscripts that the Vikings stole from the tomb in Egypt.'

'And the Thingvellir Scrolls . . .'

'. . . Are the Hebrew version of those same texts, together with a new Coptic translation.'

'Sira Magnus knew nothing about all this.'

'That's true. But he had, by accident, got hold of an ancient document, the Snorri Codex, which held the clues that the sheikh had been searching for, for twenty-five years. The codex contains maps and codes that led to all the Norwegian tombs and the cave in Thingvellir where Snorri had hidden Asim's copy of the manuscript.'

'Sira Magnus had no idea about what he'd found.'

'Not exactly, no. And he didn't know how to interpret the text, drawings and maps. But he knew enough to know that the codex was worth millions of dollars on the black market. That was why Sira Magnus contacted us.'

'I don't believe you.'

'Sira Magnus needed money. Well, perhaps not him in person, but his church. A new organ. More art on the walls. Sira Magnus wanted to sell us the codex.'

'I still don't believe you.'

'Over the years, Sira Magnus has managed to get hold of quite a number of Icelandic manuscripts and documents which he has then sold to the sheikh. None of them was of any great historic or financial value. But how else do you think a priest could afford to drive a four-wheel-drive BMW?'

. . .

'I don't think he sold anything for personal gain,' Stuart continues. 'Even though he treated himself to a nice car. I think he primarily wanted to get money for the church, for research, the congregation and the Friends of the Snorrastofa. And maybe because it was more exciting than giving the historical artefacts to the manuscript institute.'

I remain silent.

'I got to know Sira Magnus at the end of the nineties,' Stuart says. 'We met at a conference in Barcelona about the spread and importance of Carolingian minuscule in medieval manuscripts. I liked him . . .'

'You killed him!'

'He got in touch a few months later. He had some manuscripts that he thought I might like to see. He must have known that I had connections with the sheikh. That's how it all started.' He looks down. 'What happened this time, and what made it all so messy, was that he regretted it. He realised that he was about to overstep the mark by selling a rarity like the Snorri Codex. So he changed his mind. That was when he phoned you. He needed support. He was desperate. When you came to visit him at Reykholt, he had pulled out of the deal. He had cancelled the whole thing.'

'But he was still terrified of you.'

'Sira Magnus knew that we were on our way. And what we wanted. He claimed that he didn't have the codex any more. That you had taken it with you into the manuscript institute.'

'So you killed him?'

'He died of a heart attack. Read the post-mortem report.'

'You bloody well kept his head under water!'

'Hassan did get a bit violent. It's in his nature. He had the green light to offer Sira Magnus vast sums of money. But he refused. Hassan had to, shall we say, persuade him. Hassan takes his job very seriously. But no one killed Magnus. Hassan forced him to say where he had hidden the codex, yes, but he didn't kill him. Not directly. Though Magnus did die at their hands.'

I let this pathetic explanation fizzle out between us. Stuart is uncomfortable. I let him suffer. Then finally I ask: 'How did you know that Thrainn and I were at Thingvellir?'

'Hassan knew what you were up to as long as you were at Snorrastofa. But when you moved into the hotel in Reykjavik, they lost track of you for a while. They started to investigate. We knew that you were in contact with Professor Thrainn Sigurdsson, so we rang the institute and pretended to be your colleagues. One of the secretaries told us where you were.'

'And in Norway? You kept pretty close tabs on me there.'

'It's not that difficult, if there are enough of you. Several of the sheikh's men have worked in intelligence. They used all sorts of tracking equipment. Infrared surveillance cameras, GPS tracking, mobile phone tracking. The problem was that you kept leaving your mobile phone behind and doing unexpected things. You are not easy to follow, Bjørn.'

'You found me in Lom. I didn't have my mobile with me there.'

'But your colleague, Øyvind, did.'

'Why did you never find me at Nesodden, then?'

'We knew you were there. But we never managed to locate the house. Our equipment isn't that advanced.'

'So it really was you I saw . . .'

'We followed your car, using GPS . . .'

'I found the transmitters.'

'We thought you'd look. So we put four transmitters on the Citroën. We reckoned you'd find a couple of them. And couple of them you would never find. That was how we managed to find you at Ringebu.'

'Where you killed the priest and set fire to the stave church.'

He sighs. 'Another accident.'

'Accident! I was there. I saw what happened, Stuart!'

'The sheikh's men can be a bit rough. Things like that happen. Unfortunately. The sheikh was furious when he heard about it.'

'Spare me! A killer is a killer.'

'They are paid extremely well do the sheikh's dirty work.'

'And yet no one found what I did?'

'You have a unique talent, Bjørn. The sheikh is impressed. Even though he has a battalion of people at his disposal, no one has managed to see the patterns in the drawings. Maybe it's because you're Norwegian. Maybe it's because your brain is configured to see patterns where others don't. But mainly, it's because you have a phenomenal talent.'

I don't respond to his clumsy attempt at flattery.

'We chose a new tactic when you came to the Schimmer Institute. Me. We knew that you would seek me out. After all, I am the world's leading expert on Viking raids down the Nile. So instead of sending his orcs to the Schimmer Institute, the sheikh let me look after you. By letting you in on all the secrets that I knew, I won – at least for a while – your trust.'

'So the sheikh didn't have anyone at the institute?'

'He had me. And a guy who was keeping you under surveillance. We put a camera and microphone in the lamp in your room. He was going to watch you, see what you knew. The sheikh also paid a handful of other researchers to look at the artefacts, like the statue of St Lawrence.'

'On the last night you said that the sheikh had sent several men to the institute?'

'It was a bluff. Sorry. When I pretended to get a phone call from the SIS telling me that the sheikh's men were on their way, it was actually reception calling to say that my clothes had come back from the dry cleaner's. The fact that you happened to come across the St Lawrence statue and chose to confide in me gave me the opportunity to get even closer.'

I take a deep breath and hold it. How easily fooled can you be? I should have seen through him the minute we met.

'You took me with you to Egypt. To the tomb. To the Forgotten Town. To Rome. To Luigi. Why?'

Stuart gets up, then he sits down again. Had I not known better, I might have thought he was struggling with his conscience.

'Because, Bjørn, I hoped that you would manage to find all the things I never found. I wasn't getting anywhere. I had a lap full of ceramic shards, but I couldn't make them into a pot. Only you could do that, put the pieces together.

I hoped that by feeding you with information, you would help us progress.'

'But it was the Thingvellir Scrolls you were after, the whole time?'

'Absolutely.'

'What is it about the manuscript that makes it so valuable to the sheikh?'

'I can't tell you that.'

'The Schimmer Institute. Egypt. Rome. It was *you* who kept tabs on me the whole time.'

'The sheikh also sent a few men to help. But you were under my protection the whole time, Bjørn. And believe me, I would never wish you any harm. I wanted to borrow your talent. The fact that the sheikh's gorillas killed Luigi was a mistake.'

'A mistake . . .'

'They should of course have waited until we had left Rome before dealing with Luigi. It got us into trouble. We realised we were losing control. You were surrounded by a growing number of security guards and policemen. So we kept a low profile. But when the SIS and the Directorate for Cultural Heritage gathered together the leading experts from all over the world to excavate the St Sunniva Cave, we saw our chance to infiltrate the project. We managed to get three of our people selected for the project team. But unfortunately they weren't very good tomb raiders.'

'And here in the USA?'

'Bjørn, you have to understand . . . over time you have been under more surveillance than a CIA agent suspected of spying! The sheikh has his people everywhere. The Schimmer Institute, the SIS, the Directorate for Cultural Heritage. We knew perfectly well that Laura was working for you. We also know that the Guardians took the mummy and the texts with them from Iceland to Greenland and then on here, to Vinland.'

'And now? What now?'

'The Thingvellir Scrolls could make you extremely rich.'

'Extremely rich . . .' I repeat his words with a hint of irony. To me, money is like women. I crave it most in my fantasies.

'Think about it. A life of luxury. A villa with a swimming pool. Sports cars. Holidays on the French Riviera and in the Caribbean. Fine wines. Steaks. Attractive women.'

A normal man might toy with the idea, whereas I only become more obstinate. Stuart thinks that my silence is because I'm giving it some consideration.

'The sheikh is willing to pay you ten million dollars for the Thingvellir Scrolls.'

'Ten million dollars.' I taste the number. 'What makes a text so unbelievably valuable?'

'Ten million dollars!'

'I don't know where they are.'

And that is not even a lie, just a slight distortion of the truth.

'Fifteen million?'

I shake my head. 'To be frank . . .'

The FBI do not knock on the door. They take it in with them.

With a loud tearing sound, the door to the room next door is rammed open. A stun grenade is detonated. Running boots. Loud voices.

'FBI! Down! Down! Down! FBI!'

I learnt in Rome how special forces teams enter a room. The tactic is the same all over the world. They come when you least expect it. And they come fast and show no mercy. And they make a terrible noise.

'Down! Down! Down!'

Neither Stuart nor I moves.

The door to our room is kicked open. Three armed policemen storm in.

'FBI! Down! Down! Down!'

This is not a request. It is a threat of sudden and quick death if we do not do as we are told.

I slip off the sofa and on to the floor like something that is melting.

'FBI!' they roar again. In case we are deaf or incredibly stupid.

Stuart puts his hands above his head. 'I think there's been a misunderstanding . . .'

'Down! Down! Down!'

Stuart slides reluctantly down on to the floor. As if *this* was truly below his dignity. He looks at me. Then he spreads his arms and legs.

'Cleared!' shouts one of the FBI men.

The police swarm into the room. Some look like front-line soldiers from an intergalactic spaceship. Some are wearing windbreakers with FBI written on the back in big yellow letters. Some have MP5s, others pump-action rifles, and some revolvers. And then finally come the men in suits.

'Mr Beltø?' one of the agents asks.

'Yes, sir!'

He helps me to my feet and hands me my crutches. 'We'd like to have a chat.'

9

Laura and I spend the rest of the day and evening with the FBI.

To have Hassan, Stuart and the rest of the gang tried and sentenced for murder and attempted murder in three European countries is no easy task. But, with the exception of Stuart, they are all Arabs. Muslims. And they all have handguns which they are not licensed to carry.

'Islamic terrorists,' I repeat, again and again.

I don't know what will happen to Stuart and his chums, but it is not likely that they will be released imminently.

When we are finally done with the police, Laura and I go out into the Washington night. We eat at a Japanese restaurant before taking a taxi back to the hotel.

10

The next day I buy a brand-new mobile phone, which is registered in the name of one of Laura's friends. I send the number to a handful of people I trust. Terje Lønn Erichsen is one of them.

We spend the next twenty-four hours trying to crack the code.

I have sent him pictures of the manuscript, and we each have a copy. So, using MSN messaging, we play with various code keys and combinations. Even though the letter from the Caribbean was written several hundred years later than the coded texts in the stave churches, it is encrypted in exactly the same way.

Every second word is encrypted using a combination of Caesar 7 and 8, and every third word is written backwards.

It is a remarkable document.

In the letter to Archbishop Valkendorf, the Guardians thank him for his previous correspondence, as they were naturally not certain of who the bishop in Trondheim was or whether the Fraternity of Guardians still existed in Norway. They confirm that the bishop has replied with the correct symbols – ankh, *tiwaz* and the cross – and apologise for not having sent word for so long, but it is only now that they have found a safe harbour in a village called Santo

Domingo on the island of Hispaniola (which today is the island that is split into the Dominican Republic and Haiti). Here they were met by a European they call Barolomé Colón, brother of Cristóbal Colón, otherwise known as Christopher Columbus.

They write that following the massacre on Greenland, the group fled to the country to the west of the horizon. They have travelled south with the Holy One for the past fifty years. They knew that according to Norse tradition, they would find an easterly wind that would take them back to Europe.

They have spent many years in various Norse settlements along the east coast and cultivated relations with the native *skrælings*. They have left rune stones behind them. Many of them have died along the way, from age or in fights with the natives. Some have stayed in the settlements. Some have settled with the *skrælings*. Even though children have been born, the group of Guardians has now shrunk to nineteen men, nine women and eight children.

They let the archbishop know that they have decided to return the mummy to Egypt, as Asim wished them to.

I read the translation of the letter again and again with Laura. Where do we continue our search?

Santo Domingo is the oldest European town in the Caribbean, now a big city with over two million inhabitants. Did the Guardians' journey stop there? Or did they sail back to Europe? Did the mummy end up in the Vatican after all?

11

We select a pile of books about the history of Santo Domingo from the library. And we start searching.

Later in the day, I call Professor Llyleworth at the SIS to find out whether he can help us. I can tell from his voice that the connection with Santo Domingo gives him an idea.

'Have you looked at the Miércoles Palace?'

I feel a flicker of hope. I have heard about the legendary palace in Santo Domingo.

'As far as I know, Esteban Rodriquez is a rather eccentric man. Check it out!' Professor Llyleworth says.

In a reference book from 1954 called *The World's Ten Greatest Palaces*, Laura looks up the chapter on the Miércoles Palace. The magnificent palace is a five-hundred-year-old Renaissance building with large grounds, on the edge of the old town in Santo Domingo. According to local folklore, the palace was built by Christopher Columbus, which can hardly be the case as he was already dead by the time construction on the palace started. His brother, Bartolomeo, however, was involved in procuring the site for the palace at the then centre of the town. The Miércoles Palace today is like an oasis in the middle of a vast city.

The article also has a short section about the Rodriquez family, who own the Miércoles Palace, and who staunchly protect their past. According to the article, Rodriquez was a European aristocrat who accompanied Christopher Columbus's brother, Bartolomeo, on one of his expeditions to the newly discovered countries. The text also mentions speculation that the Rodriquez family's wealth stemmed from what remained of the lost treasure of the Knights Templar; that they had been bribed by Queen Isabella not to reveal the secret of her origins; that Henry VIII financed the building of Miércoles Palace in order to keep the Rodriquez family out of Europe, following a scandal; and that Leonardo da Vinci persuaded the Sforza dynasty in Milan to build the palace as part of a plan to establish an aristocratic bridgehead to the New World. But the truth is that no one actually knows much about the background of

349

the Rodriquez family before they arrived in Santo Domingo in the sixteenth century and built the Miércoles Palace, moved in and then closed the doors with a bang that still resounds through history.

Miércoles.

Miércoles means Wednesday in Spanish. The word is derived from the Roman god Mercury, who is the same god as the Germanic Wotan (Woden, *Wōdinaz*) and Old Norse god Odin. The English *Wednesday* is derived from *Wēdnes dæg*, in the same way as Odin's name appears in the Norwegian *onsdag*.

Miércoles Palace.

Wednesday Palace.

Odin's Palace . . .

Laura points to a black-and-white photograph of the coat of arms of the reclusive aristocratic Rodriquez family.

I see, surrounded by dragons, lions and sword-bearing seraphs, three symbols.

Ankh, *tiwaz* and the cross.

INTERMEZZO

Bård's Tale (III)

'King Olaf fought most desperately. He struck the lenderman before mentioned (Thorgeir of Kviststad) across the face, cut off the nose-piece of his helmet, and clove his head down below the eyes so that they almost fell out.'

SNORRI

'You are from the immortal realm of Barbelo.'

THE GOSPEL OF JUDAS

HE SHIVERED in the damp monk's cell and pulled his cloak tighter around him. He dipped the newly cut quill in ink. In the evening, when the sun had gone down, he carried on writing in the dim light of two candles that the monks replaced every morning. The stench of the melting tallow blended with the sharp smell of the ink, and the steam from the fish, cabbage or mutton that was being cooked in the kitchen. Sometimes he heard the monks laughing, which always made him smile, and later he closed his eyes and listened for the harmonies when the monks gathered for evensong. Outside, the sea fog had wiped out the horizon and the contours of the islands and mountains. As dusk fell, he often remembered the feeling that filled him on the boat, when they finally saw land again . . .

EXTRACT FROM BÅRD'S TALE

. . . after many years spent away on Viking raids. We saw the coast of our homeland through the banks of fog. We were home! Even King Olav was excited and happy. The only one who did not find any joy in seeing the mountains and fjords was Asim. He stood silent and solemn by the reliquary and stared at the shore with a sombre expression.

Once land had been sighted, King Olav sailed south and then east along the coast to land at Viken, together with one hundred of his loyal men. From here, the King of the Sea walked back to the farm where once he grew up, and to his mother, Åsta, and stepfather.

Much has been told of the King's work to spread Christianity. I, who stood by my king's side through all those years, recognise little of all that is said. The truth is that the land which our king was trying to unite was split by clans and families, with no sense of country. It was a patchwork of independent regions, ruled by strong-willed chieftains and petty kings. Before he could Christianise the country, he first had to seize power. He was not helped by angels, as they said in the south-west, and the gates of heaven were never opened, as they believe in the west. The White Christ never stood by the king's side. Oh no, the spread of Christianity was the result of hard work. And discipline! Olav spoke well to the petty kings, chieftains and important farmers in the inland regions. They accepted Olav as their king. Bit by bit, he also gained power along the coast, to the south and then up the west to Trøndelag. As ruler of south and middle Norway, he now made peace with the Swedish king and married one of his daughters. A magnificent wedding it was! My lord Olav was now the strongest king in Norway. But in the country he wished to Christianise, many people still worshipped the gods of their forefathers.

King Olav was an impatient missionary. This caused his people to turn against him, stirring the old Viking in him when they resisted the word of the Lord. He razed their places of worship and farms. He maimed and killed his enemies. And all in the name of Christ. If Norway was to be converted, the old gods had to be banished, with force and threats. Jesus's message of forgiveness and charity was not embraced with enthusiasm. And I sympathised with those who resisted.

*

Asim had a monastery built on Selja, where he gathered around him a group of Guardians to protect the mummy and treasure we had taken with us from the desert land. I visited him there every third year.

All people looked upon Asim with veneration. He was more than a priest or monk. Asim was a sorcerer, an astrologer, a prophet who could listen to the gods. At the monastery, he instructed the king's men in astronomy and astrology, geography and history. He sent regular expeditions out to travel the length and breadth of the land. With the help of measurements and astronomical observations, he gathered information about the land and sea, the rivers and mountains, until he was able to draw a map of Norway. This map enabled King Olav and his men to travel around the kingdom faster and with greater safety.

Asim was a man of habit. Each morning, as the sun rose, he would climb up to the ledge in front of the cave and look out to sea. The monks said that he was waiting for someone to come over the ocean.

Many of Olav's enemies gathered together with Canute the Great, King of Denmark and England, who came sailing to Norway with his army – the fleet was a terrifying sight with its billowing sails and dragonheads. No one took up arms against the Danish king. To the contrary. People were tired of King Olav's threats and attacks. The Christian king had insulted many a proud man. Canute, on the other hand, promised the chieftains power, riches and freedom. He lined the pockets of his most important allies well. Even Olav's soldiers deserted him.

The king sank into despondency. His life's work lay in ruins. The Christianisation of Norway was no great holy triumph. King Olav felt like a dog, when, with his tail between his legs, he was forced to flee east. The King of Norway! The Viking! The great warrior who had always looked fear in the eye. Champion of Our Lord! He had to flee from King Canute and the irate farmers.

I was with the company that followed the king east, through the great forests. He left his wife and daughter with King Anund of Sweden and we rode and sailed on, until we came to the Grand Prince, Yaroslav of Novgorod in Gardarike.

The chieftains at the Øreting Assembly hailed Canute as the new king of Norway, and Håkon Eiriksson as his regent. Olav was inconsolable. The Grand Prince Yaroslav offered Olav the crown of Bulgaria, which the king declined. His only desire was to win back his country, his rightful inheritance, Norway.

In the summer of 1030, Olav received the joyful news that Earl Håkon had drowned when his ship was wrecked. Norway was without a leader! With renewed vigour, Olav returned.

Proud and confident of victory, King Olav rode through the valley of Verdal in Trøndelag. We numbered fifteen hundred strong. Our forces met on the flats at Stiklestad. Olav had led his army up on to a horseshoe ridge, which gave us a good view of the enemy ranks, who arrived separately in groups. To the north lay marshlands and to the south a river. A ravine to our right prevented the enemy from attacking. If they were to take us, they had to come up the slope on to the ridge where Olav had gathered his troops.

I rode over to the king's side and said despondently: 'The enemy looks to have three times as many men!' The king's friend, Dag Ringsson, had not yet arrived with the thousand men whom we so sorely needed. Olav smiled without fear. 'We have God and Divine Providence on our side,' he said. I said nothing. Down on the level ground, thousands of warriors gathered in formation. Olav's scouts reported they were at least five thousand strong: farmers, chieftains and leaders who had turned against Olav. My hand clenched the hilt of my sword. I had not the king's burning vision and confidence, and saw only a superior force.

'You have been a good squire and loyal friend, Bård,' the king said. I can still see him in front of me, with his coat of armour and helmet, armed with a sword and an axe, carrying his white shield with the cross of the White Christ in gold. I said: 'Thank you, my lord.' The king spoke again: 'Do you recall that at Karlsrå I told you of my dream in which a man with fire in his eye told me that I would go home to become King of Norway?' I told my king that I remembered. Then Olav furrowed his brow and said: 'As I slept with my head in Finn Arnesson's lap, I dreamt of a ladder that went straight up to Heaven. And at the gate to Paradise, the same man with fire in his eye was waiting.' The king looked at me askance. I believed that such a dream could be taken as an ominous sign. Then the king laughed. 'Quite the opposite, Bård,' he said. 'A promise!'

Olav had gathered his strongest and most courageous men – together with some more anxious skalds – behind a wall of shields. At the front, he positioned some berserkers and bandits who were not trained in the art of war, but who were wild and mad and thirsty for blood. Around him, Olav had the Swedish soldiers from King Anund, warriors from the Grand Prince Yaroslav and the army that had accompanied his fifteen-year-old half-brother Harald from Oppland.

We swooped down the ridge towards the waiting army of farmers, our battle cry resounding. To me it felt as though we were riding straight into Ragnarok. I was not afraid of fighting at my king's side, but I soon saw that, being so outnumbered, all we could do was delay the inevitable: the death of our king.

The battle was fierce and bloody. We gathered speed as we came off the ridge and ploughed straight into the enemy lines. Some fled our attack, others retaliated. Some fought with spears, others swung axes and swords. Showers of sharp arrows whined through the air. Yet others threw spears and stones. Men screamed and roared, some with rage, others in pain and fear. The ground was sodden with blood. The rank smell of intestines floated like an invisible mist over the battlefield. Tore Hund, the king's old enemy, came forward. 'Olav!' he said in a thunderous voice, and aimed his spear. He mercilessly thrust his spear up under the king's coat of armour and deep into his belly. 'My king,' I whispered, but was overpowered by the noise of hundreds, no, thousands of men fighting. Olav gasped his last. And thus, at Stiklestad, my lord and master died, the Viking king Olav Haraldsson, the man we now know as *Óláfr hinn helgi*.

He lifted his quill, screwed the lid back on the ink and rolled up the parchments. With a deep sigh, he leant back.

Forty years had passed since that sun-filled day at Stiklestad when the king had died. But he could still recall every moment with a clarity that he otherwise lacked in old age. The July sun shimmering in the sky, the smell of blood and intestines mixing with the scent of the earth and the meadows and the forests; the screams of dying men and the threatening roars of those who fought wildly and valiantly.

Outside the window, a seagull bobbed on the wind. The waves crashed against the cliffs.

The eternal breathing of the sea, he thought to himself. The sea's salty breath.

The monks found him not long after vespers. He was lying on his bed with his hands folded on his chest. They knew immediately that the old Viking had died.

The abbot, who had himself sworn allegiance to Asim the Egyptian, sent word of his death without delay to the Grand Master of the fraternity in Nidaros.

PART IV

The Last Guardian

♀ ↑ †

'. . . And he lifted up the rod and smote the waters that were in the river, in the sight of Pharaoh, and in the sight of his servants; and all the waters that were in the river turned to blood.'

EXODUS 7: 20

'Sufficientia Scripturae Sacrae'
(ON THE SUFFICIENCY OF SACRED SCRIPTURE)

The Miércoles Palace

1

LIFE IS full of sounds.

I hear the traffic from the street below, a constant muted roar beyond the closed window. The air conditioning hums happily. A door closes somewhere. A lift door pings open.

I am sitting on the edge of my bed in my hotel room, surrounded by guidebooks and maps. The hotel is not one of the cheapest, but then it is not me who is paying.

I have sent a text to Laura to say that I have arrived safely. She is no longer needed. I would have been very happy for her to come to Santo Domingo with me, but the SIS thought it would be safest for her to return to London.

I am obviously someone who can be sacrificed.

Stuart, Hassan and the sheikh's gunmen are in prison, Laura tells me. The FBI is going to charge them with kidnapping and terrorism.

I ask a taxi driver to take me to the Miércoles Palace, which is on the outskirts of the old town, not far from the *Catedral Primada de América*, the first Catholic cathedral on the American continent.

The palace lies in the middle of such a vast park that it is almost impossible to see it between the ancient trees. Here and there, shallow ponds shimmer under arched bridges.

The park is surrounded by a wrought-iron fence that is nearly four metres high. At regular intervals there are carefully made brick pillars with inlaid panels showing biblical motifs.

Building on the palace started in the early 1500s, but it was not completed until a century later. According to the guidebook I bought at the airport, the Miércoles Palace and park were used as a model for the design of Versailles.

Today, it is Esteban Rodriquez who rules in the Miércoles Palace. A reclusive philanthropist who occasionally makes an appearance at royal events in Europe – always as a friend of the king or prince – but who generally avoids the limelight. The family has funded hospitals, churches and schools in the Third World via the more or less unknown Miércoles Foundation, based in Washington, DC. Esteban Rodriquez is married to Sophia Goldsmith, who was about to make her breakthrough as an actress in the USA when she met Rodriquez in 1958. They have two children: Javier, born in 1964, and Graciela, born in 1968.

I struggle down the pavement beside the overly high fence on my crutches, until I come to the main gate, which is locked and guarded by armed security men in neat uniforms. I look for a bell or intercom, but it seems that the occupants of the Miércoles Palace are not interested in door-to-door salesmen, tourists or missionaries. I try to call over one of the guards, but he is well practised in ignoring curious passers-by.

Eventually, I give up and go back to the hotel.

In the evening, I write a letter addressed to *Señor Esteban Rodriquez, Miércoles Palace* on the hotel's thick, headed and watermarked notepaper, telling him a bit about myself and my project. I ask whether it would be at all possible to meet him. I should perhaps have called it an audience with him.

I hand the envelope in at reception and ask them to courier the letter to the Miércoles Palace. The otherwise utterly correct concierge raises an eyebrow and says: 'Of course, sir, right away.'

2

I am woken early the next morning by someone knocking on my door.

I fumble to find my glasses. It is eight o'clock. I pull on some trousers and then open the door.

There are three men standing outside. The receptionist, whom I recognise, and behind him two immaculately dressed men in their thirties.

'Mr Belto,' the receptionist says with some excitement, 'these gentlemen are from the Miércoles Palace.'

The two men bow. One of them hands me a piece of paper with the Rodriquez coat of arms printed in gold at the top. The message is handwritten:

Dear Mr Beltø
At the risk of being presumptuous, I would like to invite you to breakfast at the palace and have therefore sent two of my trusted men to collect you. This will spare you the inconvenience of having to find your own way here in the morning traffic.
Respectfully,
Esteban Rodriquez

The shining black limousine that awaits outside the hotel resembles a three-hundred-metre-long pantechnicon. It has dark windows and white leather seats in the back.

The limousine accelerates smoothly and proceeds to break every traffic rule in the Dominican Republic. It therefore takes us no more than fifteen minutes to get to the Miércoles Palace. The gates open and we sweep past the guards. The wrought-iron gates then close behind us and shut out the rest of the world.

We drive through the park on a wide gravel road. I spot four swans on a pond by the trees and farther off in the distance, I see people riding on thoroughbred horses.

Then we leave the shade of the trees and I finally get a full view of the Miércoles Palace.

There are those who think that when you have seen one palace, you have seen them all. But the Miércoles Palace still takes my breath away. Its size and detail again make me wonder who on earth the Rodriquez who built the palace five hundred years ago was.

Five livery-clad servants are waiting when the limousine comes to a halt in front of the wide granite steps that lead up to the main entrance. I am welcomed with a bow and led into the palace.

The entrance hall must be three storeys high, and the staircase is so large that I wonder where they got all the marble from. I am taken up to the first floor, past huge paintings, pillars and endless corridors. We stop outside some double doors that must be at least four metres high, and the servants then bow as I enter the room.

They close the doors behind me.

In the middle of the room is a table, set for breakfast. It somehow looks a bit out of place in this enormous room.

The ceiling is decorated with religious motifs framed by gold ornamentations. Huge mirrors with gilded frames hang on the walls. There are bay windows at the far end of the room that lead out on to a terrace.

I walk slowly into the room. A door opens. I don't hear it, but I feel the draught on my cheek.

3

He stops on the red carpet runner and looks at me, smiling. My mouth falls open. We stand there staring at each other.

I have met him before.

At Luigi's gentlemen's club in Rome.

Esteban Rodriquez is the long-haired, distinguished gentleman who held my hand for so long.

'You?' I say simply.

His smile is like a scar.

'I met you in Rome,' I add to fill the silence as he comes towards me. Again we shake hands. Again he looks me in the eye.

Esteban Rodriquez has his hair combed back. His face is sharp and intense. He reminds me of a 1940s film star whose name I can't remember, and he is dressed as though he is expecting a supper invitation from the Great Gatsby.

'I've been watching your progress,' he tells me, in a pleasant baritone voice. He speaks English with only the slightest Spanish accent. 'You are a very determined young man. A bit like a terrier or a pit bull. When you get hold of something, you don't let go.'

He snaps his fingers. A maid materialises with two glasses of cognac on a tray.

'A good start to the day,' he suggests. We raise our glasses. The cognac burns down my throat and coils up in my stomach.

He rotates the glass in his hand and sniffs the bouquet. His thin nostrils quiver.

'And you? Who are you?' I ask.

'Who am I?' he replies, with a playful, questioning look. 'Most people can trace their family back four or five generations. But how many people know anything about their great-great-grandparents? The oldest preserved parish register in Norway is from 1623. But in my library, I have a genealogy where I can trace my family back, by name, to 930.'

'In Norway?'

'Of course.'

I look at him for a long time. My certainty grows.

Outside, the breeze strokes the trees and lifts the leaves.

'I was born here, on the fourth floor of the palace. My mother was a Cuban aristocrat, renowned for her beauty and her singing voice. My father first saw her at a ball and immediately sent her a luncheon invitation by courier. She came, of course. No one turns down an invitation to the Miércoles Palace. My father was blond, pale and blue eyed. My mother had nut-brown eyes, black hair and golden skin. It has always astonished me that my father's genes won over my mother's. But that has always been the case in our family, on the male side. There is something defiant about us.'

'You're a Guardian!'

He drinks the rest of his cognac down in one go and closes his eyes while he inhales deeply.

'You are the last Guardian!' I exclaim.

'I have taken the liberty of settling your bill at the hotel and having your belongings brought here to the palace. I have had a room prepared for you in the guest wing. I hope that you will accept my invitation?'

'No one turns down an invitation to the Miércoles Palace.'

We sit down at the table in the middle of the room. Servants immediately swarm around us with warm rolls, jam, scrambled eggs and cheese, and freshly squeezed orange juice. When we have finished eating and drinking, he shows me through the vast corridors to a guest room that is bigger than my entire flat. My suitcase is standing in the middle of the floor. Between the windows is a four-poster bed that is large enough for the largest orgies I could ever imagine. There are two Empire-style suites in the room. I also have a separate toilet, bathroom and dressing room. Heavy curtains have been pulled across the windows, which must look out to the park. One wall is lined with an impressive book collection that is locked behind crystal-glass doors.

I send Professor Llyleworth a text message to let him know where I am. For some reason, I get an answer from Diane's mobile phone.

The Miércoles Palace? Lucky you! Wish I was there!

A few minutes later, the professor replies:

You're privileged. Not many people get into the Miércoles Palace.
Greetings to Esteban. He is one of the SIS's most loyal donors.

4

When I have unpacked and showered, Esteban Rodriquez takes me on a tour.

'Graham Llyleworth sends his greetings,' I say.

'Ah, the professor! I give the SIS financial support every now and then. A very nice gentleman, indeed.'

It takes us well over an hour to wander through all the rooms: large and small drawing rooms and lounges, ornate bedrooms and boudoirs, all joined by a network of endless corridors. At regular intervals I have to sit down for a rest. I am getting blisters on my palms from my crutches.

I hear the dying notes of a clarinet somewhere in the palace. Esteban turns to me: 'Apologies. The son of my wife's chambermaid has just enrolled in a wind orchestra.'

We pass through two conjoining ballrooms, each as large as a concert hall, and extremely ornate. We then go on to a music room, where there are Steinway grand pianos, uprights, spinets, a Hammond B3 organ and a gilded harp. A cat that has been sleeping on a piano stool looks up with such a patronising gaze that it might as well have been the emperor of the universe.

But Esteban Rodriquez keeps the most amazing thing until last: the library.

The Miércoles Palace library occupies an entire wing on the west side of the complex. Not only does it contain tens of thousands of works from the Renaissance, Baroque and Romantic periods, it also houses thousands of original manuscripts relating to the European discovery and colonisation of America from the 1500s on. Esteban Rodriquez shows me handwritten letters from Christopher Columbus to Queen Isabella, and other important clerics and aristocrats.

'Come,' he says, and takes me over to an exhibit case. Under the heavy glass I see a document, written on parchment that has darkened with age. 'A letter from one of the people who survived the massacre in Greenland. A group of trappers in Newfoundland were supposed to take the letter back to Iceland, but the messenger was killed by native Indians, and the letter somehow ended up in the possession of a settler family. It describes how they escaped from Greenland when the Fraternity of Guardians realised that the Vatican had traced them and the Pope's army was on its way.'

I carefully read the Old Norse text: *We sought refuge with the holy treasure in the country to the west of the horizon.*

Esteban repeats almost inaudibly: 'The country to the west of the horizon.'

'The USA . . .'

'Hmm. Remember that this was in the middle of the fifteenth century and, strictly speaking, neither the USA nor Canada existed. The fugitives from the east coast of Greenland followed the route of Leif Eriksson and the Vikings; they rounded the southernmost tip of Greenland and sailed up the west coast, crossing the Davis Strait to Baffin Island, and then continued south to places that are known today as Labrador, Newfoundland, Nova Scotia, Maine and New Hampshire. Vinland . . .'

We look at the document in silence as we imagine the difficult voyage in freezing-cold waters.

The clarinet continues to complain somewhere so far off that it's almost inaudible.

'Bjørn, you found something on Iceland.'

I'm immediately on my guard.

He puts his hand on my shoulder. 'A manuscript . . . have you read it?'

'No.'

'Let me guess – it was a Hebrew text with a Coptic translation?'

'You're good at guessing.'

'You have no idea what that manuscript is worth.'

'Three murders. A broken leg and a broken finger. And a figure of fifteen million dollars has been mentioned. So yes, I do have a fairly good idea.'

'Where is it?'

'We're in the process of translating it.'

'But *where*?'

The intensity of the question convinces me that he actually doesn't know the answer.

'In a safe place,' I reply.

5

'Bartolomeo Columbus laid the foundation stone for the Miércoles Palace.'

It is late in the afternoon. Esteban Rodriquez is leaning back in a wicker chair out on one of the terraces that over-look the park. He lights a cigar. A breath of wind snatches some grey flakes of ash from the tip. The air is scented with mimosa. A tern plays on the sea breeze. A gardener has turned on the sprinkler, which produces a smell of moisture.

'The Spanish colonial powers were established here in

Santo Domingo when Christopher Columbus first came to America.'

'Rumour has it that your family came here with him.'

'You've obviously understood the connection.'

'You are the last Guardian.'

He takes a puff on his cigar. 'Santo Domingo was the first European settlement in the New World – if we disregard the Norse settlements in North America, that is. They still argue about which island Columbus landed on first when he came here in 1492. What many historians refuse to acknowledge is that Columbus was familiar with the Vikings' voyages to Vinland.'

'You're talking about his visits to Iceland and Greenland in 1477?'

'Columbus and the other sailors talked to fishermen and trappers who told them about a country to the west of the horizon. Columbus thought they were talking about Asia.'

'A slight misunderstanding.'

'The problem was that he had miscalculated the circumference of the world. Columbus knew, as all sailors did, that the world was round. He based his calculations on those of the geographer Marinus, from Tyre, but he believed that the degrees represented a shorter distance on the earth's surface than was in fact the case. And to top it all, he worked with the Italian linear measure that was equivalent to 1,238 metres, and not the Arabic measure that was equivalent to 1,830 metres. With this flawed starting point, Columbus calculated that the circumference of the earth was roughly equivalent to 25,000 kilometres and that the distance between the Canaries and Japan was 3,700 kilometres. His critics were not so much frightened that his ships would fall off the edge of the world, but rather that the sailors would die of starvation and thirst long before they reached Asia.'

'So in fact, America blocked their way to certain death.'

'And Columbus could return to Europe triumphant, convinced that he had sailed to Asia. It was only on his third expedition in 1498 that he set foot on the South American mainland. And he never actually went to North America. He returned to Europe in 1504, and died there two years later, in Valladolid in Spain.'

'I read recently that they've discovered where he is buried.'

'Columbus was first buried in Valladolid, but his remains were then taken back to Seville and later over the ocean to the cathedral here in Santo Domingo. In 1795, the French took his remains with them to Havana, and in 1898 the bones were returned to the cathedral in Seville. In 1877, a box of bones, bearing the inscription *Don Christopher Columbus*, was found here in Santo Domingo. Many people believed that they had moved the wrong body.'

'So where is he buried?'

'They are all wrong. He is buried here at the Miércoles Palace.'

My breathing gets stuck.

'That is what they wanted, his family. They made an agreement with the court. Columbus's remains were buried in a grave here in the park of the Miércoles Palace in 1569. The bones that everyone thought were Columbus were in fact those of his son, Diego.'

'I don't understand what the connection is between Columbus and the Guardians.'

He taps his cigar, making the ash fall all over the terrace as fine dust. A breeze catches his white hair, which he tucks back behind his ears.

'A long story,' he says, and stubs out the cigar. 'A story that spans hundreds of years.'

And then he tells it to me.

The History of the Guardians

1

ESTEBAN RODRIQUEZ presses his fingers together like a tower.

'To understand the history of the Guardians, you first have to understand the Egyptian high priest, Asim. He was a very learned man, and knew a great deal about many disciplines and faiths. He tutored those closest to him in Egypt, and later in Norway, in religion, mythology and magic. To understand the stars. To see into the future. To commune with the dead. To write coded messages and secret script. To draw maps. To interpret dreams. To find holy geometric patterns in nature. Asim was an experienced mystic.'

Esteban tilts back his head and closes his eyes. Then he leans forward again and locks his eyes on to mine so suddenly that I jump.

'Asim was a composite of beliefs and ideas that we might not see as being compatible in the West. As a high priest, he worshipped the Egyptian gods. But Amon-Ra must have been a tolerant god, because he also worshipped Abraham and Moses, Jesus and Muhammad. He was an astrologist and practised occult magic. But he was also well read, good with languages and had mastered many of the disciplines of his day. A learned and wise man. And he had dedicated his life to one thing: to protecting the tomb of a holy mummy and the treasure and texts that had been left in the deceased's tomb. The mummy was already two and a half thousand years old when Asim became high priest, which is older than Jesus's remains would have been if they existed today. So when the Vikings attacked the temple and emptied the tomb, they not only desecrated his faith, they also robbed him of his mission. Asim would have given his life for the mummy. But when he realised that they were so much stronger in force, he chose to go with them. If he went with the enemy, he could at least try to protect the Holy One and, in time, have everything returned to the mummy's eternal resting place in the tomb in Egypt.'

'An ambitious project.'

'An ambitious man.'

'How did Olav find out about the tomb if it was such a secret?'

'In Cleopatra's day, a disloyal and discredited priest from the Amon-Ra cult drew a map that showed not only where the tomb lay in relation to the Nile, but also where the entrance to the temple was and the two outer chambers that camouflaged the inner burial chamber. He was presumably trying to curry favour with the Romans. But the Romans did not trust the traitor. All we know is that the map ended up in Rome, by way of Cleopatra's husband, Mark Antony. It was later sent, presumably by accident, to King Athelstan of England with some other gifts. He then left it to his foster son, Håkon the Good. And so the map fell into the hands of the young Olav Haraldsson.'

Esteban rubs between his eyes, as though he has a headache. He looks away, and it is as if he suddenly changes into a different person. I am reminded of the poor souls at my nerve clinic, who are lost in the wilds of madness.

'Asim sent a plea for help to the Caliph of Egypt when they were with Duke Richard in Rouen. He attached the first Coptic translation of the papyrus manuscript from the tomb. Some years later, from Norway, he sent another plea to the caliph, which was hidden in a clay statue along with a map. But the postal system was not reliable in those days. The pleas, the map and the translation were all snapped up by the Pope's intelligence, which intercepted all suspicious post.'

Esteban takes out another cigar from an exclusive wooden box, and lights it with great ceremony. He sits with half-closed eyes and enjoys the tobacco before continuing with the story.

'Asim sat waiting to be rescued at Selja, while King Olav Christianised Norway with threats and violence. Asim must have realised at some point that none of his countrymen would find their way to the icy wastes. So he devised a plan that would not only protect the mummy, but would also ensure its safe return to Egypt.'

'What sort of plan?'

'He formed a fraternity, an order of guardians. The first Guardians were monks that Asim knew from the abbey and men who had fought with the king. So the order was a mixture of monks, skalds, rune masters and Vikings who still believed in the Old Norse gods. Asim added Coptic and Egyptian mythology to this already heady mix. He believed that the mummy would be resurrected as a god in human form. The Christians were waiting for the resurrected Christ and then, later, their fallen king, St Olav the Holy. In a complete chaos of religion, numerology, astrology and sacred geometry, the wise man Asim's Egyptian mythology was fused with the Norwegians' Old Norse beliefs and Christianity. It was from this that the symbols ankh, *tiwaz* and cross arose. This combination of the three sacred symbols represented the Fraternity of Guardians, but also formed a kind of occult protection across the religions. Asim instructed the Guardians in religion, astrology and esoteric arts. They submitted wholeheartedly to their master with great loyalty and swore to dedicate their lives to the task.'

Esteban puffs on his cigar before blowing the smoke right in my face. I wave it away with my hand.

'Asim also used supernatural powers. In Egyptian mythology and tradition, it is important to honour the gods by building monuments. The world is, as you know, full of sacred places that have been established according to mysterious patterns that escape most of us. Asim consulted the stars and made a horoscope in which he aligned the earth's sacred geometry with a particular constellation. By positioning five burial chambers so that they formed a pentagram that accorded with the constellation of Gemini, the tombs would then be protected by a supernatural power. And, as you also know, the locations were chosen based on his own rather basic map: St Sunniva's Cave, Nidaros, Hamar, Tunsberg and Bjørgvin. It took those who came after him, the newly Christianised nation-builders, well over a hundred years to complete this grand plan. When the "monuments" were finished, they all concealed a secret tomb. Nidaros Cathedral, Hamar Cathedral, Tunsberg Fort and Lyse Abbey.'

'What about the stave churches? How do they fit into all this?'

'That's another chapter. I'll come to that.'

Esteban goes over to a drawer and takes out a worn document written with a pen plotter on perforated paper.

'Asim's own account, in a rather clumsy translation.'

My heart and hand tremble when he passes me the copy.

The Story of Asim

All glory to you, Amon-Ra, almighty god and lord of truth; all glory to you, Osiris, king of eternity; all glory to you, Jesus, merciful saviour and son of god; all glory to you, Muhammad, most praised prophet of Allah. I am Asim, high priest of the temple of the Humble Servants of His Holiness, the Sun God Amon-Ra and the Guardians of the Covenant, close to the walls of Thebes and the tombs of the kings. I write these words as a prisoner in the land of torment. In truth, I say to you: I have been taken to the end of the world, a kingdom of eternal ice and cold, of snow and stone and mountains that scrape the skies. Men as brutal and wild as the most terrible demons of hell wreak havoc on the deep fjords and the dark forests. I hope that it will please the gods when I relate that I have found a new tomb for THE HOLY ONE.

Here, gods of gods, is my story:

The barbarians came at daybreak, when Amon-Ra's breath coloured the skies red. I stood barefoot on the rock with the night chill still in it, and stared at the strange ships that came sailing down the river; elegant longboats with great sails and snapping dragon mouths raised on their prows. Ships filled the river as far as the headland to the north. And ever more boats rounded the head.

I had woken long before the others. I had washed away the night's sweat with water that was stored in ceramic pots in the coolest corner of our sleeping quarters and picked and eaten some fruit. Refreshed, I left the temple and walked out into the morning. I stopped at the rock when I saw the ships. I looked up to the heavens and asked why the stars had not warned me. Why had the gods not prepared me? Which strange gods watched over and aided these wild men? It was not possible that they could be more powerful than my gods. Why, then, had my gods closed their eyes and turned away?

The barbarians were as silent as cobras. The most cunning and dangerous animals are the most silent. You never hear a crocodile before it locks you in its teeth, or a snake before its poison paralyses you. Ill at ease, I followed the ships with my eyes. They were so much faster than our river boats. How had they managed to pass the forts and ports of entry? They must be invincible. I hoped that they would sail on to Karnak or Waset or the Valley of the Kings, or even farther south to Swenet or Abu Simbel. But this hope died when the ships that were closest lowered their sails and made for the shore. Long rows of oars came out from the ships' sides and moved rhythmically through the water. Without a sound. No shouts. No war cry. Just silence. The demonic dragon-heads stared at me. I ran back into the temple and sent the priest Fenuku to warn the temple guards and men from the village. Then I hurried back to the rock. Down on the riverbanks, the barbarians were starting to come ashore. Mighty Anubis, they were many; they came in their thousands, and they were warriors, giant, tall and muscular men with long, unkempt hair and beards. Each one carrying swords, axes, spears and decorated shields.

They leapt out of their ships in a mass that made the ground tremble and ran up towards the temple. They were led by a tall, thickset and strong young man. I did not move. I proudly raised my head and folded my arms. Now my gods would come to my aid. Now Egypt's eternal rulers would protect THE HOLY ONE. The young man stopped a few paces from me. His face was broad, pale and ruddy, his hair light brown and tangled. His blue eyes shone like sapphires in the rising sun. I had now understood who they were. In diplomat Ibn Fadlan's account from a journey on the River Volga nearly one hundred years since, I had read of the fearless and barbarian Rus. In al-Yaquabi's geographical work he talks of barbarians who had sailed as far as

Seville on the great Córdoba river. Al-Magus. Fire worshippers.

Leave! I thundered, and raised my arms to the skies. Turn back! The mightiest gods protect this temple.

In the Book of the Dead they talk of the hour of wrath. And the hour of wrath was upon us. The young man stared at me. When he took a step forward to cut me down, I was prepared to meet my ancestors. My own gods had betrayed me. In that moment of wrath, the gods whispered in my ear. To die was no heroic act. To die would merely be to flee my holy mission. I could not serve THE HOLY ONE in death. I had to submit to the barbarians. My mission was to protect THE HOLY ONE and his treasure. And therefore, mighty Amon-Ra, I fell on my knees on the flagstones and looked up to meet the eyes of the young leader. Therefore it was, great Osiris, that I laid my forehead and palms on the ground in surrender. It was in humble sacrifice, O holy lioness Sekhmet, that I surrendered to the uncivilised pagans from the ends of the world. And never, great gods, from fear.

The young leader granted me grace. Two of his subordinates dragged me behind them down to the largest ship, where they tied me to the mast.

The barbarians were without mercy. They gathered many of the priests in front of the temple, alongside a troop of armed temple guards and a large group of craftsmen with spades, picks and axes. Some had retreated into the temple to protect boldly the secret entrance to the tomb behind the altar. Others armed themselves and marched down towards the fleet on the river. Tightly bound to the mast, I watched helplessly as the barbarians slew all who resisted. One by one our courageous men were felled and hacked by the barbarians' swords and axes. None of the tactics we had practised in the temple grounds would help against this swarm of godless men; the formations to protect ourselves, the footwork and arm movements we had perfected to achieve optimal strength when thrusting the sword, all was wasted in our meeting with these wild men, who charged ahead without giving their opponents any chance at all. The fight did not last long. The blood of my men ran in the sand and dust. Clouds of flies hovered above the drying pools of blood and the gaping wounds of the dead. The sun was hot. Amon-Ra's anger was without limits.

When the barbarians returned to the ship carrying the coffin of THE HOLY ONE, I wept. Not even I, with my unworthy eyes, had seen the cypress coffin that lay in the innermost chamber. Weeping, I begged them to stop. But they neither heard nor paid heed. Four of the barbarians carried the coffin down to the ship, where they covered it with layers of sacking, straw and hemp, and then wrapped it in the cloth they used to repair the sail. Finally, they tied a rope around it and stowed the cushioned coffin in a hold under the deck. The sacrilege filled my eyes with tears and my soul with sorrow. The barbarians left behind the Canopic jars with THE HOLY ONE's mummified organs, but took with them all that they could carry of the gold and jewels, and magnificent gifts, such as the statue of Anubis, the gold caskets, the gold statues, amulets, scarabs, the magic figures, two boat models and some of the ushabti who were there to serve THE HOLY ONE on the other side. To my horror I also saw the sealed casket that contained THE HOLY SCRIPTURES. They left nothing untouched.

As a prisoner on the large ship of the young leader with the blue eyes, I sat bound to the mast until the Nile ran out into the open sea. From the shadow of the Lighthouse of Alexandria, we sailed west towards the cradle of the sun.

The horror! Holy Osiris, they stink! Like unclean animals – yes, pigs with rotting intestines and badgers with gangrene – they infect the air around them with their bodily odour, the pungency of stale sweat, acrid belching, fermenting intestinal gas, confined feet and unwashed sexual organs. Their clothes reek of old urine and excrement, of sweat, blood and the rotting entrails of their victims. Just as ibn Fadlan described, they are dirty and oblivious to their own odours. But they also have human qualities: they are proud and spirited and care for their families and property. They have sailed the seas and rivers, plundering and wreaking havoc, for two hundred years. I understand well why the coast folk fear them. They are fast and merciless. Long before any enemy has managed to raise an army, they have come ashore and left again, with riches, women and slaves. Their speedy warships are flat bottomed and so shallow that they can sail up on to the riverbank. Their courage in battle knows no limits. They are bloodthirsty lions. They are cunning and shrewd. In battle they are fearless, crude and brutal. They fight savagely against any enemy. Even with fatal wounds and missing limbs they continue to fight. This courage is easily understood: courageous men who die in battle are taken to a paradise they call Valhalla by the Valkyries, where the fallen warriors can fight, eat and drink eternally. The end of the world is called Ragnarok.

I learnt many words from the slaves who brought me food, and picked up others by listening to the men's talk. I have a quick ear. By the age of eight, I had mastered the languages of the six countries around Egypt. When I was twenty, I spoke twelve languages. Some are born with beautiful singing voices; I was born with the ability to learn the tongues of others.

For days and weeks we sailed west, and then north.

The air became cooler. Soon they let me wander around freely on the ship.

The barbarians attacked towns and villages along the coast. They raped and pillaged and killed and torched. At what I thought was the end of the journey, we sailed into a town, far inland, on a river that twisted and turned like a snake in the sand, just as the Nile. Here no one drew their weapons. They were among friends. The town was called Rouen. Their host was a ruler they called duke. From the duke's palace I sent a letter and a transcript of THE HOLY SCRIPTURES to the caliph. Then later we sailed across the sea once more to an island in the west, where we stayed for a while.

It was autumn when we set sail farther on to the end of the world and the frozen chill of the kingdom of death. We travelled from the kingdom of the sun and the fertile banks of the Nile to the barren stony coast of the land of snow. We left behind the beneficence of Amon-Ra, the warm breath of Osiris, and submitted to the barbarians' gods. O Gods of my ancestors, give me strength! When I was a child and my nightmares showed me to the gates of the kingdom of death, it was always a landscape such as this – cold, desolate and wild – that I thought I could see through the mists of death. We sailed for days along the coast of a land they called Norðrvegr. The mountains towered into the skies and vanished in the clouds. Ragged islands of cliffs and sharp rocks stood between the shore and the open sea.

One afternoon, the ship came to an outlying island. I stood with both hands on the rails and looked at the rounded mountain on the small isle. I caught the scent of what I had learned to know as earth and marsh, forest and mountain, heather and moss. I drank in the unexpected smells; they reminded me dimly of my lost homeland when the Nile receded after floods.

We moored the boats to two timbers that were stood between boulders. A small wooden chapel had been raised at the foot of the steep mountain. While the king and bishops went in to pray to their god, I and a Viking by the name of Bård clambered up the mountainside. High up in a rock face that was difficult to reach and impossible to see was the opening to a great cave.

My thanks, mighty Amon-Ra, for leading us to this place.

I have never left the abbey that we built on that island in the country where the sickle moon stands.

In a letter that I sent to Egypt, I described the long voyage north. I told where I would hide THE HOLY ONE. The letter, which was written on vellum, was then rolled up and sealed and hidden in a glass bottle in a ceramic statue of Anubis, ruler of the afterlife and god of mummification. I gave two loyal warrior-monks gold from THE HOLY ONE's treasure and sent them to the nearest trading centre to find a boat that was sailing south. They were to take Anubis, who contained my letter, all the way to Egypt. I do not know if they succeeded, for I never heard from them again. But I doubt that they reached their destination.

With them, they had the verse that my fellow countrymen were to show when they came to find THE HOLY ONE, and that the GUARDIANS would recognise. Only the learned in Egypt would know and use the words from the Book of the Dead. The GUARDIANS would take such men who came bearing the key to the tomb of THE HOLY ONE.

~ The Key ~

Courtiers of the Royal Court accompany
The Osiris King Tut-ankh-Amon westwards.
They proclaim: O King! Come in Peace!
O God! Protector of this land!

At this time, I set the men to making a burial chamber in the cave. The rock here was far harder than in Egypt, but we were fortunate that the cave formed a natural chamber. The work took many years. As in Egypt, I had an inner chamber built, and in the middle of the tomb there was a stone plinth for THE HOLY ONE's sarcophagus. I placed all the treasure that Olav had left in my care in a side chamber. I also prepared a plinth for my own coffin hard by the back wall of the chamber, lest I be called to the underworld before my people came. Together with the five best men, I decorated the walls with painting and old hieroglyphs, cartouches and runes. We raised an inner wall with an arched entrance that is to be sealed on the day that the last body is brought to its final resting place in the sanctuaries of the pentagram. Thereafter the wall and entrance will be concealed by many tons of stones, such that the rock fall appears to form the bottom of the cave.

A cold sun wandered across the heavens. We shared little of Olav's battles here on the island. The winters were hard. The cold cut into my body like a knife. The merciless frost of the snow land always remained a stranger to me. When I could, I transcribed the holy scriptures and translated them into Coptic. The days were filled with instruction, map drawing, contemplation and rituals. Out in the barbarous wilds, King Olav fought to share his new god with his people. I understood now who Olav was. He was, in truth, a holy man. King Olav was the resurrected Jesus. Christ returned after a thousand years in the body of Olav to create God's kingdom on earth.

When I was told of King Olav's death at Stiklestad, I sent ten monks to fetch the deceased. His body was exchanged with one that resembled him in appearance. In a boat, the king's body was taken from Nidaros along the coast to Selja. Here I taught the monks how the Egyptians embalm and treat their dead. With the monks around me, I mummified Olav's body and asked that they do the same for me – in order that I too could meet my gods when I left this life. We built a new plinth in the tomb so that the king can rest with THE HOLY ONE. Together they will be resurrected when one thousand years have passed.

When Olav was in the tomb, I gathered thirty-three of the most faithful warriors, monks, bishops and skalds from the circle around King Olav. And I exhorted them to form a secret fraternity of GUARDIANS, a holy order. With their very lives they would protect THE HOLY ONE, his scriptures and treasure, and the secret of THE HOLY ONE's final resting place. Each of the GUARDIANS must swear to initiate a worthy successor in an eternal cycle. I asked them to communicate using codes in order that the uninitiated may not read the message. On a mystic map of southern Norway, I drew the holy symbol and explained that the form of the pentagram pleased the gods. Everything submits to the harmony of the pentagram and is protected by its divine power. I told the GUARDIANS: in the next hundred years, you must build four magnificent sanctuaries. Beneath each sanctuary, in the greatest secret, a tomb shall be built. The men for whom these tombs are intended shall rest here on this island until their own tomb is complete. There shall be a total of five tombs that form a powerful alliance in the divine form of the pentagram. The most important tomb was that which was already completed here on the island. Here King Olav would rest with THE HOLY ONE. In Nidaros, they should build a cathedral over the burial chamber of Bishop Grimkell. In Hamar, they should build a cathedral over Bishop Bernhard's tomb, and in Tunsberg, they should raise a fort over the tomb of Bishop Sigurd. In Bjørgvin, they should establish an abbey over the tomb of Bishop Rudolf.

These words are dedicated to you, Great Amon-Ra, and to you, JAHVE, and to you, Allah.

2

I feel overwhelmed after reading Asim's version of the events that took place a thousand years ago. I hand the copy back to Esteban.

'My sister translated it as well as she could in the eighties.'

'She knows Coptic?'

'Beatriz knows a lot of strange things.'

'I still have so many questions.'

'Not surprising, really.'

'One thing I don't understand is Asim's loyalty to King Olav. He didn't try to escape. He didn't turn against the king who had kidnapped him and emptied the tomb. Quite the opposite, in fact – it almost seems that Asim started to idolise the king.'

Esteban folds his hands on the table in front of him. 'Something happened to Asim. Perhaps on the journey back to Norway, perhaps in Rouen, perhaps at the abbey. King Olav must have appealed to his religious longings, and the fact is that Asim started to see the king as a prophet, someone who was in contact with the gods. Remember, Asim was a mystic who worked with numbers. It was a thousand years since Jesus had walked the earth. He got it into his head that King Olav was not only a prophet, he was the resurrected Christ. And from there, the leap to his next prophecy was not so great: that THE HOLY ONE and Olav would be resurrected in a powerful religious union after one thousand years.'

'And he really believed that?'

'Since when have religions been rational? Religion is about dreams and longing. Many people who feel that life lacks meaning look to religion for the answer. Asim's sect wanted to unite all faiths. They wanted to roll all religions together into one. Asim's message was that everything is one, only we interpret the same truth in different ways. For Asim, it was completely natural to mummify Olav and put him to rest with the thousand-year-old mummy. That was how he kept in favour with the gods.'

'Asim was not a prisoner. Couldn't he have taken the mummy back to Egypt?'

Esteban wags his head a couple of times before answering. 'In theory, yes, he could have left Selja. But how? It was risky to travel all the way from Norway to Egypt with such a treasure. On land he would have to confront bandits, local armies, tariffs, mad sovereigns and blood-thirsty landowners. And also witches and trolls. He had to traverse great tracts of land, cross rivers and mountain ranges of dizzying heights.'

'But by sea . . .'

'He would need an impressive Viking fleet in order to protect himself against pirates, marauders, more tariffs and enemy armadas.' Esteban's face is split by a fleeting smile. 'But of more importance was the prediction that Asim found in the stars; his astrological prophecy that THE HOLY ONE and King Olav would both reappear in Egypt in a thousand years.'

Even though I don't believe in astrology or predictions,

Asim's prophecy gives me an odd feeling, like seeing the reflection of something that doesn't exist.

'And a thousand years have passed now,' I say in a very quiet voice.

3

Esteban apologises that he has to go and make some urgent phone calls. While he is away, I listen to the sounds of the park and ponder on the mystery of Asim. A beetle that is as big as a Matchbox car scuttles over the terrace tiles. A hysterical bird flaps past. When Esteban returns, we carry on talking about the Guardians. Esteban knows more than what is told in Asim's story. His library is presumably bursting with letters and writings from his ancestors.

'The Fraternity of Guardians was carefully selected,' he says. 'It was bound by secrecy, loyalty and pride, based on Old Norse ideals. But Asim was wise. He only told a chosen few the whole secret. Otherwise, they each knew only what they needed to know, as they do in intelligence services and criminal gangs. Only a handful knew about the tomb on Selja, and they were known as the Inner Circle of Seven.'

'And the codes?'

'The codes were used to guide and instruct the other members of the fraternity and the next generation of Guardians. Every time the mummy or other parts of the treasure were moved from a stave church or burial chamber, the Guardians left messages to say where the treasure had been taken. They signed it out, if you like. The code told who had taken over responsibility. No one other than the Guardians would be able to decipher these riddles.'

'So the codes were an internal communication system between the Guardians.'

'You could say that. Imagine if one of the Guardians died

unexpectedly. It would be catastrophic if he had not left a message for the other links in the chain. The Inner Circle of Seven always had a complete overview, whereas the other Guardians were local masters who had no idea of the fraternity's structure. They had their instructions to initiate and share their knowledge with the next Guardian and the Guardians in the neighbouring parish, so that there was always someone there with the necessary knowledge. When the treasure was moved from one church, the Guardian wrote a coded message to let the others know where. Today, a Guardian would send an encrypted text message or email. Back then, they carved their messages in runes.'

'How did the Guardians find the messages from their predecessors?'

'In the same way that you did – they looked. But unlike you, the Guardians knew exactly what they were looking for and where to look. That was part of the fraternity's shared knowledge. Codes, messages, instructions, directions and clues were left in places where the Guardians had been taught to look. The Guardians left behind clues in coded rune texts and cryptic messages for their fellow Guardians and the next generation. The Urnes Guardians would, for example, know that the treasure had been moved from their church to Flesberg around 1180. But they wouldn't know that it was then divided, and one part was sent out of the country and the other went to Garmo in Lom. Let's say in 1250 the Grand Master of the fraternity knew most of the Guardians had been killed by war or disease, so he instructed the Guardian from Urnes to move the treasure to a safe place. The Urnes Guardian would not know where the treasure was, but the Guardian who initiated him would have told him that the directions were on a rune stick in one of the staves in the church. The rune stick would then direct him to Flesberg, and the word *sonorous* would be a hint that he should look for the church bell. There he would find the runes which he, unlike most other people, would be able to interpret. You remember the text on the bell? *The bell rings Urnes fifty years Flesberg fifty years Lom fifty years*. To a Guardian, the text was self-explanatory. I'll come back to the fifty years later. But, given the knowledge he had about the codes, the Guardian would now go to Lom. There he would find the message that *the sacred scripts and the sleeping god are brought to safety; they are with our Guardian kinsmen in the land where the sun goes down*, in other words, with Snorri in Iceland, and that the next clue is waiting *where the sun rises*. As the Guardian knew that the stave churches had been positioned to make a cross, he would know that *Lars* was in the stave church at Ringebu, and that he would find the next instructions in his *Bible*.'

'A kind of treasure hunt across the centuries . . .'

'A treasure hunt for the initiated. The Guardians initiated their own successors. The initiates were told where the clues were hidden and how they should be interpreted. In this way, the codes were unintelligible to most people, whereas a Guardian would not only find them, but would also be able to decipher and read them. So the new generation of Guardians could then follow the treasure from stave church to stave church, and from hiding place to hiding place.'

'What would the Guardians have done if Asim's Egyptian priests had in fact turned up?'

'The Guardians knew that the worthy successors of Asim would have the key, a rhyme. It is a prayer from the Egyptian Book of the Dead, which was painted on the wall of Tutankhamen's burial chamber: *the courtiers of the Royal household accompany Osiris-King-Tut-ankh-Amon to the west. They shout: O King! Come in peace! O God! Protector of this land!*'

'The text from the Snorri Codex . . .'

'The key was never used. The Egyptians never came. But the Vatican did.'

'Too late.'

'Correct. The Vatican had stowed away the confiscated manuscripts and maps without really looking at them. Another hundred years would pass before the Vatican found time to study the texts. In 1129, Cardinal Bishop Benedictus Secundus sent the knight Clemens de'Fieschi to Norway to look for the treasure. In 1152, the Pope's envoy Nicholas Breakspear, who not long after became Pope himself, was close to finding the tomb in Hamar, where he established a diocese. In 1180, Pope Alexander III sent another expedition. Ten years later, the Hospitallers established themselves in Norway when they were given Værne Abbey by King Sverre Sigurdsson. Then in 1230, Pope Gregory IX made yet another attempt.'

'How did the Guardians know that the Vatican was looking for the cave on Selja?'

'They were warned. It wasn't possible for the Vatican to keep secret the fact that an armed unit was on its way north through Europe, complete with scouts and spies. When they heard the warnings, the Guardians thought it was safer, certainly in the meantime, to change hiding places.'

'Even though the tomb at Selja was sacred?'

'Asim had left behind lots of instructions to cover all eventualities. The Guardians knew what they should do. Based on astrological predictions, Asim had decided that if the mummy was under threat, it should go on a sacred journey in accordance with the magic number fifty.'

'What's magical about fifty?'

'In the Bible, fifty is the jubilee number. The jubilee year was a time when sinners were forgiven, slaves and prisoners were released, and debts were waived. The Guardians loyally followed Asim's instructions. So, when they got wind that expeditions from the Vatican were on their way, they built a burial chamber under Urnes Church, which was already under construction. Urnes was built exactly one hundred years after the death of Olav. Fifty years later, they moved the treasure to Flesberg Church, et cetera.'

'And the Vatican could not work out what was going on?'

'They never worked out what was going on with the stave churches. Nor did they know about the cave. When Clemens de'Fieschi followed Asim's rather imprecise map, he ended up at the Dollstein Cave. The next expedition did in fact check St Sunniva's Cave on Selja, but the tomb was hidden so well that they didn't discover it. Everything was done according to Asim's plan until 1239, but then the Guardians panicked. The *Birkebeiner* king, Håkon Håkonsson, was getting too close, so they didn't want to take any chances, and smuggled the most important thing out of the country.'

'Most important thing?'

'The mummy. And the gold casket that contained the six pots with the original papyrus manuscript.'

'To Iceland.'

'Two years earlier, Snorri Sturluson had been initiated as a Guardian by Duke Skule. Snorri took over responsibility for the coffin and the sacred manuscript and took them home with him to Iceland. He also took with him the Norwegian Guardians' parchments.'

'So the codex that Sira Magnus found in Reykholt was Snorri's heritage to the Guardians who would come after him?'

'Thordur the Stammerer, to be precise. The parchment codex included Snorri's own handwritten instructions, as well as the parchments that he had taken with him from Norway. The documents revealed – with the help of codes and maps – where the hiding places were in Norway and Iceland.'

'You suggested that King Håkon Håkonsson was looking for the treasure?'

'Someone had told the secret to King Håkon and he got a fellow conspirator, Gissur Thorvaldsson, to put pressure on Snorri in order to force the truth out of him. Snorri remained silent, and was killed.'

'So then Thordur the Stammerer was the Guardian.'

'Snorri had initiated Thordur the Stammerer as his successor. Håkon summoned Thordur to Norway in order to interrogate him. The king was frantically searching for the treasure. He married his daughter off to the Castilian king's brother and sent diplomats to the Sultan of Tunis, all in the hope that something would lead him to the treasure.'

'Caves ... stave churches ... codes ... It's all a bit confusing.'

'For you. For us, today. But you have to remember that you have been picking up loose ends. You have not discovered things in the correct, chronological order. Quite the opposite, you have arbitrarily uncovered fragments of the past. The copy of the manuscript that you found at Thingvellir was put there by Snorri over two hundred years after Asim had transcribed it. The stave churches were built long after the tomb in the cave on Selja.'

'Do you know why Snorri divided the treasure?'

'Probably for safety's sake. He built a tomb on his own farm in Reykholt, where he then kept the mummy and the papyrus manuscript. Asim's translation of the manuscript was hidden in the cave at Thingvellir.'

'And the rest of the treasure continued to be hidden in the stave churches?'

'At the time, confusion prevailed among the Guardians. The treasure had been spread, but they still completed the work on the four stave churches. And just as the sanctuaries had accorded with the pentagram, the stave churches were also positioned in a sacred pattern, in the

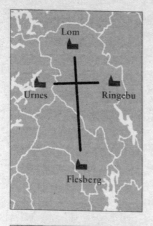

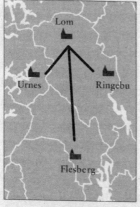

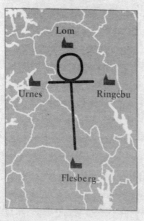

form of an Egyptian ankh, the rune *tiwaz* and a cross. The cave on Selja had been empty for a while, so around 1250 the rest of the treasure was moved back to Selja. The last instructions – which involved the clever twist of the two statues of St Lawrence in Ringebu and Borgund – completed the Norwegian end of the cover operation. And by this stage, the most important part of the treasure, the mummy and the manuscript, were out of the Norwegians' control.'

'This is not easy to follow.'

'It is precisely because the cover operation was so complex and tangled that the treasure never fell into the hands of the Vatican.'

'And then the mummy was moved from Iceland to Greenland when Norway was devastated by the plague.'

'That's right. And after a century in Greenland, the Vatican once again started to catch up with them. In 1447, a papal expedition to Greenland landed slightly too far to the south, which gave someone time to warn the Guardians, so fifty men and women managed to escape by boat. The rest of the settlement was simply slaughtered.'

'And the Guardians sailed to Vinland?'

'The Guardians established five settlements in Vinland over the next fifty years. They moved steadily south, leaving behind them rune stones, longhouses and stone towers.'

'Why did they never go back to Norway and Iceland?'

'Because they had decided to return the mummy to Egypt. It had been known since Viking times that there were trade winds that would take you east from what we today know as Florida and the Caribbean. These winds would take them to Europe and the Mediterranean, via the Azores. So that was why they moved steadily south. They were looking for the wind that would take them home. When they reached the Caribbean, they came into contact with seafaring natives who told them about the white people on the islands that lay even farther south. The Guardians' ships were now so decrepit that they were in no real condition to cross the Atlantic, with all its storms and weather, so they hoped that they would be able to return home with these European explorers. And it was here at Santo Domingo that they met Bartolomeo Columbus. And it was from here that they sent the encrypted letter to the archbishop in Nidaros, the letter that you are rumoured to have found in Washington.'

I don't say anything and Esteban continues: 'Archbishop Erik Valkendorf was a Guardian himself, in what was by then a very diluted order that no longer knew exactly what it was protecting. Valkendorf did, however, confirm that this happened exactly five hundred years after the events in Egypt and five hundred years before the mummy was due to be resurrected at home in Egypt, according to Asim's prophecy. The magic of numbers again.'

'Just like the Seal of the Guardians that you showed me

in Rome, where the combination of symbols always comes to six six six. What was that, by the way?'

Esteban starts to chuckle. 'My friends in the gentlemen's club are quick to exaggerate. Numbers can be anything you want them to be. I think Bartolomeo was simply enjoying himself, writing out the three symbols in different sequences. And if you give the symbols other numerical values, you get different answers. If there really is a *Satan's Bible*, it has nothing to do with this.'

'What happened to the Guardians once they had met the explorers? Did they ever return to Europe?'

'Some sailed home. Some stayed and got involved in looking for treasure in Central America. The unbelievable amounts of gold and precious objects that they found financed the building of the Miércoles Palace and are the basis of my family's wealth.'

'And the mummy?'

'A sad story. It disappeared some time towards the end of the seventeenth century. Strictly speaking, it disintegrated. By that stage, no one was loyal to Asim or their ancestors any more. They were living the good life here at the palace.'

'The mummy disintegrated?'

'All that remains of the mummy is some bone fragments and dust, and they are kept in a pot.'

I feel my eyes fill with disappointment.

'It's possible that all the changes in climate were what caused it to disintegrate. From the dry heat of Egypt, to the cold, damp air of Norway. The sea, the salt, the transport.'

'And what about the papyrus scrolls?'

'We still have some of them. The Vatican was presented with a couple as a gift. The others are here in the library. But they are nothing special. They are really only of interest to scholars and specialists. Fragments of Bible transcripts from the fifth and sixth centuries, descriptions of daily life in Egypt, paeans, things like that.' He pauses. 'Bjørn, Asim's transcript from Thingvellir . . . I'll ask again.' He looks straight at me. 'Will you give me the Icelandic manuscript?'

I say nothing.

'It belongs here. At the palace, together with all the others.'

'It's not even in my possession.'

'Who has it, then?'

'The manuscript is a historical artefact,' I say, evasively. 'It would be a criminal offence to hand it over.'

'The manuscript . . .' he starts, then pulls himself together. 'Please trust me. Don't you want to complete Asim's project?'

'Asim's project was to protect the mummy. And it no longer exists.'

'Maybe not physically . . .'

'The Guardians betrayed him. They failed to fulfil their mission.'

He remains silent. After a while he says: 'You know, you could have been one of us. A Guardian! You have some unique qualities. It was men like you that Asim and King Olav gathered round them. Persistent, fearless, concerned with the bigger picture.'

'Does it still exist? Is that what you're trying to say? Does the order of the Guardians still exist?'

His gaze turns inward, looking back to all that has been.

'Now we just guard the memories and shadows of the past.'

Beatriz

1

TWO LIVERIED servants knock on my door as the great Doomsday clock out in the corridor strikes eight. With slow steps, I am escorted by the two penguins through the carpeted labyrinth of the Miércoles Palace, where every limping step on my crutches is a step back in time.

Esteban Rodriquez is sitting waiting with his family in the dining room, under a huge chandelier that could easily be confused with the Northern Lights from a distance. Esteban's wife, Sophia, shakes my hand with a smile that never warms her eyes. She is a dark-haired beauty who reminds me of an Inca high priestess before she tears out the heart of her victim. The best plastic surgeons have fixed her face and figure at an age in the past that she will never give up. Their son, Javier, is a suntanned playboy with sparkling eyes and a smile full of white teeth and sweet promises. He spends parts of the year in Bel Air and St-Tropez. He is radiant, as if he has just come from a great party with plenty of free cocaine and women. Graciela has inherited her mother's beauty and distance. She is my age but, like her mother, looks a lot younger. Her handshake is flaccid and she withdraws her hand quickly as if she can't bear to touch me.

Then I am introduced to Esteban's sister.

Beatriz is in her late fifties, and her eyes have the spirited quality of a strong, smart and mature woman, who still has a playful young girl inside. Her hair is light brown, wild and curly, and tumbles to about halfway down her back. She has a small diamond in her nose. Her posture and shape bear witness to many painful hours spent in the gym. She shakes my hand with a firm grip and a twinkle in her eye.

'So, you are the man who found the Shrine of Sacred Secrets.' Her voice is warm and husky, as if she needs to go to bed, and preferably with someone.

I can see that she has just read my thoughts and blush. Then we all sit down at the table, which is so long that we could also have invited the National Assembly.

While the waiters bring in plates full of exotic hors d'œuvres, Esteban tells me about the history of the Miércoles Palace and the Rodríquez family's line of statesmen, good-for-nothings, knights and pickpockets, virgins, nymphomaniacs, saints and black sheep. He makes small, snide comments to Beatriz every now and then. She ignores his tactlessness with patronising dignity and cold eyes. Sophia doesn't say a word. She has disappeared into her own world of indifference. Javier delights in telling us about a party at Cap Ferrat where Mick Jagger sprayed champagne in the face of a finance man who had helped himself too liberally to the host's wife. When he speaks English, Javier has a Spanish accent that could make the clothes fall off women. His laughter erupts in lavish cascades. Sophia and Graciela pick at their food. Esteban asks Beatriz whether she has got any farther with her thesis. She is evasive and seeks refuge in Sophia, who looks away and chews her food with mechanical jaw movements. Javier tells an amusing story about George Michael in a shoe shop on Fifth Avenue, but the point is lost in his laughter.

We sit at the table conversing for well over two hours.

I feel like an outsider. The others eat Caribbean dishes like *pelau*, chicken with curry and chilli, spicy *channa* and salted fish with aubergines. I am given raw, fried, boiled, grilled and marinated vegetables that I have never heard of or tasted before. We drink exclusive wines from the palace wine cellar. And all the time I look at Beatriz whenever I can. I don't know whether she notices or not, but I think she does. She is extremely beautiful. If she can read my thoughts, she hides it well. Perhaps she is playing with me. Fortunately there are parts of my brain where I can quarantine my fantasies without them being seen.

2

After dinner, the men drink cognac and smoke cigars, while the women sip port in the adjoining room. We meet again in what they call the lobby, where great glass doors lead out on to the terrace. Around half past ten, Esteban and Sophia say goodnight. Graciela loosens up once her parents have gone and I hear her laugh for the first time. But after fifteen or twenty minutes, Javier and Graciela also retire.

In the silence that they leave behind, Beatriz and I stand looking out of the door. I am filled with the tingling knowledge that I am alone with her and that I could theoretically take those few steps towards her and sweep her up in my arms, hold her tight and feel her body against mine.

'Shall we go out for some air?' she asks.

She looks at me in a way that I find hard to interpret. I assume she is reading my thoughts again, which embarrasses and excites me. She laughs gently and then takes me by the arm and leads me out on to the terrace. I want to kiss her, but would of course never dare do anything so bold. We sit down in some deep, soft garden chairs. Santo Domingo twinkles between the trees like a faraway galaxy. The noise of the city reaches us only as a distant hum. The park is filled with the mating calls of birds, frogs, crickets and small animals.

'Can you believe that I was once a hippy?' Beatriz smiles.

I try to arch an eyebrow, but seem to have problems with my muscle coordination, so it probably looks more as if I've got a tick in my eye.

'I lived in San Francisco for three years from 1966. Haight-Ashbury, the summer of love, LSD, flower power.' Her voice has a touch of the sun and warmth that comes from somewhere deep inside. 'Perhaps it was my way of rebelling against all this,' she says, throwing her arms wide.

'Poor little rich girl?' I comment, slightly more acerbically than I had intended.

Her smile twists into a bitter, cold grimace, so I know that I have insulted her deeply. But then the warmth and charm return again.

'I grew up like a princess in a royal family with no kingdom and no people. My father was an alcoholic, my mother comforted herself with lovers, and my older brother, Esteban, well . . .' She looks up at the sky. We both follow the flashing lights of an aeroplane. 'You know, Bjørn, my family has never really been part of this community or culture. The Miércoles Palace could have been in the middle of Hyde Park or Central Park, for that matter, or in Bombay or Tokyo, and we would have been just as isolated and cut off from the world as we are here.'

I grew up in an old white, wooden house in a quiet suburb of Oslo, but I still know what she means.

'Many envy us our wealth.'

'I should imagine so.'

'But it's not such a good life.'

'That's what the rich always say.'

'I hope I don't come across as blasé, but I'm sure I do.

Wealth does something to you. And it's not attractive.'

She runs her fingers through her hair. Her skin glows golden in the half-light. I can't believe that she is probably about twenty years older than me. She is like a fragile and timeless elfin.

'The sixties, and everything that came with it, were paradoxically what saved me. If I hadn't rebelled, I would have gone under. I had to become someone else, in order to be myself, if you see what I mean.'

'I think so.'

'My family had no idea. They thought I was living a quiet, secluded life at boarding school.'

'How did they find out?'

'I was admitted to hospital after an overdose. The doctors didn't think I would survive. The principal called my parents and told them to come to San Francisco. And what do you think they did? The alcoholic and the demi-mondaine disinherited me. The ultimate hypocrisy! I wasn't worthy. And Esteban, of all people, inherited everything!'

She looks straight at me, and draws breath to say something, something important, but then stops herself and looks away. When she continues, it is about something completely different. I wonder why she hesitated. Maybe she doesn't know me well enough, or what she has to say is difficult to bear.

'After rehab and my exams, I went to live in London, then Rome and Rio de Janeiro. I never married, but that doesn't mean that I was lonely. I only moved home again long after my parents had died. By then Esteban had grown into and perfected the role of my father to the point where I sometimes wondered if they were in fact one and the same person.'

'Why did you want to come back?'

She lowers her eyes. 'Because this is where I belong,' she

says with an edge of defiance. 'And no one can take that away from me. Not my mother, my father nor Esteban. And certainly not Esteban.' Then she lightens up. 'But most of all, because this is where I work best. Close to the library and the historical manuscripts. And the Curator, of course.'

'Who?'

'A colleague, and a friend. You'll meet him.'

In a ridiculous moment of jealousy, I wonder whether he is more than a colleague and friend.

'Your brother mentioned that you were working on a thesis . . .'

'Pah, what does he know! But yes, I am. I studied theology and history at Berkeley. I now have a part-time position as a guest professor at the Universidad Autónoma de Santo Domingo, but I mostly work here in my office at the palace.'

We sit there talking until two in the morning. And all the time, I imagine her naked in my bed, with her hair flowing over the silk sheets; warm breath, glowing eyes and small, pointed breasts and a pierced navel. We talk about the differences between New Age and religion, about living conditions in South and North America, about emigration from Africa and the formation of the first tribes. I imagine her wrapping her legs around my hips and her nails scratching my back. She tells about her friends in the Grateful Dead and Jefferson Airplane, and about hallucinations brought on by LSD and mescaline. I say, ambiguously, that I don't need to take drugs to hallucinate. She replies, equally ambiguously, that she knows.

When we say goodnight, she gives me a hug and a peck on the cheek, as if to say that if I had been in San Francisco in 1967, it could have been us. Or am I just flattering myself? I was but an egg in 1967.

When I go to bed, the impression of her body burns on my skin.

3

I spend the whole of the next day in the library.

I don't see anything of Beatriz or Esteban. Instead, I have books, letters, manuscripts and drawers of ancient maps of the Caribbean islands and coastline of mainland America to keep me company.

The library is on the ground floor, and has windows facing out to the park. There are ten aisles that branch off from the main hall. Some of them are full of books from floor to ceiling; others are filled with cupboards and drawers with documents, letters, maps and other texts that are systematised geographically, thematically and chronologically. At the far end of the library is a set of impressive double doors with brass door handles. I try one, but the door is locked. I notice a code lock, a fingerprint reader and an iris scanner on the wall.

I come across a section dedicated to pirates in the Caribbean. Among all the court transcripts and death sentences, I find some xylographs of famous pirates, kidnappers and buccaneers posing like kings. In one disintegrating cardboard file there are long letters to Esteban's ancestors from pirate legends such as Henry Morgan, Francis Drake and Edward 'Blackbeard' Teach. One drawer is full of documents from the USA, from the time when there were only thirteen colonies: letters, agreements, and even one of Thomas Jefferson's early drafts of the Declaration of Independence. After lunch, which I eat alone under a parasol on the library terrace, I discover a Nordic section that contains a wealth of rare first editions and original manuscripts, and a bitter correspondence between Hamsun and Ibsen.

Esteban comes into the library in the late afternoon. He pretends that he didn't expect to find me there, as if he had just come by to get some exciting bedtime reading.

I ask what is behind the locked doors. He tells me that it is a specially secured section where they keep the most valuable, rare books and documents.

As if a thief could steal so much as a full stop from the Miércoles Palace . . .

'Bjørn, about the manuscripts you found in Iceland.' Again. 'Is it a question of money?'

This question takes me aback, so I can't think of an answer.

'Because if that's the case, I'd like you to know that I have the means to make you very wealthy indeed. And then you would be able to do far more exciting things than you do as an associate professor at the University of Oslo.'

'I like my job.'

'You would like your new life even more.'

'Why is the manuscript so important?'

'It would complete my collection.'

Not a lie, but not the whole truth either.

'Let me think about it.'

I have no intention of selling him anything. But I need more time, time to understand everything.

From the expression on his face when he looks at me, you might think that we had just signed a contract and were waiting for the ink to dry.

I left my mobile phone in a drawer in the bedside table. Professor Llyleworth has rung eight times and sent a text:

Hassan and Stuart Dunhill released. Call me!

The professor answers after only one ring. He tells me that Stuart and Hassan were released by a district court in Washington, DC.

'How is that possible?' I ask.

'The court's assessment of the evidence was that the district attorney had nothing on them. Nothing.'

Neither Stuart nor Hassan was armed when they were arrested. Their lawyers argued convincingly that they had been called in as middlemen to what they had assumed was a normal business meeting about the sale of a collection of Middle Age documents. They were not aware that Laura and I had been kidnapped, or that some of the people there were armed. Yeah, right.

'Hassan is a wanted war criminal and murderer,' I protest.

'Hassan is dead.'

'What? What did you say?'

'Officially, he is no longer alive. His passport, birth certificate, the Iraqi embassy and various international registers, including the International Court of Justice in The Hague, all confirmed the accused's identity as Jamaal Abd-al-aziz. The lawyer also produced a valid death certificate for Hassan.'

'But . . .'

'Don't ask me. But it says a lot that someone has managed to manipulate all those registers. Even the pictures of Hassan had been changed. The court didn't believe the prosecution.'

'But it's all a cover-up.'

'The judge was not to be swayed.'

'The sheikh must have bribed him, then. With a few million.'

I ask the professor where Stuart and Hassan are now,

but he doesn't know. 'If it's any comfort, all the others in the group were remanded in custody. They were all carrying unregistered, illegal handguns.'

'Cold comfort.'

'Relax, Bjørn. They can't possibly know where you are.'

'I don't feel so sure about that.'

'We have to respect the ruling. Constitutional rights can work both for and against us.'

But what about my safety?'

'The Miércoles Palace is probably the safest place you could be right now.'

The Sacred Library

1

'BEATRIZ, CAN I ask you something?'
'Of course.'

She has invited me for dinner, and we are sitting by the window in her dining room. She has her own flat in the north end of the palace. It is just the two of us, Beatriz and me. Makes you wonder.

'What is behind the locked doors in the library?'

'More books.'

The cook has prepared a vegetarian dish of steamed, buttered asparagus, grilled tomatoes and paprika stuffed with rice and spices. Beatriz has a white-wine-marinated quail's breast. She raises her glass. We drink together.

She is not herself. She tries to smile as if she doesn't have a care, but something is bothering her. The dam bursts as I eat my last asparagus. First she looks down at what is left of the quail's breast. Then she looks up at me.

'Are you considering giving him the manuscript?'

I chew slowly. Asparagus has always been one of my favourite vegetables. It must not be cooked for too long, and there should still be a firmness to it when you get it in your mouth.

'Who? I haven't made any promises to anyone.'

'Esteban. He said that you were going to sell the manuscript to him.'

'Then he misunderstood me. He said he needed it, and I

said I would think about it. And that is it. The manuscript isn't even mine. Why would I sell him something I don't own?'

'He'll tempt you with millions of dollars.'

'I don't care much about money.'

'He'll trick you. Don't let Esteban get hold of the manuscript.'

Beatriz wipes the edges of her mouth with a linen napkin that carries the family monogram.

'To be perfectly frank, Beatriz, I am not quite sure what you're trying to tell me.'

She looks out of the window. The floodlit trees shine and glisten in the blue dark of the night. The lamp on the terrace lures in swarms of insects and holds them captive.

'You must never trust Esteban. Never.'

'He's your brother.'

Something flares up from deep inside her and is reflected in her eyes.

'Can you imagine what it feels like to belong to a family of traitors and liars?'

I can, in fact. Before she died, my mother asked me whether I had forgiven her for what happened to my father when he fell from that rock face in Telemark. I stroked her cheek and said of course. But I wasn't telling the truth.

I don't tell Beatriz that, not now. But she still stretches her hand over and puts it on mine. A graceful, brown hand on top of my own milk-white one.

'Esteban says that he has told you everything.'

'Yes, but not truly everything.'

'No, not everything.'

We sit in silence for a while.

'When you look at me, it's hard to imagine that I come from Viking stock,' she says. 'No, you don't need to say anything. The Caribbean genes have long since defeated the Nordic genes in me.' She gives my hand a little squeeze and then lets it go. 'Being ashamed of your family and your forefathers is very painful.'

'Do you have any reason to be ashamed?'

'You have no idea . . .'

'I would be proud of your ancestors' steadfastness. Just think of all the hundreds of year that they protected the mummy.'

She lets out a short, cutting laugh, the same response a call girl might have if one of her regulars asked whether she loved him.

'I can just imagine what Esteban has told you.'

'Was he lying?'

The door opens and a parade of waiters come in to collect our plates and serve dessert: warm berries with homemade vanilla ice cream. They pour dessert wine into small crystal-cut glasses and then close the doors behind them so quietly that I have to turn round to check whether they have in fact gone.

'Yes, he is lying. No doubt a lot of it was true. Most of it, possibly. But he was lying about the most important thing.'

'Why?'

'Esteban has been poisoned by the past.'

'What do you mean?'

'We are all products of our ancestors' choices.'

'Well, we also have free will.'

'Some people are corrupted by their own free will.'

'Esteban?'

'My brother has been corrupted by centuries of betrayal, double standards and a lack of principles.'

She drags out the words, as if each one were a ball and chain.

I look at her with surprise and discomfort as I suck on a

warm raspberry. The repressed anger brings a flush to her cheeks.

'What are you trying to say, Beatriz?'

She uses her silver fork to chase a blueberry round in the melted ice cream. Her eyes fill with tears.

'How do you think my ancestors could afford to build a palace like this?'

'Inca gold?'

Quiet laughter. 'I'm sure the gold from the Incas and the Aztecs helped. The Guardians allied themselves with the conquistadors and, true to their Viking blood, plundered all the riches from the Caribbean islands and the mainland. León, Velázquez, Cortés, Pizarro, de Soto, de Coronado – we were with them. Legend has it that it was in fact my ancestors who found the South American city of gold, El Dorado. That our wealth originates from El Dorado.'

'Isn't El Dorado a myth?'

'So they say. But who knows. The foundations of my family's incredible wealth were laid in the sixteenth and seventeenth centuries. A lot of the money came from the conquistador raids, but we also got considerable amounts from Europe.'

'From who?'

'From the most powerful institution in Europe in the sixteenth century.'

'Which was?'

'Let me ask you a question: for how many centuries do you think the fraternity that you call the Guardians were loyal to Asim and their mission?'

I had for some time now cherished the hope that Esteban was a Guardian, one who had sincerely honoured the promise that his ancestors had made.

'My ancestors were traitors, Bjørn. They betrayed Asim; they betrayed everyone who had sacrificed their lives. They betrayed their mission.'

'How?'

'Many people believe that Columbus brought European depravity and decadence with him to America. The fact that Europe discovered America was the downfall of the indigenous people. Well, it was certainly the downfall of the Guardians. They were corrupted, one and all. By money, by power, by status. Esteban and I come from a family of thieves and riff-raff.'

I don't know what to say.

'The Caribbean was never the final destination for the Guardians,' she continues. 'They were going to return to Europe. They were searching for the winds that would take them home. But they stayed here, all the same. Have you ever asked yourself why?'

'Why?'

'Greed.'

'I don't understand . . .'

'In a way, I suppose, they continued to be Guardians, they just switched their allegiance. They kept the same secret, but for someone else.'

'Who?'

'If you put two and two together, it's obvious.'

'I've never been good at maths.'

'They stayed here in Santo Domingo, in the palace that was built with the help of the best architects and engineers in Europe. They took Spanish names. Some of the Guardians stayed right here in the Miércoles Palace. My ancestors. Others sailed back to Europe with Spanish merchant ships. They were all given aristocratic titles, large properties and more money than they could dream of. The few that protested were killed. The most honourable were killed by the Inquisition on the direct orders of the Vatican. The only ones who survived were the ones who betrayed the promises they had once made. Their descendants live, to this day, in castles in Italy, France and Spain.'

'Who was behind it all?'

'At the time when the Guardians first came to Santo Domingo, the Pope was Julius II. He is remembered for many things. He was also known as *Il Papa Terribile*. He was a scheming, authoritarian figure. In 1506, he established the Swiss Guard, who still guard the Vatican and the Pope today. He initiated the plans to construct St Peter's Basilica as it now stands. He employed Michelangelo to paint the ceiling of the Sistine Chapel. Michelangelo was also commissioned to make the Pope's tomb, with the famous statue of Moses.'

'I still don't get the connection.'

'The connection is the Vatican.'

'But why? With all due respect, we're talking about a mummy, some papyrus scrolls and a Viking raid.'

'Neither Asim nor the Guardians could have guessed the significance of what they were hiding. Without knowing it, they were guarding a mummy and a manuscript that would change the world's understanding of Judaism, Christianity and Islam.'

I don't know how to react. The words sound pompous and unreal.

'I really hope that I am not being disrespectful when I say that this all seems a bit out of proportion.'

She spears the blueberry with her fork and eats it.

I ask: 'What kind of secret could take on such proportions? Was the mummy God?' I attempt a laugh, but it comes out as a dry croak.

Beatriz takes a drink of wine and closes her eyes. The subdued lighting wipes away her wrinkles and makes her look as young as she was when she danced in the moonlight at Haight-Ashbury.

'I have to ask you something, Bjørn.'

'Ask away.'

'The manuscript . . .' She stops, as if she doesn't

quite know how to formulate what she wants to say.

'Yes?'

'What do you know about it?'

'It is a copy and a translation from the eleventh century of an older, original Bible manuscript.'

'Have you read any of it?'

'It's still being translated.'

'I hope that you have hidden it well.'

'Of course, it's in the best hands.'

'Do you have a copy?'

That was a question that Esteban had never asked.

'Of course.'

Her mouth will not shut.

'Would you like to see it?' I ask and offer her my hand.

I turn on one of the PCs in the library and log on to the Gmail account that Sira Magnus set up. In the inbox, under Snorri Codex, is Thrainn's email with the digitalised version of the Thingvellir Scrolls.

'Oh my word,' Beatriz exclaims as I open the pdf file.

The parchments appear on the flat screen in front of us, clear and sharp.

'The Curator won't be able to believe his own eyes. Do you think . . .' She hesitates. 'Could I have a printout?'

I press the print icon. She squeezes my shoulder in gratitude. The great laser printer comes to life. When the document is printed, I say: 'You actually never answered my question.'

'What question?'

I nod towards the locked doors.

'Oh, that. Come along.'

She pulls me over to the door, where she stares into the iris scanner until the green light clicks on. Then she punches in a code. The locks hums, and she opens the heavy door.

2

We enter into an atmosphere of mystery and ancient times. The frescoes on the walls and ceiling depict important events from the Bible. Had I not known better, I might have thought that Michelangelo had been here with his palette and brushes. Three chandeliers hang from the domed ceiling. There are icons and reliquaries on the shelves and in niches. I hear the echoes of Gregorian chants in my mind. On the end wall hangs a cross, with the crucified Jesus. *Elí, Elí, lemá sabaktáni?* My God, my God, why have you forsaken me? In a glass case on top of a high pedestal, I see a crown of thorns. Surely it can't be *the* crown of thorns? I can't bring myself to ask. Under the cross, on a table covered with a white cloth, tall white candles burn in a menorah, a seven-branched candelabrum. Along the walls, between the frescoes, are cabinets with bookshelves, glass doors and drawers. The deep windows are secured with wrought-iron grilles and there is a CCTV camera on the ceiling.

'Welcome to the Sacred Library,' Beatriz says. 'This is where we keep our most valuable and rare treasures.'

We walk into the room on a carpet runner that is as soft as moss.

Beatriz stops by one of the cabinets. She takes out a codex with wooden covers. I stand behind her and look over her shoulder.

She opens it with great care.

'This is the original text of *De Transitu Virginis*, about the assumption of the Virgin Mary, written around AD 169 by St Melito of Sardis. As Mary was the mother of the son of God, she could not die a physical death, so she was assumed body and soul into heaven when her time had come.'

I look at the letters in awe, each of them written with love and faith.

Beatriz then moves on to another section where she

opens a drawer. On a silk cushion lie two gold coins.

'These coins are ascribed to Nicholas of Myra, or St Nicholas, better known as Santa Claus in the modern day. He saved a man and his three daughters from poverty and prostitution by throwing three purses of gold coins in through their window and down their chimney, in secret.'

She takes a gold casket out of a gilded writing desk. In it, pressed between two glass plates, is a cracked parchment.

'This is Christ's execution order, drawn up by Pontius Pilate.'

'Where do you manage to get all these things?'

'We have always been on good terms with the Vatican. Various popes, cardinals and bishops have used us in a number of ways. When theological debates get overheated, it is sometimes expedient for them to remove documents that they don't want the opposition to get their hands on. The Miércoles Palace is more secure than the Vatican's own archives. Perfidious archivists and cardinals are a constant risk to the Vatican. They have always been able to trust us.'

'That's incredible, Beatriz, absolutely incredible!'

'Not everything comes from the Vatican. We have also bought manuscripts, letters, books, codices and parchments on the open market and the black market. We have financed excavations. We have bribed archaeologists, explorers and thrill seekers. And by securing these treasures, we have at least prevented them from getting lost.'

'It doesn't make any difference to scholars and the general public if they are locked away in the Miércoles Palace or with Sheikh Ibrahim in the Emirates.'

'The sheikh has snapped up many a manuscript from under our noses. But then, he would no doubt say the same about us. Come, there's a man I would like you to meet.'

3

He is so tall, so thin and so pale that he might easily vanish if the light was behind him. His complexion is as white as mine. Perhaps that is why I feel an immediate affinity with him. I can trace a map of liver spots on his skull, through his wispy grey hair. His nose is hooked and sharp. His whole being is inward looking, to a world he has kept to himself.

His bedroom doubles up as a study. When we knock on the door, he is sitting having a cup of tea at his desk, which is covered in papers, books and documents.

'This is the Curator,' Beatriz says by way of introduction. 'That's what we call him, the Curator.'

He holds out a bony hand. It is like shaking hands with a skeleton.

'I've read about you,' he says in a voice that is as dry and delicate as the handmade paper on his desk.

Beatriz tenderly puts her hand on his thin shoulders. 'We are old friends. I have known him all my life. He was my first babysitter. He became my friend and mentor. He has lived and worked at the Miércoles Palace since 1942, when he fled from Warsaw . . .'

'As a boy, let me tell you, as a boy!'

'. . . and ended up here, via Copenhagen, Boston and Havana. My father took pity on him in a rare moment of compassion. It was the Curator who sparked my interest in history and theology. And all that lies hidden in old manuscripts.'

'I understand that you share our passion for the treasures of the past,' the Curator says. He speaks in a quiet voice, almost a whisper, like the wind playing with a forgotten book on a park bench. When our eyes meet, it is as if he opens some inner door, and for a hallucinatory second, I look into an endless corridor filled with books covered in centuries of dust. Then the illusion vanishes and I see that his watery eyes are full of broken vessels.

He bobs his head. 'Beatriz is a wonderful person, isn't she? Be grateful for her friendship and devotion.'

I am not quite sure what to say. Behind the gracious façade, I sense a playful irony and that he is somehow testing me.

'When I lived abroad, it was the Curator who phoned me and sent me letters, and kept me up to date on life in the palace,' Beatriz tells me. 'And whenever I came home, it was the Curator who I looked forward to seeing.'

The Curator looks curiously at the printout that Beatriz is holding in her hand. She nods imperceptibly. He chews his lower lip. She hands him the printout. With trembling hands he takes the papers. He pulls out a pair of glasses from his breast pocket and holds his breath when he squints at the paper. His eyes run along the lines.

'Finally,' he repeats several times in a whisper. He looks up at Beatriz. 'This is it!'

'That's what I told you.'

'I didn't dare believe it. But this is it!'

4

The Curator pours three glasses of sherry. Beatriz and I are sitting on his bed. He is sitting on the chair by the desk.

'The Viking king, Olav, did not know what he had stolen,' the Curator says. The sherry has left a damp shadow on his upper lip. 'He just wanted the gold casket that the scrolls were in.'

'We have the original manuscript here in the palace,' Beatriz tells me.

'Esteban said there was nothing special about it.'

'Esteban was lying.'

'Would it be possible to see it?'

'It's not as simple as that. Only Esteban and I have access to it. A security measure. Each time the door is opened, it is recorded in the security logbook. Esteban would start to wonder.'

'Unfortunately, the original manuscript is not complete,' the Curator says. 'The dry desert air in Egypt is perfect for preserving papyrus. The damp Norwegian and Icelandic sea air is, to put it mildly, not so good. Parts of the papyri have disintegrated, so the manuscript is full of lacunae. Much of it is illegible. In order to be able to read it correctly and translate it, we need the undamaged copy from Thingvellir.'

'Could you please tell me soon what it is that makes the manuscript so special?'

'It is the original of a biblical text.'

'I've understood that already. But what is in it that frightens the Vatican so much?'

The Curator gets up and fills our half-empty sherry glasses, then puts the top back in the bottle.

'Frightens . . . hmm, it's not that simple. A thousand years ago, the Vatican had very different views from those it has today. I'm not sure how the Vatican would have dealt with the matter if the manuscript had been discovered in our time. But a thousand years ago, they panicked.'

'Why?'

'Because the Church has over the centuries propagated the illusion that the Bible is the word of God.'

There is an underlying defiance to his words.

'Is that not the whole purpose of the Church?' I ask.

'For precisely that reason, the authority and position of the Church and the Bible would crumble if the Vatican acknowledged that the Bible is . . . well, a collection of good and edifying stories, written by people, modified by people, collected and selected by people. And nothing else.'

'Everyone knows that the Bible can't be taken literally. It

represents something greater. There aren't many people these days who believe in the Bible in a literal sense.'

'Is that so? Ask the homosexuals. Ask women. For two thousand years, the Church's interpretations have been drummed into us. You would be surprised how many people read the Bible as God's word to us mortals, as though God had written it himself. Some Christians do see the Bible as a source of understanding, worship and contemplation. But, nonetheless . . . the very forces that initiated the Crusades, the Inquisition and slavery are still flourishing today.'

'I thought that all that changed with Luther?'

'Well . . . What does Paul have to say about homosexuality? The same apostle who preaches love, forgiveness and compassion condemns homosexuality, and this view is supported by many of the seniors in the Church.' The words erupt in a shower of spit. 'What do you think Jesus would have to say about the hate that homosexuals inspire in some Christians?'

'Calm down.' Beatriz leans forward and pats him soothingly on the leg.

'Paul lived in a different age,' I argue.

'Exactly! Which only goes to demonstrate that the Bible belongs to a bygone age. Nowadays, today in fact, the Church condemns the very same slavery that it once wholeheartedly condoned. But homosexuals are still persecuted with blinding fervour and hateful passion.'

This outburst leaves the Curator breathless, and he leans against the desk.

'Are you all right?' Beatriz asks.

'Yes, yes, yes!'

'The Curator gets easily worked up,' she says to me. 'But I agree with him. The Bible is a literary and mythological masterpiece. Which belonged to a certain time, people and world. Today, we can choose whether we want to read it as a religious message or a philosophical manifesto. Whether or not the Bible is seen to be God's word depends entirely on the faith of the reader. The Bible's authority is dependent on the power and infallibility of the text.'

Beatriz pauses and the Curator jumps in: 'The Bible was given a stamp of approval by the Church fathers over fifteen hundred years ago. And since then, popes and religious clerics, priests and preachers, have stood united in backing it as absolute. To criticise the Bible is to deny God. Wars have been fought in order to defend and spread the word of the Bible. Millions have been killed in the Bible's name.'

The Curator has a coughing fit, and I am able to squeeze in a question: 'How do the Thingvellir Scrolls undermine all this?'

Beatriz answers, while the Curator recovers. 'The most essential texts that, in fact, form the theological foundations of Judaism, Christianity and Islam are the Five Books of Moses. The Creation, the history of the Patriarchs, the exodus, Canaan, Cain and Abel, the laws, precepts and Ten Commandments, all the stories that form the foundations of our shared cultural heritage and understanding.' She thumps the Curator on the back as he is still coughing. 'Moses is one of the most influential figures in world history. The beliefs and religions of half the world's population are based on his word. The Almighty God who appears in the Five Books of Moses is the same God who is still worshipped by Christians, Jews and Muslims.'

The Curator has managed to stabilise his breathing again, and empties his sherry glass in one go. 'What would happen if someone could document that the whole thing was a sham?'

'A sham?' I repeat like an echo. 'What is a sham?'

'How would you react if I said that the Books of Moses

are the culmination of numerous texts and thoughts from ancient times?'

'That's more or less one of the first things that theology students learn at university.'

'But isn't it strange how they protect their knowledge? Most people don't know that the Five Books of Moses are a composite of Babylonian myths, Phoenician and Hittite sagas and Egyptian stories, woven together with the depiction of an autocratic god to create a monotheistic religion. And a new state. Many would dismiss the whole thing as a myth, yet another conspiracy theory. Some – experts, critical theologians and scholars – would admit that the Old Testament *is*, to a large extent, precisely that, a unique collection of ancient texts, in a new guise with a new label.'

'You could of course choose to ignore the whole issue because you are convinced that the Bible is the word of God,' Beatriz chips in.

'Or you could see the Bible as one culture's portrayal of a mythological past and the hope of an idealised future,' the Curator suggests. 'About humanity's inherent dream of beauty and the ethereal. More sherry?'

He uncorks the bottle. I hold out my glass, which he fills to the brim. Beatriz still has half a glass left and covers it with her hand.

The Curator continues as he puts down the bottle: 'Imagine – imagine if someone could produce indisputable evidence of how and why the Books of Moses and the new religion evolved.'

'What sort of evidence would that be?'

'The Thingvellir Scrolls!'

Beatriz and the Curator look at me askance, challenging me.

'There are two billion Christians in the world, and half of them are Catholics,' the Curator states. 'There are one and a half billion Muslims. Fourteen million Jews. For many of them, the Books of Moses are the very foundations of their faith. Moses paved the way of faith for Jesus and Muhammad.'

'That is why this manuscript is so important,' Beatriz explains. 'It tells another story.'

'The Pope could never come forward and say that the scriptures upheld by the Church fathers are incomplete,' the Curator exclaims. 'He could never say that the Bible needed to be rewritten. That would be unthinkable! He could never say that the Old Testament contains errors that have to be rectified. He would be stabbing all his predecessors over the past two thousand years in the back. And he would also be acknowledging that the Bible, for all its literary splendour, is not the word of God, but in fact the word of man.'

'The Bible would become a well-written, beautiful storybook full of wise people's visions of a god and a paradise that we can all long for,' Beatriz says.

'And which is in fact simply an illusion,' concludes the Curator.

The Sixth Book of Moses

1

W̲E̲ H̲A̲V̲E̲ moved out on to the terrace. Beatriz has taken with her some wine, a large, square candle and a mosquito coil, which bothers me more than the mosquitoes. The Curator has gone in to get three glasses.

'Why is he so angry?' I nod in the direction of the terrace door and the Curator.

'During the war, he and his parents sought refuge in a church in Warsaw. The priest turned them away. He didn't want to give asylum to Jews. An altar boy ran out on to the street and told some soldiers. His father was shot on the church steps and his mother was sent to a concentration camp, where she died. Only the Curator managed to get away. He was ten years old.'

The Curator comes back out with the glasses. 'How quiet you both are,' he says as he opens the bottle of wine and fills the glasses.

'You're such a chatterbox, you talk enough for us all,' Beatriz teases. She lights the candles.

'I'm just passionate,' he retorts. We raise our glasses.

The Curator sinks down into one of the terrace chairs and stares at the red of the wine. 'Can you bear any more of my lectures?' he asks, humorously.

'Do I have any choice?' I chuckle.

'No,' replies Beatriz.

The Curator turns the stem of his wineglass before putting it down.

'The Bible . . . It is so easy to think of the Bible as something holy, defined and constant. But in fact it is the result of purposeful editing by very human hands, and is influenced by the personal beliefs of its editors, as well as their political and theological agendas. There is no one Bible that all believers can accept. Jews, Christians, Orthodox, Catholics, Protestants – they all have their own version of the Bible. To cut a long story short, the Thingvellir Scrolls are a complete Hebrew copy and a Coptic translation of a collection of ancient texts. Call it a first draft, if you like. A rough text. Unedited. At some later stage, various writers have edited, reworked and adapted the texts so that they become one cohesive story.'

'And that story is called the Five Books of Moses,' says Beatriz.

A tremor runs through me.

'The Thingvellir Scrolls,' the Curator continues, 'are the original texts on which the Books of Moses are based.'

'The original texts reveal not only how the Five Books of Moses evolved, chapter by chapter, page by page,' Beatriz explains, 'but also what was omitted.'

'Wow,' I say. I should perhaps have said something more eloquent, but that was all I could think of.

'And there's more,' Beatriz adds. 'The texts also include another book.'

'Another book? What do you mean?'

She nods.

The Curator takes a sip of wine. 'The manuscript also contains a Sixth Book of Moses.'

I take a few moments to gather my thoughts. An unknown Book of Moses. It's a ridiculous claim. At the same time, it makes sense. All the secrecy. The sheikh and Hassan. The Vatican. The SIS. All the loose ends suddenly tie up neatly.

'I know that it's difficult to take in,' the Curator says.

Somewhere in the town a shot is fired. Or an exhaust backfires.

'All we have been able to read until now are the incomplete extracts from the partially decayed original manuscript that we have here in the palace. That is why the Thingvellir Scrolls are so incredibly important. Because they contain the text, word for word, in its original form.'

'And according to the incomplete fragments,' the Curator expands, 'this Sixth Book of Moses is about his childhood and youth. It includes new precepts that would have a considerable impact on Judaism, Christianity and Islam. God tells more about who He is, why He created the world and what He expects from mankind. He intimates that there are other gods, but that he is the creator of mankind and the world.'

'God talks of visions that the Gnostics and Cathars were to champion much later,' Beatriz says. 'The Sixth Book of Moses includes much to weaken the position of the Church and the clergy. God condemns all who wilfully misinterpret Him. We each have God and the true faith in us. *Holiest is the temple that you will find in your own heart*, it says. God warns Moses against false priests who use the Church as a means of bolstering their own position.'

'Four chapters are dedicated to Satan and three to known and unknown angels and archangels. God calls Satan his fallen son and talks of him with great paternal love. What is understood as *evil* is primarily the absence of the divine.'

I take a sip of wine and try to keep up.

'The Sixth Book of Moses will completely change our understanding of the other books,' the Curator says. 'Someone has, for reasons we don't know, omitted the sixth book. If it was to be included in the canon, it would mean that the three major world religions would have to adapt parts of their belief system in line with the new scripture.'

'In what way?'

'We can only know that when we have read the complete text. To draw conclusions based on the translations we have already done would simply be guesswork. This is an example of why we are so dependent on the Thingvellir Scrolls . . .' He takes a piece of paper out of his inner pocket, with the following short text on it:

> When you pray to the Lord, your God, He is . . .
> (illegible) . . . and you shall find . . . (illegible) . . . is one,
> thus he is . . . (illegible) . . . has created. You shall . . .
> (illegible) . . . already found, and it is . . . (illegible)

'We have translated the parts of the spoiled original papyrus manuscript that we have that are legible,' the Curator explains. 'But in order to fill the gaps where the papyrus has disintegrated, we need Asim's copy. The text is basically meaningless when it is not complete.'

4

Moses and the Israelites wandered in the wilderness for forty years. They have my greatest sympathy. My own journey through the wilderness is starting to take its toll and it is not over yet.

The Curator goes in and comes back with a worn, bound edition of the Old Testament. He leafs through the thin pages with his long fingers.

'The first thing we have to do if we are to read, understand and interpret the Books of Moses correctly is to acknowledge that they were never written by Moses.' He then reads:

> So Moses the servant of the LORD died there in the land of Moab, according to the word of the LORD. And he buried him in a valley in the land of Moab, over against Bethpeor: but no man knoweth of his sepulchre unto this day. And Moses was an hundred and twenty years old when he died: his eye was not dim, nor his natural force abated.

'So, did Moses write that?' the Curator asks. 'How could he describe his own death and burial?'

He leafs on to another section.

> Now the man Moses was very meek, above all the men which were upon the face of the earth.

The Curator has a little chuckle. 'Now, would the world's meekest man write that about himself?'

'That doesn't prove anything,' I argue. 'Even if Moses didn't write everything in the Five Books of Moses, it doesn't mean to say that he didn't write any of it.'

'That's what a lot of people think,' Beatriz says, 'that an editor has embellished Moses' manuscript. By far the majority of theologians and priests today agree that Moses did not write the Five Books.'

'If you read the Five Books,' the Curator continues, 'it is easy to become confused by all the repetition, all the different names for God and people, and conflicting versions of the same events.'

'There are two different versions of the story of Creation in Genesis,' Beatriz states.

'Two?'

'Two related stories that are woven together into one,' the Curator explains. Then he reads:

> In the beginning God created the heaven and the earth. And the earth was without form, and void; and darkness was upon the face of the deep. And the Spirit of God moved upon the face of the waters.

'That is how the Creation, as we know it, begins. But a conflicting story of creation has been incorporated into the same text – written by someone else and then woven into the first version. It is so seamlessly done that the reader doesn't even notice that the story is starting again.'

'Where?'

The Curator looks for the passage, and then points to it: 'See for yourself. Genesis, chapter two. This is where a *new* story of Creation starts. You don't need to be theologian or a linguist to see that the passage is the introduction to a separate story.' He reads:

> These are the generations of the heavens and of the earth when they were created, in the day that the LORD God made the earth and the heavens, and every plant of the field before it was in the earth, and every herb of the field before it grew: for the LORD God had not caused it to rain upon the earth, and there was not a man to till the ground. But there went up a mist from the earth, and watered the whole face of the ground. And the LORD God formed man of the dust of the ground, and breathed into his nostrils the breath of life; and man became a living soul.

'Can't you hear that this is a separate introduction to a free-standing story of Creation?' Beatriz asks me.

The Curator adds: 'In the first version, God creates heaven and earth, light and dark, water and land, plants, birds, fishes, animals of the sea, animals of the land, and finally, humans. Man and woman. In that order.'

'In the next chapter,' Beatriz continues, 'the order is different. Here God creates the earth, heaven and water first. Then he creates man, and then plants, animals and birds, and finally woman, or Eve.'

'How can both versions be correct?' the Curator asks.

'And so on and so forth,' Beatriz says. 'Read the stories about Noah. They don't tally at all. In one place in the Bible it says that Moses goes to the Tabernacle – before he has even built it! The Books of Moses are full of contradictions.'

'Inaccuracies,' the Curator corrects. 'Errors.'

I need to go to the toilet.

5

When I come back, the Curator has opened another bottle of wine. A moth flies into the glass of one of the terrace lamps again and again. The moon shines through the leaves and a sea breeze caresses the park.

I sit down and take a sip of wine. Both Beatriz and the Curator watch me, as if trying to gauge whether I have had enough.

'Theology is full of known "secrets",' the Curator begins. He takes a deep breath before continuing. 'Theologians, rabbis and priests have always known about these imprecisions. For a long time, the fact that there was a greater truth behind it all was used to dismiss any contradictions. As early as the eighteenth century, critical theologians were saying that Moses could not possibly have written the Books of Moses. Theologians have known this for centuries. If you go into any theology faculty around the world, this now forms a cornerstone of their understanding of the Bible. Moses did not write the Pentateuch.'

Beatriz watches me as she drinks her wine.

'All this leads to the documentary hypothesis,' the Curator says.

'Or the JEPD theory,' Beatriz adds.

'Which means?'

'That there are four main sources on which the Books of Moses are based. J stands for Jahwist, E is for Elohist, P is for priestly and D is for *Deuteronomium*,' Beatriz explains.

I squash a mosquito that has settled on my lower arm.

'Work on the Five Books started nine hundred years before Christ, and a number of manuscripts were then edited into five books in the period to roughly four hundred BC,' she says.

'The authors of the books tell the same basic story, but from different perspectives.' The Curator folds his hands. 'They angle the material depending on their own political and religious beliefs, and then try to modify each other and correct the previous version.'

'Ironically, all these varying and conflicting versions are then sewn together.' Beatriz smiles.

A light in a window not far from us, in the servants' wing, is switched off.

'Based on their knowledge of theology, history, politics and linguistics, theologians have separated all the chapters and verses in the Five Books of Moses and then tried to put them back together again in their respective contexts,' the Curator expands. 'However, this process actually led theologians to believe that the Pentateuch is in fact derived from far more complex sources than even JEPD.'

'So who wrote the Five Books of Moses, then?' I ask.

6

My mobile phone rings.

I don't answer at first. I am no slave to my phone. And I am curious about Moses. But then I remember that the only people who have this number are those who might need to get hold of me.

It is Professor Llyleworth. He is distressed. The SIS has made some enquiries, and a certain Jamaal Abd-al-aziz, Hassan in other words, boarded an American Airlines plane from Miami to Santo Domingo about an hour ago.

'How does he know I'm here?' There is a stammer in my voice.

'The sheikh's intelligence is second to none.'

'What should I do?'

'Stay where you are. It's safest.'

'Safest? When Hassan's on his way?'

'I've already spoken to Esteban Rodriquez and the security at the Miércoles Palace is being stepped up as we speak.'

I tell the Curator and Beatriz about Hassan. They agree with the professor that it would be more dangerous for me to leave than to stay.

'He'll find you, no matter what,' Beatriz says. 'At least you're safe here.'

I stare out at the vast, dark park.

'There are so many alarm systems out there, that any intruder would be caught before he even climbed over the fence,' the Curator assures me.

7

'Back to the Books of Moses,' I say, and empty my wineglass in one go. 'Who wrote them?'

Beatriz fills my glass. 'Theologians operate with at least four sources, but there are in fact many more,' she says.

'The Jahwist, who consistently calls God *Jehovah*, the English rendition of Jahwe or Yahweh, is the foremost of the Old Testament theologians and literary masters,' the Curator explains. 'He lived around nine hundred years before Christ and is responsible for the basic structure and the ingenious framework. He gave the ancient myths and stories a new epic form and theological significance. The Jahwist's perspective, storytelling technique, vocabulary, literary style and religious views would indicate that he was a Jew. All his heroes are from Judaea. He was possibly a scribe at the court in Jerusalem, maybe the court of King Solomon.'

Beatriz takes over: 'The Elohist, who talks about God as *Elohim*, not Jehovah, wrote the Israelites' response to J, a hundred years later. All his heroes are Israelites, as opposed to Judaeans. He replaces the Judaean perspective with an Israelite one.'

'P is for priestly,' the Curator says, 'and these sections were written by a group of priests from Judaea in the time after the Second Temple was built, that is around five hundred years before Christ, and before Jerusalem fell into the hands of the Babylonians. The priests also had their own theological and political agenda.'

'*Deuteronomium*, the Fifth Book of Moses, was written six hundred years before Christ,' Beatriz concludes. 'Many people believe that Deuteronomy was written by the same Jeremiah who also wrote the Old Testament's Book of Jeremiah.'

A door slams somewhere in the palace. The Curator stops talking. Esteban Rodriquez appears in the door to the terrace. 'Is this where you are?' he says, out of breath, looking straight at me. 'You've heard?'

'Professor Llyleworth just called me.'

'We have doubled the security here. We've called in more security guards and stepped up the monitoring of the park area.'

'Thank you. I'm really sorry to cause so much extra work. If it's best that I go . . .'

'Don't even think about it!' His eyes move from Beatriz to the wine bottle. 'Well, I won't disturb you any longer. I have to phone the chief of police.'

Beatriz leans forward and pats my hand. 'It'll be fine,' she whispers.

When the Curator hears Esteban closing the hall door, he continues: 'Ironically enough, all these conflicting versions are then edited into one. It's a bit like cutting apart an aggressive newspaper debate and pasting together the various contributions as one cohesive argument that apparently argues for the same thing. As a single text it comes across as a powerful authority that bound the north and south, Israel and Judaea, together in terms of religion, politics and society.'

'How did all this end up with Asim?'

'The various manuscripts that made up the Five Books of Moses were taken over by the Amon-Ra cult four hundred years before Christ. They were rolled up and wrapped in cloth, then placed in ceramic pots that were sealed and stored in a gold casket. In *Aegytiaca*, which is based on Egyptian archives in the Heliopolis Temple, the historian Manetho writes about a religious ceremony where the gold casket and papyri were carried into the tomb and placed at the mummy's feet.'

'And the casket remained there, undisturbed, until 1013,' Beatriz finishes.

I lean back, look up at the stars and take another sip of wine as I think to myself: Well, that's the way it goes.

The Third Guardian

1

THE NIGHT is full of insects. The sirens from the city sound like a train whistle on a prairie. We tuck into a third bottle of wine.

'So,' I say, eventually, holding my wineglass against my chest, 'why have you told me all this?'

'We have been waiting for you,' Beatriz says.

'For me?'

'Ever since the Curator and I started to study the material at the end of the sixties, we have been waiting for the third Guardian.'

An abyss of confusion opens beneath me.

'Wait, wait, wait. What do you mean?'

'Bjørn,' Beatriz says, 'you are the third Guardian.'

'I'm not a Guardian.'

'We had no idea that it was *you*. But we knew there would be something special about the third one, something that made him stand out.'

'You,' the Curator repeats.

'When we heard that a Norwegian was coming to the Miércoles Palace and that the Norwegian was you, we realised,' Beatriz continues. 'Bjørn Beltø . . . the man who saved the Shrine of Secrets.'

'Beatriz and I have a task,' the Curator tells me.

'Which is?'

'To complete the mission of the Guardians.'

'You mean . . .'

'To return the mummy to the tomb in Egypt.'

'Does the mummy still exist? Esteban said . . .'

Beatriz interrupts: 'You shouldn't listen to Esteban! He's lying, lying, lying. The world deserves to read these texts as they were originally written.'

'I don't share the Vatican's fear,' the Curator says. 'Those who believe will continue to believe. Another dimension will be added to their faith. And the theologians will have something to argue about for the next hundred years.'

'But what's all this about waiting for *me*?'

The Curator takes out another folded piece of paper from his inner pocket. 'This is a translation of something that Asim wrote on Selja before he died, an astrological prediction, a prophecy, call it what you like.' He hands me the page.

And there will come a time when the GUARDIANS will bring THE HOLY ONE back to his resting place, under the sacred sun, in the sacred air, in the sacred rock; and a thousand years will pass; and half this period will be shrouded in the mists of depravity and corruption; and of the great multitude of GUARDIANS only three shall remain; and they are true, they are pure of heart and their number is three; for the holy number is three and three pleases THE HOLY ONE, just as three holds GOD's pillars: Judaism, Christianity and Islam, and the Holy Trinity, and the three holy cities of Islam, the three patriarchs, the three pilgrimage festivals Salosh Regalim, the three wise men, the Israelites' three leaders in the wilderness: Moses, Aaron and Miriam, the three sections of the Tanakh, and the three eternal truths: Heaven, Hell and Purgatory.

2

Beatriz rubs her nose and says that she thinks it is time to go to bed.

She glances over at me as she says this. For a few seconds, I imagine that she wants me to go with her. But then she adds that she is exhausted and that the wine has given her a headache. She stands up and gathers together the empty bottles.

'It's hardly a coincidence that it is a thousand years since the mummy was moved from its resting place,' she says.

'Or that it's five hundred years since the Guardians were morally shipwrecked here in the Caribbean,' the Curator adds, and blows out the candle.

'And now, at last, we are three,' Beatriz finishes.

The Mausoleum

1

'COME WITH me,' the Curator says.

A bat chases an insect through the night. It is some time now since Beatriz swept into the palace, leaving us alone in the dark and the numbing silence.

'Where to?'

The Curator gets up, with the brittle movements of old age. 'I want to show you something. Follow me.'

We leave the big candle, mosquito coil and empty glasses standing on the table, and close the terrace door behind us.

2

He leads me back to the Sacred Library. 'Just a moment,' he whispers, as the iris scanner struggles with his bloodshot eye. Then he punches in the code and once again I hobble into the church-like library.

He opens a cupboard between two shelves marked *Guardas nórdicos* and *Textos santos*. And from a drawer labelled *Aventuras de los caballeros*, he takes out a rectangular cardboard box. He opens the lid and folds back the tissue paper.

'I think this might interest you.'

I look down into the box, full of curiosity. There I see a text written in runes on vellum, the finest calfskin. The rows of Nordic letters form symmetrical blocks of text. I lean closer and translate the first lines:

> Odin, grant me strength.
> My hands, they shake. My gnarled fingers resemble more the claws of an eagle. My nails are scabrous and broken. Each breath is a rattling wheeze. My eyes, that once could see a buzzard high beneath the clouds, or a flag atop the mast of a ship over the horizon, are now prisoner to an eternal mist.

'We call this manuscript *Bård's Tale*,' he tells me. 'The text was written by Bård Bårdsson, Holy Olav's man-at-arms and squire, at Selja forty years after the battle at Stiklestad.'

'Bård?' I exclaim. *Barðr!* The crumbling mummy in the stone coffin beside Asim at Selja.

'An unusual manuscript. The text differs from the prevailing style of his day.'

'The Guardians must have sent it with Snorri when . . .'

The door crashes open. Esteban marches into the room with two security guards, for all the world like a furious field marshal who has been betrayed. The Curator and I jump. Surreptitiously, though obviously not surreptitiously enough, I hand the box with *Bård's Tale* in it back to the Curator.

'Has anything happened?' I ask. 'Is it Hassan?'

Esteban snarls something in Spanish that I can't understand. Deflated, the Curator hands him the cardboard box containing the manuscript.

Esteban takes a quick look in the box. *'Historia de Bård,'* he says. *'Porqué?'*

'Perdóneme, Senõr Rodriquez,' the Curator mumbles.

Esteban turns suddenly towards me. 'Interesting?' he asks, his voice as cutting as glass.

'I only read a few lines,' I reply, feebly. 'Have you heard any more news about Hassan?'

The security guards grab the Curator and escort him out of the library as if they have arrested him.

'What's happening?' I ask.

Esteban looks at me like a headmaster.

'I apologise if I . . .' I start.

'It's the Curator who should apologise!'

'We . . .'

'This far exceeds his authority.'

'As you had shown me Asim's manuscript, I thought . . .'

'What *I* can show you and what the Curator can show you are two entirely different things.'

'Of course. I'm so sorry. We didn't mean to . . .'

'*Bueno*,' he interrupts. 'Come with me!'

Esteban takes me by the sleeve and drags me through the library. I have quite a job keeping up, on my crutches.

3

We exit the palace via one of the side wings, go down some wide steps and along a paved footpath. We pass playing fountains and marble statues with their gaze fixed on eternity. The park is thick with trees that vanish into the darkness. I hear the rustling of leaves and the cooing and chirping of nocturnal beasts, as in the jungle. Esteban leads me down a gravel path to a meadow. And there, in the middle of a colourful carpet of flowers, floodlit by concealed lights, is a metre-high standing stone.

A rune stone.

I run my fingers over the symbols that have been almost worn away by the centuries. Symbol by symbol, I translate for myself:

☥ ↑ ✝

Tord carved these runes far from the land of his ancestors
Over stormy seas and unknown mountain ranges
Through forests and over peaks
We have carried the Holy One
We were born to protect
By the mercy of the gods
As instructed by Asim
To the island of the sun
Hispaniola
1503

In the middle of the park, surrounded by flowers and a high wrought-iron fence with long, sharp spikes, lies a white mausoleum.

The walls are decorated with a red-stone frieze, but there are no windows. The domed roof is verdigris copper.

We stop at the gate. 'Watch,' Esteban commands. He pulls a remote control out of his pocket. An enormous grid of infrared beams lights up the dark. 'Security,' he explains. 'In case someone, against all odds, manages to get past the outer gates, ground sensors, surveillance cameras, infrared beams, detectors and dogs.'

He presses his eye to the iris scanner and then punches in a code. The iron gate swings open.

We pause at the bottom of the granite steps that lead up to the entrance. I recognise the three symbols in a frieze on the gable above the great double door. Ankh, *tiwaz* and the cross.

We go up the steps to the marble floor in front of the door. The old, solid locks have been replaced with coded locks installed in the wide doorframe. Esteban punches in a code, waits a moment, then punches in another.

The heavy doors open without a sound.

We walk into a vestibule with a mosaic floor. The roof and walls in between the carved frames and gilded ornamentation are decorated with frescoes. The doors close behind us. The bolt thumps into place. The inner and outer doors can obviously not be open at the same time.

Through the next door, a broad staircase leads us down two flights to another vestibule. Once again, Esteban has to look into an iris scanner and punch in a code.

The door opens.

And in we go.

4

I lose myself in the mausoleum's mystery and divine beauty.

The high, lime-washed vaulted ceiling is supported by fourteen marble pillars. Behind the pillars, the walls are white and shiny. The rotunda, pillars and vaulted ceiling create a sublime harmony. Whereas the Sacred Library and the rest of the Miércoles Palace are lavishly decorated, the mausoleum is simple and clean. And incredibly beautiful and blindingly white.

The tomb does not appear to be big from the outside. But once inside, I am overwhelmed by its monumental proportions and dimensions.

In the middle of the tiled floor, a gold coffin lies on a metre-high plinth, with wide steps leading up to it. At each corner, seven candles burn in equally tall gold menorahs.

We approach the plinth and coffin with veneration. The clatter of my crutches feels blasphemous, so I tuck them under my arms and limp on without support.

We go up the five steps to the plinth.

The lid of the coffin is open. It rests on four ebony posts.

Inside the coffin, with his thin arms crossed over his chest, lies the mummy.

He is bound in linen. His head is oblong and pointed.

'This,' Esteban says, 'is Moses.'

Even though I had already guessed this, the air is sucked out of me, leaving behind a prickly, blank vacuum. My heart is hammering so hard that I gasp for breath. It all feels so unreal and solemn that my eyes fill with tears.

'Moses . . .' I repeat, in awe.

5

An internal door into the mausoleum opens and Beatriz comes in, followed by the same security guards who hauled off the Curator. The guards position themselves on either side of the door. Beatriz glides over the floor.

Confused, I look from Beatriz to the mummy and then back. Why has she come here? I thought she went to bed ages ago. Why has she got the two guards with her?

'I want the Thingvellir Scrolls,' Esteban demands.

Although I had not anticipated the exact words, they hold a remarkable logic. Despite my disquiet and growing fear, I realise why Esteban has shown me the mummy.

'You are no doubt wondering why I brought you here,' Esteban continues. 'I want you to understand that the Thingvellir Scrolls are part of a greater whole. And that whole is here. At the Miércoles Palace.'

I look at Beatriz askance. *What are you doing here?* Her eyes are cold and defiant.

'Beatriz?' I plead.

She looks at her brother.

'Lovely lady, isn't she?' He nudges me. 'Attractive. Don't think I haven't seen the look in your eyes.'

'Where are the scrolls?' Beatriz asks. All the warmth has drained from her voice.

'Will you give them to us if I let you sleep with her?' Esteban laughs. 'What do you say, Beatriz? Are the scrolls worth fucking a paleface?'

Beatriz stares at me.

Esteban continues: 'I've been patient with you. Don't you agree? I have been friendly and accommodating. I have given you plenty of opportunity. But now I'm starting to lose patience.'

'I don't know where they are,' I stammer.

'Perhaps I believe you. Perhaps I don't. But to find out should be easy enough.'

He signals to the two security guards, who clump over the tiles. Esteban escorts me down the five steps. Beatriz follows. They then lead me out of the mausoleum, down a flight of stairs and through endless underground passages that have been recently painted, with heavy security doors, until eventually we end up somewhere that must be directly under the palace.

They open a great wooden door. A steep stairway leads down into the depths of the cellar.

'Where are we going?' I stutter.

Beatriz turns and walks away. Towards the light.

They push me down the steps, down into the dark, down into the stench of damp and decay. Claws scuttle across the stone floor. Yellow eyes glitter when one of the guards turns on a torch. A spider pulls back as the beam of light sweeps over it.

'Where are we going?' I ask again. I realise that we are not on our way back to my room, with its large, soft bed and chandelier. I want an explanation.

The cellar corridor is low and damp, with an arched ceiling. The flagstone floor is slippery. We turn a corner and stop outside a thick wooden door with an iron cross-bolt. A lizard zigzags over the floor and up the wall.

One of the guards unlocks the door with a ridiculously large key. The lock creaks as though it has not been used for a hundred years. Which, no doubt, is not far from the truth.

'I do not want you to think ill of my hospitality,' Esteban says. 'So I will move you up again as soon as you are willing to cooperate. In the meantime, I'm sure the conditions down here in the cellar will help you to reflect.'

He tells me to go in.

No bloody way. I stay where I am.

'I think you should know,' I sob, 'that I suffer from claustrophobia.'

One of the security guards gives me a shove, which sends me headlong into the cell. My crutches clatter down beside me on the stone floor, which is hard and cold and wet.

Then they slam the door.

The Cell

1

THE CELL is pitch dark. It reeks of age, mould, urine and stagnant water and moss, and something that has died and decayed a long time ago.

I stand up and bang my head on the stone ceiling. I groan. It is difficult to find my balance in the dark.

I have to concentrate to repress the onset of claustrophobia. I know that I must not give in to panic. Three, two, one . . . Deep, regular breathing. No danger. Enough air. Three, two, one . . . I pull the air deep into my lungs, down to my stomach.

Even though my eyes must have got used to the dark, I still can't see anything. Not a single thing.

With my hands in front of me, I take a few limping steps over to the wall. This is also made from solid stone. I run my fingers through my hair. I've got a bump on my head.

My breathing is now regular enough to register something other than my own sobs.

I hold my breath and listen.

Someone is breathing.

I am not alone in the cell.

Fear paralyses me. I am frozen to the wall and press myself against it even more as I listen to the faint, rasping breathing of another being.

A person? An animal? A Gollum-like creature that has lived in the dark for four hundred years and will now have its hunger satisfied?

My throat constricts. The sobs come out in convulsive explosions. My hands and knees are shaking.

'It's only me, Bjørn.'

My heart stops.

Then I recognise the voice.

The Curator.

My body remains locked in the paralysis of fear for a few more seconds. Then my lungs empty in a rush of air.

With my back to the wall, I sink to the floor.

'These cells have been used for all sorts, from slaves and pirates to mutineers and political agitators. We are in the second dungeon. They could accommodate up to fifty or sixty prisoners. Some lived here for years before they died. It's now used as a cold cellar and store.'

I can't see him. But from his voice I would guess he is about three or four metres to my left.

'I apologise that I've managed to get you caught up in all this,' I say.

'It's not your fault.'

'I thought Beatriz was on our side.'

'Of course she is.'

'She . . . it was Beatriz who came with the security guards to get me. In the mausoleum.'

'I'm sure there is an explanation.'

'You don't understand . . .'

'I do understand.'

'And Esteban . . . He can't treat us like this.'

'King Esteban can treat whoever he likes however he likes!'

'Normal people don't behave like that.'

'Normal? Esteban? He is obsessed.'

'It never crossed my mind that my nosing about would affect you.'

'It's all my fault. I should have realised that we would be seen by the security guards on the CCTV. Even in the middle of the night.'

'I don't understand . . . You're his employee!'

'I have been his useful fool up until now. The manuscript is now something that is between you and him. He can do without me now.'

'But why has he . . .' I look for the right words. '. . . put you under house arrest?'

'Because he doesn't trust me. Because he finally caught me red handed. He has been after me for years. Beatriz has protected me. Now he's finally caught me out. I don't think that there's anything in *Bård's Tale* that might threaten him. It's my disloyalty that bothers him. The fact that I could show you one of the Sacred Library manuscripts behind his back.'

'Why is he after you?'

'Because I have always challenged him. He has never liked me. And what's more, he's jealous.'

'Of you?'

I can hear him breathing again in the dark.

'Because Beatriz is fonder of me than she is of him.'

'So what? He is a brother and you are a friend. There's no comparison.'

He speaks quietly: 'Esteban has always had a more than brotherly interest in Beatriz.'

The darkness between us swells.

'What do you mean by that?'

'Did you know that the Egyptian pharaohs were so

concerned about keeping the family's divine bloodline pure that they married their sisters? Even Cleopatra was married to her much younger brother. There are some who believe that Pharaoh Akhenaten's relationship with his mother, Queen Tiye, was the model for the Oedipus myth.'

'Are you saying that Esteban and Beatriz have an incestuous relationship?'

'I have never wanted to ask.'

'Esteban is not exactly a pharaoh.'

'But he suffers from megalomania all the same. He is just as mad. In the sixties, before she moved to the USA, Beatriz confided in me that Esteban had sexually assaulted her.'

'What are you saying?'

'She was suicidal at the time. I had just managed to foil a suicide attempt when she told me about him. She never wanted to talk about it again later. I don't know whether it carried on or whether he left her alone.'

I put my face in my hands. 'Why are you telling me all this?'

'Because it's important that you understand how mad he is.'

'Mad . . .'

'Don't be fooled by Esteban's psychopathic charm. He is evil, through and through.'

I wonder to myself whether it's actually the Curator who has a screw loose. It pains me to think of Beatriz in Esteban's arms.

'I'm sure Esteban has a lot of powerful friends,' I say. 'But when all this is over, he will discover that I do, too.'

'Dear Bjørn.' He hesitates before continuing: 'You don't honestly imagine that he's going to let us out of here alive?'

Moses

1

I SLEEP in fits and starts through the night.

I sit on the cold, wet stone floor with my back against the hard wall. My dreams and fear twist themselves into tight knots. At regular intervals I wake up with a start and stare out into the dank darkness, gasping for air. A hypnotherapist once taught me how to calm my claustrophobic panic attacks by meditating and slowing my pulse. Three, two, one . . . I am one with my breathing. But it is not easy.

Sometimes I hear claws scratching on the floor. I imagine that the ceiling is covered in thick cobwebs and that there are fat spiders waiting in every corner for a rat to get caught in their sticky web. When I try to seek refuge in sleep, I am startled by small spasms in my body.

I hear the Curator's quiet, slurring snore. Has he told me the truth? Or has Esteban put him in the cell to fool and persuade me? Are the Curator and Beatriz and Esteban all conspiring against me? Is the Curator the one who is mad and who lusts after Beatriz? And how could I be so wrong about Beatriz? How could I fall in love with a woman who is as corrupt and cold as her brother?

I doze and dream that I have become a Guardian. One who picks up the reins where they were dropped five hundred years ago. Bjørn Beltø. Guardian.

My body aches. It is impossible to find a comfortable position.

I wake up to hear the Curator relieving himself against the wall.

I get up and do the same.

Then we both try to sleep again.

2

I don't know whether it is morning, afternoon or the middle of the night. Time has lost all meaning in the dark. My hunger is overpowering even my fear.

As I doze, the pirates and slaves who ended their days here pass before me. I can smell their fear.

3

'Bjørn?'

'Yes?'

'Shall we talk?'

'Why?'

'It's better than losing your mind.'

'What should we talk about, then?'

'Moses.'

'Again?'

'Why do you think the Vatican has paid the Rodriquez family a fortune to guard his mummy and manuscript for five hundred years?'

'Good question. If the mummy really was Moses, the Vatican would surely have built a cathedral in his honour instead, like St Peter's Basilica. A shrine for all the world's Jews, Christians and Muslims.'

'Not if Moses was not what the Church wanted him to be. Not if Moses never led the Israelites through the wilderness. Not if he was a disobedient and unfilial Egyptian prince who defied his father.'

'So the description in the Bible is not true?'

'Nearly a thousand years passed from the time when Moses is supposed to have lived until his story was pieced together in the Five Books of Moses. A story can change in the course of a thousand years, Bjørn. That's a long time.'

I agree. A thousand years is a long time.

4

People who lose their sight often say that their other senses are enhanced. I understand now what they mean. In the dark, I hear water running somewhere deep in the walls, claws scratching the stone and the mucus in the Curator's lungs. I smell the passing of time and the urine in the corner. I taste my own metallic breath and feel the blood coursing through my veins. I can't see the Curator, but I feel the shape of his aura.

'In the Bible, events that took place over several centuries are concentrated down to a single stock cube of drama,' the Curator says. 'Only when everything falls into place in the right chronology and at the right pace do fact and myth meet.'

'For example?'

'The ten plagues of Egypt, say. The waters of the Nile turning to blood. The plagues of frogs and insects, dying livestock, boils, hailstones, darkness. Do you remember?'

'Yes, I did go to Sunday School.'

'In biblical times, an enormous volcanic eruption split the Greek island of Santorini in two. The entire Mediterranean area was affected by tsunamis. Volcanic ash was thrown up into the stratosphere and clouded the sun. The ash fallout caused a climatic catastrophe. Thousands of people and animals died. The Nile was poisoned. The fish were wiped out. The ecosystem was thrown off balance. There were no fish to eat the larvae, so they matured into insects and the swarms of insects were good food for frogs. You see? It's all connected.'

'But what about the Exodus?'

'A historical mystery. All we know about the Israelites' flight from Egypt is what is written in Exodus. But based on historical events that can be dated archaeologically, we know that the Exodus must have taken place some generations after the rule of Pharaoh Thutmose III, who laid the foundations for a new and powerful Egypt. By then, the country was wallowing in wealth. His great-grandson, Amenhotep III, had magnificent buildings made all over Egypt. He built the Malkata Palace in Thebes, and started to reconstruct the destroyed town Avaris, which lay to the north on the Nile Delta. The new town was named Pi-Ramses – Pithom and Ramses – but the area is better known as Goshen. Now, in the Second Book of Moses, it says that *therefore they did set over them taskmasters to afflict them with their burdens. And they built for Pharaoh treasure cities, Pithom and Raamses.* So, the story of the Bible and archaeology are more or less in line here: according to Exodus, the Israelite slaves were involved in a mammoth building project. And archaeologists have found evidence that foreign slaves worked on the reconstruction of Pi-Ramses.'

'So that means . . .'

'. . . That Amenhotep III was the pharaoh in the Bible. He was the father of Akhenaten, who wanted to replace all the Egyptian gods with one almighty god.'

'The same project as Moses.'

'Exactly. And I know who Moses was.'

Promises

1

WE HEAR heavy steps out in the corridor.
We both take a deep breath.

We hear the key turning in the reluctant lock.

The door opens in an explosion of light. The Curator and I are both blinded. We protect our eyes against the sharp beam of the torch.

When my eyes adjust to the light again, I see the cell properly for the first time. It is not big. Four metres by five, or thereabouts. The Curator is sitting in a corner. The walls are made from great blocks of granite. The flagstone floor is uneven, smoothed by the dragging feet of many prisoners. The roof is vaulted.

'You!'

One of the guards points at me.

I grab my crutches. The Curator gets up to come with me, but is pushed back down again. They slam the door shut. I hear him hammering on the door, but the sound is muffled, unreal, as if coming from faraway.

The guards let me have a shower and go to the toilet. I wouldn't be surprised if the stench from the cell still clings to my damp, dirty clothes.

2

They are waiting for me by a rococo-style table of newly polished mahogany. Esteban is dressed in an expensive suit. Beatriz is wearing a sweet, tight summer dress.

'*Buenos días*,' Esteban greets me. 'Did you sleep well?'

I don't answer.

Beatriz looks at me with empty eyes. 'Everything would be so much easier if you would just tell us where you have hidden the Thingvellir Scrolls.' Her voice is cold.

I'm good at keeping silent.

'Isn't she lovely?' Esteban shows the tip of his tongue. He gives a roguish smile and strokes her bare arm. 'Quite something, eh? Proof that God created woman! You should have seen her when she was young. Oh-la-la!'

Beatriz's expression remains blank.

'We have a question for you,' Esteban says.

'And if I answer?'

'Then we stop bothering you.'

'Will you let me go?'

'Of course.'

'The Curator, too?'

'Naturally.'

'And if I don't answer?'

'You will answer. You are not stupid. You will have plenty of time to come to your senses,' Beatriz replies.

'Time?'

'To think. In the cellar. With the Curator.'

'What do you think I should do, Beatriz?'

'I think you should do what Esteban says.'

'I'll think about it.'

The Crown Prince

1

AFTER OUR little interview, I am taken back down to the cell. I have been given two rolls, two apples and two bottles of water.

The stench hits me.

The security guards push me in and leave me in the dark with the Curator's history lessons.

'How did it go?'

'Beatriz was there.'

'Oh . . .'

'Did you hear what I said?'

'Yes.'

'She's part of it.'

'Of what?'

'Esteban's operation.'

'Beatriz? Never.'

'I don't understand it, either.'

In the dark, we wolf down the rolls and the apples, but we save the water.

We listen to each other's breathing in the silence.

'So who was he?' I ask.

I hear the Curator sitting up and clearing his voice.

'The Moses of the Bible never existed.'

'But you still know who he was?' I sniff.

'The prince we know as Moses was an Egyptian of royal birth. He was not the son of a slave. Those who compiled the Bible have moulded him to suit the Israelite project. Like so much else in the Bible, the story has been touched up and manipulated.'

'Why?'

'They had a nation to build. A people to unite. A religion to establish. They needed a prophet. They needed a fantastic story that would inspire people and keep them in check.'

'So they made up Moses?'

'A stroke of genius. By creating a literary character, Moses, they could build up the story using actual and fictional people, myths and historical events.'

'In what way?'

'Moses' origins are a good example: the son of a slave who becomes a prince. We all know the story from Exodus where the pharaoh's daughter finds the baby Moses floating down the Nile in a rush basket. The problem is that an Egyptian princess would never be allowed to adopt a son, as she does in the Bible. The bloodline in the Egyptian royal family was so divine that the pharaohs had to make their own sisters and daughters pregnant in order to keep that bloodline pure. The idea that one of the king's semi-divine daughters would be allowed to adopt the son of a poor Hebrew slave is unthinkable.'

'How did the story evolve, then?'

'The story of the adopted son has its roots in a similar story from Babylonian mythology, but there is also an

Egyptian story. Many pharaohs married princesses from other kingdoms in order to form political alliances. Some of them were given their own palaces and the title *tet-sa-pro*. Now, what do you think *tet-sa-pro* means?'

I shake my head in the dark.

'*Tet-sa-pro* means pharaoh's daughter, Bjørn. These poor women lived lonely, celibate lives and could not have their own children. A sad life. If they took a lover, they were killed. From historical sources, we know about the fate of one such woman. The Syrian princess Termut was a *tet-sa-pro* during the reign of Thutmose III. She had no children. But the sources still say that she raised a son.'

'An adopted son?'

'Yes. We don't know his name, but we know that Princess Termut was allowed to adopt a son because she was only a *tet-sa-pro*, in other words married into the family, and not of divine lineage. This story, combined with the Babylonian myth of a baby floating downriver in a reed basket, gave the writers of the Bible the idea for Moses' journey from the slave camp to the Egyptian royal court.'

3

'So who was Moses?'

'A rebellious crown prince.'

'Akhenaten?'

'Akhenaten took the throne in place of his older brother.'

'Which means?'

The Curator pauses. 'Moses was Akhenaten's brother.'

'Brother? Which brother?'

'Amenhotep III's oldest son and crown prince was called Thutmose. He was also known by the name Djhutmose and is one of the greatest mysteries in Ancient Egypt.'

'I haven't even heard of him.'

'Exactly. Whereas all the others in his family are well-known names: his father, Amenhotep III, his mother Tiye, his younger brother Akhenaten, and of course Tutankhamen, who was the son of either Akhenaten or Amenhotep III – but no one has heard about Crown Prince Thutmose. He could have gone down in history as the great pharaoh Thutmose V. But instead, he disappeared. Without any elegies or tributes from his people and family. Without any explanation. The country's crown prince quietly vanished from history.'

'Why?'

'He fell from grace. He disappeared suddenly and unexpectedly in the twenty-third year of Amenhotep III's reign, like dust in the wind.'

'What happened?'

'It's a sad story. Crown Prince Thutmose was a celebrated war hero and religious leader, a courageous general in his father's army. Like Moses, he rebelled. There are too many similarities between the crown prince and Moses for it to be coincidence.'

'Such as?'

'In the Bible we are told that Moses killed an Egyptian who mistreated a slave in Goshen. Crown Prince Thutmose also fought against the abuse of slaves. According to an alternative version of the Bible story, Moses did not flee to Midian but to Ethiopia. Here he fought so heroically that he was crowned king. The Koran says quite plainly that Moses ruled as king in Ethiopia. The Jewish Talmud also speaks of Moses as a king.'

'So?'

'Crown Prince Thutmose was also King of Ethiopia for a period.'

'And that makes him Moses?'

'No, there's more. Moses and Crown Prince Thutmose were both great generals. They were both deeply religious. After one successful foray, Thutmose was made the high priest of the temple of Ra in Heliopolis in the north of Egypt and was also linked to the Ptah cult in Memphis. That is to say that the crown prince prevailed over all the priests in Upper and Lower Egypt from this base, which was not far from Pi-Ramses.'

The Curator coughs. I think to myself that he is far too fragile to survive being in a cell for days.

'Are you following me, Bjørn? Crown Prince Thutmose was high priest in the land of Goshen, which was revitalised by his father – and which is where, the Bible tells us, the Israelites were the slaves of the pharaoh.'

4

Following a short pause, in which he blows his nose, the Curator continues: 'There are more links between Crown Prince Thutmose and Moses in Manetho's history, *Aegyptiaca*. He talks of a slave uprising in Avaris, that is Pi-Ramses or Goshen, during the reign of Amenhotep III. Manetho writes that the pharaoh was advised to rid the country of the *undesirables*, and to put them to work in the quarries of Avaris.'

'Who were the undesirables?'

'Who could they have been other than the much-hated Israelites? According to Manetho, the slaves worked there for many years until the arrival of a priest from the Temple of Ra in Heliopolis. Crown Prince Thutmose! The priest had abandoned his Egyptian religion and gods and worshipped an almighty god. Manetho also writes that this priest had previously been a soldier, like Crown Prince Thutmose, and he taught the undesirables to fight. In the Bible, it says the Egyptians *were grieved because of the children of Israel*. Manetho relates that when the priest led the undesirables in an uprising, many of them fled back to their homeland. Do you see the parallels? A slave rebellion . . . An Egyptian helper . . . Flight to the homeland . . .'

'Exodus . . .'

'Precisely! Centuries later, the people who wrote the Bible transformed this story into an epic and dramatic tale of betrayal and courage, rebellion and flight – a departure to God's Promised Land. Naturally the story in the Bible is far grander and proud. A spectacular exodus . . . A god who actively interferes with events on earth . . . A majestic leader of Moses' calibre . . .'

5

'Does that mean that the mummy that is kept in the mausoleum here at the Miércoles Palace is Crown Prince Thutmose?'

'The mummy is Crown Prince Thutmose, son of Amenhotep III and Queen Tiye. The black sheep of the family. Rogue and rebel.'

'What happened to him when the slaves fled?'

'After Thutmose had helped the Israelite slaves to flee, he boldly returned to his father's palace. Home to Daddy. Well, Amenhotep III was no gentle, understanding father. He sentenced his disobedient son to death. Not only had the prince rebelled against his family and the Egyptian gods; not only had he helped the slaves to escape; he had, more importantly, dishonoured his father, the king and god of Egypt. And for that, there was no forgiveness.'

'So he was executed?'

'Because he was of royal birth, he avoided public execution. For the pharaoh, his son's betrayal was a state secret, a non-subject, a disgrace to the family. Crown Prince Thutmose was allowed to choose himself how he would die. He chose poison. When he had drunk the poison and breathed his last, he was embalmed and mummified. He may have been a traitor, but he was still royalty and therefore divine. But he was not laid to rest in the company of his forebears. Instead, he was buried in a secret tomb on the west bank of the Nile, beyond the Valley of the Kings and the Valley of the Queens. He was hidden away behind two other tombs, and thus he was wiped from history. Amenhotep III ordered all evidence of him to be destroyed. Any written references were burned and statues were pulled down.'

'But he hasn't been forgotten?'

'The prince left behind many writings, some of which we have here at the Miércoles Palace on the decayed papyri. In brief, these texts were the beginnings of a new religion. The crown prince's supporters – and there were many – never forgot their leader. They looked after his teachings and even older traditions, and they studied his writings and religious visions. Priests were also converted to believing in one absolute god, who was greater than all the Egyptian gods. And so people started to cultivate Crown Prince Thutmose as a religious leader. More and more people started to worship his god. One branch developed into Judaism. Another smaller branch became the Amon-Ra cult. The crown prince's mummy, which they guarded, became their god. In terms of the Bible, visionary writers gathered together many texts and thus created a new and powerful protagonist, and named him Moses.'

The Sheikh

1

TIME PASSES slowly in the dark.

The Curator and I discuss various theories about Moses and the history of the Guardians. How much did they know? How much did they understand? How has the story been distorted over the centuries?

I am taken up to talk to Esteban and Beatriz twice. They ask me to tell them where the Thingvellir Scrolls are. I am frightened, but I say nothing.

2

The next time they come to get me, the guards put a hood over my head. My fear tips over into panic. I hyperventilate. I try to break free. I cry like a baby.

The guards drag me through the cellar and carry me up the stairs and along a long corridor into a room, where they tie me to a chair.

I twist and turn.

The door shuts.

'Help me, help me!' I scream.

I try to bite a hole in the hood with my teeth.

'No reason to panic,' Esteban says. 'The material lets air through. You'll get enough oxygen.'

'Take it off!'

'Breathe deeply.'

'Take it off!'

'You're a tough cookie, Bjørn Beltø.'

'Take the hood off!'

'Soon.'

'I can't breathe!'

'In a while.'

'Now!'

'Of course you can breathe.'

'Please, take it off! Please!'

'If you hold still for a moment and let me speak, then I'll take it off.'

I try to calm down in the clammy warmth of the hood. Three, two, one . . .

'There now. That's better.'

'Please. Be quick.'

'Bjørn?'

'Yes . . .'

'You're going to meet the sheikh.'

'Sheikh Ibrahim?'

'Face to face.'

In the same way that I imagine a monk feels the presence of God in a chapel, I feel the presence of the sheikh in the room. As if his very existence swallows up all the oxygen.

'So you're both in it together?'

Esteban laughs. 'Well, you could say that. Almost nobody has met the sheikh.'

I gasp for air and breathe in my own warm breath. By introducing me to the sheikh, he is also signing my death sentence. I realise that.

He loosens the rope around my neck and takes the hood off. I gulp down fresh air while I squint in the bright light and look around for the sheikh. But the only person I can see is Esteban, with the hood in his hand. It is dark outside. A clock on the wall shows that it is eleven thirty. I breathe heavily and deeply. The panic attack and claustrophobia have left me drenched in sweat.

'Where is he?'

'He is here.'

Confused, I look around again. But there are only the two of us in the room.

Esteban's eyes meet mine.

'I am the sheikh,' he says.

3

I look at him for a long time, waiting for him to laugh and say that it is a joke, for the door to open and Sheikh Ibrahim to come in, in all his pomp and glory.

Or maybe I realise that he is telling the truth.

Esteban circles my chair.

'Ever since I was a boy,' he tells me, 'and my father told me the history of the Guardians, the manuscript and the mummy, only one thing has mattered to me and that is to find Asim's copy. The Thingvellir Scrolls. As you know, the palace and I are under the protection of the Vatican, in all kinds of ways, including financial. So I had to find another way. I inherited my father's obsession: to complete the manuscript collection at the Miércoles Palace with a complete version of the manuscript. And I realised very early on that I would need an alter ego to do this. Too many people knew who I was. They would start to ask questions if I turned up at manuscript auctions or poked around in the best antiquaries, archives and libraries in the world. So I created the sheikh and let him employ a team of workers.'

'Why a sheikh?'

'Why not? Ibrahim al-Jamil ibn Zakiyy ibn Adbul-aziz al-Filastini. A well-educated, sophisticated, rich and reclusive sheikh, based in the United Arab Emirates. A generous sponsor, donor and supporter and philanthropist. As the sheikh, I have funded university departments and research institutes. But everything that I have done, all the transactions and investments I have made, have had one sole purpose: to provide me with information that might lead to the parchments you found in Thingvellir. I allied myself with scholars and thugs. I employed academics and antiquarians. But I always operated through middlemen. Always. No one met the sheikh personally. No one knew who he was. Not even my dear sister, Beatriz, knows that the sheikh and I are one and the same person. He has never stayed in the same house for more than one week. No one ever knows where he is. The sheikh operates through his organisation. A network of lies and deceit. An illusion.'

'Why are you telling me your secret?'

'Because I want you to understand how important it is for me to get the Thingvellir Scrolls. I want you to understand that you have to tell me where they are.'

'And if I don't?'

He goes over to a side door, opens it and waves in someone who has been sitting there waiting.

Hassan

1

HASSAN STRIDES into the room, all muscle and might. Hassan the stone crusher.

'If you don't cooperate,' Esteban says, 'I will ask Hassan to persuade you. But we don't need to go to that extreme. I have told you the truth in the hope that it will convince you that this is of the utmost importance to me, and that I take my work very seriously. I will let nothing stop me. Nothing!'

I can't answer. Esteban cuts the ties that keep my hands attached to the chair.

'And if I tell you, you will let me and the Curator go?'

'Of course.'

But we both know that he can, in no way, risk that his secret be revealed.

He breathes in sharply through his teeth. Then he goes over to a desk and takes something I recognise out of the drawer.

'I'm curious, Bjørn. Show me how you managed to find the cave at Thingvellir based on what you read in this manuscript.' He puts the Snorri Codex down on the table beside me.

The sight of Sira Magnus's lost manuscript stirs my emotions. I see my friend sitting at the table in the rectory, and I hear his voice.

'I know that you think we stole this from Sira Magnus.

And that we killed him. But the truth is that he tried to sell it to us initially. I can't help the fact that he changed his mind. We didn't want to kill. But his heart couldn't take the strain. That's all.'

Esteban looks over at Hassan. The enormous Iraqi is staring straight ahead, without saying a word, as if neither Esteban nor I is there, as if his thoughts are somewhere far away in the autistic universe.

That's all . . .

My hands are shaking so violently that it is difficult to hold the manuscript. I turn to the verse on the last page and show how it led us to *The Saga of the Holy Cross*, which in turn contained the directions to the cave. Esteban clucks to himself. Then he looks again over at Hassan, who is dozing off.

'It's late. Hassan has just arrived. I think that you and he should have a serious chat in the morning.'

I shudder at the thought of a serious chat with Hassan.

'He's not very sophisticated. But he is extremely efficient, as you can imagine. Think about it. Before he starts. You would be wise to cooperate from the start, before he breaks more fingers, or does some damage to that broken leg of yours which appears to have healed so nicely. I wouldn't annoy him. Breaking bones is one of Hassan's more moderate methods. Back in Iraq, he poked out a man's eyes because he refused to speak. With his own bare hands. I thought I'd just mention that in case you were reluctant to give me that answer I want. For your own sake, Bjørn, it would be wise to cooperate.'

2

Kierkegaard once said that our fear is of tomorrow. I understand what he means now.

I can't sleep. With my back to the stone wall, I stare into

the blackness of the cell. Although I know there is a wall just a few metres in front of me, I could as well be looking out into endless space. Nothing quells the fear of what awaits me at dawn. Terror has wrapped me in its embrace. Only one thing exists: Hassan.

Of course I'll tell them what I know. I'm not stupid. I will not sacrifice my fingers, eyes or life for the Thingvellir Scrolls. But there are two problems. One is that they are going to kill me in any case, and the other is that I have no idea where the manuscript is. I would guess that the SIS safe house is somewhere in the London area, but it might equally be in the quiet, idyllic village of Llanfairpwllgwngyllgogery-chwyrndrobwllllantysiliogogogoch in Wales, for all I know.

What will they do to me, when I tell them I don't know? Will they break some fingers just to make sure I'm telling the truth? They will no doubt ask me to call the SIS. What will Professor Llyleworth or Diane say when I phone out of the blue – *Hi, it's Bjørn* – and ask where the Thingvellir Scrolls are? At best, they will understand that I am doing it under duress, and at worst, they will refuse to tell me. No matter what happens, the scrolls and the SIS folk will be somewhere else when Hassan's troop turn up with the cannons. And there is little doubt that I will be anywhere other than here, in the cell, in the dark, when they check out whether I have fooled them or not.

I have always been a coward when it comes to pain – dentists, throat infections, blisters, ripped nails. No one has suffered as I have.

The thought of the pain that Hassan will inflict on me makes me feel sick. I want to cry.

My breathing is irregular. The Curator is snoring peacefully.

The Plan

1

T HIS TIME I don't hear the footsteps. I just hear the rattling in the lock and the rusty mechanism's objections.

I tense. *Already?* My breathing stops. My heart stops. My brain freezes, leaving only one emotion: wild, primitive panic.

The hinges creak. The door is pushed open.

I can't breathe. My throat is constricting.

The shattering edge of a torch beam shines in through the opening.

For a moment I know exactly how people who have been sentenced to death feel when they are about to be led to the electric chair.

I whimper.

'Shhhh,' whispers a voice.

Beatriz.

Beatriz with the wild hair and the beautiful smile. Beatriz with the twinkling eyes.

Beatriz the traitor.

Why have they sent her to get me? Tiny Beatriz?

'Quick!' she whispers.

The Curator jumps to his feet. 'Bea!' he exclaims, and gives her a hug. I have problems gathering my thoughts and limbs at the same time.

'Phew, it stinks in here,' Beatriz says.

What's happening? Where are the security guards? Is Hassan waiting outside the door?

Frightened and confused, I edge along the floor farther into the cell. Away from Beatriz and the fear she brings with her.

'Bjørn?'

I cringe when the beam from the torch strikes me across the face like a whip.

Beatriz sighs. 'Oh, Bjørn.'

Oh, Bjørn?

I squint into the light.

'Dear Bjørn, you really haven't understood, have you?'

Understood? I don't answer. *Dear Bjørn?* I haven't understood.

She comes into the cell. She hands the torch to the Curator and helps me to my feet. I'm shaking. And I'm embarrassed because I'm shaking so much. Even in the face of death, I'd like to have a bit of dignity. In my last minutes on this earth, I don't want to be a shaking, whimpering wreck.

She puts her hands on my shoulders and looks me straight in the eye. My short-sighted eyes that Hassan will gouge out with his thumbs before he kills me.

'Bjørn?'

I look away.

'Hello? Hello, my friend?'

'What do you want?'

'Oh, Bjørn.'

'Are you going to watch? When Hassan tortures me?'

She pulls me to her.

'Bjørn. Listen to me. Bjørn! *Bjørn!*'

'What?'

'I was acting!'

Acting! So she says.

'I pretended to be on Esteban's side.

Pretended. So she says.

'It wasn't hard. I know the role well. My whole life has been one long charade with Esteban as my opposite. He . . .' She decides not to say what she had thought of saying. 'That evening when Esteban surprised you and the Curator in the library, one of the guards who I pay a little extra to be . . . well, to be on my side, shall we say, tipped me off. I realised that I had to pretend to play along. I had no choice. It was the only way I could find out what Esteban had in mind. I offered to take the guards over to the mausoleum so that he could talk to you, alone, before he threw you in the dungeon. He was so happy when I offered to help. Now it was him and me against the world . . . Esteban is a smart bastard, but when it comes to me, I have him eating out of my hand. He's so gullible, he always lets himself be fooled. It's always been like that.'

There is an edge of deep bitterness in her voice.

'How do I know that you're not acting now?'

'I think you know that, Bjørn.'

'Why did you ask me to tell you where the Thingvellir Scrolls were?'

'Because I had to pretend to be the evil Beatriz, Esteban's ice queen.'

'And what if I had told you?'

'Bjørn, I know you. I knew that you wouldn't say a word.'

'She's telling the truth, Bjørn,' the Curator assures me. 'I know Beatriz. You can trust her.'

'And even if you had been forced to say where they were,' Beatriz says, 'it's not the Thingvellir Scrolls that are most important to us.'

'What's more important?'

'To save the mummy and the original manuscript.'

I am still sceptical and analytical in my reasoning. Why

should I believe her now? But my body has accepted the explanation. I can feel my muscles relaxing. The fear is receding. I can't resist those warm eyes. She gives me a gentle pinch on the cheek.

'Here,' she says, and hands the Curator a gun.

'Is everything sorted?'

'Is what sorted?' I ask.

'Everything's ready,' Beatriz confirms. 'No one suspects anything. I have behaved as normal. I've done my nails. I went up to the university, phoned my friends around the world, just as I always do. Esteban has no idea. And all the time I've been getting things ready.'

'Ready for what?' I question.

'I have chartered a cargo ship with a controlled environment container, and several tons of sugar and coffee for delivery in Italy.'

I look at her, nonplussed.

'The ship is called *Desideria*,' she says, 'which means longing.'

I am obviously a bit stupid. 'Why are we transporting several tons of sugar and coffee to Italy?' I ask.

Neither of them answer. They presumably think I'm joking.

'I've also got hold of two identical vans and an articulated lorry,' Beatriz continues. 'And I've bought fourteen sacks of yams and two kegs of home-made rum. I have bribed the customs men, the guards and the dockers down at the port. I have chartered a freight plane, which is waiting at the airport. I've spoken to Professor Llyleworth of the SIS, who is assisting with a group of operatives – former professional commando soldiers – who have been flown over from London. Everything is ready.'

'Good work!' the Curator says.

'What are you talking about?' I say.

They both look at me in disbelief.

'Bjørn, surely you remember our conversation,' Beatriz says. 'We're going to take the mummy back to Egypt. We're going to make sure that the right people get the papyrus manuscript.'

'How are we going to manage that?'

'We have to steal the mummy and the manuscript. No, steal is the wrong word. Take back. We're actually fulfilling the task that the Guardians should have done five hundred years ago.'

'Shall we go?' The Curator is standing by the door, impatient.

'Yes, we don't have much time.' Beatriz brushes some imaginary dust off me, then she hands me my crutches.

2

We take another route through the cellar.

'Esteban has a guard at the top of the stairs,' Beatriz explains.

The cellar is a labyrinth of narrow, dark corridors. We walk and walk. A lizard shoots over the floor. For a while I worry that we have got lost in this underground maze, but Beatriz turns left and right with the confidence of someone who knows where she is going.

With a firm grip on my crutches, I hobble after her.

'The security system is so advanced that it is almost impossible for an outsider to steal the mummy and manuscript,' Beatriz tells me. 'A stranger would barely get past the main gate. Even a squirrel can't move in the park without the guards knowing about it. But the system does not cover the possibility of an inside job. Such as me.'

Finally, at the end of the corridor, we come to some steep, narrow steps that lead up to the first cellar. We then walk along another corridor to some stairs that lead up to the hall outside the library.

'We will get the papyrus scrolls first. From here, we have to watch out for security cameras,' Beatriz instructs. 'There are forty-five cameras that transmit images to fifteen monitors every ten seconds, so that the palace is constantly under surveillance, both inside and out.'

I'm not particularly good at maths, but manage to work out that each camera must then have about twenty seconds when it is not recording.

'We don't have much time,' the Curator points out.

'There are two cameras covering the library,' Beatriz says. 'One is in the right-hand corner on the ceiling, and the other is in the middle of the library. Both cameras have dead zones. Follow me. Don't move before I say so.'

The Vault

WHEN BEATRIZ gives the signal, we slip into the library; that's to say, Beatriz and the Curator slip in; I scramble in with my crutches, stumble on the edge of the carpet and hit the doorframe with my shoulder, so that the arm cuff and handgrip of my crutch slams against the woodwork. I groan with pain. Beatriz turns, gesticulates and rolls her eyes.

'No one knows yet that I've let you out of the cell,' she reprimands under her breath. 'The minute someone finds out, we're done. If they discover us, we'll never escape.'

'Message received loud and clear!'

We flatten ourselves against the wall between two porcelain vases, in the ceiling camera's dead zone.

When the red light on the camera goes off, we sneak along the bookshelves to the next blind spot. Beatriz has to run over to the iris scanner and code panel in two stages in order to open the door to the Sacred Library.

I don't hear any alarms or running steps. But my heart is hammering so hard that it feels as if there should be echoes as far as Key West.

We close the door to the Sacred Library and flatten ourselves against the wall right under the camera. When the red light goes off, Beatriz and the Curator run through the library and I follow.

We turn into a lobby where there is a reinforced-steel vault door. Fortunately there are no cameras here.

Beatriz puts her eye to the iris scanner, waits for the green light and then taps in two six-digit codes. Each times she touches the keypad there is an electronic peep. The door clicks.

As she opens the heavy steel door, a low light comes on.

'If Esteban has discovered what I've been up to, it's now we'll be caught,' she says.

I hobble into the vault.

The white room reminds me of an operating theatre. It is sterile and cold; you can hear the constant humming of the air conditioning, and there is a steel table with glass panels in the middle of the room.

Beatriz goes over to the table, and I follow. The rubber ferrules on my crutches squeak on the tiled floor.

Under the thick glass plates, between finely calibrated instruments that measure the temperature and humidity, lie six papyrus scrolls.

The papyrus has disintegrated into fibrous dust in several places.

'The Books of Moses,' Beatriz says.

With great reverence, I lean over the table and look at the papyri, which are covered in grubby hieroglyphic script that I can't understand.

The Curator drums on the glass with his fingers.

'The Vatican is happiest for the scrolls to be kept here, far away from prying eyes and untrustworthy employees, who might reveal their content. For five hundred years, the Vatican has paid the Rodriquez family handsomely to look after the manuscripts.'

While the Curator and I had amused ourselves in the dark cell, Beatriz had prepared the papyri for transport.

She packs them in silk, which is of just the right tension. Under the steel table, she has hidden a lined aluminium case with six bespoke sections. She carefully moves the scrolls into the moulded-form inserts.

The aluminium case is so light that the Curator can carry it on his own. We leave the vault and close the door, and then walk along a servants' corridor that is not watched by the beady eye of a camera. At the end of the corridor, back stairs lead us down into the cellar again. There is less risk of bumping into anyone down here. Beatriz goes in front with the torch, followed by the Curator and the aluminium case. And I hop along behind.

Once again we go through a labyrinth of cellar passages. I have no idea if they are the same ones we came down earlier. It is dark in this network of corridors and impossible to distinguish one from the other. But Beatriz knows her way. She opens a metal door that creaks as in a comedy film, and we come out into an underground garage, with harsh neon lighting.

'Esteban had the garage built in the seventies, as there were storage rooms down here,' Beatriz explains.

She opens the back door of a red van with the Coca-Cola logo blazoned on each side. There are two heavy wooden cases in the back. One is long and rectangular; the other is small and square. The Curator puts the aluminium case and the six papyrus scrolls into the smaller box and then packs it with bubble-wrap and wood wool.

The rectangular box is just big enough for the mummy's coffin.

I lean one of the crutches up against the garage wall. I need one arm to be free if I am going to help carrying.

3

From the garage, we enter another maze of corridors, this time on the west side of the palace. We turn right through some burgundy metal doors, and I suddenly recognise the newly decorated corridor that leads to the mausoleum.

It is actually easier to walk with just one crutch, and I wonder why I've carried on using both. The doctor in Italy said nothing about how long I would have to use them, and the Norwegian doctor who replaced the plaster cast with a support bandage didn't mention the crutches either. Maybe I could have got rid of them ages ago. That would be bloody typical of me.

One floor down from the mausoleum, we stop outside the door with the time lock. There are no cameras here. Beatriz punches in the code. Once we are through the door, we have to wait for it to lock behind us before Beatriz can use the iris scanner and tap in the second code. The second door opens.

We go up the stairs into a back room behind the mausoleum.

'OK,' says Beatriz. She turns to face me, and takes a deep breath. 'This is the crucial part.'

'What do you mean?'

'As there are two cameras in the mausoleum, the security guards will always be able to see the coffin on one of the monitors, so we have to cut the transmission.'

'Is that not a bit risky? If we do that then they'll definitely know that something is up. Is it not better to hope that they won't be paying attention?'

'They watch those monitors, believe me. If we cut the transmission, we can win a few extra minutes before they work out that it's not a technical fault. One of them will have to come down here from central security on the first floor, to reset the cameras. If he moves fast, that takes four and a half minutes. Then he'll discover that the cameras have been turned off manually and that the coffin is gone. He'll activate the general alarm after about four minutes and fifty seconds.'

'General alarm?'

'There are various alarm systems in the palace. The local alarms are only activated in certain areas and in central security. The general alarm is worse, as it activates all the sirens both inside and out. All doors and gates are locked automatically and the external floodlighting, including red and orange flashing lights on the main fence, is turned on. The alarm goes straight to the police, who will have the palace surrounded within four to five minutes. They will also block the main routes out of Santo Domingo and stop all outbound traffic from the airport.'

'In other words, we have three minutes to get the coffin from the mausoleum to the van, and half a minute to drive through the park and out into the city,' the Curator says. 'Are we going out by the western side gate?'

'Yes.' Beatriz nods. 'Carlos is on duty at the west gate tonight.'

She gives another nod to the Curator, who opens the front of the alarm panel.

'The siren will make a terrible noise,' he says. 'Are you ready, Beatriz?'

'Yes.'

She punches in the code.

The Curator stands with his finger on the button that will turn off the cameras.

Beatriz counts to five.

'Go!'

The Shot

1

THE ALARM starts screaming.

'Quick!' Beatriz shouts. She opens the door and chases the Curator and me into the mausoleum.

The siren bounces off the walls, floor and vaulted roof. The echoes vibrate at different tempos and are thrown into disarray.

The flickering candle flames project an interplay of light, shadow and muted colour onto the white marble pillars.

'Go, go, go!'

We run – and stumble – over the shiny tiled floor of the mausoleum and up the five steps to the plinth.

We all stop respectfully in front of the mummy, as if the same thought has struck us all.

Moses . . . Crown Prince Thutmose . . . The defiant prince . . .

The linen-wrapped body looks so fragile. His crossed arms resting on his sunken chest. To move him feels like a sacrilege, disturbing his thousand-year sleep . . .

Beatriz closes the coffin. She and the Curator secure the lock.

'Hurry!' she shouts over the shrieking alarm.

We grab the golden handles – Beatriz and the Curator at the front and me at the back – and lift the coffin out of the sarcophagus.

I was worried that it might be too heavy to carry, but it weighs almost nothing.

2

Keeping the coffin as level as possible, we go down the steps and across the floor. The noise of our footsteps is drowned out by the alarm. The Curator holds the door to the back room open, and then it slams behind us.

My ears are ringing. The alarm is adjusted to a frequency that affects your hearing and mind.

We struggle to keep the coffin level as we descend the stairs to the security doors. Beatriz and the Curator lift it up above their heads and I bend down so that the bottom is only just above the treads. I drag my one crutch behind me and it bounces down the stairs.

I expect to bump into a security guard at any moment, or even worse, Esteban and Hassan.

Once we are down, the alarm becomes a distant annoyance. Beatriz scans her eye and waits for the green light.

Nothing.

'Can they lock us in here?' I ask.

'Of course,' Beatriz replies. 'The whole system is controlled from central security.'

'It always takes a bit of time,' the Curator says.

A bit of time . . .

Then the green light comes on. Beatriz taps in the code. We hear the electronic hum as the door opens, and run out.

We hurry down the corridor with the coffin between us. One of the strip lights is flickering. The soles of our shoes slap against the floor. My pulse is thumping in my ears.

As the Curator opens the door to the garage, I expect to see a squadron of guards there, ready to shoot. But the garage is empty, except for the faint smell of diesel and engine oil. An old-fashioned alarm bell is ringing up on the wall, just like the ones that used to ring at break time when I was at school.

We carry the coffin over to the Coca-Cola van. Beatriz opens the back door.

3

Hassan is sitting on one of the flip seats in the back of the van.

His face is without expression. He looks like the manager of some small bank branch in a foreign town far off the beaten track. The kind of manager who refuses to give you the money you so desperately need because you don't have the right form stamped by the authorities in both countries.

His bald head shines, even in the murky light of the back of the van. His moustache is well trimmed and robust. He is wearing a white shirt, blue tie and a neatly pressed grey suit.

The Curator, Beatriz and I don't move. None of us says a word. We stare at Hassan and wait for him to do something. I hold tightly on to the golden handle of the coffin.

He is not armed. But he is so big that he doesn't need to bother with minor details like guns. He is used to getting what he wants. There is something about his size which makes him seem totally unassailable and invincible.

But he is not.

4

At first I don't realise where the shot came from. There is a loud, sharp cracking sound that echoes off the concrete walls. Beatriz and I jump.

Hassan opens his mouth and twists his face. A red rose blossoms on his white shirt and grey suit.

He gurgles. Pink foam appears in the corners of his mouth.

With a heavy thud, he falls to floor in the back of the van. The flip seat jumps back to the wall.

The Curator takes his hand out of his pocket. He is holding the gun that Beatriz gave him. There is a smouldering hole in his jacket.

'I had to,' he says, simply.

We put the coffin down on the floor and try to haul Hassan out. But he is too heavy. Even though there are three of us pulling him, he doesn't move.

'We haven't got time for this,' Beatriz cries.

So we leave him where he is.

'I didn't have any choice,' the Curator says. Then he adds, insistently: 'Did I? I didn't have any choice.'

'You didn't have any choice,' Beatriz and I chorus.

We lift the coffin into the van and put it into the wooden box, which we then fill with wood wool and cover in bubble-wrap.

I try to look everywhere other than at Hassan. But he is so big that it is difficult to avoid him.

'No choice,' the Curator mumbles.

The Escape

1

BEATRIZ JUMPS out of the back and dashes round to the front of van and gets in behind the wheel. The Curator and I have to clamber over Hassan to get to the two flip seats behind her. I get blood on my knee.

Using a remote control, Beatriz opens the garage door and accelerates past the rows of parked cars and concrete pillars. A loose drain rattles as we pass over it. Only now do I remember that I have forgotten to take the other crutch. Oh well.

The wheels screech on the garage floor as Beatriz swings round and then brakes in order to drive up the steep, ridged exit. We come out into a big backyard and then turn on to the road through the park.

'Half a minute behind schedule,' the Curator says.

Beatriz speeds up. Gravel and small stones pummel the undercarriage.

'Strange,' Beatriz says suddenly.

'What?' the Curator asks.

'If Hassan knew what we were up to, Esteban must know too. Where is he? Why isn't he stopping us?'

This part of the park is not floodlit. Myriads of insects are illuminated by the headlights. Beatriz is driving as fast as she can. Dark tree trunks merge to become a black wall outside the van windows. A small animal – a rabbit or a squirrel – sitting in the middle of the road freezes in the deadly embrace of the front lights. The second before we are about to mow it down, it throws itself into the undergrowth.

Beatriz is gripping the wheel so fiercely that her knuckles are white.

Between the trees, we see the lights of the car park by the west gate lodge. The Curator and I close the curtains between the front and the back of the van.

Beatriz brakes and rolls down the window. The guard asks good-humouredly for something. I catch the word Coca-Cola. Beatriz replies. The guard laughs. They are talking in Spanish so I don't understand what is being said. The double gates rattle and swing open. Beatriz says something more and laughs. '*Sí, sí, sí!*' laughs the guard. '*Bueno, Carlos,*' Beatriz says. '*Buenas noches.*'

At that moment, the general alarm goes off.

The name is appropriate. The general hubbub and racket might lead you to think that World War III had broken out. An alarm that sounds like a cross between an air-raid siren and a fog horn goes off at a volume that will no doubt wake everyone in the Dominican Republic, Haiti, Puerto Rico, Jamaica and south-east Cuba.

Through the back window I see that the Miércoles Palace and the park are now floodlit like a hotel complex in Dubai.

The gates stop moving. Then they automatically start to close.

Beatriz puts her foot to the floor. The van lurches forward and gets caught between the gates, which scrape the sides of the van.

The guard is banging frantically on the back door. 'Stop! *Qué pasa?* Stop!'

With a noise that sounds like ripping metal, the gates lose their grip and we are out.

2

The driveway from the west gate down to a wide avenue is lined by a low wall covered in mimosa, which continues to climb halfway up the wrought-iron fence. We hurtle down towards the main road and Beatriz does not look left or right before turning on to it. A grey Mercedes brakes and skids across the road. The driver hoots his horn in a rage.

Beatriz pushes the Coca-Cola van up to a speed of one hundred and twenty kilometres an hour.

'People must think that we're on our way to some very thirsty customers,' the Curator remarks.

Fortunately there are not many cars on the road at this time of night. The middle of the avenue is planted with trees. Red and orange lights are flashing all along the fence of the Miércoles Palace.

We spin to the right at the next crossing. An identical red Coca-Cola van is waiting here. And behind it, an articulated lorry, a Lexus, a Ford Transit van and two Hummers.

Beatriz comes to sudden halt. The other Coca-Cola van turns out into the avenue and carries on in the same direction. Beatriz concentrates as she drives up the aluminium ramp into the back of the articulated lorry. The gates to the Miércoles Palace have scraped the Coca-Cola logo off the sides of the van. While the door is being locked, Beatriz, the Curator and I run over to the Lexus. The lorry drives off with a slight hiccup, in a cloud of black diesel exhaust. We follow in the Lexus, with the Transit van and the two Hummers, carrying the storm troopers from the SIS, behind us. We drive in convey around the block before moving back out on to the main road.

After a couple of hundred metres, we are overtaken by the police and security from the Miércoles Palace. They come thundering down the avenue like a Roman legion: a black Ford Excursion, two Land Rovers and eight police cars with sirens and flashing blue lights. We let them pass. Just then, Beatriz gets a phone call. She listens and then turns to us when she has hung up. 'The plane that I chartered has been cordoned off by the police.'

'Shit,' I say.

'Not at all.' Beatriz laughs. 'They are doing exactly what I want them to.'

While Esteban's troops continue to follow the other Coke van and his police cronies surround the plane, our modest convoy turns left, then we turn round at a roundabout and head for the harbour.

3

Ten minutes later we are down by the port, which is situated on a headland at the mouth of the river.

The driver of the Lexus is called on his walkie-talkie. It is the driver of the Coca-Cola van. He says that the police and security guards from the Miércoles Palace are about to catch up with him. They are out in the country now.

'They will find nothing more than fourteen sacks of yams and two kegs of rum in the back,' Beatriz explains. 'Oh, and fifty crates of Coke.'

We drive past sheds, warehouses, barracks, oil tankers, cranes, a container park and mounds of what looks like sugar cane, bark chippings and fine sand, ready for export.

'Ah, here we are,' Beatriz says.

Desideria

1

THE *DESIDERIA* lies in front of us, moored to the quay with so many hawsers that it looks as if she is being held against her will.

She is an elegant ship. The bridge is lit up and I see the ghostly faces of some officers in the light of the lanterns on the first deck.

The articulated lorry pulls up alongside the ship, and the Lexus and Transit van stop behind, whereas the two Hummers disappear off into the dark again, heading for the nearest warehouse.

We get out of the car. The streets behind us are full of sirens. The harbour smells of oil and salt water and foreign spices. A pelican that looks as if it has just swallowed a small calf waddles around on the end of a pier.

Beatriz reverses the van out of the articulated lorry and over to the gangway. The dockers are already loading the ship with goods. Beatriz wants us to take the two boxes, with the coffin and manuscript inside, on board ourselves and then down to the special container in the hold.

The Curator opens the back of the van. Suddenly he turns, and I too turn to see what he is looking at.

2

Three black cars, with no lights on, roll down the quay.

They stop a few metres from us.

The doors open.

And eight men get out. I recognise a couple of them from the Miércoles Palace. And one of them I met in Iceland. They are all armed.

Esteban Rodriquez gets out last.

'You surprise me, Beatriz,' he says.

With a weary expression, he leans against the open car door.

Beatriz stands between the Curator and me, staring at her brother.

'I'm impressed,' Esteban continues.

'Spare me,' she hisses.

'I would never have guessed that you were so meticulous. The chartered plane, the boat, two vans, the ploy to throw us off the scent. You had me fooled with your false charm and lies. Impressive! Truly impressive!'

'I have always managed to fool you, Esteban. Always.'

He moves away from the car door, then step by step he comes closer. His smile is forced.

'There has always been something special between you and me, Beatriz.'

'Only in your perverted fantasies.'

'Beatriz!'

He holds out his hand. She takes a step back.

'Dear sister, come back to the palace with me. I am willing to forget and forgive everything. You know that I will take the coffin and manuscript back with me, no matter what. And you know that I have no choice with regards to *them* . . .' He nods at the Curator and me. '. . . but you and I can go home and forget all this.'

Beatriz's mouth is a grim line.

'I'm not unreasonable,' Esteban continues. 'I understand. You're a woman. You let your emotions and naive idealism get the better of you. I forgive you, dear Beatriz. Now please, come back to the palace with me.'

'Ever since we were children, you have always believed that I looked up to you, loved you. But the truth is, Esteban, that I have always detested you.'

'Beatriz . . .'

'And you know very well why. You are sick. You have always been sick. Only you're not aware of it yourself.'

Tears run down her cheeks.

'Come home with me, darling Beatriz. Home to the palace.'

'Never!'

'You belong at the palace. With me.'

He struggles with feelings that are reflected in his face. His voice hardens. 'If you don't come back with me of your own accord, I will be forced to punish you. Do you really think that I didn't know what you were up to? Do you really think that I'd let you sail away on that ship? I'm no fool. I know how to keep my eyes and ears open. As you can see, there are eight armed men behind me. They are all experienced soldiers. And you have six bodyguards from the SIS in those two Hummers. My guess is that they are armed with MP5s. And you probably have a gun each. Well, you don't stand a chance. Your friends will be dealt with in a matter of seconds. But no one will touch you, Beatriz, you know that. I would never harm you.'

The pelican out on the pier turns towards us, swallows and then waddles off again.

'I guessed that you would be watching me,' Beatriz says.

'You know me so well, my sweet.'

'So I made some contingency plans.'

Esteban cocks his head.

'Plans that you couldn't monitor. That you would never discover.'

A look of surprise flashes over his face.

The pelican is trying to decide whether to take off or not.

On an invisible signal, they appear. Commando soldiers. Ten or fifteen of them have been lying in wait on the ship. Ten more up on the containers. Four or five appear on the roof of the nearest warehouse. And they are armed with everything from submachine guns and heavy machine guns to sniper rifles.

Esteban gives a flustered laugh. 'Well, well, Beatriz, well, well.'

The pelican unfolds its great wings and throws itself off the pier and lands in the water with a splash.

Esteban looks at his sister with an expression that is difficult to read.

With slow movements he puts his fingertips to his lips and blows Beatriz a kiss.

3

Suddenly everything happens very fast.

Esteban grabs something from his inner pocket. His men instantly raise their submachine guns.

But the commando soldiers are faster.

The shots ring out: ten to twenty sharp cracks.

Esteban stands swaying for a while before he falls. He curls up like a foetus in a pool of his own blood.

His body spasms a few times and then he lies still.

Beatriz heaves in great sobs.

Esteban's eight security guards lie dead too. None of them had time to fire a shot.

'I'm no fool, either, Esteban,' Beatriz says bitterly.

'Beatriz . . .' I whisper.

'Shush, not now.'

One of the uniformed commandos appears in front of her. 'Excuse me, ma'am,' he says. 'Everything according to plan?'

'Yes, do everything we agreed on.'

'Agreed?' I ask.

'Let's get out of here.'

'But . . .'

Beatriz takes me by the hand. 'You don't need to know any more, Bjørn.'

'I want to know more. That has always been my problem.'

She laughs and nods to herself.

'What now, Beatriz?'

'We sail.'

'What about all of this?'

'The bodies, with the exception of Esteban, will be buried in a derelict churchyard ten miles north of the city. *This* never happened.'

'And Esteban?'

'We have a family mausoleum, of course, at the Miércoles Palace.'

'But the police . . .'

'I've sorted everything out in relation to the police.'

'How?'

'The Miércoles Palace was attacked during the night by armed robbers, terrorists, I don't know. My courageous brother tried to stop them. And I managed to escape.'

She throws one last look at her brother's body.

'Goodbye, Esteban,' she says coldly.

4

While the bodies are being put in the back of the two Hummers, we carry the boxes with the coffin and manuscript on board. Undaunted, the dockers start to unload Beatriz's pile of suitcases and bags from the back of the Ford Transit.

Everything is done swiftly and efficiently.

Someone takes me by the arm and helps me up the gangway.

The crew cast off and the *Desideria* turns round to face the sea.

5

Half an hour later I go up on deck and rest my elbows on the railing as the boat heads south-east. The engine has a rhythmical throb that makes the hull vibrate.

I look at Santo Domingo for the last time. I see the thousands of shining windows, flashing neon lights and queues of cars trailing a veil of red lights behind them.

I throw the remaining crutch overboard. It drops into the water like an errant arrow.

A door opens and then bangs shut.

For a moment there is silence.

'So this is where you are,' Beatriz says so quietly that I barely hear her. She pulls her sleeves down over her bare arms before she leans against my shoulder. It sounds as if she is crying. I put my arm round her waist. The ship rolls on the waves. Drops of spray wet my face. The sea air is robust and salty. After days spent in that stinking cell, the ocean offers hope and promise. We stand there, close together, without saying a word, watching the town shrink in the distance until the lights are swallowed by the night and the sea.

Epilogue

♀ ↑ ✝

'I have left life, no fault was found with me when I stood before Osiris and his judges. I stand before you, lord of the gods. I have joined the dead and the kingdom of justice. I have come to the land of those who rest on the horizon, I am approaching the holy gates.'

THE EGYPTIAN BOOK OF THE DEAD

'And there will come a time when the GUARDIANS will bring THE HOLY ONE back to his resting place, under the sacred sun, in the sacred air, in the sacred rock.'

ASIM

LONDON (Reuters) – A mummy, believed to be the body of the biblical Moses, and an original papyrus manuscript containing a sixth Book of Moses, were today returned to the Egyptian authorities.

A group of international scientists and experts appointed to examine the mummy and the manuscript will start work on Monday.

The find is in some way connected to the discovery of several old burial chambers in Norway and Iceland, though any links between the Egyptian and Nordic archaeological finds are as yet unclear.

A spokesman for the Vatican, Cardinal T. K. Bertone, said that they had learned about the discovery of the mummy and the manuscript from the media. They are certain that 'the blasphemous claims' that have been made in connection with the find will soon be dis-proved. The Five Books of Moses, as told in the Bible, are 'the word of God', according to the Vatican.

'WHAT DO you mean, the Vatican has a copy of this . . . this *manuscript* . . . Cardinal Bishop?'

The Pope was apoplectic, and the cardinal bishop fiddled nervously with the gold chain and cross that he wore round his neck.

'Holy Father,' he said, 'our forebears confiscated a copy of the Coptic translation of the manuscript by the high priest Asim in the eleventh century. So when the mummy and the original papyri turned up again in Santo Domingo five hundred years later, Pope Julius II and Cardinal Bishop Castagna thought it best that they remain there.'

The cardinal bishop handed a faded document to the Pope, which contained the minutes of the meeting between Julius II and Castagna.

'But why?' asked the Pope.

'I guess they did not want to create a fuss, Your Holiness.'

The Pope stared at the cardinal bishop. His expression was one of anger and dismay.

'And this has all been kept secret . . .'

'Of course, Holy Father!'

'. . . from all the popes since Julius II?'

'It is best that your humble servants look after certain things on your behalf, Holy Father, so that you are in no way tainted by the knowledge.'

WASHINGTON, DC (Reuters) – The world's largest private collection of books, documents, letters and maps has been donated to the Library of Congress.

The collection from the Miércoles Palace in Santo Domingo, which includes several million titles, was released following the unsolved murder of Esteban Rodriquez and the discovery of the so-called Moses mummy and the original manuscript of the Books of Moses.

According to Tommy Manning, a senior curator at the Library of Congress, the donation is priceless in terms of the cultural historical value.

CAIRO, EGYPT (AP) – Heads of state from over fifty countries will be present when the so-called Moses mummy is laid to rest tomorrow, in its original tomb outside the ancient Egyptian town of Luxor. The ceremony will be hosted by the president of Egypt.

The mummy, which is more than three thousand years old, will remain there until it has been decided whether to open the tomb to the public, or to build a new sanctuary in Luxor, Cairo or Jerusalem.

The Egyptian authorities and religious leaders have not yet decided whether the mummy will lie in state in the future, or not.

There will be no representatives from the Vatican or Jewish organisations present at tomorrow's funeral. Leading Islamic clerics are also boycotting the ceremony.

According to a Vatican spokesman, the Pope does not recognise the mummy as that of the biblical Moses. It is stated in a papal bull that the newly discovered Bible manuscripts are 'ancient forgeries created by heathens to spread doubt and unbelief'.

The spokesman says further that the Vatican is confident that the international research team will shortly uncover what they call 'a perfidious, heretical fraud'.

L ASER BEAMS criss-crossed the clear night sky on the evening on which the mummy was returned to its original tomb. The ceremony was broadcast live across the world. An impressive line-up of artists entertained the guests on a temporary stage in front of the Temple of Amon-Ra.

In several of the clips showing the audience, TV viewers saw a pale, white-haired man with thick glasses, sitting between an older woman with cascades of wild, curly hair and a thin, elderly gentleman with an impressive profile.

Bjørn, Beatriz and the Curator were invited as guests of honour. They had taken time off from their work at the Schimmer Institute, where they were helping the team of experts to restore and translate the ancient papyrus manuscript.

Earlier in the day, Bjørn had sent an email from the hotel in Luxor to Thrainn, Terje, Øyvind, Laura and all the others who had helped him. *Dear friends*, he wrote, *this may sound pompous, but tonight the promise that the Guardians made one thousand years ago will be fulfilled. We are the last Guardians, folks. Our job is done.*

The ceremony ended with fireworks around midnight. Thousands of rockets whistled up into the sky and exploded with blinding flashes, glittering colours and showers of silver. No one noticed that up on the cliffs above the temple, a white dove left its nest and flew into the silent darkness of the desert.

'And when Moses had led the Israelites out of Egypt and shown them the way to Canaan, as the Lord had commanded him to, he returned to the pharaoh.

The pharaoh, his wise men, high priests and courtiers were waiting in the palace.

And Moses fell down on his knees and said: 'The Lord commanded me to lead the Israelites out of Egypt, flock by flock. And it is done.'

The pharaoh said: 'But you have betrayed me, your father.'

And then Moses said: 'As the Lord of Israel asked me to do, so I have done.'

And then the Egyptian king became angry and said: 'You have betrayed me, your people and your kingdom, and are therefore sentenced to death.'

And Moses said: 'Such is the king's word.'

Because Moses was of royal birth, they allowed him to choose how he would die, and Moses chose a blend of poison, honey and wine.

They led him away from the pharaoh, to one of the palace chambers, and there they gave him a cup filled with poison, honey and wine.

And lo, a dove flew by and cast its shadow into the

chamber as Moses emptied the cup of poison. And while he waited for the poison to stop his heart, he said:

'Holiest is the temple that you will find in your heart. When you pray to the Lord God, He is one with you. He is always with you and by you, and you will find Him in you, for you and the Lord are one, just as He is one with all that he has created and with Barbelos, the True God. You should not seek Paradise, for you have already found it, and it is in you.'

And then he fell.

Thus died Moses, servant of Our Lord, in the pharaoh's palace. And they buried him in secret in a tomb by the river. And Moses will rest in the hidden tomb for ever, for unto this day, none knows where the tomb is.'

Extract from the newly discovered Sixth Book of Moses

'God has no religion.'
MAHATMA GANDHI

Acknowledgements

S O MANY people have been willing to help and share their expert knowledge with me – though they may perhaps have felt a twinge of anxiety when I then proceeded to wreak havoc with their discipline – and I would therefore like to thank all those trusted advisers for their invaluable ideas and information. I am solely responsible for any errors that may have occurred and, of course, for all the ideas, fantasy and speculation that I have spun around historical reality, and the historical and theological theories on which this fiction is based. I would like to reiterate that *Guardians of the Covenant* is a novel, and one in which I have taken many liberties. The historical framework and theological theories have been adapted to the fictional reality of the book, and none of my advisers or sources are in any way responsible for how I have used the information they provided. Like any novel that evolves in the grey zone between fact and fiction, *Guardians of the Covenant* is pure speculation, a mind game that starts where reality and science end.

I would like to thank my editor, Øyvind Pharo, and literary consultant, Alexander Opsal, at Aschehoug Publishing House, and Eva Kuløy, my rights manager at Aschehoug Agency, for their painstaking work and their contribution in assisting me to fully prepare the manuscript for launch.

I would also like to thank my friend and colleague in Iceland, the author and film director Thrainn Berthelsson, for his unflagging support. Many thanks go to Dr Gisli Sigurdson at the Arní Magnússon Institute, who opened the vaults so that I could see the ancient manuscripts, and who then patiently answered all my questions. My thanks also to the Reverend Geir Waage at Reykholt for his tour of Snorri's old stamping grounds. And thank you to the authors Harald Sommerfeldt Boehlke, Bodvar Schjelderup and Einar Birgisson for sharing their knowledge of sacred geometry. My thanks to Professor Terje Stordalen of the Faculty of Theology at the University of Oslo, and to Dr Jørgen H. Jensenius, architect and expert on Norwegian stave churches. I would also like to thank Professor Michael Brett from the School of Oriental and African Studies at the University of London, a specialist on the history of North Africa, Egyptian defence and the Fatimids. Thank you also to the Secretary-General of the Vatican Secret Archives, Luca Carboni, and to Thomas Mann, the Reference Librarian at the Library of Congress in Washington, DC.

There are also a great many more individuals who deserve my thanks for their contributions, big and small, comments, suggestions and support. So my sincerest thanks go to: May Grethe Lerum, Arnt Stefansen, Bjørn Are Davidsen, Jørn Lien Horst, Vegard Egeland, Fredrik Græsvik, Knut Andreas Skogstad, Davy Wathne, Kjell Øvre Helland, Viggo Slettevold, Øyvind Egaas and Astrid Egeland. Thanks also to Gunn Haaland and K. Jonas Norby at the University of Oslo, district sheriff Lars Smestadmoen, archaeologist Jan Bill at the Viking Ship Museum in Roskilde, and Professor Doris Behrens-Abouseif from the University of London. I would also like to thank my Icelandic publisher, Jóhann Páll Valdimarsson, Thora Sigridur Ingolfsdottir and all the others at JPV Publishing, and my Italian editor, Elisabetta Sgarbi, and her colleagues, Beatrice Gatti and Valeria Frasca, at Bompiani. My thanks also to the advisers at the Norwegian Directorate for Cultural Heritage, the church warden at Ringebu stave church, Statens kartverk, Statistics Norway and the University of Oslo.

I would especially like to thank my long-suffering family and in particular my wife, Åse Myhrvold Egeland, who not only is one of my most candid readers and consultants, but who also puts up with being a literary grass widow.

And finally, *woof* to Teddy and thanks for the company.

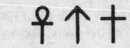

Bibliography

No book is ever written in a vacuum. While working on *Guardians of the Covenant*, the following sources have been of particular help:

The Bible
The Egyptian Book of the Dead
Sturluson, Snorri, *The Heimskringla*

NORWEGIAN BOOKS

Aartun, Kjell: Runer i kulturhistorisk sammenheng, Pax, 1994
Alnæs, Karsten: *Historien om Norge*, Gyldendal, 1996
Boehlke, Harald Sommerfeldt: *Det norske pentagram*, Eutopia Forlag (1st edn), author (2nd edn), 2005
Grambo, Ronald: *Djevelens livshistorie*, Ex Libris, 1990
Hauken, Aage: *Teologene som skapte Det gamle testamente*, Land og kirke/Gyldendal, 1980
Ingstad, Helge: *Vesterveg til Vinland*, Gyldendal, 1965
Langslet, Lars Roar: *Olav den hellige*, Gyldendal, 1995
Lindh, Knut: *Leiv Eriksson – Oppdagelsen av Amerika*, Farhenheit/Pantagruel, 2000
Mykland, Knut (ed.): *Norges historie*, Cappelen, 1976

Myklebust, Morten: *Olav – viking og helgen*, Fantasti-Fabrikken, 1997

Schelderup, Bodvar: *Loggbok for en helgen*, Genesis forlag, 1997

Schelderup, Bodvar: *Paktens tegn og den femte tavlen*, Periscope Vision, 2004

Sparkland, Terje: *I begynnelsen var futhark – norske runer og runeinnskrifter*, LNU og Cappelen Akademisk Forlag, 2001

Thiis-Evensen, Thomas and Eva Valebrokk: *De utrolige stavkirkene*, Boksenteret, 1993

Valebrokk, Eva and Thomas Thiis-Evensen: *De utrolige stavkirkene*, Boksenteret, 1993

BOOKS IN ENGLISH

Birgisson, Einar Gunnar: *Egyptian Influence and Sacred Geometry in Ancient and Medieval Scandinavia*, self-published, Iceland, 2002

Carter, W. Hodding: *A Viking Voyage*, Ballantine Books, 2002

Dodson, Aidan and Dyan Hilton: *The Complete Royal Families of Ancient Egypt*, Thames and Hudson, 2004

Eskeland, Ivar: *Snorri Sturluson, A Biography*, Grondahl Dreyer, 1993

Finkelstein, Israel and Neil Asher Silberman: *The Bible Unearthed – Archaeology's New Vision of Ancient Israel and the Origin of Its Sacred Texts*, Touchstone, 2001

Friedman, Richard Elliott: *Who Wrote the Bible*, Summit Books, 1987/1997

Graham-Campbell, James: *The Viking World*, Frances Lincoln, 1980/2001

Haagensen, Erling and Henry Lincoln: *The Templars' Secret Island*, Windrush Press, 2000

Haywood, John: *Historical Atlas of the Vikings*, Penguin, 1995

Murdoch, David: *Tutankhamun, the Life and Death of a Pharaoh*, Dorling Kindersley, 1998

Osman, Ahmed: *Moses and Akhenaten – The Secret History of Egypt at the Time of the Exodus*, Bear & Co., 1990–2002

Phillips, Graham: *The Moses Legacy, the Evidence of History*, Sidgwick & Jackson, 2002

Prytz, Kåre: *Westward before Columbus*, Norumbega Books, 1991 (translated from Norwegian)

Rohl, David: *A Test of Time – The Bible from Myth to History*, Century, 1995

Sigurdsson, Gisli and Vésteinn Ólason: *The Manuscripts of Iceland*, Árni Magnússon Institute, Iceland, 2004

BOOKS IN NORWEGIAN TRANSLATION

Bowker, John: *The Complete Bible Handbook*, Dorling Kindersley, 1998

Bowker, John: *God. A Brief History*, Dorling Kindersley, 2002

Keller, Werner: *The Bible as History*, Hodder & Stoughton, 1965 (translated from German)

Singh, Simon: *The Code Book: The Science of Secrecy from Ancient Egypt to Quantum Cryptography*, Anchor, 1999

WEBSITES

The following websites have been of particular value:

www.arild-hauge.com (about the Viking age, runes and folklore)

asv.vatican.va (Vatican Secret Archive)

www.stavkirke.info (about Norwegian stave churches)

no.wikipedia.org
en.wikipedia.org
www.katolsk.no
www.bibelen.no